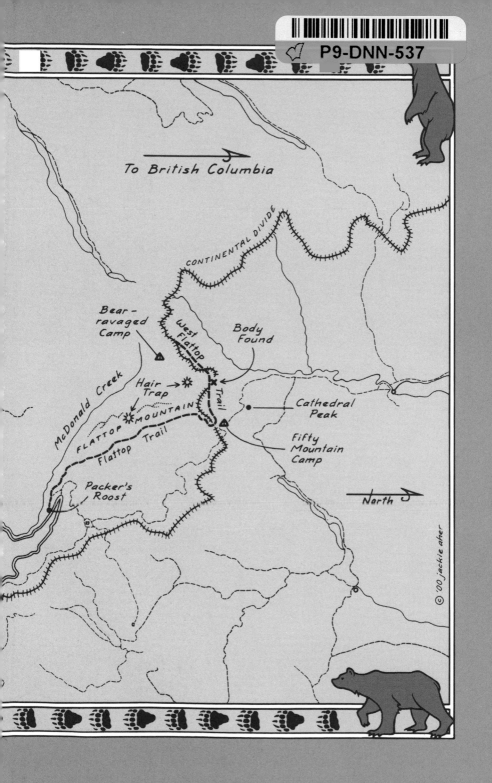

To British Columbia

CONTINENTAL DIVIDE

Bear-
ravaged
Camp

West
Flattop

Body
Found

McDonald Creek

Hair
Trap

FLATTOP MOUNTAIN

Trail

Cathedral
Peak

Fifty
Mountain
Camp

Flattop Trail

Packer's
Roost

North

© '00 Jackie aher

Blood
Lure

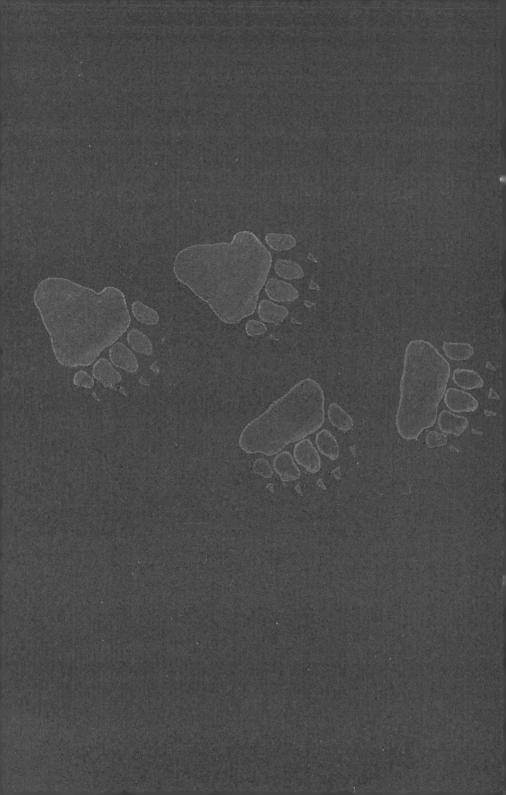

Blood Lure

Nevada Barr

G. P. PUTNAM'S SONS   NEW YORK

G. P. Putnam's Sons
Publishers Since 1838
a member of
Penguin Putnam Inc.
375 Hudson Street
New York, NY 10014

ISBN 0-399-14702-0

Printed in the United States of America

BOOK DESIGN BY AMANDA DEWEY
ENDPAPER MAP BY JACKIE AHER

Acknowledgments

I needed a great deal of help with this book, help that was generously given by the staff at Waterton-Glacier National Peace Park. Special thanks must go to Dave Mihalic, my guide and inspiration, Butch Farabee, my landlord and friend, and Kate Kendall, who answered countless questions. Jack Potter, Steve Frye, Gary Moses and Larry Fredrick, I am grateful for your time, wit and expertise. Fred Van Horn, I thank for information; Barry Wollenzien and Ron Goldhirsch for showing me the park routines. Thanks also to Joan and Geoffrey for the loan of their auras, and Bob because he is Bob.

Here at home I thank Dave Wetzel of the Jackson Zoo for telling me about the care and feeding of grizzly bears.

FOR BOBBI,
a gracious and
faithful friend

Blood
Lure

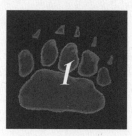

With the exception of a nine-week-old Australian shepherd puppy, sniffing and whining as if he'd discovered a treasure chest and sought a way inside, everyone was politely pretending Anna didn't stink.

Under the tutelage of Joan Rand, the biologist overseeing Glacier's groundbreaking bear DNA project, Anna had spent the morning in an activity so vile even garbage men had given her wide berth, holding their noses in awe.

Near Glacier National Park's sewage processing plant, behind an eight-foot chain-link fence sporting two electrified wires, and further protected in an aluminum shed the size of an old two-holer outhouse wrapped in six more strands of electrical fencing, lay the delights the excited black and white pup whiffed: two fifty-gallon drums filled with equal parts cows' blood and fish flotsam, heated and left to steep for two and a half months in what was referred to as the "brew shed."

Joan, apparently born without a gag reflex, had cheerfully taught Anna how to strain fish bits out with one hand while ladling red-black liquid into one-liter plastic bottles with the other.

"Fingers work best," Rand had said. "Pure research; the glamour never stops." With that, she had flashed Anna small, crooked, very white teeth in a grin that, in other circumstances, might have been contagious.

Standing now in the offices of the science lab, the puppy beginning to lick her boot laces, Anna was glad she'd not succumbed to the temptation to smile back. Had she done so, her teeth would probably be permeated with a godawful stench that could only be described as *eau decarrion,* the quintessential odor of Death on a bender, the Devil's vomit.

"It wears off." A kindly woman with shoulder-length brown hair looked up from a computer console as if Anna's thoughts had been broadcast along with her smell. "It just takes awhile. Have you worked with the skunk lures yet?"

"That's for dessert," Anna replied grimly, and the woman laughed.

"That's the lure of choice. Joan says they roll and play in it like overgrown dogs. That lure is so stinky you've got to pack it in glass jars. Goes right through plastic."

Anna thought about the blood lure, the skunk. Both had been painstakingly researched, other scents tried and discarded, till those most irresistible to grizzly bears had been found. And she was going to be carrying these scents on her back into the heart of bear country in Montana's side of the Waterton-Glacier International Peace Park, nothing between her and the largest omnivores in the lower forty-eight but a can of pepper spray.

The puppy woofed and put portentously large paws on her shins, his black-fringed tail describing short, fat arcs. "You want to roll in me, don't you?" Anna asked. He barked again and she quashed an urge to pick him up, defile his soft new fur with her tainted hands. Turning away from the importuning brown eyes, she studied the color photocopies of *Ursus horribilis* thumb-tacked to a long bulletin board situated over a conference table: the muscular hump between the shoulders developed, it was thought, to aid in the main function of the four-inch claws—digging. Fur was brown, tipped or grizzled with silver, earning the bear its name. Ears were rounded, plump, teddy-bear ears; teeth less sanguine, the canines an inch or so in length, well suited to their feeding habits. Grizzly bears ate carrion, plants, ground squirrels, insects and, sometimes, people.

Anna thought about that. Thought about the olfactory enticements she would carry, handle, sleep beside at night.

Stepping closer, she studied the pictures of massive heads, long jaws, paws that could topple a strong man, claws that could disembowel with ease, and she felt no fear.

Members of the bear team, who monitored bear activities in

the park and settled bear/visitor disputes, and the Glacier rangers routinely lamented the fact that the American people were such idiots they thought of these wildest of animals as big cuddly pets. One man had been stopped in the act of smearing ice cream on his five-year-old son's cheek in hopes of photographing a bear licking it off.

Anna was too well versed in the critter sciences to believe the animals harmless. She fell into a second and equally dangerous subspecies of idiot: those who felt a spiritual connection with the wild beasts, be they winged, furred or toothed. A sense that they would recognize in her a kindred spirit and do her no harm nullified a necessary and healthful terror of being torn apart and devoured. This delusion didn't extend to the lions of Africa. One couldn't expect them not to eat an overseas tourist; everybody enjoys an exotic dish now and again. But American lions, American bears . . .

She laughed aloud at herself. Fortunately she wasn't fool enough to put interspecies camaraderie to the test and never would she admit any of this to anyone. Least of all Joan Rand, her keeper, trainer and companion for the nineteen days that she was cross-training on the Greater Glacier Bear DNA Project, gleaning knowledge that could be put to use to better manage wildlife in her home park, the Natchez Trace Parkway in Mississippi.

"Ah, my stinky little friend, your vacation package is ready," Joan said as she emerged from an inner sanctum. Rand was American by birth, French-Canadian by proximity, and she sounded precisely like Pepe Le Pew, the cartoon Parisian skunk, when she chose to. Anna laughed. Joan would remember Pepe. She was near Anna in years, somewhere in that fertile valley of middle age between forty-five and fifty-five.

Anna had liked Joan right off. Rand was on the short side— five-foot-two—and stocky, with the narrow shoulders of a person who couldn't carry much weight and the solid butt and thighs of somebody who could hike a Marine drill sergeant into the ground.

Anna liked the quickness of her mind and the gravelly quality of her voice. She liked her humor. But in the two days they'd lived and worked together, she'd not felt an ease of companionship. It seemed she was always looking for something to say. Mostly silences were filled with work. Those that weren't had yet to be-come comfortable, but Anna had hopes.

The bear researcher dropped the skunk accent, adjusted her oversized glasses and said, "Take a seat. This is Rory Van Slyke. He's our Earthwatch sherpa, general dogsbody and has promised, should a bear attack, to offer up his firm young flesh so that you and I might live to continue our important work."

Rory, the individual to whom Joan referred, smiled shyly. In her years with the National Park Service Anna had only had oc-casion to cross paths with the Earthwatch organization once be-fore. Some years back, when she was a boat patrol ranger on Isle Royale National Park in Lake Superior, Earthwatch—an inde-pendent environmental organization funded by donations and staffed by volunteers—had been working on a moose study with the National Park Service. They had the unenviable task of hiking cross-country through the ruggedest terrain of a rugged park seeking out dead and rotting moose, counting the ticks on the carcasses, then packing out the really choice parts for further study. They did this not merely voluntarily, they paid for the priv-ilege, suggesting that the altruism gene was not a myth. All of the Earthwatchers she'd met, including Rory Van Slyke, were young. Probably because the work they did would kill a grown-up.

"How you do?" Anna said mechanically.

"Well, thank you. And yourself?"

A long time had passed since anybody had bothered to finish the old-fashioned greeting formula. Evidently Rory had been raised right—or strictly.

"Fine," she managed. The boy—young man—had a light, high voice that sounded as if it had yet to change, though he was clearly years past puberty. He didn't look substantial enough to be much of a sherpa, but as bear bait, he'd do just fine: slight build, tender-looking skin, coarse sandy hair and dark blue eyes fringed with lashes so pale as to be virtually invisible.

"Here's the plan." Joan spread a topographical map on the table in front of Anna, then leaned over her shoulder to point. She, too, stank to high heaven. It was good to be a member of a group.

"We've gridded the park into cells eight kilometers on a side," Joan said as she dropped a transparent plastic overlay on the top-ographical map, aligning it with coordinates she carried in her head. "Each cell is numbered. In every square—every cell—we've put a hair trap. This is not to trap the bear in toto but merely designed to ensure visiting bears leave behind samples of their hair for the study. Traps are located, near as we can make them, on the natural travel routes of the bears: mountain passes, the confluence of avalanche chutes, that sort of thing. So we're talking some serious off-trail hiking here, bushwhacking at its whackingest. These asterisks," she poked a blunt brown forefinger at marks made by felt marker on the overlay, "are where the last round of traps are located. They've been in place two weeks. The three of us will take five of the cells: numbers three-thirty-one, twenty-three, fifty-two, fifty-three and sixty-four. Here, on the central and west side of Flattop Mountain. What we'll be doing is going into the old traps, collecting the hair, dismantling the traps and setting them up in the new locations, here." She put another plastic overlay on top of the first, and a second set of asterisks appeared. "Or as close to these respective 'heres' as we can get. Mapping locations out on paper in the cozy confines of the office has very little relationship to where you can actually put them when you get out into the rocky, cliffy, shrubby old backcountry.

"Once the trap wire is strung, we pour the elixir of the gods—that's this blood-and-fish-guts perfume you are pretending not to notice on us, Rory—into our new trap and leave for another couple of weeks. While wandering around up there we'll also cover the Flattop Mountain Trail from below Fifty Mountain Camp to the middle of the Waterton Valley and the West Flattop Mountain Trail from the continental divide to Dixon Glacier. Bears are like us: they like to take the easy way when they can. So we've located and marked a number of trees along the trail system that they are particularly fond of scratching their backs on. We'll collect hair samples from these, as well as any samples of scat we happen across."

The lecture was for Rory. Anna had heard it before when Joan and her boss, Kate, explained the daunting task of data gathering for the DNA project, the inspiration of Kate Kendall, a researcher working jointly with the USGS—the United States Geographical Survey—and the NPS. From the hair and scat collected, the DNA of individual bears would be extracted. Modern techniques used by the lab at the University of Idaho would establish gender, species and individual identification of the animals sampled. With this information, it was hoped an accurate census of the bears could be established, as well as population trends, travel routes and patterns. This trapping system had been designed to give every single bear at Glacier an opportunity to be counted.

"We'll be out five days," Joan finished. "Leaving tomorrow at the crack of dawn."

No one spoke for a moment, the three of them gazing at the map as if at any moment it would begin to divulge its secrets.

"Hey," Joan said, breaking the silence. "Maybe we'll see your folks, Rory."

The young man whuffed, a small expulsion of air through the nostrils that spoke volumes, none of them good, about how he viewed the proximity of his parents. Anna looked at him from the corner of her eye. Down was gone from his cheek, recently replaced by a beard so fair it glistened rather than shadowed at the end of the day. He was seventeen or eighteen at a guess. Very possibly on his first great away-from-home adventure. And Mom and Dad found a way to horn in.

Just to see if any of her surmises were in the ballpark, Anna said, "How so your folks?" and prepared to listen with an expression that would pass for innocent with the unwary.

"Mom and Dad are camping at Fifty Mountain Camp for a week. Mom got this sudden urge to get back to nature."

"Quite a coincidence," Anna needled, to see what kind of response she could scare up. No sense smelling stinky if one couldn't be a stinker.

"Mom's kind of . . . ," Rory's voice trailed off. Anna didn't detect any malice, just annoyance. "Kind of into the family thing. Sort of 'happy campers all together.' She knows I won't see a lot of her, if at all. She can always amuse herself. And of course Les had to come if she came."

Now there was malice. A pretty hefty dose of it for a lad so green in years.

"Les?" Anna prodded because it was in her nature to do so.

"My dad. Carolyn's my stepmother."

Had Anna for some unfathomable reason chosen to go forth and populate the earth with offspring of her own, it would have cut her to the heart to hear herself mentioned in the tones Rory used when speaking of his dad. The kinder notes, poured out upon the stepparent, would have been just so much salt in the wound.

"I doubt we'll even see them from a distance," Joan said. "This itsy-bitsy chunk of map I've been pointing at represents a whole lot of territory when you're covering it on foot." There was a slamming-the-iron-door quality to her dismissal of the domestic issue that made Anna suspect her of being a mother in her other life. If she had another life. In the forty-eight hours Anna had known her, Rand had worked like a woman buying off a blackmailer. It wasn't that she lacked humor or zest, but that she pushed herself as if her sense of security was held hostage and only hard work could buy it back.

A classic workaholic.

Anna's sister, Molly, had been one until she'd nearly died; then, at the ripe age of fifty-five, fallen in love for maybe the first time. Molly was a psychiatrist. She could tell Joan that no amount of work would suffice. But if Joan was a true workaholic, she wouldn't have time to listen.

Personally, Anna loved workaholics. Especially when they worked for her. In a sense those laboring to save one square inch of wilderness, rescue one caddis fly larva from pollutants, were in the deepest sense public servants. And maybe, if the gods took pity and the public woke up, these rescuers would save the world, one species, one coral reef, one watershed at a time.

Anna'd organized a backpack so often it took her no more time than a veteran airline pilot packing for a four-day trip. The five liters of blood and guts were secured in a hard plastic Pelican case. Rory would carry that. Anna and Joan split the rest of the equipment between them: fencing staples and hammers, vials of ethanol for scat samples, envelopes for hair, a trap log to record the salient facts of the sites, like where, precisely, in the two million acres of Glacier each four-hundred-square-foot trap was located so the next round of researchers could find it. The skunk lures, five in all, weighed next to nothing. Wool, permeated with the scent purchased from a hunting catalogue, was stuffed in film canisters and stowed in a glass jar. That went in Anna's pack. In under two hours everything was arranged to Joan's satisfaction.

The women spent the remainder of the evening at a scarred oak table in Joan's dining area going over BIMS—bear incident management systems reports. Joan lived in park housing and Anna felt peculiarly at home. There was a sameness to the quarters that engendered a bizarre dreamlike déjà vu.

It wasn't merely the prevalence of the Mission '66 ranch-style floor plans: three bedrooms, L-shaped living area and long narrow kitchen circa 1966, the last time the NPS had gotten major funding for employee housing. It was the décor. Rangers, researchers and naturalists, from seasonal to superintendent, could be counted on to have park posters on the walls, a kachina or two on the shelves, Navajo rugs over the industrial-strength carpeting and an assortment of mismatched unbreakable plastic dishes in the kitchen.

The predictability of the surroundings had dulled Anna's natural curiosity. Remembering now her suspicion as to her hostess's family leanings, she took off the drugstore half-glasses she'd finally admitted to needing for close work and looked around the compact living area.

On top of the television, between a Kokopelli doll standing on an *ojo de Dios* and the skull of some large canid, were framed school portraits of two boys, either fraternal twins or very close in age. Both were stunningly beautiful, a pedophile's dream-come-true.

Thinking of the children in those terms brought Anna up short. Dark thoughts, dire predictions, a view of the world as a dangerous and dirty place was an occupational hazard of those in law enforcement—even park rangers, whose days were spent in beautiful places populated by largely benevolent if occasionally misguided vacationers.

Her promotion to district ranger on the Natchez Trace Parkway was taking its toll. The Trace was a road, hence Anna was a cop. Asphalt could be relied on to be a conduit for crime.

The boys in the picture frames: not potential victims but future promise made flesh. Attitude screwed around the right way, Anna asked, "Are those your sons?"

"Luke and John," Joan said.

Good apostolic names. Anna smiled. "What happened to Matthew and Mark?"

"Stillborn."

Anna's brain skidded to a halt; a feeble jest had struck the jugular. "Shit," she said sincerely.

"Yup."

Silence settled around them, oddly comfortable this time, more so given this silence's root.

"John graduates high school this year. Luke's a junior. I got pregnant while nursing. Another old wives' tale bites the dust. They live with their dad in Denver."

There was no need for elaboration. The park service, though sublime in many respects, was hell on marriages. Anna was all too familiar with the forlorn photographs of shattered families.

Accompanied by an alarming creaking noise that she hoped was the ladder-backed chair and not Joan's sacroiliac, the researcher rose. She crossed to the television, returned with the pictures and set them down amid the BIMS reports and scat sample tubes.

"They're good-looking boys," Anna said, to make up for her evil pedophilic thoughts.

"Their dad was a virtual Adonis. Still is. Still knows it. Still drives the little girls wild."

Another chapter in the same old story.

"Ah," Anna said.

"If I ever marry again, it'll be to a rich old hunchback with bad teeth."

Picking up a frame, Anna studied the photo simply because she thought Joan had brought the pictures that they might be pored over and admired. "John?"

"Luke. Though he's younger, he's the bigger boy."

Around the eyes—brown and, because of a slight down-turn at the outer corners, sad-looking—Luke resembled his mother. In all else he had followed along the Adonis lines. "Looks a little like Rory Van Slyke," Anna said. "Looks" wasn't quite the right word. The two boys did have a surface resemblance, but it was the eyes that made them so alike, a depth of vision that boys shouldn't have. As if, during what should have been carefree childhood years, they had seen enough of life to become weary.

"I noticed that," Joan said.

Wistfulness permeated the words. Joan missed her sons, maybe picked the Van Slyke boy from the Earthwatch litter because he reminded her of Luke. Evidently Joan heard her own vulnerability and was shamed by it. At any rate, the moment of intimacy was over.

"BIMS," she said overbrightly. "Never a dull moment. Let me read you one." The forms had been made up in an attempt to keep a record of every bear sighting in the park. They were filled out by visitors and park personnel alike to gather information on the activities and whereabouts of the grizzlies and their less alarming cousins, the black bears. Each form had places for writing the location of sighting, date, time, observer, color of bear, observer's activity and, the most entertaining if not always the most illuminating, the comments section where the activities of the bear were described.

Joan shuffled through her pile of BIMS and, Anna noted, in the process managed to turn the photos of her sons so they faced away. "Here it is. Listen to this. 'Big bear. Major, mondo, hippo of a bear. Thousand to twelve hundred pounds.'"

"Too big?"

"By half. In Glacier, grizzlies don't reach the size they do in Alaska, where they have access to all that salmon protein. Here an average male weighs in at three-fifty or four hundred pounds, the females a little less. We get a lot of exaggerated reports. I can't say as I blame folks. When you see a bear and you're all alone in the big bad woods, they do have a tendency to double in size."

Joan's jocularity was forced. Equilibrium was not yet reestablished. The ghosts of Matthew, Mark, Luke and John still hovered over the scat bottles. Anna wondered whether the situation with the boys was intense or if it was just Joan.

"I got a good one," she offered in the spirit of denial. She paged back till she located a form filled out in lavender ballpoint. "August fifth. No location. No time. No observer name. Species: grizzly. Age: twenty-six. Color: blond—don't know if this means the bear was twenty-six and blond, or the observer was."

"Blond for our bears is rare."

"That's not the rare part. This is." Anna read aloud from the "Comments" box. "'Bear activity: juggling what looked like a hedgehog. Observer activity: standing amazed.'"

Joan laughed and the air was clear again. Tales of visitor silliness could always be counted on to bring back a sense of normalcy to park life. "Reports like that reassure me that Timothy Leary's alive and well and doing drugs with Elvis," the researcher said.

After ten o'clock, in Joan's spare room furnished, as was every spare room in every park service house Anna had ever slept in, with peculiar oddments of furniture heavily representing the 1950s and Wal-Mart, and a closet full of backpacks, coats and sleeping bags good to ten below zero, Anna lay awake. Her book, an old well-read copy of *The Wind Chill Factor*, was open on her chest. Seeing the shapes of animals in the water stains on the ceiling as she used to do as a child, she contemplated the upcoming backcountry trip.

Months had passed since she'd done anything more strenuous than sit on her posterior in an air-conditioned patrol car. The most weight she'd lifted with any regularity was a citation book and government-issue pen. In desperation, she'd joined an aerobics class at the Baptist Healthplex in Clinton, Mississippi, but she'd only gone twice. One of the requirements for inclusion in this cross-training venture had been the ability to carry a fifty-pound pack. Anna hadn't lied. She could carry fifty pounds. Just how far remained to be seen.

She hoped she wouldn't slow everybody down. She hoped Joan wouldn't have Rory Van Slyke unwittingly bearing, along with the blood of sacrificial cows, the burden of stillborn apostles because of an uncanny likeness to long-absent sons.

She hoped she'd see some grizzly bear cubs.

And that the cubs' momma wouldn't see her.

2

Because Joan Rand was a small woman with a great brain, their packs weighed closer to forty than fifty pounds, a fact Anna knew she would be increasingly grateful for as the day wore on. The first three miles of the twelve-mile hike were fairly straight and level. The second three ascended twenty-five hundred feet in steep switchbacks.

Rory's pack was somewhat heavier as befitted the younger, stronger, taller and, more to the point, junior member of the team. Twenty-five hundred feet was the ascent Anna'd used to climb twice a week from the ranger station in Guadalupe Mountains National Park to the high country. She'd been younger, stronger and taller herself in those days and still it was a bitch of a climb.

A member of the bear team assigned to handle bears that clashed with visitors gave them a lift partway up the famous Going to the Sun Road that cut through some of the most scenic country in the park, a road made in the 1920s and '30s, when labor was cheap and so was wilderness. He dropped them off at Packers Roost, a horse and hiker staging area at the bottom of Flattop Mountain.

Unlike some of the parks Anna'd worked, Glacier was a pristine rather than a rehabilitated wilderness. Most of the land had never been logged, mined or grazed. The trees were old growth, the land scarred only by the natural phenomena of fire, flood and avalanche. An unusual departure from this purity was the old fire road they followed to the beginning of the ascent.

Because it had once been cut clear of trees then left to heal, it had a fairy-tale quality. A wide swath of delicate green moss grew in from the road's edges to a narrow trail kept barren by foot traffic. This living carpet was starred with tiny white star-shaped flowers. Overhead, feathery branches of fir and cedar closed out the sun. A tenuous heady perfume, found only in the mountains of the west, scented the air. With each breath, Anna was transported. As she walked she enjoyed flashbacks to the southern Cascades at Lassen Volcanic and to the tip of the Rocky Mountains in Durango before they let go their alpine greenery and flowed into the red mesas of New Mexico.

Those native to Montana had been complaining of an uncharacteristic heat wave that was pushing temperatures into the eighties, but Anna, having so recently fled a Mississippi August, reveled in the cool and the shade.

Joan went first, followed by Rory. Anna took up the rear. Over the years she'd found by slowing down and dropping back a little, she could slip free of the chatter zone and enjoy the solitude of the hike. And, here, the silence.

Nothing stirred. No birds fussed above or scratched in needles and leaves. Insects didn't buzz. Squirrels and chipmunks didn't clatter through the treetops scolding her for trespassing. She wondered if the western forests had always been so preternaturally quiet, or if her ears had merely become accustomed to the ongoing concert of life that played in the woodlands of the deep South.

Or perhaps there was a great toothy predator that had momentarily struck dumb the lesser beasts of the forest.

Anna waited for a titillating frisson of fear to follow the thought, but it didn't. Fire ants: now they put the fear of God into her. Not grizzlies. Rory, she could tell, was not so sanguine. On the ride up, the bear-team guy had regaled them with the story of an attack he'd worked on two summers before. Three hikers had been mauled in the Middle Fork area—the southern edge of the park.

Joan, kindly disposed to the damaged hikers but clearly protective of the accused bear, had given her take on the events. Once or twice a year a bear mauled a visitor. Usually the person was not killed. Grizzlies, Joan told them, did not customarily attack with the idea of eating one. Grizzlies kept their cubs with them two or even three years. With the exception of humans and the great apes, they were the animals who spent the most time educating their young. They taught them how to survive, where to find springs in dry years, what plants to eat and where they grew. A female grizzly didn't bear offspring until she was six and would only have five to ten cubs in her lifetime. This made her extremely protective of them. When she perceived a threat, whether another bear or a hiker, her goal was not to eat it but to teach it the meaning of fear.

Seldom would she charge a group of four or more people. The threat to her and hers was perceived as too great to overcome and she would run away. That was why the park suggested backpackers never hike alone.

The bear under discussion had been surprised by two hikers, charged them, mauled them—"Couldn't be too bad," Joan said, "they walked out"—then fled up the trail and smack into unfortunate hiker number three.

"Nobody died," Joan pointed out. "If the bear wanted them dead, they'd be dead. If the bear wanted to eat them, they'd be dragged off and eaten, their remains cached in a shallow hole and covered over for later. *Ergo*, the bear did not want to kill them. *Ergo*, the bear did not want to eat them."

From the look on Rory's face, all he'd heard was "kill them and eat them." Since they'd been on the trail he'd been peering into the woods like a man being stalked.

If a bear had been watching or following, there was no doubt in Anna's mind that they'd never know it was there. Because Glacier was blessed with a heavy snowpack in winter and afternoon rains throughout the short summer, it lacked the open, cathedral aspect of the woods on the eastern slope of the Sierra or the southern tip of the Cascades. In Glacier, the forest floor was thick with dead and down trees, never burned, never logged, fallen in places as thick as pick-up sticks in the child's game. Fern, huckleberry, bearberry, service berry, the shoulder-high broadleafed thimbleberry, and a plethora of plants Anna couldn't put a name to, tangled in the cross-hatching of rotting timber.

A bear wanting to hide would do so.

Following her thoughts into the woods, she realized for the first time what an arduous task it was going to be fighting through the underbrush off-trail to service and reset the traps.

Selfishly, she was glad they were covering the high country. Some of it would be above tree line. A good chunk was encompassed by the burn left from the 1998 fire. The going was bound to be somewhat easier.

Lost in thought, she rounded a bend in the trail and nearly walked on the heels of Rory Van Slyke. Next to "never hike alone" on the rangers' list of safe behavior in bear country was "stay alert." So far Anna was oh-for-two.

"Here's one," Joan was saying when Anna bumbled into the meeting. "This is one of the hair trees we've marked. This yellow diamond is what you'll be looking for." She pointed to a piece of reflective plastic that had been nailed to the tree about as high as the average person could reach with a hammer.

"We also number them to be sure we know exactly which samples came from which tree. The numbers are behind the trunk at the bottom. We want to notice these trees but we don't want to advertise them to every hiker down the pike."

"What's the barbed wire for?" Rory asked at the same time Anna noticed segments had been stapled to the bark in an uneven, widespread pattern.

"That scratches them a little deeper is all. Pulls out some of the underfur that's more likely to have a little bit of tissue clinging to it so that we can more easily get a DNA sample."

"Doesn't that make them mad?" Rory's concern at an enraged grizzly in the neighborhood was clear on his face.

"No," Joan reassured him. "They like it. We didn't know if they would or if they would abandon the wired trees. But they seem to actually prefer them. See the tracks?"

Worn into the moss from the paws of many bears following the same path from the rubbing tree to the trail were two prints made larger by repeated use.

"Cool, huh?"

Anna agreed it was cool.

Rory asked, "Does pepper spray really work?"

"It's the same stuff we use in law enforcement," Anna told him. "It's made from the essence of red-hot peppers. I guess it would work on bears. Unless they've developed a taste for Mexican food. Then I think it would only serve to whet their appetites."

Joan shot her a look that was not without humor but made it

clear that tormenting Rory was not an acceptable form of entertainment. "We're not going to get ourselves into a situation
where we have to find out," Joan said firmly.

"Rory, you're an exception to the rule. Most boys love bears.
I actually get fan mail because I am the Bear Lady at Glacier."
Joan's voice was pleasant as ever, but it was clear that in harbor-
ing fear of bears, Rory had impugned them and the researcher's
feelings were hurt. "One boy e-mails me every couple of days.
He's drawing a map and has to know where the bears go to eat at
any given time."

"I like bears," Rory said defensively.

"You will," Joan promised.

"They would certainly like *you*," Anna said ominously.

To distract the children from their squabbles, Joan made the
mistake of introducing Anna to huckleberries. Arm in arm with
thimbleberries and bearberries, they grew wild over much of the
park. In late summer and fall, when they were at their peak, they
were the favored food of bears, both black and grizzly. They con-
sumed them by the ton as they stored up as much sugar and fat as
they could for a long winter spent curled in dens at the higher elevations.

For the next mile or so, Anna played catch-up, foraging for
the delicious dark purple berries then trotting to catch up, pack
slamming down on hip and knee joints that weren't nearly so forgiving as they once had been.

Joan couldn't resist a few berries herself but took her responsibilities to her job more seriously than those to her immortal
berry-loving soul.

The Van Slyke kid had gone about his berrying with zeal till
Anna gave into the temptation to muse aloud as to whether bears
would find huckleberry breath an irresistible enticement. For that
she earned an exasperated look from Joan Rand and Rory's share
of the berries.

When they crossed Kipp Creek, glittering over stones of vivid
red, green and gold—not the murky, brown, cottonmouth creeks
that prevailed in Anna's new home in the south—interest in
berries gave way to interest in breathing.

Unbeknownst to him, Rory got some of his own back. He
was stronger than he looked. And younger than some of Anna's
towels. On the climb, much of it on an exposed southwest-facing

mountainside, the sun proved its strength. After a mile Anna was hurting. Sweat poured into her eyes. Lungs pumped and burned. Breath sawed through a mouth dry from hanging open gasping for air like a landed trout.

Periodically Joan called a rest stop in the shade offered by the occasional towering white pine. For this Anna could have kissed her feet had she not known that if she did so, she'd never get up again. During these brief respites, Anna swatted deerflies obsessed with the backs of her thighs and split her concentration between enjoying the view and hiding her physical weakness from her compatriots.

From their ever-higher vantage points they could see seven mountains. Four, along the Continental Divide, formed a wall encircling them from west to east. Mountains, not green but blue, were still streaked with snow at the summits, and long mares' tails of water cascaded over the rocky faces in tumbles and falls tracing through stone and forest for thousands of feet.

The canyon they labored so hard to climb out of was no exception. A ribbon of white water, now falls, now rapids, now fishing holes, appeared and disappeared as the mountain's magic act unfolded.

Between sweating, faking fitness, and mentally promising Amy, her aerobics teacher back home, that she would attend classes religiously if she survived this hike, Anna was dimly aware they pushed through an array of wildflowers that she should be appreciating.

By noon they reached the top. Sheered off by glacial movement, Flattop was a peculiarity among its steep-sided neighbors. To the east, the argillite cliffs of Mount Kipp in the Lewis Range rose over alpine meadows. Six miles north, the planed top of Flattop Mountain dropped away, wrinkling down into the Waterton River Valley and on to Canada.

Once on Flattop they left the comforts of the trail and struck west through the burn, heading toward Trapper Peak. Between Flattop and Trapper's imposing flanks was a deep cut, much like the one they'd followed during their ascent, where Continental Creek carved its way down three thousand feet to McDonald Creek to empty its glacial melt. The first of the hair traps was located in a small avalanche chute above the gorge, a place made as attractive as its grander competition by several springs that ran even in the driest years.

The fire of 1998 had burned slowly and exceedingly fine, consuming everything in its path. Blue-black snags clawed at the sky. Without shade, without greenery or moisture, the sun weighed as heavily on Anna's back as her pack. With every step, cinders crunched under her boots. Black dust boiled up to stick in the sweat and DEET sprayed on her legs. Despite the insecticide, horseflies, deerflies and mosquitoes followed. With only a brief window of opportunity in which to slake their thirst, they were fearless.

Despite the ash and grit, she blessed the fire that had torched ten thousand acres of America's crown jewel, taxed the Glacier superindent's courage, not to mention the Waterton superintendent's faith in the good sense of the U.S. superintendent as he watched the NPS "let burn" policy crackle toward the Canadian half of Waterton-Glacier International Peace Park. Waterton-Glacier was a unique and highly successful experiment. The only park of its kind, one half was in Canada, the other in the United States, with major environmental decisions and park regulations worked out jointly between the two countries.

The Canadian superintendent was less optimistic than the American superintendent when it came to letting nature burn where she would, but Glacier's superintendent stood firm. The fire had been left to burn itself out and Anna was glad. She was no great devotee of trees; they blocked one's view of the forest. And fire cleaned out the deadwood, exposed the soil to light and air, making possible the riot of life that followed fire's necessary cleansing and renewal.

Against the scorched earth, with the liquid gold of the lowering sun, a carpet of glacier lilies glowed with an electric green so intense she could remember seeing it only in the altered states of consciousness of the late sixties and the paintings of Andy Warhol.

Glacier lilies were fragile yellow blooms, smaller than a half-dollar, that hung pointed and curling petals in graceful skirts around red stamens heavy with pollen. Their leaves grew from the base, sharpened green blades as tall as the blooms. Under this glamorous show, according to Joan, they hid bulbs rich in starch. The bulbs were routinely dug by the grizzlies in late summer and early fall as they followed the huckleberries into the higher elevations. At the height of the season great swatches would be dug up, leaving areas that looked as if they'd been rototilled.

This year, the flowers were spectacular. Glacier had gotten nearly twice its normal snowfall. Snows hadn't melted above six thousand feet until July. Spring, summer and fall were happening simultaneously as plants, so lately released from their winter sleep, rushed through the stages of life to reseed before the first cold nights in September.

"Hey," Joan said, "we've got company."

Anna dragged her eyes up from where they frolicked in fields of green and gold.

On a low ridge to the north, black as everything was black from a fire that had burned hot, fast and to the bone, stood a lone hiker. Behind him was a wall of exposed stone, probably once fawn-colored but now the gray-brown of rotting teeth where the rains had imperfectly washed it free of soot and char.

It wasn't against park rules to hike off trail. Or camp off trail for that matter, though that required a special permit. It was unusual. For a man alone it was also foolish. Bears were the least of the dangers of hiking by oneself in the backcountry. The greatest were carelessness and stupidity. A slip, a fall, a badly sprained ankle or shattered kneecap, and one could die of exposure or thirst before anybody thought to begin a search.

Rory, sensing a social—and so, static—occasion, was quick to drop his pack and dig out his water bottle, a state-of-the-art model with the filter built in. Anna allowed herself a fleeting moment of envy.

"Hello," Joan called cheerily, because she was that kind of person.

A happy "hello" from a small middle-aged lady was scarcely the stuff of nightmares, but even at twenty yards, Anna could swear she saw the hiker flinch, cast a glance over his shoulder as if deciding whether or not to make a run for it. Like a hound that hears the clarion call, fatigue fell away and Anna's mind grew sharp.

"Wonder what in hell he's been up to." She wasn't aware she'd spoken out loud till she noticed Joan and Rory staring at her. "What?" she demanded.

Joan just chuckled. Few people chuckled anymore, that low burbling sound free of cynicism or judgement that ran under the surface of mirth.

Anna's attention went back to the hiker. He was walking toward them. Reluctantly, she thought. This time she kept her suspicious nature under wraps. At first she'd resented the heightened awareness that law enforcement duties forced upon her. But somewhere along the line she'd come to enjoy it, as if looking for trouble was a desirable end in itself.

The interloper was in his teens at a guess, though maybe older. His beard was nonexistent, but an accumulation of grime aged him around the mouth. He'd been in the backcountry awhile. Hazel eyes, startling under beautifully shaped brown brows and shaded by a ball cap with a dolphin embroidered above the brim, moved nervously from place to place, as if he looked beyond their tiny band to see if there were reinforcements hiding, waiting to ambush him. The pack he carried was big, too heavy for day hiking but not packed for overnight. Judging from the way the ripstop nylon bagged inward it contained neither sleeping bag nor tent. He was camped out somewhere. So why carry the frame pack? And why the haunted look?

"You're a ways from anywhere," Joan said and stuck out her hand.

After the briefest pause, he took it. Workman's hands, Anna noted, callused and scarred, the nails broken and rimed with dirt from too long between baths. Odd for a boy so young. His shirt was streaked with soot and he wore a chain wrapped twice around his waist.

"You all just out camping or what?" he asked. The question didn't seem particularly neighborly to Anna but didn't bother Joan in the least. She launched into an explanation of the Greater Glacier Bear DNA research project, the wording geared for the ears of laymen. Anna set her pack down and freed her water from a mesh side pocket. Joan was proselytizing, converting the masses to greater respect of bears. Anna tried to figure out where the boy's accent was from. Henry Higgins aside, few people could place others by their dialect, except within the broadest of areas. Americans made it more difficult by swimming around the melting pot: kindergarten in Milwaukee, third grade in San Diego, high school in Saint Louis. The south was as close as Anna could place him, anywhere from Virginia to Texas.

Out of long habit she committed his physical description to memory. He was a big kid, though not tall, around five-foot-eight, chunky without being fat. The kind of body that's a good deal stronger than one would think. Shoulders sloped away from a round handsome neck. What hair she could see poking from beneath the ball cap was silky brown with a natural wave. One day soon his face would be chiseled into classic good looks. Anna could see it in the aquiline nose and the rounded prominent chin.

She took another drink. Sat on a rock.

The boy never loosed his pack, made none of the comfortable settling-in gestures she and Rory engaged in. When Joan had done with her sales pitch, he asked her where they were going for their traps. Obligingly Joan began showing him on the topo. Anna found herself wishing she wouldn't. His interest was overly specific, having nothing to do with the project and all to do with where the three of them were going to be at any given time.

"I'm Anna Pigeon," she interrupted none too subtly. "This is Joan Rand, Rory Van Slyke." Stepping up to him, she thrust her hand out much as Joan had done. No better way to get the feel of somebody literally as well as figuratively. Despite the afternoon's heat, his palm was clammy. He was scared or had serious problems with circulation. A rank odor came off him. Not just the accumulation of unwashed body odors but something muskier, almost an animal smell. "What's your name?"

Again the flinch. "Geoffrey . . . uh . . . Mic-Mickleson."

"Nicholson?" Joan asked helpfully.

"Nicholson."

Now Anna knew he was up to something. "Where are you from, Geoffrey?" Had she been on the Trace, in uniform, she would have had this boy out of his car, his driver's license in her hand quicker than a swallow can change directions in flight.

"Oh. You know. All over. I'd better be going. It's a ways back to camp." He smiled for the first time and Anna resisted the temptation to be charmed. Not only was it pretty—his straight, white teeth probably the cleanest part of him—but sparked with a hint of apology and an innocence that bordered on goodness. The smile was at odds with the rest of the package. Anna chose to ignore it.

"Be seeing you around," she said as he turned and walked back the way he had come. It sounded more like: "We'll be keeping an eye on you." Anna meant it to. Some people bore watching. She was sure this fellow was among them. She was just as sure they wouldn't be seeing him. Not if he saw them first.

Burbling notes drew her back into the present. Joan was smiling, her eyes full of altogether too much fun. "I do declare, in another minute or two you were going to frisk that boy and read him his rights. Frisking I could understand. A smile to make you lie right down and die."

Rory found a lump of charred wood to fix his attention on, evidently uncomfortable with women his mother's age—or older—having impure thoughts.

"He was so fishy I thought he was going to sprout gills and swim away," Anna defended herself.

"Aw, he was just shy."

"He was carrying a half-empty frame pack."

"Maybe he lost his day pack."

"It was too full for a day hike."

"Maybe he's a photographer, carrying cameras, tripods, film."

"Maybe," Anna said, but she didn't think so. "Why the big interest in where we were going, where we were camping?"

"Because he's a *nice* young man and *nice* young men pretend to be interested in what their elders and betters are saying. Isn't that right, Rory?"

"That's true," Rory said with such sincerity Anna wanted to laugh but didn't for fear of alienating him.

"See? Proof," Joan said.

Anna didn't say anything. She was getting entirely too crabby over the whole thing. "Are we almost there?" she asked plaintively.

B y the time they reached the vicinity of the first hair trap, too
little light and too little strength remained for anything but
setting up camp.

With the departure of the sun, the mountain grew cold. The thin, dry air did not retain heat. Horseflies and deerflies took themselves off to wherever it was they went during the dark hours but the mosquitoes remained, a cloud of mindless hunger hovering over the camp.

Despite their carnivorous attendance, Anna hauled water from a startlingly beautiful creek, a ribbon of green that cut through the burn scar, sparked by a joyous multitude of mountain wildflowers. Staying clean in the backcountry was an arduous undertaking, results obtained for effort put forth seldom satisfying, but for Anna, it was a necessary if she was to maintain anything close to good cheer. Tonight's ablutions were brief as every square inch of flesh was assaulted by flying proboscises the moment it was exposed.

Too tired for culinary frills or witty conversation, the three of them ate their freeze-dried lasagna, then crawled into their sleeping bags. Rory was restless and noisy in the tent beside theirs; Anna lay next to Joan, scratching insect bites and wondering if all earthly paradises had been infiltrated by something wretched, all ointments incomplete without the requisite fly. Yet she was uniquely happy. From time and use, cloth walls and hard ground had come to symbolize a freedom that loosed her mind and soothed her soul in a way she'd never been able to duplicate between cotton sheets.

Sleep curled down and she went willingly into freefall.

The trap they tended in the morning was in as awkward a locale as nature and researchers could devise. Glacier National Park was slashed with avalanche chutes. These cuts were scoured year after year when snow grew unstable in springtime and was carried by its own prodigious weight down these natural passages. Because snow and ice cleared the chutes of larger vegetation, the rocky soil had little to bond it to the steep-sided gorges. When rain followed snow, mudslides followed avalanches.

The only plants that could survive these inhospitable conditions were fast-growing, supple and ever-renewing. From a distance the chutes appeared as paler green pleats in a mountain-green robe: nearly barren, at best knee-deep in ground cover. Up close they were head-high in a riot of color: red paintbrush, lavender fleabane, hot-pink fireweed, white cow parsnip, lacy green false hellebore, the flashy red of chokecherries, white pearls of baneberry, rich purple huckleberries, fierce yellows of butterweed and arnica. Of these, the bears enjoyed all the berries, hellebore and cow parsnip. A veritable salad bar and a perfect place for the trap.

The trap itself was marvelously low-tech. Eighty feet of barbed wire was strung from tree to tree or, in this case, tree to rock to snag to tree, fifty centimeters above the ground. Inside this ephemeral corral was a litter of rotten pieces of wood strewn haphazardly about and a single sapling twenty feet high.

"What do you think?" Joan asked.

Such was the pride in her voice, Anna dug deep to find something nice to say. "It doesn't stink," she ventured.

"That's right!" Joan said as if Anna was a very clever student. The researcher dropped her fanny onto a rock, letting the stone take the weight of her pack as she squeezed free of the shoulder straps. "The smell of the DNAmite—"

"*DNAmite?* You're kidding," Rory said incredulously.

"That's what we call the blood lure," Joan admitted.

"A lot more civilized than what I'd call it," Anna contributed.

"Be grateful for DNAmite," Joan said. "We've tried Runny Honey made of blood, fish and banana, and Blinkie's Demise with fish blood and fennel oil. My personal favorite, Cattle Casket Picnic in a Basket, a succulent mix of blood, cheese essence and calamus powder. Then there was one with Vick's VapoRub—Licorice Whip with blood, anise and peppermint."

"DNAmite is sounding better all the time," Anna said.

"Anyway," Joan went back to the original thought, "the smell goes off in a week or ten days. The love scent lasts somewhat less."

"The skunk in the film canister," Rory said. He too was divesting himself of his pack. Anna followed suit.

"That's right!" Joan exclaimed. Two excellent pupils in one day. "Only this one was a sweet cherry scent. Every two-week round, we change this lure. Bears are terrifically smart. It only takes them once to learn something. And they teach it to the cubs, usually in one lesson they remember for a lifetime. The bears come for the DNAmite and have a good roll but there's no food reward. We didn't want to get them habituated to traps as food sources. So next time maybe they're not so interested when they smell the blood and fish. That's why we've got the love scent; a little something new to pique their interest. We started with beaver castor, then fennel oil, smoky bacon—a real winner—then sweet cherry and now, last round of traps, bears with jaded palates, we bring out the *pièce de résistance*: skunk."

Free of her pack, Joan stood and shook each of her parts—feet, legs, hands, arms, trunk—like she was doing the hokey-pokey. Ritual completed, she turned her attention to the trap. "The love scent's hung up high to broadcast on the breeze and to keep it out of reach so the first bear doesn't take it down—" She paused a moment, then muttered, "Harumph."

Anna laughed. She'd never heard anyone say "harumph," though she'd read it a time or two when she was working her way through the old dead English authors.

"Hung it too low," Joan said. "Heads will roll. Look. It's gone."

Anna hadn't coupled Joan Rand with the activity of rolling heads, but watching her face, she had little doubt the threat was not empty. Clearly, incompetence was not tolerated in pure research. Anna made a mental note never to screw up.

"Maybe a bear climbed up and got it," Rory offered. He'd felt the chill as well and tried to deflect the anger from the hapless hanger of scent.

"Grizzlies don't tend to climb trees," Joan said. "Not the adults. Cubs can climb some. This little tree is not big enough around to climb. No. If it had been hung properly, a bear couldn't get it, not unless he had a fifteen-foot reach."

"Where does the hard stuff go?" Anna asked. "The DNA-mite?"

Rory snorted.

"Okay, okay," Joan said. "Let's just call it the lure. Now, that wonderful catnip of bears is poured on a pile of rotting wood in the middle of the trap. Or if the middle is *ocupado,* as in this case," she waved at a four-foot-high piece of rock nearly obscured in the brush that choked the enclosure, "at least five feet from the wire. We don't want 'em getting the goodies without squeezing under the wire first. We save that lure for last. Pour it, then get upwind before it permanently saturates our nose hairs. Take a look at this." Joan poked at a bit of the widely scattered pieces of rotten wood. "It's everywhere. Our bears must have had a regular jamboree."

A painting, "Teddybears' Picnic," came to Anna's mind: a bucolic scene of bears depicted in human poses picnicking in the woods, indolently pursuing human entertainments. She'd always found the picture disturbing. "I was told dead bears, bears that have been skinned, look like people," she heard herself say, and wondered where the comment had sprung from.

Joan hesitated before responding. Her usually clear greenish eyes narrowed and clouded briefly. Anna got the feeling she'd been out of line but couldn't guess how.

"That's so," Joan said. "It's unsettling. Not something I'd care to look at more often than I had to." She glanced at Rory. He'd lost interest in them and washed trail mix down with water.

Anna realized what the problem was. Joan suspected her of trying to creep-out the Van Slyke boy for the sheer evil fun of it. "Oh," she said and closed her mouth to reassure the researcher that her motives were pure.

Joan handed out latex gloves, envelopes and pens from where they were cached in her pack. Anna and Rory were set to work collecting the hair while she took scat samples from the many opportunities with which ecstatic bears had provided her.

Approximately every foot along the wire was a barb. Wearing gloves so as not to contaminate the samples, Anna carefully plucked the fur free of each barb and deposited it in its own small envelope. Rory then sealed it and wrote the date and location of the trap on the back. Using an alcohol-based disinfectant, the metal was then cleaned to remove any remaining tissue or hair cells, and they moved on to the next barb to repeat the process. When they were done collecting, the wire would be rolled up and packed out to be reused at the next trap site.

The trap they currently worked had been extremely success- ful. Nearly every one of the rusted points was tufted with fur. The chore was tedious. The footing uneven. The deerflies hellacious. Still Anna preferred it to the soulless air-conditioned patrol car she'd spent her days in for too many months.

"You're good at this," she said to Rory, because she was feel- ing generous and it was true.

Despite Mother Nature's considerable aggravations, Rory worked with a quiet diligence Anna found admirable in a boy his age. The patience he exhibited with the fussy and exacting nature of their task was admirable in a person at any age.

"My dad—Les," he corrected himself, or punished his father, "and I used to put together airplane models when I was in grade school. When he used to do stuff."

"Used to? What does he do now?" Anna asked, ready to change the subject if he brought up any touching stories of crip- ples or lingering illness. No sense getting to know him that well.

Rory's coarse blond hair, not yet as sweaty as Anna's, fell from underneath the brim of his ball cap. He pushed it back and she noticed how small and fine-boned his hands were. He proba- bly fought against being perceived as delicate or wimpy. There was something in his silences that could be attributed to an at- tempt at toughness. "Les is a low-level number cruncher," he said with an unbecoming sneer.

Careful not to lose any, Anna brushed three hairs from a gloved fingertip into the envelope he held pinched open. "Low- level number cruncher" sounded like a quote. Anna wondered who had called Rory's dad that and why the boy had embraced the derogatory term.

"What does your mom do?" she asked, hoping for a little more enthusiasm to pass the time.

"Mom's cool," Rory said as they crabbed over half a yard to the next section of wire. "She's a lawyer."

"Trial lawyer?"

"Divorce. We live in Seattle. Carolyn's my stepmother. My real mom died when I was five. Dad married Carolyn a couple years later. She doesn't take shit off anybody."

Rory meant that as high praise indeed. Anna could tell that not taking shit was of great importance to him. At eighteen that boded ill. Refusing to "take shit" translated in Anna's experience to taking pride in the character flaws of impatience, intolerance and insecurity. Any law enforcement officer who refused to "take shit" was not doing his job. Or at least not well.

"Speaking of taking shit . . ." Joan came up behind them. "Got four superb samples. Come look at this one." She had tucked the vials into their padded carrying case so Anna could only assume she wanted them to follow her back to the source. Rory rose from his knees in a single fluid movement. Anna pushed belatedly up from hers, none too excited about exerting herself in the mad-dog-and-Englishman sun to go look at bear excrement.

Joan had squatted down on her heels, Rory in like posture at her elbow. Content not to toy with gravity any more than need be, Anna remained standing.

"Looky," Joan said. "This bear's been into something he oughtn't." Poking through the excreta, she turned up a couple of reddish fragments. "Paper. Maybe he got into a pack. Or an outhouse. It's illegal, but people sometimes still dump their trash down the toilets at the camps rather than carry it out. Bears go after it. Or he might have got into garbage. See this? Probably tinfoil."

Joan pondered that a moment. Anna slapped at the flies trying to skinny-dip in the sweat at her temples. "Did you read anything in the BIMS about bears in garbage, campsites, anything like that?" Joan asked Anna after a moment.

Anna hadn't.

"Ah, well," Joan said. "Could have been a backcountry outhouse the rangers haven't checked in a couple of days." She looked worried. One of her four-hundred-pound charges had misbehaved. The concern wasn't misplaced, considering what penalties humankind often extracted from other species for even the slightest infractions.

Joan stirred around in the pile some more. "These lumps, dog food or horse pellets is my guess. Bears don't have what you'd call careful digestion. Food passes through them almost in its original form sometimes. See? You can see the edge of this pellet. Hardly dulled. Grizzlies have a terrific range but it's a safe bet this fella got his ill-gotten gains here in the park. This trap is far enough from any of the borders; for it to be going through his system here, he'd've got it locally, so to speak."

Researchers lived in the details. Anna accepted this preoccupation as necessary but couldn't embrace it as her own. "Must be," she said and went back to her furgathering.

The new trap to be set up in cell sixty-four was plotted on paper just under three miles as the crow would fly from the old trap. Dismantling the traps and setting them up was the work of an hour or two. Getting their decidedly uncrowlike selves to the next destination was the time-and-energy-consuming part of the job.

Anna's body was as tired as it had been the first day out but it was settling into its wilderness mode. Aches dulled or vanished as muscles began to realize no amount of whining was going to deter her. She began thoroughly enjoying herself. On the west side of Flattop, still in the burn and away from improved trails, lakes, glaciers or much else that would recommend it to tourists, the isolation felt complete. They followed game trails where they could and scrambled over the broken serrated stone of the sheared-off mountain where they had to.

Hidden gardens occasionally appeared with such sudden and unexpected beauty they ratified Anna's belief in magic. On some of the steep and rocky hillsides, where the soil was too thin to support trees, the fire had leapt over, leaving the stony steps unburned. White and gold rocks, rimmed round with purple butterwort, Indian paintbrush and feathery yellow stonecrop, created magnificent tumbles of color in the desolate landscape.

At one such oasis, where they broke for lunch, Joan pointed out an area that had been dug up, the charred soil turned over in a rough square, eight feet on a side.

"Bears digging glacier lilies," she told them.

Glad to be free of her pack with a few minutes to do as she pleased, Anna wandered over to where the dirt was disturbed, hoping to find some good tracks. Instead of bear prints, she found boot prints and, in the dig itself, the sharp-edged marks that could only be made by a shovel.

"I think I know what our Geoff Mickleson-Nicholson was up to," she called back. Joan came to join her and Anna pointed out what she had found.

"Son of a bee," Joan said. "Somebody's sure been digging them up. No proof it's our guy."

"Hah," Anna said rudely.

"It happens," Joan said.

Anna knew that. People routinely—and illegally—supplemented their gardens by digging up rare or merely desirable plants on park lands. Though why anyone would come so far to dig the plants and go to the effort to pack them out was a mystery. There were plenty of places near the Going to the Sun Road where a reasonably stealthy individual could get all the lilies he wanted and dump them in the waiting trunk of his car.

"People are stinkers," Anna said philosophically.

"People don't know any better," Joan said charitably.

"They're just weeds," Van Slyke offered and was nonplussed by the severe looks he got from both his elders.

"Lecture, after dinner tonight," Joan forewarned him. "Be there."

She radioed the site of the disturbance and the extent of the damage to dispatch so it could be passed on to law enforcement. It crossed Anna's mind to tell her to give them the description of the young hiker they had met, but she didn't. The crime wasn't worth the investigation. And, too, Joan had liked the boy with the beatific smile. Earlier in the year, when Anna had first reported for duty on the Natchez Trace, she'd worked the murder of a child—a girl, really, sixteen. The experience had ruined her taste for making the world a little darker for any reason.

Because the burn had denuded it of trees, leaving them no way to string the wire, the second trap couldn't be put where it had been marked. Joan found a place nearby that would suffice. At the confluence of three game trails, tried and true paths through the broken country sure to be favored by bears, they strung their wire around the snags of several white pines and the branches of an alder.

A tall snag, looking as sere and crippled as a mummy's fingerbone, thrust up near one edge of the enclosure. Joan, working as carefully as if she were handling nitroglycerine, took one of the film canisters containing the skunk lure from the glass jar and perforated the hard plastic with an ice pick so the love scent could broadcast its charms.

While she strung it up in the top of the snag, Anna and Rory foraged down the still-green slope of the ravine for downed wood. When they had a pile a couple feet high and twice that in diameter, they came to the moment of truth.

Desirous of proving himself on the battlefield of the thoroughly revolting, Rory volunteered to do the honors. Anna and Joan watched as he uncapped the liter bottle of blood lure and poured it over the wood. The liquid was black and thick. Out of self-preservation, Anna had forgotten how unbelievably strong and unremittingly vile the smell was. The makers of stink bombs could take a lesson from bear researchers.

The trap set, the three of them departed as quickly as they could. Rory walked beside and just behind Anna, Joan taking the lead since she was the only one who knew where they were going.

"I think I got some on my hands," Rory said.

"Oh, ish," Anna said unsympathetically. "Stay away from me."

"No. Seriously. I think I got some on me."

This time she heard the panic in his voice and stopped.

Rory's face was tight and young with fear. His eyes had gone too wide. Anna could see a narrow line of white between the pupils and the lower lids. She enjoyed tormenting young people as much as the next person, but fear, real fear, could not be ignored. "This is really bothering you, isn't it?"

He stopped beside her. He clasped his hands around the shoulderstraps of his pack to stop their shaking then let go suddenly as if afraid the taint on them would spread to his equipment. "No big deal," he said, the need to hide his fear as great as the fear itself. "I just thought if I got that smell on me . . . well, you know."

Anna could think of no way to deal with Rory's obvious terror of wild animals. She realized some of what Joan had taken for orneriness earlier had been her knee-jerk attempt to kid him out of it. At a loss, she let her sight turn inward. A picture came to mind. She had been very small. A rotten boy, Daryl Spanks, a boy terminally infected with cooties, had put them all over her tuna sandwich at the end-of-year school picnic.

Mrs. White, her first grade teacher, had not told her how silly she was being. Instead, she had taken the sandwich and painstakingly picked every single cootie off of it.

"Let's have a sniff," Anna said and shrugged out of her pack.

Rory put out his hands palms up in the universal pose of inspection. Anna sniffed both arms carefully up to the elbow. "I don't think you got any on you," she said finally. His eyes had lost their panicked glaze but he was still wound too tight for comfort.

"Just to be sure," Anna said. She dug her liquid soap from her pack, doused his arms with her drinking water and made him lather and rinse twice. Fear was a killer. Anna had seen people die of it when their wounds weren't anywhere near mortal. Rory wasn't in that kind of trouble, but fear distracted. That in itself was a danger with off-trail travel.

The second rinse completed, she conducted another sniff test. "If there was any residue, that got it. Smell."

Rory smelled his arms. The cooties were gone.

"What are you guys doing?" Joan called. She'd turned around, discovered she was alone and backtracked.

Alarm returned to Rory's face. This time it didn't take an adept to divine the cause. He didn't want his boss to know he was a weenie.

"Rory had a splinter," Anna said. "We got it out."

Rory could no more thank Anna for this face-saving lie than she could have run a four-minute mile. Instead, he offhandedly helped her on with her pack and she understood the gratitude implicit in the gesture.

They followed the rim of the canyon inhabited by Continental Creek. Though they walked always through the black and dusty shadow of the old fire, the ravine had escaped the flames. By contrast the growth in it seemed the more miraculous and verdant.

Late in the afternoon they came out of the trailless country to the improved and maintained West Flattop Trail. Travel became so carefree, had her pack been lighter, Anna would have skipped. Nothing like a little hardship to bring about appreciation of the finer things. Two hours before sunset they hiked out of the burn. Fir trees closed around the trail, breathing cool, clean air and a reassurance of peace the burned area lacked.

They camped off trail, midway between the next trap they would dismantle and the site where they hoped to set the new one.

Joan had picked a lovely place half a mile off West Flattop in a small meadow ringed with fir and pine. A stream no more than a foot wide with silky grasses growing nearly over the top of it, so tiny it did not show on the map, cut through one edge of the clearing. In the startling way of glacier-carved country, near the stream, apparently fallen from the sky, was an immense slab of gray-and-sand-streaked stone.

The beauty of the place did as much to knit the raveled sleeve of care as sleep might and they stayed up late, lying shoulder to shoulder on the rock, watching for falling stars and telling the inconsequential truths strangers thrown together in the woods often do.

There was no discrimination between male and female, old and young, they just existed, unimportant and free under the infinity of Montana's sky. Anna told them of her new sweetheart in Mississippi, a southern sheriff who moonlighted as an Episcopal priest. And who had a wife who refused to grant him a divorce. Mississippi took the sacrament of marriage seriously. There were only three reasons a person could get a divorce without his or her spouse's cooperation: adultery, felony or mental cruelty.

"I think it'd be mental cruelty to make somebody stay married to you who didn't want to," Rory said, sounding as if he spoke from experience.

Rory talked about his stepmom, telling them of this great joke she'd pulled on Les: telling everybody at a party that he had a penile implant and making cracks all evening about pumping things up.

That brought on an extended silence as Anna and Joan tried to figure out what the funny part was. Rory seemed to need them to laugh with him but neither managed it.

Joan talked about wanting a dog and how life in the parks made that an impossibility. Had she been able to hear the loneliness underlying her wish, she probably wouldn't have told them, but with their backs on good mountain rock and their eyes full of nothing but stars, they had slipped free of the social taboos not to feel too much—and never let on if they did.

It was after midnight when they finally crawled into their sleeping bags.

Without warning, Anna's eyes were open, blind and useless in the claustrophobic dark of the tent. Something had signaled an abrupt end to sleep. A sound. Cracking. Wood on wood or a twig snapping under a heavy foot. Or hoof. Or paw. Perhaps Rory, up in the night to answer the call of nature. Though the poor boy was so afraid of critters he'd probably suffer till morning in the imagined safety of his tent. Not for the first time, Anna wondered why a young man still frightened of the monsters under his bed would pay to work in bear country.

Not yet concerned, she waited for the sound—the quality already forgotten, left in the sleep it had so rudely jerked her from—to come again, attach itself to meaning so she could call off the internal watchdogs and close her eyes.

A soft exhalation, the sigh of the wind or a ghostly child penetrated the tent wall, then brushing, gentle, the sound a soft-bristle brush would make on nylon. Anna had heard it before when furry denizens had come to visit in the night: skunks, raccoons and, once, a porcupine. The noise their coats made rubbing against fabric as they explored her campsite.

Tonight's brush was painting strokes high on the tent wall. Deer. Elk. Bear. Anna felt the first tingling along her spine as a race memory of untold millions of years of being hunted by night stirred deep in her primitive brain.

Making no noise, she reached over and touched Joan.

She woke quickly. "What—"

"Shh." Anna listened. Though she could see nothing of her tentmate and no longer touched her, she could feel Joan's tension, along with her own, charging the atmosphere inside the tent.

Shushing, susurrating sound. All around them now as if the animal circled the tent. Not once. Not to probe and, curiosity satisfied, move on. Circle after circle. No sound but the soft brushing and the periodic gusts of air, voiceless woofs. A bear. Grizzly. Black. Full grown. Shoulder touching high on the domed wall of nylon.

With each circuit, Anna's Disney-born sense of oneness with her fellows of the tooth and claw faded. It was replaced by the lurid pen-and-ink illustrations she remembered from a sensationalized account of two women killed when she was in college, both dragged from their tents, mauled, killed and fed on in *Night of the Grizzlies*.

She pushed her lips as close to Joan's face as a lover might and barely breathed the words, "What's it doing?"

"Don't know," Joan whispered back.

The circling stopped, as if at the thread of sound the two women spun between them. A silence followed, so absolute in the perfect darkness of the tent, Anna felt dizzy, as if she were falling into it. Her senses stretched: blind eyes trying to see through two layers of tenting, deaf ears trying to hear movement beyond the insubstantial walls.

A barely audible rustle as Joan pushed herself up on her elbows sawed across Anna's nerves with the impact of sandpaper on a sunburn. No second hand to measure it, time did not tick by but pulsed, expanding and contracting like the air in her lungs as Anna forced herself to breathe.

"Do you think—" she whispered.

A snap of wood.

"Shh."

A growl broke the night above them and both women screamed. The growling increased in volume and moved down the length of the tent. On this circuit the bear leaned in, no longer brushing but caving the tent walls in with its weight. Formless, terrifying, Anna felt the nylon push hard against her shoulder, the side of her head.

Hands—Joan's—fumbled over the front of her sweatshirt, closing on the cotton. "Down," she was hissing. "Fetal position."

Anna's training came back to her. Play dead. Try and protect the soft white underbelly. Curling in on herself when every ounce of her being urged her to break out of this North Face sarcophagus and run, actually hurt, stomach and leg muscles trying to cramp.

The growling ebbed and flowed but remained in one direction as if the animal stood outside the front-zippered fly talking to itself, deciding whether they were to live or die.

Anna flipped through her brain looking for anything she'd done to attract the animal, to hold its attention for so long. Nothing. Under Joan's watchful eye she and Rory had put everything that could be of any interest whatsoever to bears into the red bear-pack: lip balm, insect repellent, sunscreen, deodorant, tooth-paste, virtually anything liquid and/or scented. Even if it was sealed in glass, Joan insisted it go in the bear-bag, which was hung with the food fifteen yards from camp.

The mental listing was cut off. The bear was roaring, raging. "Holy shit," Anna said. Her own voice scared her. "Is it hurt, you think? Wounded?"

"God, I hope not," Joan said fervently.

A blow struck the tent then and they heard nylon ripping.

"Shit," Anna said.

"Quiet."

Nylon tearing. Roars that cut through the dark and tore into Anna's bowels. Joan breathing or crying on her neck. Her, gasping or sobbing on Joan's.

Noise from without went on for what seemed like forever but was probably only half that long. Crashing. Roars. Fabric ripping. Thumps as if the bear threw or batted things from one place to another. Swooshing and flopping. Digging. Bass gutteral grunts pushed out with the sound of frenzied destruction. Impacts against tent and earth as if the beast tore at the ground.

"What in hell?" Anna whispered.

"Beats me," Joan whispered back.

Soul splitting, a roar broke close and vicious. Blows began falling first to one side of the tent then the other. Anna felt a cut through to her right shoulder.

Blood. Now there would be the smell of blood.

The lightweight metal tent frame collapsed with a second blow and Anna felt weight slam down on the back of her neck. Habit or instinct, she threw her arm over her face and pushed down tighter around Joan.

The animal had gone mad. The deep-throated anger of nature turning on humankind. Then came crunching and a prolonged rustle. Rolling on the downed tent? Burrowing through the thin stays in the fabric? A high wild roar, a shriek in gravel and glass.

"Rory," Joan whispered.

"Shh."

A crack. Maybe a tent pole, maybe a peg jerked from the ground by the elasticized cord and shot into a tree.

Abruptly everything stopped. Deathlike stillness. Anna was

dizzy with the quiet. The rage of the attack ended as a candle's light is ended when the wick is pinched.

Nothing moved: not Anna, not Joan, not the bear. For what seemed a very long time, Anna waited, muscles in body and mind drawn tight, waiting for the slash of claws to rake blood from her back, the smell of an omnivore's breath before the puncturing canines pierced skull and bone.

The crunch never came.

Fear did not diminish but increased. The fear that if she moved, even so much as an eyelash, if her pulse fluttered or her skin twitched, the narrowly averted disaster would be brought down upon them. Either Joan felt the same way or she'd fainted.

After a while Anna thought she heard the passage of a large creature a few yards away. Maybe the bear had crossed the meadow soundlessly and now pushed into the underbrush at the edge of the clearing.

"Gone?" Anna whispered. Her throat was dust-dry. The word came out as a croak that sounded scarcely human.

"Wait," Joan replied.

Handfast like children lost in the wood, Anna and Joan lay in the wreckage of their tent. Anna could feel the nylon fallen over the side of her head and neck. A cold draft came in through a tear someplace.

Unmeasured, time passed. With no new horror to stimulate it, the fear response began to wane. Anna's heart rate dropped, muscles unclenched, breathing slowed and deepened. She began to be embarrassed by her hold on Joan's hand and pulled free.

"I've got to move," she whispered. "See what's going on."

Joan thought about it so long Anna feared she was going to have to prove insubordinate their second night out. She couldn't lie there any longer, unable to see, to move, to think.

"Okay," the researcher said at last. "One at a time. Move slowly. You see the bear, stop. Stop everything. Just lie wherever you are."

"Got it."

"Don't fight."

"No."

"Don't run."

"No."

"Okay."

Trussed in tent, fly and sleeping bag, Anna found escape impossible without some squirming and thrashing. An unpleasant image of her cat, Piedmont, waiting in total stillness till an unwitting mouse or squirrel thought in its silly little rodent brain that the world was safe once again. Then, as the helpless nitwit began to creep from its hidey-hole, Piedmont would pounce. The ending was seldom a happy one for anybody but Piedmont.

With each twitch and rustle she made as she turned her body around and pushed her way feebly toward the end of the tent that held the zippered entrance flap, Anna was reminded that it was infinitely better to be predator than prey.

The front of the tent had suffered the worst. Poles were bent or broken but still strung together by the elastic cord running through the sections of hollow tubing that fitted together to form the tent's infrastructure. The result was a laundry basket of funhouse corners and shredded walls.

Without a light, finding first the tent zipper then the fly was proving impossible. Spending more time head-down in the suffocating folds of night and nylon was unthinkable. Anna was not yet so far gone that she slept with her Swiss army knife in her pajama pocket. She regretted that inconvenient sign of sanity.

Then she discovered that the bear had done for her what she could not do for herself.

A long gash had been opened through tent and fly. Resisting the impulse to fight her way clear of the entrapping ruin of fabric, she pulled the nylon open a finger's width and peeked out.

After the pitch dark of the tent, the clearing, lit by a half-moon and stars, appeared as bright as a staged night for actors. When she'd satisfied herself the bear was gone, she crawled out.

For a long moment she crouched just outside while the shakes took control of her body. She felt like laughing and wanted to cry. Breathing deeply to dispel the hysteria, she let it pass. Having pushed herself to the balls of her feet, knuckles down in a runner's starting position, she turned a slow circle, searching the black woods pressing close—surely closer than when they'd retired for the night—seeking any sign of movement or sound.

Finding none, she said, "All clear." It came out in a weak kitten's mewl. Clearing her throat, she said it again. Better.

"Help me," Joan's muffled call came from within the pile.

Anna held the tear open, and within a moment Joan wiggled free, caterpillar from cocoon.

"Rory!" they both called at once.

"Flashlight," Anna demanded and Joan grubbed in the tangle for her day pack.

"Rory!" Anna called again.

His tent was in worse shape than theirs. In the colorless light of the moon, it lay like a ripped and punctured balloon. Anna grabbed handfuls of nylon. "Rory," she called a third time.

Joan had found the flashlight but Anna didn't need it to know Rory was gone.

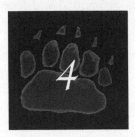

"Luke!" Joan screamed the name of her younger son, the one who bore such a striking resemblance to the Van Slyke boy. Dropping the flashlight, she fell to her knees and began digging frantically through the collapsed tent, clutching at the lumps of his pack and boots as if they were severed parts from his torn body. The courage and control she'd exhibited when the danger was merely to herself were gone. She was reacting as a panicked mother might.

"Joan," Anna said, then more sharply: "Joan!" The researcher was beyond the reach of human voice. Anna waded into the mess of fabric and aluminum tubing, knelt and grabbed her around the shoulders, holding her tight, pinning her arms to her sides. For an instant she thought Joan was going to fight but the solid reality of the embrace brought her down from panic. She tried to get up.

"Stay," Anna commanded.

"The bear must have dragged him out, taken him into the woods," Joan said. She sounded stunned, incredulous, but no longer out of control. Anna let go of her shoulders but kept a firm grip on her hands. Joan fell back and they sat face to face, knee to knee on Rory's tent.

"Maybe not," Anna said. She'd been hoping for calmness, rationality, but her voice shook, tremulous and childlike. "Do bears do that?" she had to ask, *Night of the Grizzlies* notwithstanding.

"Not often," Joan said. "Rarely. Almost never." She was reassuring herself. Anna let her.

A quick glance at her watch told her it was at least three hours till dawn. The faint light of the clearing, seemingly so bright after the inside of the tent, would not penetrate the thick canopy of forest. Had the bear dragged Rory into the woods to feed on, there was a chance the boy was still alive. An even better chance he wouldn't stay that way long.

Pursuing a grizzly into the forest in the dark, a grizzly already enraged by something and now, perhaps, with food in the form of Rory Van Slyke to defend, was the rankest madness. If the bear took the boy, they would most likely find his corpse half eaten and buried in a shallow grave raked out of the duff. If they found him at all.

Not going after Rory was going to be one of the hardest things Anna had ever done. Because, if he was still alive and they could find him, there was a chance—always a chance—that they could frighten the bear away before it killed him.

Crazy to try and save him.

"Stay here," Anna said, retrieving the flashlight from where Joan had dropped it. "It's too dark to find anything, but I can check the edges for—for anything obvious."

"I'm not staying."

Anna could delude herself sufficiently to put her own life at risk but not so completely she could endanger anybody else.

"You've got to," she said. "If Rory ran off, then comes back and we're both gone, he'll freak. You know he will."

"If Rory ran, the bear would have chased him," Joan said stubbornly. "That's what they do."

Anna couldn't remain still any longer. "You'll stay?"

"I'll stay."

"I'm not going far. Not out of earshot."

Cold and cutting, a new wave of fear met Anna at the edge of the clearing. Standing beside the tiny stream, moonlight silver on the grass, the music of water over stones in her ears, she stared into the ragged, unremitting night beneath the fir trees and she could not move.

Since she was a child Anna had felt a kinship with animals. She'd never been afraid of them. As she grew, she came to respect their ways and not tread on their taboos, putting them and herself in danger. The animal that had circled their tent, ravaged their camp, was different. Though it went against logic she felt, on a level too deep to argue with, that it had been toying with them. The circling and circling, the sudden rage, the fury of the violence, the abrupt cessation, as if a malevolent plan were behind it.

Walt Disney lied. It was the Brothers Grimm who had the right idea: witches baked little girls, stepmothers poisoned them, bears ate them.

"Get a grip," she whispered, dizzy with the nightmare she'd just dreamed. "A bear's a bear's a bear." It crossed her mind that by demonizing the animal, she might just be seeking an excuse not to step across the stream into the woods.

"Make noise." Joan's shout woke Anna to her responsibilities.

"Right," she called back. The objective was not to sneak up on the bear but to frighten it away should it still be in the vicinity.

"Rory," Anna called and, "Hey, bear," indiscriminately as she pushed under the draping branches of the first fir. Between cries she listened. There'd been no special reason she'd entered the woods at this point. In darkness, if the bear had left any mark of its passage over the meadow, she'd not seen it. She just had to start somewhere.

Anna had been working wilderness parks for many years but held no illusions about her own powers. Better outdoorsmen than herself, without compass or a view of the stars or horizon, would get lost in these woods at night. Keeping the clearing in sight on her left, she worked her way around the edge of the meadow. A complete circuit revealed nothing. It was too damn dark.

"Anna," Joan called.

"Here." She flashed her light toward the camp and stepped out of the trees. The search was as futile as she'd feared it would be. Joan's hail gave her the impetus to give it up.

"The bear didn't take him, at least not from his tent."

Joan was so cheered by her good news Anna hesitated but had to ask. "What makes you think that?"

"The zipper. Look."

Anna crossed the small clearing. Joan held up the tattered remnants of Rory's tent and rain fly. "Both unzipped. Bears don't do zippers. No thumbs. No patience." She laughed, the burden of the boy's life lifted from her. At least for the moment.

So bleak had been Anna's thoughts, she resisted the optimism as she might a trap. "Rory could have been sleeping with them open," she said.

Joan gave her a look that even in the ghost light of the moon glowed with mock scorn. "Yeah. Right."

"Right." Of course he wouldn't. Mosquitoes had disappeared around eleven when the temperature dropped below their comfort zone, but Rory would have been closed up tight, keeping the scary outside out. Thin, man-made cloth against four-inch godmade claws; an illusion, only, of safety.

Unzipped zippers didn't mean Rory was unharmed. They only indicated he'd not been dragged from his tent. Several scenarios, equally grim, presented themselves in Anna's brain. Panicked, the boy might have fled the tent. Maybe the bear did chase him when he ran. That would explain the abrupt end to the bear's attack on their tent. Anna had heard nothing to indicate Rory'd made a break for it, but then she couldn't swear she hadn't had her hands over her ears like a little kid. Rory might have been outside the tent when the bear arrived, taking a leak or whatever. If that was the case, he might have gotten away. Then again, he might have made a noise or a movement that drew the bear away from camp and down upon himself.

These alternatives to salvation-by-zipper would occur to Joan soon enough. Anna wasn't sure how she'd react. The frantic call of "Luke!" still resounded in Anna's skull bones. Motherhood was an alien world. Who could predict which forms of insanity were fostered there?

"Hot drinks," she declared, naming the universal panacea for all wilderness ills.

"Shouldn't we . . . We've got to . . ." Joan cast vaguely around for an action. Logic won. "Okay."

Glad to be doing something, Anna headed to the far side of what had been their stargazing rock and now looked unsettlingly like a sacrificial altar, to where they'd hung the bear-pack. Each step closer to the black beneath the trees drove fear up into her innards. Beyond fear: a rudimentary, gut-wrenching terror of the dark and the ravening beasts that have awaited there for tens of hundreds of thousands of years. To give in to it would be to crawl into a cave in her mind that she never wanted to visit again. Once was enough. She'd seen those cold blank walls in Mississippi when a man had beaten her nearly to death.

Narrowing her mindscape to the next few seconds and the task at hand, she forced fear to a level that didn't impede her functioning. Eyes and ears open for movement from the woods, she and Joan kept up a running patter, meaningless, to provide a level of human noise a bear—a normal bear—would find off-putting.

As she loosed the rope from the tree trunk to lower the bear-pack, a moment's panic knifed through her: a sudden vision of herself, arms laden with food, becoming an irresistible target, the shadows in the wood coalescing, the gleam of teeth, a rake of claws.

Breathing it out as if it were poison, she blew the image away and watched the red pack, colorless without the sun, separate from the greater darkness overhead and descend to the ground.

Once past the idea that the aroma of Constant Comment tea would bring certain death rushing from the trees, they began to enjoy the hot drinks working their dependable cure. The night was no less cold, the ruin of the camp no less stark, but sitting in the warmth of down bags, their backs against the solid reassurance of the rock, both Anna and Joan felt less afraid. Anna was able to let her thoughts off such a tight leash, and Joan's motherhood was being shoved back into its box by the scientist and researcher. Neither spoke of Rory Van Slyke. Until the sun rose he was in the hands of the gods. Or the belly of the beast.

"You're hurt," Joan said. "Your arm."

Anna looked down her right shoulder and remembered the pain slicing through it in the tent. In the feeble light of the setting moon it showed only as a black stain on the pale sleeve of the gray turtleneck she slept in. She'd not felt a thing since. Too much adrenaline in her system. Now that Joan called attention to it, she was aware of a burning sensation.

"It's not deep," Anna said.

"Only a flesh wound?" Joan laughed and it made Anna feel better than even the hot tea had.

The role of caretaker slipped over the researcher's own fears. She found the flashlight and shined it on Anna's arm. The jersey was torn and there was some blood. Joan set the flashlight on the rock, the beam pointed toward Anna. Pinching up the sleeve she said, "May I?"

"Tear away."

Joan tore open the sleeve over the wound. "Thanks. I've always wanted to do that. So dramatic."

Using water still warm from the stove, she washed the scratch clean. Anna watched with surprising disinterest. The events of the night left her with a detached feeling of unreality. *Like shock,* she warned herself and took another drink of hot sweet tea.

"You're right," Joan said. "It's not bad."

With the blood wiped away Anna could see it was shallow and only three or four inches long. Enough to break the skin and tear down a few layers but nothing more.

Obediently she held her tea in her left hand and let Joan clean the wound with peroxide, smear it with antibiotic ointment and dress it with gauze. It was the right thing to do. Bear's claws, she assumed, weren't sterile weapons. Left to herself, though, Anna might have ignored it. Lethargy: another sign of shock. Delayed onset. Bizarre. Anna drank more tea.

"I've been researching bears for twenty-one years," Joan said as she finished putting away the first-aid supplies. "Since I graduated from the University of Minnesota. Black bears, brown bears, polar bears, Kodiaks. I even petted a koala bear once, though they are not members of the family. And I've never experienced anything like this. It was like the bear was having a psychotic break."

People went insane every day. Hospitals were built all over the world to house them. Animals didn't. It went against nature. The unnatural was more frightening than murder, mayhem, flood or famine.

Anna sipped. They sat shoulder to shoulder, almost touching, both staring out over the toes of their sleeping bags at the crushed and pillaged tents. "Do bears get rabies?" Anna asked, her wound suddenly more interesting. In Guadalupe Mountains National Park, she had dealt with a rabid skunk. In Mississippi she'd had to put down an infected porcupine. When she was eleven years old, she'd seen her dad shoot a rabid dog, an Airedale that seemed nearly as big as a camel to her child-sized eyes. Rabies sickened an animal until it became vicious. The movie version of a blood-crazed creature hell-bent on human flesh was largely a myth, but such was the misery an infected animal suffered, they did become deranged.

"That's a good question," Joan replied. "I don't see why not. Their nervous systems are not so radically different from a dog's or a human's. But every time there's a bear attack, we check and

I've never heard of it happening. Probably because of their size. Bats, dogs, skunks—nothing bites bears."

"This bear sounded sure-footed," Anna noted. She was thinking of the staggering gait of animals far enough gone with rabies to exhibit strange behavior patterns.

"Your arm, did he bite you or scratch you?" Joan asked suddenly.

"I was wondering when you'd think of that," Anna said. "I don't know."

"If you start frothing at the mouth, can I shoot you?"

"No gun."

"I'll be creative."

They thought about that for a while, Anna reliving remembered footage from *Old Yeller*. "I wish we'd gotten a look at the bear," she said after a while.

"We may yet," Joan said. Put in the future instead of the past, the concept wasn't nearly so attractive.

They waited through the false dawn in silence. By half past five the light grew strong enough to again think about the boy and the bear.

Both tents were destroyed. Anna and Joan spread them out to assess the damage. The shredding was excessive for any animal not seeking a food reward. Multiple rips two and three feet in length cut down from dome to ground in seven places on Rory's tent and one on theirs.

The ground around the tents had been dug up. A stuff sack containing fencing tools was torn to pieces, the tools scattered in the grass. Rory's day pack, clothes and sleeping bag had been dragged from his tent and littered the clearing.

Having gathered what they could find of the young Earthwatcher's belongings, they took inventory: the clothes he'd worn the previous day, his boots, baseball cap, three and a half pairs of socks, four of underpants, shorts, T-shirts, tennis shoes, water bottle. Everything he would logically have carried was accounted for. The only items missing were the sweat pants and shirt and a pair of soft flat-soled black slippers, the kind for sale in any Chinatown, that he'd worn the night before.

If he had escaped the bear, the wilderness could kill him if they didn't find him fairly soon. Dressed in pajamas and slippers and without food, the nights in the fifties, he would have a rough time of it. Had they been in the desert, his time would be even shorter. Glacier's high country had water. If he was lucky and didn't panic, he wouldn't die of thirst.

Joan radioed park dispatch. In short, efficient sentences she gave them the information they'd need to plan the search for Rory Van Slyke. Radio traffic built in volume as one ranger after another was dragged out of bed by the phone and called in service over the radio. Come sunup, the search was park business as usual. Anna and Joan would begin from the campsite. Six members of the bear team from the frontcountry would start in on horseback. The ranger stationed at the backcountry cabin halfway down to Waterton Lake would head up their direction.

Given the night's events, odds were good Rory was either dead or would be found close to camp in fairly short order. The machinery was set in motion because if he was truly lost or alive and injured, time was the single most important commodity they had to offer.

By six-thirty it was light enough to track. Anna had little confidence in her abilities in lush woodland; the bulk of her experience had been in the desert. But their quarry weighed an estimated four hundred pounds. That would help. Joan Rand was not an experienced tracker in a general sense, but she had been following bears by track and spoor most of her adult life.

In the clear gray light, unencumbered as yet by the shadows of the rising sun, the two women stood by the rock, day packs full of food, water and first-aid supplies.

"There." Joan pointed southwest.

"I see it." Faint elongated depressions, which would vanish as soon as the sun's heat reached the dew, formed an irregular line in the grass between the circle of trees and where they'd packed up the scrapped tents; the bear traveling through high grass.

Moving slowly, one to either side of the ephemeral trail, they walked, eyes to the ground.

"No scat," Joan said.

"Is that odd?"

"Everything about this bear is odd. Pooping—" Anna found comfort in the silly nonscientific word. "—is one of the ways bears let you know they've staked a claim. Often at sights of severe maulings, especially if the bear has fed on the victim, you find a big pile of poop. We solved a bear murder case three years ago. Got DNA samples from the poop and, lo and behold, they matched up with hair samples we'd taken the year before from another bear/human interface. So we knew we had the right bears and weren't just killing them to make the victim's family happy."

"Bears plural?" Anna asked. Could there have been more than one bear in their campsite last night?

"Mother and two two-year-old cubs. We had to kill them all. They had all partaken of the feast." Joan seemed to remember that maybe this time Rory Van Slyke and not some nameless stranger was the main course. She shook her head as if ridding herself of bad thoughts. "Anyway, I thought our bear might have left a mark, is all."

Not conversant with how grizzlies left their calling cards, Anna said nothing.

Items from Rory's tent were dropped along the way as if flung aside by a spoiled child. "Flashlight," Joan said, stooping to pluck the named item out of the grass. She held it up to the first rays of the rising sun. "Teethmarks."

"The bear took a flashlight?" Anna asked stupidly.

"I doubt it."

A bear wouldn't take it, wouldn't carry it. Rory would. The bear would have taken it from Rory. Maybe as the boy batted at him with it. Anna took the plastic cylinder from Joan's hands to see the marks for herself. "No blood," she observed. "That's good news, I guess." The optimism was forced. There wouldn't necessarily be blood. Not at first. She dropped the flashlight back in the grass. There'd be time to police the clearing later. As it fell, a tiny sound escaped Joan's lips as if this tossing aside of Rory's possession was in some way a slight to Rory himself.

In the morning light the woods weren't nearly as formidable as they had been the night before. At the higher elevations the undergrowth wasn't as dense. Trees were tall and widely spaced, the ground between waist-deep in fern.

Hope of tracking the bear or the boy was quickly laid to rest. No scat, no hair, no blood; the big animal had slipped invisibly into its element like Br'er Rabbit into his briar patch. Likewise had Rory Van Slyke disappeared, either carried in the bear's jaws or of his own volition, the soft, slick soles of his Chinese slippers leaving no trace.

Anna did find a peculiar bit of wood, a two-by-two of mahogany or cherry about ten inches long and polished until the edges were rounded. Because it showed no signs of weathering she knew it had come from Rory's tent. No teethmarks scarred the surface, so it was a good guess the bear hadn't carted it into the forest. What it was or why Rory needed to tote it with him on research treks or when fleeing from, or being abducted by, enormous omnivores, Anna hadn't a clue.

They spent two hours searching the woods around the camp. Calling Rory's name repeatedly they hoped to scare off the bear if it was still nearby, or scare up a response from a lost or injured boy.

Their homemade racket was assisted by the almost constant commentary from Joan's radio. The usual business of the park went on: an illegally parked horse trailer on the north side, a rockslide east of the weeping wall, but most of the talk regarded the search.

The number one-oh-two came up repeatedly. "District ranger?" Anna asked.

"Chief and, till we get a new one, acting superintendent."

Since her promotion and move to Mississippi, district ranger was the position Anna held. As was true in many middle management jobs, district rangers had tremendous responsibilities. It was they who were called upon to search, to rescue, to handle law enforcement situations beyond the field rangers' capabilities. Though they were the ultimate authority available when the chips were down or the proverbial shit hit the fan, they had very little authority in the greater NPS hierarchy. The first hint of real power was reserved for the chief rangers.

"He any good?" Anna asked.

"Harry Ruick? He's good," Joan said. "Sides with the bears when the public isn't clamoring."

"And when they are?"

"Pours experts on them."

"Does he usually go out on searches?" Some chiefs stayed active in the field, but more often than not they didn't. Several times a year they'd make some sort of publicized trek of the brass into the backwoods for management reasons but, particularly in the bigger parks, chief ranger had become an administrative position.

"Not usually," Joan admitted.

The search wasn't three hours old and already the big guns

were rolling out. Harry Ruick was guessing Van Slyke was dead.

By eight o'clock a light rain began to fall. August's warmth was co-opted by weather and altitude. It had yet to reach sixty degrees. The low ceiling of clouds would keep out any assistance by air. Rain was light and the wind calm, but visibility on Flattop had dwindled to nothing.

Joan radioed Ruick, who headed up the team, and told him they had nothing. He advised them to eat, rest, stay warm and meet the team on West Flattop Trail around noon, when horses and searchers should be arriving.

"Rory's father and stepmother are camped at Fifty Mountain," Joan said into the radio. "Has anybody been sent to inform them?"

"We'll work on it," Ruick promised and Joan left it at that.

They followed directions, eating as much as they could, resting, then hiking down to the trail. The day shared its misery, cool and rainy: warm enough that rain gear left one overheated and sweating, cold enough to give a severe chill if one got thoroughly wet. A day without a whole hell of a lot to recommend it, as far as Anna was concerned.

Shortly before noon they met up with the search party and led them the three quarters of a mile back to their camp.

Ruick hadn't wasted his time in the saddle. On the ride up he'd worked out the search area and the pattern to be used. The area around the clearing from where Rory'd disappeared was divided into quadrants. The search pattern, Anna noticed, was tight and intense. Ruick was looking for a body or an injured person, not a young man still able to cover any amount of territory.

Anna and Joan went with the chief ranger on the section west toward Trapper Peak and south to the precipitous descent into McDonald Creek. As often as not, park higher-ups went soft. Some went down this road out of laziness; even more did so because in their mountain-climbing, water-rafting youth, they'd trashed knee and ankle joints. Like aging football players, they found themselves stove in and going to fat in their middling years. By midafternoon Anna was wishing one of those fates had befallen Harry Ruick. He was no *wunderkind* rocketed up to the exalted rank of chief while still a lad; Anna put him in his early fifties. His dark hair was grizzled, and through the open neck of his uniform shirt, it looked as if the thick pelt on his chest had gone completely white. He wasn't a tall man, but built, as Anna's father might have said when waxing uncouth, like a brick shit house: squat, thick and rock-hard.

Ruick set a brutal pace and showed Anna and Joan the compliment of never doubting they could match it. Unencumbered by weight—they carried little but their own drinking water—they did.

Drizzle turned to rain and back to drizzle half a dozen times. The three of them ran rivers of sweat. Rain gear was pulled off and stuffed in packs. Rain washed sweat away and water streamed off their faces and arms. The woods dripped, their silence moving from mysterious to oppressive. Ruick led them down ragged slopes toward McDonald Creek through thickets of alder ten and fifteen feet high and so dense they crawled on hands and knees till mud caked their undersides.

They found no trace of Rory Van Slyke or the bear.

Radio traffic from the other three quadrants, two east into the burn, the other northwest across West Flattop Trail, let them know the hunting had been no better for the other team members.

Just after six that evening, they took a break and ate the sandwiches the team had packed in on the horses. Ruick was as wet and dirty as Anna. And, bless his heart, had the grace to look every bit as tired. "One more hour," he told them. "Then we're getting into dark. One more hour and we'll head back to your camp." Anna lowered her eyes to her cheese sandwich so he wouldn't see the relief in them.

Joan didn't suffer Anna's vanity. "Good," she said. "My dogs are barking." University of Minnesota, Anna remembered. Dogs were feet, barking was tired. Where that strange code fit in with lutefisk and Lutherans she'd never discovered.

Harry Ruick radioed the rest of the team with the quitting time, then they pushed themselves up for another hour of calling and crawling and swearing at the dogged weeping sky.

The last hour did not pass quickly. Time was slowed by a compulsion that had developed in Anna forcing her to look at her watch every few minutes. Finally Ruick said, "That's enough," and they turned back. The search technique he'd opted for was meticulous and labor intensive, the ground they covered rugged, rife with hiding places. As a result, they'd traveled less than three miles from the campsite.

When they were nearly to the clearing, the rain stopped. Clouds were thinning in the west, letting in a flood of orange light that lifted Anna's spirits as much as the thought of dry clothes and hot cocoa.

Joan was not similarly cheered. She wasn't sufficiently self-centered for rescue work, Anna decided as she watched her, head down, slogging along in Harry Ruick's wake. If Anna had to guess, she would have said Joan wasn't thinking of dry clothes and hot drinks, but of a boy who was facing a cold wet night without them. Or a boy who would never need them again.

"One-oh-two, two-one-four." Joan and the chief ranger's radios came to life in stereo. Two-one-four was Gary Bradley, one of the frontcountry bear-team guys. Anna had met him when they'd gathered before the search and come to know him by proxy, eavesdropping on their radio conversations. Gary was young and bearded and idealistic and interchangeable with a thousand other seasonals who gave up security and the American Dream for an intensely private dream of what the world could be.

Ruick drew his hand-held from its cordovan leather holster on his belt. Anna hadn't noticed before, but the back of his hand was crisscrossed with scratches and jeweled with bright beads of blood where thorns had broken the skin. The sight of blood reminded her of her own wound, the groove dug in her shoulder by the grizzly bear. She half hoped it would leave a scar. The story would be well worth the disfigurement.

"Go ahead, Gary," the chief ranger was saying into his radio.

"We got something here you better come look at."

"What have you found?"

"We're up near Kootnai Pass, off West Glacier Trail half a mile. How far away are you?"

"Maybe three miles. We can get there before dark."

"I'll have Vic wait on the trail."

Ruick replaced the radio on his belt and picked up the pace.

Gary Bradley wouldn't say what they'd found over the public air waves. The only thing that made people that circumspect was a corpse.

Anna sighed. So much for the cocoa.

According to Anna's internal hiking pedometer, it was approximately two miles from their camp to where the man called Vic was waiting for them: forty minutes walking. The sun had gone behind Nahsukin Mountain, but the snow on Trapper Peak still reflected molten fire. So far north, the twilight would linger.

Vic was another of Ruick's seasonals, on four months, off eight. The image of these economic nomads was that of rootless college students collecting life experiences with the safety net of Mom and Dad's income still stretched beneath them. That hadn't been true for ten years or more. Certainly not since Anna had joined the service. Vic was in his late thirties. A gold band on his left hand proclaimed him a married man. Chances were good he had a kid or two to support while he waited for the park service to offer him a full-time job with benefits.

An ugly man, tubular and tight and pointy-headed, the seasonal began waving the minute they appeared on the trail. Both hands waved a welcome ratified by an accompanying shout. Given this gay greeting Anna began to think things weren't as bad as they had feared.

Then they got close enough so that she could see him clearly. It wasn't welcome that animated his tin-woodsman form but relief. He trotted up the trail babbling about times and distances and rockfalls, only half of which they could understand. Ignoring Anna and Joan, he stopped in front of the chief ranger. Though he hadn't run more than twenty feet, he was panting, his long face with its tight little features had a grayish cast and he was sweating profusely. Anna could smell the unmistakable reek of vomit boiling off him with his body heat.

"Take it easy . . . Vic." Ruick read the man's name off the brass plate over his left front pocket. Harry Ruick had reached that rarified stratum of management where the names of the little people ran together.

The chief ranger might not know his seasonals' names, but he knew his job. Keeping his voice light and confident, he said, "Anybody going to die in the next five minutes?"

"No," Vic admitted, "but—"

"Then let's slow down. I don't know about these two," he jerked his chin at Anna and Joan, "but I need to catch my breath." The trail where Vic met them ran along the northern edge of the burn. To the south, sinking into an oblivion of inky darkness with the going of the sun, was charred land, burnt spikes of trees snagging the skyline. Tiring of its grim aspect, Anna looked north to where the mountain fell away in green and stone, tumbling steeply into the canyon cut by Kootnai Creek. In mist and blue velvet the Rockies rushed like water frozen in time across the Waterton Valley toward Canada. For the first time she had the sense she was on top of a mountain. Fragments of the rainstorm had settled beneath Flattop, clouds clinging to the sides of the far mountains. Sun-touched tops were pink, bottoms gray, leaching night up from the canyons.

Transfixed by this glimpse of paradise, she found herself standing alone. Harry had led Vic to a log, where he sat between the chief ranger and Joan, seeming to take comfort from the authority of the one and the mere presence of the other. Anna had nothing to offer so she remained where she was, acutely aware that the pleasure she took in this asymmetry of perfection would soon be blotted out by whatever nasty sorrow humans had brought upon themselves with their meddling.

That in Rory's case she was one of the prime meddlers was not lost upon her. She would feel no guilt at the boy's death, but she would not escape a heavy sense of wrongness, of not having fit seamlessly enough into the fabric of nature.

Ruick got up and came to where she stood. "Vic's going to stay here with Joan. We won't be doing much tonight. He's pretty shook. You come with me."

The bear team had marked where they were to leave West Flattop Trail with orange surveyor's tape. According to the two scraps of tape, the path led down a scree-and-alder-choked side of a ravine cut through the rock of the mountain's flank. Anna hoped Harry didn't want her to come with him too far. She'd managed to trick her tired body into moving along at a respectable clip, but if she had to climb the hill she was now skidding down for any great distance, she was going to begin to show a definite strain. If Harry wanted her to carry any dead weight, she would be in trouble.

"The boys found a body." Ruick talked as they went, sliding and clinging to spiny alders, his words flashing back with the whip of released branches. "From what Vic says, it's torn up bad. Face pretty much gone."

People live behind their faces. When rescuers had to deal with victims whose faces had been destroyed, it was immeasurably harder than dealing with severed or mangled limbs. Unfair as it was, facial mutilation turned the victim into a monster of the most unsettling kind: one to be feared and pitied at the same time.

Anna was glad Joan had been left behind to look after the seasonal ranger. Unless she was a whole lot harder than Anna took her for, she'd superimpose her son Luke under the mangled features and give herself nightmares for a year. Another terrific reason for not having children: it was so disturbing when animals ate them.

"Have you located Rory's folks yet?" Anna asked, her mind running along parental lines.

"This is not our boy."

They slid further into the night. Into dense brush, the kind favored by predators. Anna's mind closed itself off so she would not think of the roars that had ripped them from the false sense of civilization they had enjoyed the night before. She concentrated on keeping her footing and keeping the tangle of low-growing branches from raking the flesh from her face.

"Bear! Hey, bear!" jerked Anna out of survival mode. A jolt of fear so strong she twitched with it brought her to a stop.

"It's us, Gary," the chief ranger called.

"Thank God," came an answering voice.

"Thank God," Anna echoed.

Moments later they broke through the brush into a clearing no bigger than a living room rug. Like a character in a horror movie, Gary Bradley stood over a body, his flashlight held in front of him.

The last of the light had retreated to the west. Anna fumbled her own flashlight from her pack and for a moment the three of them blinded each other, needing to reassure themselves that the faces ringed around the corpse were more or less human.

Gary was pale under the beard, his lips bloodless in the harsh light of the flash. At the sight of Harry Ruick, Anna could see the young man regathering his wits. Being alone in the creeping dusk with nothing for company but a dead body and whatever killed it would unnerve anyone. Bradley was glad not to be alone and gladder still to be able to hand over the reins of leadership.

"We were covering West Flattop," he said. "Vic saw what looked to be drag marks going off the trail up there where he met you. We followed them down and found this. Her."

Anna was standing back five or six feet from the crumpled form at Bradley's feet, waiting for instructions. Ruick squatted down and she moved slightly, training her flashlight on the body to give him more light to see by.

The dead woman was lying on her side, knees drawn up as if she slept. Her right arm was thrown up, obscuring her face. Blond hair, shoulder-length, permed and dyed, frothed out from under a red-billed cap with the Coca-Cola logo on it. She wore an oversized man's army jacket. Her legs were bare between the bottom of flared rayon skirtlike shorts and the tops of her hiking boots. Anna didn't see much blood. What there was would have soaked into the ground.

Ruick settled into deep calm, his manner deliberate, his words measured. Anna had seen it a hundred times, done it herself at least that many, still she found comfort in it. Things were under control. Help had arrived.

Harry felt for a carotid.

"We checked first thing," Gary said. "She'd been dead awhile, I'd guess. She was sort of cold. But that might have been the rain."

"Any ID?"

"None that we could find."

Ruick handed Anna his flashlight and she trained it along with hers on the corpse as he carefully turned it over.

As the body rolled onto its back, Gary looked away. He'd seen what was there and made the choice not to see it again. Anna looked from the seasonal ranger back to the body then wished she'd followed his lead, traded the sight of the woman's face for the scrap of sky Gary studied.

"We just kind of started to roll her—you know, see if she was—then figured we'd better leave well enough alone. Bear'd been feeding on her," Gary explained disjointedly, eyes still fixed on a place only the gods call home.

His words pattered meaninglessly. Anna and Harry were locked in their own horror show. Half of the woman's face was gone. From just above her left eyebrow down to her jaw was a red ragged mass. Cheekbone and teeth were exposed, bone and enamel crusted brown with dried blood. The eyeball was still in its socket, staring in cloudy malevolence, the flesh around it eaten away.

Eaten. Anna pushed closer, knelt beside Harry and shined both lights on the carnage. "Look at the edges of the wound. Here and here." She pointed to the cut on the forehead and the vertical slash that had taken out half the woman's nose. "Not eaten. This was done with a knife, a razor, an axe, something like that."

Ruick stayed where he was, squatting on his heels, till Anna's knees began to ache. Dutifully she held her post, keeping the lights steady.

"I'd rather it had been a bear," Ruick said at last. "I'd whole hell of a lot rather it had been a bear."

"A person killed her?" Gary said, and for the first time Anna heard outrage in his voice. A sentiment she shared. Working with wild animals one might never lose the sense of tragedy a deadly encounter brought down on both species, but it was a tragedy untainted by evil. Or at least that's how Anna had felt before the bizarre sense that had pervaded her the night before, the feeling the beast was not merely wild but somehow intentionally malicious. People killing people was a different story. Always there was evil. Sometimes it was several times removed, as when soldiers fought to the death for someone else's ideals. But it was always there.

"Looks that way," Harry said. "Did you check the rest of the body?"

"No, sir, just the face." Clearly that had been enough for Gary.

Ruick rocked back on his heels. In the spill of light from the flashlights, he studied first Gary then Anna and made a decision.

"Anna, hand Gary the lights and help me with this. Gary, keep us lit here. I don't suppose anybody's got a tape recorder? Pen and paper?" Anna did have that in the form of the small yellow pocket notebook with the ten standard firefighting orders printed on the inside cover. While Ruick rooted around in his pack, she and the seasonal waited, wishing they had more to do, some positive action to take. Having found what he sought, a 35-mm camera, Harry clicked off half a dozen pictures. The flash burned the photos into Anna's brain as they did into the film. Scene recorded, Ruick began his work on the dead woman.

Gary held the lights as best he could while keeping his eyes off the ruin of the corpse's face. Anna took notes. Ruick opened the army jacket. The dead woman was built along apple-on-a-stick lines. The bulk of her weight was carried between pubic bone and collar bone: big breasts, thick waist, meaty hips ending abruptly in skinny and shapely legs. There wasn't much to write about. Except for the butchered face, she appeared unharmed. Internal injuries would be determined by the autopsy. Trauma to the face suggested enough force to snap the neck, but there was surprisingly little blood; none of the flowing spillage one might expect had the cuts occurred while the heart was still beating. The carving had been done after the woman was dead.

Harry's check of the body was cursory. No defensive cuts on hands or arms. Nothing apparent under the nails. Given the lack of light it was impossible to ascertain much in the way of detail. The woman had no identification on her. The pockets of the army coat produced unused rolls of film, a three-by-five card, much battered, with measurements written on it, lip balm, three pennies and a topographical map of the park. The pockets of the victim's shorts were empty.

Ruick finished the search, then lacking anything with which to cover her, he rolled the body back on its side and the ruination of her face was lost in shadow. He and Anna reclaimed their flashlights and the three of them did a perfunctory search of the

tiny clearing, using only light and eyes for fear extraneous movement would further contaminate a crime scene that had already
been severely compromised.

"No pack," Anna said.

"No water bottle anywhere," Gary added.

"Film suggests she was carrying a camera. Could be the pack
was stolen. Could be it just got left off if she was chased or killed
someplace else," Ruick said.

He got on the radio and set the machinery in motion for the
body recovery. With the weather clearing, a helicopter would be
able to come at first light to airlift it out of the park.

While he talked, Anna was shutting down. Night, too much
hiking, scrabbling and thinking, too little sleep, too little food:
her brain was blanking. Though she moved the light around in a
desultory fashion she knew she wasn't seeing what was there.
Gary and the chief ranger were in slightly better shape. Their
sleep had not been ravaged by a psychotic bear. Still, she doubted
any of the three of them would be good for much till morning.

Finally Ruick put his radio away. For a long minute no one
said anything. Anna knew she had fallen into a dangerous state.
She was abdicating, turning over not only the problem of the
dead woman but her own well-being to the solid, reassuring
Harry Ruick. *Snap out of it,* she ordered herself and scrubbed her
skull with her knuckles to wake up the gray matter. Abdicating in
the backcountry was commonplace. It was also a coward's way
and a fool's. Nobody could guarantee another's safety in the
wilderness.

Brain nominally in gear, she said, "We carry her out?"

"Can't see how to avoid it," Ruick replied. "Can't leave her
here. We're between a rock and a hard place. We carry her out
and trash what might remain of the crime scene or we leave her
here and the scavengers do the job for us. They may anyway. The
smell of blood is bound to attract some."

There was nothing in which to wrap the corpse. To facilitate
carrying, they removed her arms from the sleeves of her jacket,
zipped them inside and tied the sleeves over her chest. Anna secured
her feet by the simple expedient of tying her bootlaces together.

Harry Ruick took the head, Gary Bradley the feet. Anna had
the awkward but not difficult task of lighting their way back up
the mountainside. The body had been located less than a hundred

yards down from the trail and they traversed the distance in a grunting quarter of an hour.

During their absence Joan had not been idle. The other members of the team had convened on West Flattop Trail. It had been too late and too dark to return to Anna and Joan's camp for their personal things, but three tents had been brought up from where the bear team cached their own gear. Camp was being set up a quarter of a mile off trail where park visitors would not see it and so have their wilderness experience infringed upon. Joan herself waited on the log where they'd left her with Vic to lead them to the new camp.

Though they'd known each other little more than five days, Anna was inordinately glad to see her. Leaving the men to struggle on with their burden across the flat and level meadow that presaged the burn, Anna walked ahead with Joan.

"So it was a woman," Joan said.

Anna heard the threadbare weariness in her voice and knew she was probably running on nerve; muscle and bone were exhausted. Joan Rand was in fairly good shape, but she carried an extra twenty pounds. Most of that, Anna guessed, was heart. Joan was carrying the pain, Anna only the work and a few ounces of the horror. Either she'd been born heartless or over the years had grown inured to the tragedies of others.

"A woman," she confirmed.

"Do we know who she was?"

"Not yet."

As if admitting a failing on her part, Joan said, "You know, I was so glad it wasn't Rory I didn't even bother to ask Vic who she was."

Rory Van Slyke. Anna hadn't given him a moment's consideration since the chief ranger had said of the corpse, "This is not our boy." If Rory's trail had been picked up by the backcountry ranger or the other members of the team, they would have heard. He was still out there lost or hurt or dead.

"At least we know our bear—presuming this was done by the same bear—has moved on," Joan said. "If it had taken Rory, cached him, it would have made a nest nearby and stayed there to feed." The logic of bear behavior was cheering her considerably. Anna was about to put an end to that. It wasn't that she was in a foul mood herself and so wanted to spread the wretchedness

around. It was that she respected Joan enough to know she'd
want to know the facts and liked her enough to guess she'd rather
be told under cover of darkness by another woman than back in
camp under the glare of Coleman lanterns and men's eyes.

"This lady wasn't killed by our bear or any bear. She was
hacked up by an edged weapon. A human being killed her. Or
something with opposable thumbs masquerading as a human being."

Ahead was the camp. Lanterns had been set up, and four men
and one woman bustled purposefully about. Three tents had been
pitched and Anna heard the familiar hiss of a gas stove. Environ-
mentalist that she was, it would still have given her hope and
courage had there been a great roaring fire to welcome them,
warm their bones and keep the monsters of the dark away. In this
group of conservationists, she wouldn't dare to so much as voice
her primitive longings.

"This is it," Joan said, stopping. Ruick and Bradley carried
the corpse past them into camp like hunters returning with the
day's kill.

"Did you hear me?" Anna asked when Joan didn't fall into
step behind them.

"I did," Joan answered quietly. "I just couldn't think of anything to say."

They stayed a moment in silence on the edge of the circle of
light carved out of the night.

"Hot drinks?" Anna said finally.

"Hot drinks," Joan agreed.

Between Anna and Harry they had thirty-one years of law enforcement in America's national parks, yet the body of the murder victim created a dilemma neither of them had faced before. Because
of Glacier's active grizzly bear population the remains were not
only evidence but meat, carrion. Trails in the park were routinely
closed by the bear management team if a dead deer or elk was
found on or near them. A carcass attracted bears. What they'd so
laboriously carried out of the ravine might be a corpse tomorrow
in a morgue. Tonight it was a carcass, just beginning to get ripe
and alluring.

Faced with a problem pertaining to *Ursus horribilis,* Joan regained her equilibrium and took charge. The body was wrapped in plastic garbage bags—not because it would keep the smell from the keen noses of any bears in the neighborhood but to shield the delicate sensibilities of the humans—and hung up in a tree thirty yards from camp along with the other edibles.

That more than anything seemed to bring a bleakness of mood over everyone. Though several people made a weak joke or two and nobody stared at the ghoulish tree decoration outright, Anna was sure everyone was as acutely aware as she that it was hanging there, high in the branches, just beyond the reach of light, like a Windigo in the north woods.

They ate in silence and crawled into the tents. There were six bear-team members, plus Harry, Anna and Joan. Though as strays, Anna and Joan were invited to make a third in somebody's tent, Anna opted to sleep in the open.

Better to face down the devil than blindly hear him circling.

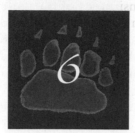

6

Despite the fact there seemed to be a bear in Glacier with Anna's name on it and a lunatic who sliced off women's faces, she slept very well. Harry Ruick woke her just after five by clanging around with stove and coffeepot.

Having only the truly vile clothes she'd worn the day before, Anna had slept in nothing but her shirt and had to spend an awkward minute struggling into underpants and shorts in the narrow confines of a sleeping bag. Trained in backcountry etiquette, Ruick did not deign to notice her until she was decent.

Joan had selected their camp with foresight. Two downed logs, fallen at right angles to one another, formed a natural seating area. Having stuffed the borrowed sleeping bag into its sack, Anna made herself a cup of coffee from a flow-through bag and joined the chief ranger where he sat on a log.

"Buck got to the Van Slyke boy's dad up at Fifty Mountain yesterday afternoon, so the folks know the kid's missing," Ruick said in lieu of "good morning."

Anna nodded. Buck was probably the backcountry ranger from down toward Waterton Lake.

"The helicopter will be able to land as soon as it's light. If I remember right, there's a good flat spot on the burn less than a mile from here. We'll need to go check it and flag it."

Harry wasn't so much talking to Anna as planning his operation. She was content to serve the passive role of sounding board. Till Harry Ruick arrived on horseback the day before, she'd never met him. He struck her as the new breed of administrator—infused with a genuine love of the resource but a political animal for all that, with an eye to the next rung up the ladder. Old-school park rangers—or at least the lingering myth of them—would have it that they put the needs of the park before their own. Enlightened self-interest was the current trend.

"You're here sort of apprenticing on Kate's bear DNA project, that right?" he asked. Despite the time they'd spent together floundering around in the shrubbery, Anna had the feeling this was probably the first time he'd really seen her.

"Yes," she said. "My home park's the Natchez Trace Parkway in Mississippi."

"You know John Brown?"

"He's chief ranger there."

"John and I went to FLETC together," Ruick named the Federal Law Enforcement Training Center, which NPS enforcement rangers filtered through at some point in their careers. "Tell him I said 'hey' when you see him."

Anna promised she would. She wasn't surprised the two men knew each other. The National Park Service was spread over a lot of real estate but there weren't that many full-time employees. The game of "who do you know" was played successfully from Joshua Tree to Acadia.

Amenities observed, he returned to the issues at hand. "We're going to do double duty today. Split our forces. You and I will go over the crime scene this morning. Two of my district rangers and about a third of my field rangers are in California on the Angeles National Forest. The damn annual pilgrimage to keep the movie stars from being burned out of house and home. Talk about a prime location for a 'let burn' policy. But be that as it may, I'm short-handed. So if you wouldn't mind playing step-'n'-fetchit for me, I'd appreciate it."

In one sentence he'd managed to give Anna the illusion of a gracious request and at the same time let her know her official status in the investigation was that of a gofer. A manager's manager.

"Glad to help any way I can," she said, and meant it.

"Good girl."

The "girl" offended Anna not in the least. Being a woman of a certain age, she'd learned to pick her battles. That, and she'd been called a whole lot worse.

"Gary, Vic, the others'll continue searching for the Van Slyke boy. As soon as the body"—he pushed his jaw at the plastic-wrapped lump of bear bait hanging in the tree at the far edge of their camp—"is taken to West Glacier, the helicopter will join the search. If the kid is up and around we ought to be able to find him today."

He didn't add the obvious, that if Rory wasn't up and around it probably wouldn't make a whole lot of difference whether he was found today or a month from today.

They sipped their coffee in companionable silence awaiting the sun. Anna was cold. Her green uniform shorts and short-sleeved gray shirt offered little in the way of warmth. In a minute, when she was more awake, she would get her raincoat from her day pack.

"Have you ever had a murder at Glacier before?" she asked.

"You mean since it's been a national park?" Harry thought about that for a bit. "Glacier was made a park in 1910. We joined up with Canada in 1932. There's bound to have been some foul play but nothing in recent history," he said finally. "They used to be rare as hen's teeth."

Used to be. Anna was thinking of the beheading in Yosemite a few years back, the death of the child in her own park only months before.

Population was at an all-time high. Park visitation was up. Anna remembered reading *Future Shock* in college, the experiments crowding too many rats in too small a space. Now, nearly thirty years later, it was happening in the parks. The rats were starting to kill each other.

Twenty minutes after first light, before the sun had scraped over the jagged cliffs rising from the eastern edge of the mountain, camp was broken, gear was stowed. Joan and the rest of the bear team headed southeast to mark the helicopter landing area, their sad cargo belly down across a saddle like a gunslinger's trophy. Needing the full light of the sun to properly examine the shrub-choked crime scene, Anna and Harry decided to first walk West Flattop Trail.

The woman had been butchered after death. The kind of precision knife or hatchet job that had been done on her face was the work of ten or fifteen minutes, maybe more considering the flesh cut away had been removed from the site. Butchering was a job requiring privacy. Consequently the body had been carried off the trail, as the drag marks attested. Corroborating this theory was the fact that the body had none of the scratches or scrapes that might be expected on the arms of a healthy live woman forced through a thick alder copse.

Had the murder occurred any distance off trail, most likely the killer would have had all the privacy needed to mutilate in peace and would have had no need to move the victim after death. Logic dictated that the murder had been committed on or near West Flattop, and fairly near where the body had been dumped. In August, with visitation at its peak, the killer would have wished to get the body out of sight as quickly as possible.

The burn covered both sides of West Flattop but for the small patch of green bordering the trail above where the body was found. It was an educated guess that the kill had occurred in the burn zone, where the perpetrator had little or no cover. He'd carried the victim till he found enough undergrowth he could hide in.

Anna and Harry walked, one to each side, three to five yards off the trail in search of the place the original violence had taken place. Just under half a mile from where they started, they found what was probably the victim's backpack. It was forty feet into the burn, stuffed under a downed tree. Char and ash had been hastily pushed over it. The scorched soil would have proved an ideal surface for tracking if it hadn't been for the rain the day before. What prints there might have been were melted into amorphous depressions that would keep their secrets.

Anna stood by, notebook in hand, while Harry photographed the pack and log with a different 35-mm camera than he'd used the night before. This one had been brought in by the helicopter. The other was his own. He'd come to the high country for a search and rescue, not to investigate a murder.

That done, he and Anna made a series of measurements so the exact location and lie of the pack could be reconstructed later on paper, should that prove necessary. Then Ruick pulled on latex gloves, carefully swept the debris off the pack and pulled it from where it had been stashed. He handled it as if protecting possible fingerprints, but it was just good form and training. The stained gray canvas, soaked with rain and grimed with soot, wouldn't hold any latent prints.

From the way the pack moved, Anna could tell it contained something heavy. Harry emptied the zippered front pouch. "Mosquito repellent, tissues, topo—careful woman, carried two topographical maps."

"Not careful enough," Anna remarked as she wrote down the items he'd removed.

"No. I guess not. Let's see what we got here." He unzipped the main pocket of the day pack and lifted out three cameras and four lenses. "A photographer. From what little I know about camera equipment, my guess is this is pretty expensive stuff."

"Rules out robbery," Anna said. Robbery had never been a motive she'd considered seriously. Robbers took things and ran away. They didn't drag corpses around and slice their faces off. Why would anyone slice off a face? "Maybe he didn't want her recognized," she said, seeing again the single eye staring out of the mess.

"If that's the case he didn't do a thorough job of it. I don't know about you, but I'd recognize those near and dear to me if half their face was still there. It doesn't take that much."

That was true. With dental work, fingerprints, medical records and DNA it was nearly impossible to hide the identity of a corpse for any length of time. Unless it was a corpse nobody cared about, and hadn't for a long time. Judging by the cameras, this woman was too well-to-do to be completely unloved.

"No film in any of the cameras," Harry said after a brief inspection. He handed Anna the stuff to hold. Arms full, she abandoned the role of secretary. Ruick reached into the pack and took out four boxes of unopened film and three empties. "No exposed film," he said. "These boxes must have been in here awhile. I guess she hadn't gotten to wherever she was going to shoot before she was killed."

"Or she was taking pictures of something the killer didn't want recorded for posterity," Anna said.

The chief ranger shot her a look of surprise. "Good point," he said, and again she had the odd sensation that he was seeing her. It was as if underlings only existed as nameless cogs in a green and gray machine. Because Ruick was good at his job, he kept that machine clean, fueled and maintained, but scarcely expected the moving parts to show signs of initiative above their station in life.

Item by item he retrieved the cameras and lenses from Anna and restowed them in the pack. Another ten minutes were spent circling out from the log, studying the ground before he said, "This vein's mined out," and they moved on.

For the next couple of hours they continued to comb both sides of the trail east and west, but found no other trace of the woman or anything to indicate who killed her or why. With the sun high and bright, they returned to where the body had been and searched the path down and the area around where it had lain, but again found nothing. If the meat cut from the face had been tossed into the brush, something had dragged it away and eaten it. Gruesome as that image was, Anna preferred it to the idea that the killer was hiking around with human flesh packed along with his peanut butter and pork and beans. More measurements were taken, notes made. Anna sketched the crime scene. So tangled was it with branches and leaf litter that, as good as the sketch was, it still looked like the doodlings of an idiot.

Having done what they could, they hiked east toward Fifty Mountain Camp. Given the sinister goings-on since Van Slyke's disappearance, Harry felt it behooved him to speak to the lost boy's parents personally.

Three miles shy of Fifty Mountain they received news of Rory. Returned from hearse duty to search, the helicopter had flown over several times but it wasn't from that source that they finally had word. The call came from dispatch in the valley town of West Glacier. Hikers northbound on Flattop Trail, two miles south of where it intersected with West Flattop near Fifty Mountain Camp, had called park headquarters on their cell phone. They'd met a young man, naked from the waist up and wearing slippers. They said he was distraught. He knew his name, Rory Van Slyke, but otherwise seemed disoriented and claimed to be seeking help for two women who had been savaged by a giant bear. Except for a bad sunburn on his chest and shoulders, he appeared unhurt. The hikers would stay with him till a ranger arrived.

On receiving the news, Harry radioed the rest of the search party to stand down. After a night of bears, a day of rain, and a defiled corpse, Anna'd not realized how starved she was—everybody was—for good news. The searchers fairly chortled and glowed over the airwaves. Everyone needed to quip, joke, to say some clever thing. Understanding this phenomenon, Ruick let the good times effervesce at the cost of radio discipline for exactly two minutes. Anna saw him look at his watch timing it. Then he cut it off with orders.

Since he and Anna were closest to where Rory waited with the hikers, they would cut cross-country from West Flattop to Flattop Trail, bypassing Fifty Mountain Camp, and collect their truant Earthwatcher. Joan and Gary were to hike to Fifty Mountain and tell Mr. and Mrs. Van Slyke that Rory had been found unhurt. Buck, the backcountry ranger Anna had yet to meet, was to join them at the camp to assist Ruick in the murder investigation.

Two law enforcement men in two million acres seemed to be giving the murderer a definite edge, but there was little else to be done. A massive manhunt could be mounted if they had any idea who they were looking for. Till then it would only breed panic and ill will.

One of the great enduring joys of wilderness travel was that, in America at least, it did not require that one have one's papers in order. Campers were supposed to have backcountry permits, but hikers didn't need even that. When in the backcountry one could go to bed when tired, rise when rested and wander where the heart led, unidentified and untracked. Even had they pulled every backcountry permit issued, there was no way of knowing where the permittees might be at any given moment. No one wanted to admit it, but in a killing such as this, the murderer was likely to get away with it. If he or she—a woman could just as easily bone a chicken or filet a person as a man—was apprehended, it would have as much to do with dumb luck as good police work.

Their cross-country trek was short-lived, scarcely more than half a mile, but all of it uphill. They rejoined Flattop where it ran parallel to West Flattop. Back again on an improved surface, they made good time and reached the waiting threesome just after two o'clock, hardly more than an hour after dispatch radioed that Rory was found.

In the day Anna'd spent with the young Earthwatcher, he'd not seemed a particularly demonstrative lad; but when he saw her rounding a clump of trees behind the chief ranger his face actually appeared to light up, as the cliché would have it. His eyes, dull and downcast, crinkled and came to life. His face, slack to the point of idiocy, firmed into a boyish smile that ripened quickly into laughter. For a second Anna thought he was going to rush over and hug her. She braced herself but his inner light flickered and began to fail. Like a robot suffering a power interruption, his movements faltered. Anna realized that, though he had been glad to see her, the major wattage was reserved for the person he thought was going to round the trees in her footsteps.

The instant it came together in her mind, she jumped in to put the boy out of his misery. "Joan's fine," she said quickly, speaking overloud to penetrate the fog of trauma hovering around him. "Neither of us was hurt. Joan's gone to Fifty Mountain to tell your folks you're okay. Joan's fine," she repeated, making sure the salient fact soaked in.

"Hooray," he said. "Hooray, hooray, hooray." And he hugged himself, sunburned arms around a chest that was just beginning to show the breadth of manhood. He rocked slightly and Anna was put in mind of a cartoon dog she'd delighted in as a kid, Precious. Precious would hug himself and levitate whenever given a dog biscuit. Rory looked like he'd just been treated to Purina's finest.

When he settled back to earth he began to chatter. "I thought you were dead. You and Joan. I heard that growling and I came back—honest to God I came back. But the bear was huge. I mean huge. Like a polar bear. So I—I knew I had to get help—"

"Easy, son, time for that later. You've had the whole park looking for you for nearly two days. A lot of people are going to be real glad to see you." Harry didn't sound like one of those glad individuals. He came across as brusque and crabby. Anna noticed the hikers, not yet properly thanked for their heroic role in the saga, exchange a glance of disapproval.

Maybe Harry was a heartless s.o.b., but Anna didn't think so. At least not entirely. She recognized the unpleasant task of leadership: Harry's work wasn't done yet. Happy as he might be that Van Slyke was alive and well, there were new plans to be laid now.

The less altruistic side of the NPS leadership mantle was the deep-down belief that virtually every ranger harbored—only idiots and greenhorns got themselves lost. Purists even espoused the idea that the money and man-hours used to find them could be better spent. Anna would have been in favor of that radical view of no-rescue wilderness had she not found search and rescue work so satisfying. Enlightened self-interest; if the corporations and bureaucracies could get away with calling selfishness that, surely a private citizen could try it on for size.

"Anna," Harry called her out of her thoughts. "Are you an EMT?"

"Yes."

"Do your thing." He nodded in Rory's direction. As she led the boy a little way away from the others, she heard Ruick click into politician mode and begin to say the right things to the hikers. There was a time in the not-so-distant past when she would have quietly rolled her eyes and indulged in a small sniff of superiority. No more. Since she'd become a manager, she'd been made acutely aware of how important a part of the job being a good politician was. And what a joy it was to be a lowly flunky again for a few days.

She sat Rory on a stump, dug out the first-aid kit and, while he told his story, ran through a standard field check.

"I'd got out of my tent and gone into the woods just a little way behind that big rock. Something must've kind of upset my system or something and it wouldn't wait till morning . . . you know?"

He looked to Anna to validate that diarrhea was an acceptable reason to leave one's tent in the dead of night.

"I know," she said agreeably.

"So I was out there awhile and I kept hearing things, getting real nervous like, you know? But I hadn't finished my, uh, my business. My insides—"

"What kind of things did you hear?" Anna interrupted, having no desire to learn about Rory Van Slyke's insides.

For a moment he didn't answer. He just watched her wrap the blood pressure cuff around his upper arm with an expression of contentment on his face. Anna guessed he was comforted by the trappings of modern medicine, civilization. The things that he'd been raised to believe would keep him safe from the monsters.

She pumped up the cuff and he looked away, suddenly squeamish, as if she were sticking a needle in his vein. "What did you hear?" she asked again.

"Animals, I think. You know, maybe just little ones, though they could have been something else. Maybe mice or rabbits or coyotes or something. I know you're supposed to make a lot of noise when you go out into the woods like that, to scare the bears off. Joan told me that. It wasn't that I forgot, but you guys being asleep and all—"

"That's okay," Anna said. "Right around camp nobody makes noises. Usually just the fact we're there and stinking like humans'll make the bears give us a wide berth."

"Anyway, I don't think that stuff I first heard was the bear. Maybe it was but I don't think so. Then I heard what sounded like footsteps. It scared me pretty bad. I was, uh, done then . . ."

Anna bet he was. Probably every sphincter in his body slammed shut when he heard a grizzly bear headed his way.

"Maybe I should have shouted," he said. "Maybe it would have scared him away."

Maybe it would have. Before Anna could be judgmental, she remembered that neither she nor Joan had done any shouting once the attack began. Perhaps if they'd screamed their bloody heads off, the bear would have run away. Instinct had taken over and they'd cowered in silence, gripped by the surety that the only safety lay in being invisible, playing dead.

"Footsteps?" Anna asked. The word seemed inappropriate for the sounds a large omnivore would make lumbering through thick ferns.

"No, it *sounded* like footsteps," Rory amended. "At first. But then it broke something, a stick or something, and I heard it growl. I've been to zoos and all and I saw that movie *The Bear,* but I thought they'd mixed things to get that noise—lions or trains or whatever, like they mixed noises to get Tarzan's yodel to come out big enough. That's why little kids can't do it right."

Anna turned away on the pretense of tucking the blood pressure cuff back in its plastic case so he wouldn't see her smiling at the image of a scrawny little Rory Van Slyke pounding on his bony chest and calling to herds of imaginary backyard elephants.

"I guess they didn't have to fake anything," he concluded. "That roar was about the most awful sound. That bear was immense. I could hear it ripping into the tents. That's when I figured I'd better get help."

The scene played out in Anna's mind's eye: a terrified boy in sweats and slippers, alone in the night as every horror he'd nursed for two days in the wilderness—and for who knew how many before he arrived—took form from the darkness. Nightmare made real in fur and teeth and claws and "most awful sound." Rory had panicked, blindly, brainlessly turned and ran into the trees, Anna would have bet on it. She didn't blame him. That might very well have been the course she would have adopted had she been given any choices. If he was able to sell himself on the fiction he'd gone for help, he'd be okay. If not, this wretched indication of cowardice would scar him. Anna wasn't sure she could help, but she'd talk to Joan about it. Being a mother of boys, she might have accrued some wisdom along those lines.

"You're in fairly good shape for a man who's been without food or shelter for thirty-six hours," she told him.

"The hikers gave me fruit and granola bars," he said. "They'd've let me eat everything in their packs—and I could have—but it didn't seem polite."

"We'll see about replenishing their stores," Anna promised. "And get you some serious food. Let me see your feet." She squatted in front of where he was seated on the stump and he lifted his foot like a compliant child on a trip to the shoe store.

The Chinese cloth slippers had held up remarkably well. Though they had been pulled and squashed and pounded till they resembled third base after an eleven inning game more than they did shoes, the seams had held. The flat rubber soles, pierced through in several places, had not split.

"You sure got your four-ninety-five's worth out of these things," she remarked as she unbuckled the Mary Jane strap on the right shoe and slipped it off. His feet were coal-black from his dusty tramp through the burn. Until he had washed, there was no telling what was bruising and what was dirt. She found one cut on his heel that lined up with a tear in the slipper's sole, and no blisters.

Gently she palpated the right foot, then the left. "What happened after you went for help?" she asked. "You still owe me thirty-five hours' worth of story."

"Not much," he said vaguely. Anna couldn't tell if he was being evasive or if the hours' had run together in his mind. "Just walked, you know. Got lost. Then came out on this trail and ran into the hikers." His voice was drifty and soft.

"Did you take any falls? Hit your head or anything?"

"No. Like I said, I'm fine."

Head trauma, then, did not account for this sudden fog. Evasive, Anna decided. If, after some distance had been put between him and bear, the panic had not subsided, and come morning he'd neither tried to find help nor returned to camp to see if Anna and Joan were injured, if he'd holed up, cowering somewhere, the evasiveness made sense. Shame was as great a fogger of memory as a blow to the skull.

The faceless face of the dead woman flashed behind Anna's eyes and another reason for evasiveness came to mind. Maybe Rory didn't want her to know precisely what had transpired during the day and a half he'd gone missing because it was something he'd rather keep secret. Like murder.

She snorted abruptly, an aborted laugh gone up her nose. Rory had run off in his slippers and pj's, pursued, at least in his own mind, by a bear. Then he meets a stranger by accident, kills her for no reason, stashes her pack, finds an edged weapon, drags her into the undergrowth and cuts her face off, all without getting a drop of blood on his person. Even for Anna, suspicion had to have at least a rudiment of logic to buoy it up.

"You go barefoot a lot?" she asked. The calluses on the bottoms of Rory's feet were thick and hard. He'd suffered less from his overland ordeal than most would.

"A fair amount," he replied. "Lots of times I run cross-country barefooted. It drives Coach out of his mind. I only do it in practice. Never at a meet."

Anna put some lidocaine on his sunburn to help with the pain and, though the day had warmed to the mid-eighties, advised him to put a shirt on so the sun wouldn't do any more damage.

"I lost my sweatshirt," he said, sounding as if he was telling a lie.

Anna looked at him sharply. It was his sweatshirt. Nobody cared whether he'd lost it, burned it or given it to a passing elk. Why lie about it? Because he'd twitched, Anna was compelled to pounce. "How did you lose it?"

"I guess I must have dropped it or left it behind or something."

Vague again. Lying again? Maybe not. Maybe he didn't know how he'd lost his shirt and that lapse was scaring him. Maybe.

"It happens," she said neutrally.

"I guess."

The chief ranger came over to their outdoor clinic. "So. He going to live?"

"For a while," Anna said and gave Ruick a brief rundown of Rory's minor complaints.

"We need to figure out the best way down," Ruick said when she'd finished. "No packaging's called for. I can send the backboard down on the helicopter. We can either get him to the nearest good landing site for airlift or have Gary or Vic bring the pack horses over and ride on down the south side. From a medical standpoint, do you think it matters a whole hill of beans?"

"Half of one, six dozen of the other," Anna said.

Rory sat on his stump looking back and forth at them, apparently accustomed to being discussed in the third person when he was in the room. He came to life when Harry said, "We'll airlift you out, Rory. We've got the helicopter till sundown. May as well use it."

"I don't need to go down," Rory said, sounding alarmed at the prospect.

Ruick looked at him, cleared the irritation off his face and changed gears from logistics to public relations. Hunkering on his heels so he wouldn't be talking down, he explained, "You've been out a long time, Rory. Thirty-six hours up here is nothing to sneeze at. Your feet are battered, you've gone without food, bad sunburn, dehydrated—"

"I had water," Rory said defensively. Picking up the high-tech water bottle with the filtering system built in, the one Anna'd admired the first time she'd seen it, he shook it to prove his point.

"You still need to get checked out," Ruick said reasonably. "Your feet—"

"I only got that one cut and Anna says it's no big deal. I've run thirteen-K races with worse cuts than that. It's nothing." Rory was becoming agitated. His reaction struck Anna as excessive for the threat he faced: a free ride in a helicopter and a night or two in a comfortable bed.

Irritation revisited Ruick's face. He was not used to being thwarted. Probably he had no children. Anna had none but she'd spent the first spring in Mississippi embroiled with the students of Clinton High School. "Thwarted" was putting it mildly.

"You have to go down, son," Ruick said, striving for fatherly kindness and almost making it.

"No I don't," Rory returned. Anna was amazed that someone who could face down a chief ranger would be given the megrims by a mere grizzly bear. It wasn't that Rory had no fear of Ruick. He did. She could see it in the nervous flick of the eyes and a slight quiver at the corners of his mouth. She could also see that he had no intention of backing down.

She doesn't take shit off anybody. Anna remembered him saying that of his stepmother as if it was the highest praise he could bestow. Rory was more afraid of "taking shit," as he perceived it, than he was of what the chief ranger could do to him if he chose. Which was considerable, up to and including having him removed from the DNA project and the park if he deemed him a danger to himself, others or the resource.

What would make a boy so afraid of taking shit—Anna couldn't think of a less crude phrase that captured the essence of the phenomenon with such accuracy—off a grown man, and an authority figure to boot? Kids spent the first twenty years of their lives "taking shit" in the form of instruction, correction, insult, advice, manipulation, education and abuse by their elders. By sixteen most were past masters at the art of passive aggression. Anna wondered what Rory's parents, particularly his father to whom he referred scornfully as "Les," had done to circumvent the natural flow.

Ruick sighed, stood up and gazed around for a moment. His eyes lit on Anna and he made an executive decision. "You handle this," he said and stalked off.

Anna and Rory watched him go. Feeling suddenly weary, she sat down on a log next to the boy. "What have you got against going down, getting checked and resting up a bit?" she asked.

Rory took a few seconds to downgrade from obstinate to sullen. "I'm not hurt," he said. "There's nothing the matter with me. I'm here to do that bear thing. We got more traps to set, don't we? I don't see why I've got to go down and be messed with because I got lost. He just wants to cover his ass in case I decide I got some big injury and sue, which I'm not going to do, and make like him calling out the troops and the helicopter and everything was a good idea. Why should I be punished because I accidentally got lost?"

Punished. A kid's word. Still, Anna could see the logic and had to admit she was impressed that a boy so green in years grasped the CYA mentality a pathologically litigious society had forced upon government agencies.

"That bear tore up our tents," she tried. "Shredded them like confetti."

"They were government issue. Don't tell me they don't have more tents."

Anna didn't. As a matter of fact, they'd already been replaced. The bear team had packed in two spares. They'd been left at Anna and Joan's camp.

"I'll sleep on the ground if I have to," Rory said.

His hands were clasped together in his lap, gripped so tightly the knuckles showed white. Rory'd been terrified of bears. Then a particularly aggressive member of that club had ratified his fears. If he was willing to face another night in the open despite that, more power to him. Maybe that was it, maybe he had to prove to himself he wasn't a coward.

"Okay," Anna said. "You stay. I'll tell Harry."

Harry was not pleased but he was practical. Legally he could not force Rory to accept medical transport, since the boy was neither mentally incompetent nor unconscious. Technically he was underage, but since his parents were close at hand and he clearly had no life-threatening emergencies, it would be inexcusably heavy-handed to play the minor card. Ruick also struck Anna as fair. She doubted he would mess with Rory's Earthwatch status on the DNA project.

"You're going to have to walk back to Fifty Mountain in those things," Harry warned, pointing to Van Slyke's disreputable footwear.

"I can do that, sir," Rory said, all good manners and boyish deference now that he'd gotten his way.

"You got a shirt or something you can put on over that sunburn?"

"Anna put sunscreen on me, sir."

The "sirs" were put to good effect. Ruick was sufficiently mollified to lose interest. "Lets go, then," he said. "I expect your parents at least will be glad to see you."

At Harry's suggestion the hikers who'd found Rory had gone on ahead. Ruick led, setting a pace that was geared to Van Slyke's sore feet, though he wouldn't have admitted it. Rory was in the middle and Anna last.

As she walked behind them it occurred to her that Rory had not asked if his parents were worried. Harry had told him up front that somebody had been sent to tell them he'd been found. Even so, it seemed peculiar. Had Anna been missing in the wilderness for thirty-six hours at his age, one of her chief concerns would have been how much hot water she was going to be in when she got home and her parents' intense relief had time to transform into anger the way it invariably did.

Fifty Mountain Camp was on the northernmost edge of the old burn scar. Trees were charred snags and tents were pitched on black soil. Forty yards further on, the fire had finally exhausted itself. Beyond were green rolling hills, meadows painted with wildflowers. Rich as velvet, the meadows lay between stones the size of houses and cars that had tumbled down from the ridge; a strange Stonehenge rolling away seemingly to the edge of the world.

Fifty Mountain had five sites, all of them full. Orange, blue and green bubbles of tents poked up between the coal black spires like poisonous toadstools. Backpacks leaned against stumps, and the inevitable laundry of backpackers, socks and old towels, hung limply from spindly branches.

As part of its bear management plan, Glacier's campgrounds were laid out differently from those in other national parks. A single area was set away from the tents and designated for cooking and consuming food. It served two purposes: to confine the excessive foot traffic food areas invariably suffered and to keep this most bear-attractive of activities separate from where the campers slept.

At Fifty Mountain the cooking area was between a creek winding a life of green and silver through the burn and the developed tent sites further up a gentle slope toward the edge of the fire scar.

Hiking up from the creek, Anna thought it looked as if a town meeting was being held in the food preparation area. The rough log benches were filled with behinds and half a dozen people stood around talking in low voices. Anna recognized Joan, Gary and Vic. With them was a tall, ruddy blond with the stringy good looks of a man who spends his days walking. He wore an NPS summer uniform, shorts, no gun. Anna guessed this was

Buck, the backcountry ranger Harry'd called on to carry the bad news and then the good to Rory's parents.

The group spotted them, there was a moment of frozen tableau as new information was processed, then Joan shouted, "Back from the dead. That's my boy," and things began to happen.

A nondescript man, slightly stooped, wisps of thinning hair lifting in the breeze, stood, shaded his eyes, then smiled. The smile, accompanied by that illumination from within, identified him to Anna: Les, Rory's father. Joy made their faces alike. Les took a couple of steps around the edge of the log then the joy-light died. The dislike he'd seen in his son's face doused it. Anna watched Lester Van Slyke as she traversed the last few yards up from the creek. Rory, already being absorbed by the amoeba of people, had said only a couple of words to him before being enclosed by the crowd.

Les was left on the outskirts. Twice he sort of pushed himself up straighter, raised his chin and peered over shoulders as if steeling himself to the task of breaking through the ranks to his child. Hopelessness or cowardice stopped him both times. Finally he turned and busied himself with a day pack on one of the benches. Anna knew what he was doing. He was engaged in the occupation of being occupied, proving he had things to do, places to go, people to meet. Fooling himself or hoping to fool others into thinking that he hadn't been shut out. Or if he had, was too busy to notice the slight. Carolyn Van Slyke, the stepmother, Anna didn't see. Odds were good she was at the nucleus of the amoeba with Rory.

Though disinclined to like Lester Van Slyke for the simple reason that his son didn't, Anna nevertheless felt pity for him. "You must be Rory's father," she said and stuck out her hand. Les very nearly flinched, then recovered himself and shook hands with her. His fingers were soft and warm, his grip almost nonexistent. It was like shaking hands with a cat's tail or a draft from the furnace.

"I bet you're glad to get your boy back," Anna said, just to be saying something. Les acted a bit foggy, as if he had trouble thinking. He looked from Anna to the wall of backs to the pack he'd been fiddling with. His face was remarkably unguarded for a man his age, around sixty. Anna could almost read the choices being sorted. Continuing with the pack was rejected; trying to pry into the inner circle to present Anna was abandoned.

At length he got himself squared away. The fog lifted and Anna was treated to another one of those Van Slyke boy smiles. "Glad's not the half of it," he said. "I have been out of my mind with worry. Anything could happen to a boy out here. Just anything. You name it. And helpless? My! I wanted to go with the searchers but I guess I've let myself get out of shape some and . . . well . . ." He drifted off apologetically, spreading his arms in a half-shrug to show her his concave chest and rounded potbelly.

He was out of shape. Had Anna been in Buck's place she would have kept Mr. Van Slyke close to camp as well. He carried twenty extra pounds, all of it in the gut. The muscle tone in his arms was nil and his legs were white and spindly above the tops of brand-new hiking boots. Obviously not a seasoned backwoodsman. His forearms were grayish with old bruising and there were marks on the few inches of thigh Anna could see below his hiking shorts. Some old and a couple fresh and angry looking. She wondered if he had one of those skin or circulation disorders where the slightest bump will leave a bruise for weeks.

"Then there was the thing with Carolyn," he finished.

Anna wriggled out of her day pack, sat down by the one he'd been rummaging through and began unlacing her boots. They were old and, given they were great heavy lug-soled boots, comfortable enough, but her feet yearned for cool air and her toes for unfettered freedom.

"His stepmom pretty anxious?" she asked to be polite.

"I don't know. I mean, I'm sure she would have been. Didn't they tell you? Carolyn's been gone since yesterday morning."

That got Anna's attention. She looked up from her bootlaces. "Gone?"

"I woke up and she'd gone. She does that. I didn't think anything of it, but she hasn't come back yet."

An emotion flickered behind Mr. Van Slyke's pale clear eyes. It looked like relief for an instant then was clouded over with concern. A faint line, an old cleanly healed scar, traced white across his brow and down the side of his nose as his face muscles tensed.

"Usually she's not gone so long. Not overnight. At least not in a place like this. I mean, where would she go?"

"Have you reported it?" Anna asked cautiously.

"This noon when she still wasn't back, I got worried. I told that young fellow, that ranger, when he came with the news you found Rory. I kind of thought maybe she was with you guys."

"Not with us," Anna said, then realized that might not be strictly true. She replaced her boot. She needed to talk to Harry Ruick.

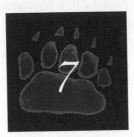

Anna crept off to be alone. It seemed like months since she'd been free of human chatter, the pressure of words on her brain, eyes on her skin. Even in times of no trauma she felt the need to escape, to decompress after a day in the society of her fellows. Distracted as she'd been by the many threads of human drama woven over the summit of Flattop, she'd not noticed how heavy the strands had become till she'd crawled out from under them.

Now, safe in a secluded crook of the creek's wandering arm, boulders as high as a horse's withers forming haphazard fortress walls between her and the squalid hubbub of Fifty Mountain Camp, she found herself imbibing huge drafts of air, sucking and sighing like a woman too long underwater. Hyperventilation brought tears. Not healing tears that flow freely and wash away grief, but the niggardly hot tears that merely sting the corners of the eyes. Peevish, self-willed tears for her own weariness and because the woman's butchered face still clung to the back of her retinas. Perhaps if she'd cried for others, the tears would have been more generous.

Joan had cried when Rory came back from the gastrointestinal tract of the bear unchewed and unclawed. Cried for joy from her warm mother's heart. Anna envied that in some unidentifiable way, envied Joan's deep connection with the human race. She was a member of the club. Anna was half convinced she'd been begotten by a passing alien life-form on a human woman. It was as good an explanation as any for the sense she had of being an outsider.

"I need my head examined," she muttered and wished she could call Molly. Instead, she forced herself to sit up, to rinse the self-pity from her face with the icy milk flowing down from the glaciers. Face free of dust, mind loosed from self-involved thoughts, she lay back again on the stone, felt the sun on her skin and began to draw strength from the earth. But for the quiet laughter of the stream, the high country was wrapped in its peculiar silence. Birds did not twitter. Squirrels did not scuffle. Even the insects did not hum.

Into this bone-deep peace, images—scenes that had made little or no sense at the time—began to resurface.

After Anna had told the chief ranger of the disappearance of Lester Van Slyke's wife, Harry took him and his son away from the others. Rory was old enough he, too, was to be burdened with the news that the body they found was very probably that of his missing stepmother. To her relief, Anna had not been asked to participate in this interaction. Fifteen feet away, leaning comfortably against a snag, she watched the three men with interest. Ruick had his back to her but she could see Rory and his father clearly.

Over the years Anna had broken enough bad news to park visitors that she knew the stages of acceptance. Predictable as sunrise, she saw them flow across Les and Rory's faces. First was blank stupidity, the brain refusing to understand, then the dawning of fear as a tide of it rushed in from the darkest oceans of the mind. Third was either disintegration or coping. Both Rory and Les coped, but before the fear had been stemmed by courage—or hope—there came a moment that didn't fit the pattern.

Shock had momentarily rendered their faces free of artifice, and the look they exchanged had been naked emotion. What emotion, was the question that troubled Anna. She could make a few assumptions as to what it was not. But she had to take them separately, father and son, because though the look had come from both at the same instant, there was no conspiracy in it and no empathy, merely two different unmasked thoughts broadcast simultaneously.

Les had not turned to his son with love or with concern. Near as she could tell, he had not been seeking to give or receive comfort. The closest she could get to deciphering the sudden dark flash of energy she'd witnessed was a flare of horror turning to shame. The vision was fleeting, quickly reverting to the blank of denial. Then Les appeared, if possible, even more downtrodden and ineffectual than he had before.

Rory's glance had been even more puzzling. Maybe anger. Maybe respect. Anna was just guessing. Reading faces was an art, not a science. Sometimes the muse was on one's side. Sometimes she merely toyed with one.

Given that the first suspect in a murder case is invariably the spouse of the victim, Anna found the exchange noteworthy. It was hard to picture self-effacing Mr. Van Slyke creeping out of his tent in the dead of night—presuming the missus had been offed in the traditional dead of night—in his brand-spanking-new boots, following or luring his wife several miles from camp, then killing her and mutilating her face. Facial mutilation usually bespoke great rage, great hatred toward the victim in particular or, less often, the gender in general. Only close friends and near enemies cared enough to rip one's face off. Lester Van Slyke didn't seem capable of that kind of emotion, but looks were consistently deceiving.

In the midst of these ephemeral and possibly imaginary weirdnesses—Anna knew she was quite capable of seeing ne'er-do-wells where only solid citizens existed—was a very real anomaly. Lester Van Slyke's wife had been missing in the wilderness between twenty-four and thirty-six hours before he bothered to report it. That in and of itself was highly irregular.

If she was right about the horror and shame on Lester's face, could it be horror at what he'd done? Or horror at what he thought Rory might have done?

Rory. Anna let her mind float over the boy for a while. He was an enigma. People of his age were such cauldrons of emotion, hormones, burgeoning pride and inherited misinformation that assigning motives to their actions was nearly impossible. Half the time even they did not know why they did a thing. From what little she knew of Rory, he was devoted to—or at least greatly admired—his stepmother. And he'd not gone out in the night intentionally; he'd fled half-dressed from the predations of a bear.

Half-dressed; something about that bothered Anna. She stretched in the sun like a lazy cat and opened her mind to pictures of Rory in dishabille.

The mysteriously missing shirt he avoided discussing was odd but not earthshaking. That was not the pea under Anna's metaphorical mattresses that bruised her thoughts each time they turned over. The sweatpants, the slippers, the sunburn, the cut foot: these things were as they should be. Anna stopped making lists and merely let the chips of memory run movies in her head: Rory talking, sitting on his stump, laughing, drinking water.

Drinking water; he'd been drinking out of his fancy filter-it-anywhere, special-order, latest-gimmick-on-the-market water bottle.

Why would someone with diarrhea, rushing into the wood to relieve himself, bring along his water bottle? According to Rory, after the bear had come on the scene, such had been his haste to "go for help" that he'd pulled up his trousers and dashed off without slowing down enough even to take his flashlight.

The water bottle could indicate nothing. Rory might have been dehydrated and thought he'd be in the woods with his loose bowels long enough he'd need a drink. Reflex might have dictated he snatch up the bottle when he fled the bear. Or it could indicate that before he left his tent, he knew he had someplace to go a long enough hike away that he'd need to bring along water. With the grim bulk of suspicion squeezing out generous thought, it came to Anna that Rory might not have wished to discuss his missing shirt because he'd purposely left it behind, hidden it so no one would see that it was covered in blood.

"Yuck," Anna said aloud and sat up. The sun had moved two fingers toward the west. There were several hours of daylight left but they'd want to start for their camp soon. Buck, bless his long-legged energy, had volunteered to walk the six miles round-trip to Anna and Joan's camp on the far side of the mountain top and bring back boots and socks for Rory.

Despite the very real possibility that the dead woman was his stepmother, Rory had refused to ride down in the helicopter with his dad and Harry Ruick. There'd been no small effort to convince him. Anna had bowed out and left it to Ruick. Again Rory had persevered and they'd flown without him.

Given her recent unsavory thoughts about the lad, Anna was sorry Ruick hadn't been a little more heavy-handed.

Having spoiled her solitude by inviting thoughts of others there, she decided to rejoin the human race even if she did so as a half-alien interloper. Her timing was good. As she was lacing up her boots she heard Joan's voice calling her name.

"Over here," Anna hollered.

A scrambling sound, then Joan appeared around the side of a boulder. Since Rory'd been found, Joan's looks had improved. The sight of the boy unharmed had eased two days' weariness from her face and eyes.

"Hey. There you are." She sounded positively chipper. Uncharitably, Anna resented it.

"Here I am," she confirmed.

Joan plopped comfortably down on the rock beside her. "You look a wee bit on the grouchy side," she said cheerfully.

"Grouchy doesn't even begin to touch it. I've been thinking," Anna explained.

"Oooh. Not good."

"Why did Rory have his water bottle with him?"

"What—" Joan looked baffled, then as her quick mind rapidly put together the pieces, crestfallen. Chipper good cheer burst like a birthday balloon. "Oh, Anna, no . . ."

"You've got to admit it's a little out of whack considering the story he gave us."

"It makes no sense," Joan said. "Surely he'd've put on his boots if he knew he was going . . . somewhere."

"Not if he didn't want to leave tracks. It wasn't that far." Anna remembered something then and added it to the soup. "He could cover a lot of country. He's a long-distance runner. He told me. He runs barefoot."

"I don't believe it," Joan said firmly.

"Neither do I, but you've got to admit it warrants looking at."

Joan sighed. "This is why I went into zoology," she said. "Animals have no hidden agendas." After that they were quiet for a while. So long that Anna began to suffer that uncomfortable feeling that comes when one suspects one has committed an awful social gaffe but can't figure out what it is.

"You know," Joan said finally. "You are in danger of going over to the dark side, Anna. You need a lot more of rainbows and roses and whiskers on kittens in the daily fare. I think you've been given to me for some serious lightening up. I've got you for two more weeks."

"God, that's not long enough," Anna said seriously.

Joan laughed, a noise so filled with that rare essence, gay abandon, that Anna laughed too, and felt sincerely lightened.

"Change in venue," Joan said when they'd subsided. "Turns out Rory is to go down. We're all to go down for a day. Harry needs us for reports, interviews and whatnot over both the search and the other. It's too late for us to head out today and ain't nobody sending an expensive helicopter for such as we. So we hike back to camp and pack out tomorrow. Harry also said, and I quote: 'Tell Anna she can nose around the campers at Fifty Mountain if she wants.'"

Tacit approval for her to investigate but with no official standing and no NPS backing. Ruick was a clever fellow. If Anna discovered anything useful, all to the good. If she screwed up, she was of little more importance than a civilian. Unless she screwed up big-time and ended up in civil court. Then they were both in deep trouble. Anna allowed herself to be warmed by the knowledge that the chief ranger counted on her not to screw up.

"Do you know if the campers have been interviewed?" Anna asked. She had been on her rock for quite some time, since before the helicopter carried off Lester Van Slyke.

"I think so. I know Harry talked briefly to everybody and told them they'll need to stop by headquarters before they leave the park in case any new questions come up or there's paperwork to be done."

"There's always paperwork," Anna said. "Always."

She followed Joan back up to camp. They had about ninety minutes to kill before Buck returned with Rory's boots. Anna decided to take up Ruick's invitation to "nose around."

Already the will-o'-the-wisp population of Fifty Mountain had undergone so much change, interviews were largely a waste of time. Rory had been missing a night, a day, and a night. During that day the body had been discovered. It was not till the following day that they'd found Carolyn Van Slyke was missing. Campers seldom stayed in one place that long. Assuming the faceless woman had been killed the night Rory ran from the bear, as the condition of the corpse suggested, two mornings had come and gone. Mornings during which early-rising campers folded their tents and moved on and new people hiked in to take their places. Witnesses, alibis, the usual round of queries brought on by homicide, scarcely applied.

Anna wandered from site to site. Only three groups that had been there the night Mrs. Van Slyke went AWOL remained. The compliment she'd inferred from Ruick's suggestion began to lose its luster. Because of unique circumstances, nosing around was a bit of a fool's errand. Still, she persevered. She had nothing better to do and she'd become accustomed to the dead ends in law enforcement. One simply followed them to their natural conclusion, checked them off the list and went on to the next. Without a good lead to follow, most investigative work boiled down to necessary tedium. Doing it out-of-doors in one of the most beautiful places on earth was a definite perk.

One by one, Anna spoke with those who had been there the night the potential Mrs. Van Slyke was probably killed. Three Canadian college girls could tell Anna nothing. Persons not young and not beautiful were of no interest to them. A couple in their late fifties from Michigan had noticed Carolyn at the food preparation area. They thought she was married to someone other than Lester. That or the wife's description of Lester was kind to the point of absurdity. She'd given him hair and four extra inches in height. They described Carolyn as a vivacious woman with a loud voice and laugh. There was little else they could recall.

The wife kindly pointed out the man they'd mistaken for Mrs. Van Slyke's husband. He was the only person Anna had yet to talk with who had been at Fifty Mountain on the night in question. His tent was pitched in the site farthest from the food area. Like every site, it had a stunning view through the teeth of rotting snags to the glacier-sheared plain that was Flattop Mountain. When Anna saw him, he was sitting on a tarp, his back against the charred bark of a pine that had survived the fire. Two years later it still struggled, half black, half green, like a scarred and wounded woman, looks and strength gone but heart still determined.

The man beneath this valiant tree wasn't doing quite as well. Like Lester, his backcountry duds and gear were suspiciously new and he wriggled like a man whose backside has known only leather car seats and barstools. Though the sun was setting and the temperature had dropped considerably, he wore only a thin T-shirt and hugged his knees for warmth. Hovering around fifty, he sported rich reddish-brown hair that was still thick. Not a trace of gray showed anywhere. Anna suspected he owed more to Grecian Formula than good genes. She could see how the Michigan couple might have mistaken him for Mr. Van Slyke. Even dead, Carolyn looked more of a match for this man than the stooped, pale, prematurely aged Lester.

"Hey, sorry to bother you," Anna said, stopping on the perimeter of an invisible circle around his camp. Anna would no more barge into someone's campsite than she would enter a house without knocking.

"Hi." He slapped at a mosquito. He made no effort to rise. Neither a backwoodsman nor a gentleman.

"I'm Anna Pigeon," Anna identified herself. "I'm a park ranger. We're asking questions of the folks who were camped here the night that woman went missing."

"I don't know anything about that. I came here to get away from people. I've stayed pretty much to myself." He delivered this piece of information to a place halfway between his eyes and Anna's knees, punctuating his words with slaps at mosquitoes.

"You want to get a coat or something?" Anna asked. It wasn't so much that she hated to see a fellow human being suffering as that she wanted his full attention.

She got it.

"A coat?" He met her eyes with sudden suspicion. "Why?"

Anna shrugged. Maybe vanity made him prickly about his outerwear.

"It's getting cold. Looks like the mosquitoes are eating you up. I thought you'd be more comfortable."

He relaxed. "No. I'm fine. You want to sit down? Pull up a chair." He laughed, the hollow angry sound of a man annoyed Glacier National Park didn't see fit to furnish their campsites. "These mosquitoes are awful. I thought you weren't supposed to have mosquitoes up here. God's country and all that."

"I've got some mosquito repellent in my pack you can use," Anna offered as she folded herself neatly on the packed ground near his tarpaulin.

He took the insect repellent readily enough and smeared it on his face and arms. "Bill McCaskil," he introduced himself as he handed it back. Sans bugs he was more personable. Anna got down to the business of interviewing.

"Did you meet a Mrs. Van Slyke around camp at all?" she asked.

"No, like I said, I keep to myself."

Anna waited. His answer had come too fast. Sure enough, pressured by silence, he amended it.

"Carolyn Van Slyke? Was she the blond lady, kind of beefy around the hips? I might have talked to her a couple of times."

Anna'd figured that. The other couple had mistakenly assumed Carolyn was married to Bill McCaskil. The only reason strangers would assume that is because they saw the two of them together. It occurred to Anna that she'd only referred to the deceased—or at the very least, the missing—woman as "Mrs. Van Slyke." McCaskil had called her Carolyn. The two of them had been on a first-name basis. Not necessarily telling. Campgrounds were informal places.

"Did you eat together, hike together, anything like that?" Anna asked.

McCaskil shot her a sharp look. "We may have eaten at the same time, I guess. There's only that one place to do it." He didn't like being questioned. Maybe he hated to get involved. Maybe he just didn't like being messed with. Still, there was something about him that set Anna's teeth on edge. She watched for a moment trying to put her finger on what it was.

He was good-looking enough. The determinedly reddish hair had a natural wave to it. A lean face and strong hooked nose over a well-shaped mouth lent him strength. The effect was marred but not ruined by acne scarring on his cheeks and chin. His body was attractive: tall and lean and gym-buffed. The kind of fit that doesn't look fit for much but modeling clothes.

Thinking that, it came to her why she felt a wrongness. He didn't want to be here. Didn't like the wilderness. Didn't like camping. His repeated desire to get away from people didn't ring true under the circumstances. He struck her as the sort who, if wanting solitude, would go to the clubs on an off night when the crowds were thinned. So why was he on a solitary backpacking trip in Glacier National Park?

Anna decided on the direct approach: "So why did you decide to come on a solitary backpacking trip in Glacier National Park?"

For most visitors this was not a trick question. It was one

they were dying to answer in great effusive gusts. McCaskil acted as if she'd asked for the solution to a complex algebraic problem.

"Why does anybody decide to go anywhere?" he countered finally.

Anna went on to ask the questions she'd come to ask but unsurprisingly Bill hadn't noticed when or where Carolyn Van Slyke was at any given time. The one piece of information he did throw out was that Mr. and Mrs. Van Slyke's marriage wasn't made in heaven.

"You wouldn't believe the way she talked to that old boy," was how he put it.

"Did they fight?" Anna asked.

"Not fight. I don't think there's any fight left in that man if there was any to begin with."

"What then?"

"She was a carper. Carped on him all the time. Snide little comments about his paunch, his bald head. He couldn't do anything right. The poor bastard. A woman talked that way to me would get a fat lip. Not that boy: 'yes dear, no dear.'" Bill laughed, showing big white teeth, the two front incisors turned in toward each other giving him a jagged animal bite. The laughter was derisive and aimed, it seemed to Anna, not at Mrs. Van Slyke but at the poor bastard who'd married her.

Leaving his camp, threading her way down the footpath past the other sites, Anna resisted the urge to break into a run. Bill McCaskil had a dark indrawn tension about him that made her uneasy. A mean streak, if his response to Lester's humiliation was any indication.

She stopped again at the camp where the midwestern couple was staying. The woman, as domestic as you please, was neatly hanging socks from a tent rope.

"One more thing," Anna said, feeling so much like Columbo she was immediately self-conscious.

"Yes?" the woman said politely.

"Do you remember why you thought the blond woman was married to the tall man camped back up there?"

The woman paused a moment, a sock held before her in two hands. "It's just that they were always together, I suppose. Not holding hands or huggy-kissy but just together. Here and there. I do remember seeing the little man, her husband I guess he is, but not so much with her."

"Thanks." Anna went on her way. McCaskil had a closer relationship to Carolyn Van Slyke than he had admitted. Why not say so? There were no laws against socializing in the backcountry. If he knew she'd been murdered, it would make sense. No one wants his vacation taken over by the tedious machinery of law enforcement. In the wilderness, no neighbors, coworkers, political opponents or extended family to focus on, there was a definite lack of much in the way of suspects. Because he was there and an unsavory type, Anna filtered McCaskil through her mind. Had he known Carolyn before, followed her or met her here at her invitation? Was he, so obviously uncomfortable away from the amenities of civilization, merely here on a hunting trip and Carolyn was unfortunate enough to be the game?

Anna found it much easier to imagine Bill McCaskil crouched over a kill, elbow deep in blood, than the unassuming Lester Van Slyke. McCaskil told Anna there was significant friction between Les and his wife. Merely a ploy to cast suspicion on Les by providing him with a motive for killing Carolyn?

Unaware she did so Anna shook her head. It hadn't felt that way. McCaskil called Lester "old boy" and "poor bastard," remarking that there was no fight left in him. That was not the portrayal of a man capable of violence. Not unless Bill McCaskil was so infernally clever and torturously subtle that he painted the picture of the quintessential worm in hopes Anna would make the leap to the idea that the worm had turned, and in a big way.

"Anna? Are you in there?"

Anna came out of her self-induced trance to see Joan peering at her from a foot away. Wrapped tight in her own thoughts, Anna hadn't realized she'd come to a stop in the middle of the trail half a dozen yards from the food preparation area.

"How many fingers am I holding up?" Joan asked.

"Sorry," Anna apologized and followed Joan's lead down the path.

"I've heard of people being in a brown study," Joan said. "I'd just never seen anybody get locked in before."

"My powers of concentration frighten even me," Anna replied.

Joan laughed. "Well, concentrate on walking. We need to get

back before dark. If you remember, Mr. Bear left our campsite at sixes and sevens."

Sixes and sevens hardly described the utter ruin of their camp. Twilight was settling toward night as they arrived. The three of them stopped on the edge of the little clearing, no one in a hurry to go into it. Overhead the sky was the sea green peculiar to mountain dusk. No shadows fell, they merely gathered beneath the trees, growing stronger as night neared.

An anxiousness as cold as the sweat of sickness balled behind Anna's breastbone. Days busy with the search and then the body recovery, bustling with people and helicopters, had driven out the rending visceral fear she'd felt the night the grizzly had come for them. In telling and retelling, the tale had grown unreal, like a war story borrowed from someone else's battle. It was real now.

The tents she and Joan had piled up were ragged with great tears. Fragments of cloth and clothing littered the grass. It was way too easy to believe the bear was nearby, just waiting for darkness.

"He's moved on by now," Joan said, as if the same fear raked her insides. "They have a huge range and he didn't get any food reward here."

"Maybe he wasn't looking for food," Anna said.

"What?"

Anna didn't repeat her comment. It didn't make sense even to her. It was just a remark the subconscious had smuggled past her censors to her tongue.

"There're the new tents." Rory pointed to two undamaged blue stuff sacks set by the boulder that dominated the green.

"Let's get to it." Anna forced herself to move. "We'll feel better after we're situated and fed."

Tents were pitched. By common, unspoken consent the shredded remains of those they'd slept in two nights before were bundled out of sight behind the rock. The "fed" portion of Anna's rehabilitative program had to be skipped except for what snacks they could find in their day packs. For reasons they could not fathom, when the bear team had dropped off the replacement tents, they had taken down the food from where it was cached and packed it out.

"What the hell do they think we're supposed to eat?" Anna groused.

"Maybe they were more concerned with what might eat us," Joan returned.

Anna decided she wasn't all that hungry anyway. What she mostly was was tired.

Anna and Joan had shoved their personal things willy-nilly into a garbage bag the morning after the attack, when their organizational skills had been somewhat challenged. As night came on, they sat around the bag, flashlights trained upon it, like brigands dividing their spoils. Anna found herself wishing for the hissing glare of Coleman lanterns, something more substantial than a six-inch Maglight to keep the terrors of the dark at bay.

From what she could observe, Joan wasn't doing much better and Rory was just about jumping out of his skin every time one of them shifted in their seat and made a scuffling noise that could be attributed to bears stalking. Cold was rushing in with the darkness; Anna's muscles tensed against it. They all needed hot food.

The divvying up went on. Joan, like Mrs. Santa, disappeared head and arms into the bag and brought out the things one at a time.

Moccasins for Anna, underwear for Joan, a single sock for Rory. Sweater for Joan, Levi's for Anna, water bottle for Rory.

Anna suddenly broke out of the Christmas rhythm and jerked her spine straight. "Goddamn motherfucking water bottle," she growled.

The other two looked at her as if she'd gone insane.

8

Anna chose not to explain her outburst. Under pressure she claimed chronic and fleeting Tourette's syndrome. The questions that the wretched water bottle brought to mind were not those she wished to pursue in the dark of night ten hours' hike from reliable backup.

Though unasked, the questions were hot and sharp in her brain and they kept her from sleep. Beside her, snuggled into her navy-blue down bag, Joan snored gently. Women snoring was a well-kept secret. Not from the world at large or husbands and lovers and roommates with ears to hear, but from the women who did it. Idly, Anna wondered if she snored. No one had ever told her she did, but then they wouldn't, would they?

It crossed her mind to wake Joan up, make her listen to scary stories. She seriously considered doing it on the "one little cloud is lonely" and "misery loves company" schools of thought. The snoring made her relent. Joan had such a happy, childlike snore. On an occasion less fraught with evil surmisings, Anna would have found it as reliable a soporific as Piedmont's deep and rumbling purr.

Curling herself into a ball like a corkscrewed cocoon, her soft underbelly protected from the predators, Anna gave herself over to the lonely contemplation of the goddamn motherfucking water bottle. Or, to be precise, water bottles plural. There were three. Three unusual, mail-order-only, hot-off-the-presses water bottles, all with a built-in filter, all by the same manufacturer.

Rory had one when they started their adventure. Rory had one when they found him after his thirty-six hours lost. Les had

had one at Fifty Mountain. Now Rory had two. The only member of the family who did not appear to have one, who, indeed, had no water bottle at all, was Carolyn Van Slyke, the dead woman. Surely the bottles had been a family affair. Probably researched, ordered and disbursed by Carolyn herself. Lester didn't appear to know or care much about backpacking. Rory was new to it. But Carolyn was a photographer and her hiking boots, if Anna remembered correctly, were old and much used.

Rory had not taken water with him when he fled the bear. It was here, in camp, in a garbage bag the whole time. Sometime in the day and a half Mrs. Van Slyke went missing, she'd lost her water bottle. Sometime during those same thirty-six hours Rory had acquired it, or one just like it.

Anna reached behind her, running her hand along the floor of the tent where it met with the nylon wall. Her fingers found the slick folds of plastic-wrap draped loosely around a cylinder, and she was reassured the mystery bottle was still in her possession. She'd lifted it quietly first chance she got. Not the bottle from the garbage bag, but the one Rory had been carrying when he turned up unscathed from his sojourn.

Ideally, to preserve the fingerprints, the bottle would have been put in a paper bag. Having none, Anna had improvised. When she arrived safe and sound back in West Glacier, she would turn it over to Harry Ruick so it could be dusted for fingerprints and tested for blood residue. If it did turn out to belong to Carolyn Van Slyke, Rory was going to be in an awkward position.

Cold swept down her spine from nape to nether regions as a *Psycho*-like image of a knife plunging through the thin nylon of the tent took over her consciousness: a picture of Rory, wild-eyed and hair awry, running amok in camp. Curling down more tightly, she suffered the craven wish that Joan rather than she slept on the side of the tent nearest Rory's.

Pushing Hitchcock's genius for evil aside, she comforted herself with thoughts of murderers. Often, in prisons it was the murderers who were chosen as trustees. Not that rare bird the serial killer, but garden-variety one-corpse–type murderers. These men and women were in reality no longer a threat to society. They had killed the person they needed to be dead and were done. Usually these were people who had killed someone they knew and, in their own minds at least, killed them for a perfectly good reason.

What perfectly good reason could Rory have for killing his stepmother? The butchery to the woman's face, done after death, suggested a desire to annihilate Carolyn Van Slyke as a person, hatred so great that merely taking her life was not adequate to slake it.

Rory spoke as if he admired his stepmom and scorned his biological father. That fit the pattern if he was an abused child. Children have an uncanny ability to know that to survive they must please and placate the abuser. To an outsider, they appear to be genuinely attached. If Rory suffered at Carolyn's hands and his dad failed to protect him, he might understandably hate him for it, cleave to Carolyn.

But Rory was no longer a little kid and, though not a beefy young man, he was strong and fit. Once the child was no longer a child the pattern shifted, fanned out. Any number of responses of the adult victim would be normal. Including a rage so long sublimated to the survival needs of a child that when it broke free it resulted in homicide.

The theory hung together after a fashion, but Anna was unsatisfied. Too many unanswered questions. If Rory was the murderer, how did he set up the assignation with his stepmother? If he didn't and meeting her was simply a coincidence happening after he ran from the bear, what did he use to carve off her face? Only the exceptionally deranged—or the marvelously foresighted—slept with a cleaver secreted about their pajamas.

It is not necessary that you think so much. Molly, in her role as psychiatrist and worried sister, had given that advice to Anna shortly after her husband died. Anna heard the words again now and resolutely cleared her mind of boys and cleavers and high-tech drinking apparatus. Into this cleared space came the gentle rhythm of Joan Rand's snore. Anna let it lull her to sleep.

The hike down was uneventful. They went back the way they had come, West Flattop Trail east to Fifty Mountain Camp then Flattop Trail south to the sheared-off edge of the mountain where the steep descent began. The country they traveled was beginning to look way too familiar to Anna. Walking through the common miracle of intensely green and living glacier lilies bursting joyously through exhausted black char, she found she looked mostly to the mountains rising above Flattop, and dreamed about new trails and new views. Cleveland, Merrit, Wilbur. *Wilbur,* for Christ's sake. Mundane names for objects of such staggering beauty.

Rory was leading the way. Anna had made him point man on the flimsy pretext that it would be good for his orienteering skills—as if a blind three-year-old could get lost on the clear tracks of Glacier's main trails. He complied. Joan looked her questions but never asked them. The answer would have been that Anna just didn't feel comfortable with Rory at her back. She wanted the lad where she could keep an eye on him until a few wrinkles were ironed out.

None of the three of them said more than a dozen words the entire trip, not even when they stopped and ate their meager lunches. Anna'd had too many words in her mouth over the past three days and was glad to be rid of the taste of them. Joan seemed lost in her own thoughts. From the expression on her face in unguarded moments, none of them were particularly jolly. Rory was silent as well but for what reasons, Anna could not fathom. He knew his stepmother, whom—if he did not kill—he presumably liked, was probably dead. Yet he did not grieve or fret in any of the ways Anna had come to expect. Perhaps he was in classic and total denial, but she didn't think so. That would require a veneer of high spirits. He appeared simply to be a man with a complex issue that drew his energies inward as he worked through the ramifications. Whatever it was it didn't seem to frighten or sadden him and it didn't slow his pace, so Anna was happy.

Harry Ruick and Lester Van Slyke waited for them at Packers Roost, the staging area near Going to the Sun Road. Harry had loftier things to attend to than playing taxi driver, so Anna knew Carolyn Van Slyke was really truly dead. Lester had identified the body. Now the hard news would be brought home to Rory.

Knowing what was coming, she maneuvered herself from the rear of the pack to Harry Ruick's left. She wanted to see Rory's face when he found for certain-sure his stepmother had been slain. So far, the emotions the probability had elicited from him—at least publicly—had been out of balance.

Clearing her mind and draping herself with what empathic tendencies she could muster, Anna watched. Lester Van Slyke was the first to speak.

"Son," he said, "Rory—" His voice broke and he stopped.

On an infant's face, every feeling is clearly manifest, as visible and identifiable as wind patterns on water. Rory was old enough to have developed the mask humans build to hide their emotions. The blueprint of the mask had probably been in place by the time he was seven years old. By the time he was thirty it would be complete, a false face that he himself might not be able to penetrate. At eighteen there were still thin places in the veneer. Anna watched emotions flow beneath the unfinished mask as one might watch a mime act through rain glass.

For the briefest of instants there was a flicker of light, a candle quickly extinguished behind his eyes. Before thought or memory came to quench that flame, Rory had been genuinely glad to see his father.

"It was your stepmom, son. She's gone," Les said, having recovered his voice. His pale blue eyes filled with tears that ran unnoticed over soft and sagging cheeks, catching in the stubble of two days' growth of beard.

Light winked out of Rory's eyes, apparently extinguished by his father's tears. The emotions that followed passed beneath the distorted glass of civilization so quickly Anna was not sure she interpreted them correctly. It looked like a draft of disappointment with a disgust chaser.

Rory noticed Anna watching him and his face firmed. Another lesson in deceit learned. Next time the mask would have an added layer of opacity. If he grieved, it was deep inside. Openly ignoring the weeping Lester, Rory spoke to Harry Ruick.

"Do you know who killed her?"

"No," Ruick said honestly. "We're hoping the forensic evidence sent to the lab will give us a clue. Till that comes back we're going to need to ask you and your dad a lot of questions, get to know everything we can about your stepmom. We might get a lead from that."

Rory nodded, looking considerably older than his years. Perhaps because nature abhors a vacuum, Les had taken on the role of the child, at least outwardly, and snuffled into a crumpled handkerchief. "I feel so lost," he said, and sounded it.

As they climbed into the sedan, Les asked Rory to join him at the motel where he was staying but the boy declined, preferring the grubby, spartan NPS researchers' dorm to greater comfort bought at the price of his father's company.

Lester took the rebuff with resignation. This was not the first time his son had slammed a door in his face. Compassion hit Joan so hard she grimaced as though she'd sustained a punch to the stomach. Anna wondered if she was merely imagining the hurt or if her sons, Luke and John, had dealt such a blow themselves.

Rory's adult façade was crumbling and Lester Van Slyke was frankly gray with exhaustion. Of necessity and not generosity, Ruick postponed the taking of statements and the interview process until the following afternoon.

Five of them squished into a sedan for twenty minutes, breathing each other's fear, anger and sweat was pressing heavily on Anna. She rolled down her window, pushed her face into the onrush of air and closed her ears. Rory, sitting in the backseat between her and Joan, jostled her at every turn in the twisted mountain road. At each nudge Anna suffered the burn of childhood fury when *her* side of the backseat was encroached upon.

By the time they reached the employee housing area and Ruick pulled the car into Joan's drive, Anna had her hand on the door handle. She pulled up on it before the car rolled to a full stop and got out with a harried sense of escaping. It was all she could do to remain in their company long enough to unload her pack from the trunk. Ruick was still throwing verbal instructions at her back as she headed toward the front door.

Once inside Joan made an incredibly generous offer. "Do you want to shower first?"

Anna managed a nod of bare civility before shutting herself into the blessed sanctity of the bath.

Neither Joan nor Anna had the desire, much less the energy, to talk shop that night. Clad in her teddy-bear print, goin'-visitin' pajamas, Anna lay on the couch watching whatever network was on, alternately blessing and cursing her hostess for being a teetotaler. Had there been alcohol in the house, given her present mental and physical condition, Anna would have dearly loved to imbibe. When the angels perched on her shoulder, she was grateful that temptation in the form of the cunning, baffling and powerful was not set before her. When demons in the form of rigorously edited memories of drug-induced bliss shrieked at her, she longed for that same temptation so she could give into it forthwith.

Joan chose to dull her brain not with television or booze but with her personal drug of choice: work. She sat surrounded by several days' worth of bear incident management system reports and a pile of faxes, e-mails and 10-343 law enforcement reports that she had, in the addict's age-old habit of stockpiling drugs, radioed ahead and asked her assistant to leave on her dining table.

"E-mail first," Joan said as she opened her laptop. "Ah, three from my map boy wanting to know where the bears will seek food this week."

"How do you know where they'll be?" Anna said.

"I don't. I just know where the food will be. What's ripe. Like that."

Anna left her to it.

She was amusing herself by cataloguing the gross errors committed by law enforcement on some cop show when Joan broke the long and peaceful silence.

"Four bear sightings since we've been in the high country," she said.

"Mmmm." Anna made a noise to excuse herself from being out-and-out rude but which she hoped would discourage any further intercourse.

"One's pretty funny," Joan said.

Anna refused to ask how so. Several seconds ticked by. She could almost feel Joan's need to talk.

Joan cracked. "Seems this one was dancing."

"Next they'll be riding bicycles and lobbying for the vote," Anna said.

Contact was made. Joan rubbed her eyes, her glasses riding up on the backs of her hands. "Do you think Rory'll be okay?" she asked. "I mean he *seemed* okay. Way too okay if you ask me."

"It's quiet, *too* quiet . . . ," Anna intoned.

"Yeah, like that. Didn't it seem to you that he kind of went away inside himself when his dad and Harry flew out to ID the body? He had to know it was his stepmom. The rest of us figured it was."

Anna thought of the water bottles and wondered if Rory had not merely thought it was Carolyn but known for a fact it was.

"He'll be okay," Anna said, then remembered it was Joan she was talking to. Not someone she wanted to blow off. She sat up, folded her legs under her tailor-fashion and muted the television.

"I don't know," she amended. She told Joan of Rory's vagueness about what had transpired during the thirty-six hours he'd been missing, about her fears his cowardice in abandoning them to *Ursus horibilis* would permanently scar his psyche. She told Joan about Carolyn Van Slyke's missing water bottle and Rory turning up out of the woods with a spare. The recitation done, Anna felt much relieved. She couldn't say the same for Joan.

Owl-eyed behind the oversized spectacles, Joan studied her as if she was a scat specimen. "How do you walk around like a normal person with such creepy thoughts in your head?" she asked finally. "It must be like being Stephen King but without the money."

"I guess," Anna admitted, feeling guilty for casting her shadow side over Joan's naturally sunny self. "I think good thoughts, too." She was remembering Joan's lecture on rainbows, roses and whiskers on kittens.

"Name one," Joan challenged.

Anna drew a blank and Joan laughed her wonderful laugh, joy and appreciation of the absurdity of the human condition running up and down the musical scale. Relenting, she said. "I know you do. It was unfair to spring the question on you at this time of night."

Anna accepted the reprieve but her failure bothered her and she finally came up with one: "Kittens. Not just the whiskers, the whole ball of wax."

Again the laughter. When it had subsided, somberness reclaimed Joan, and Anna waited for the inevitable. It wasn't long in coming.

"Do you think Rory did it?" Joan asked.

Anna wanted to say no for the sake of her friend but chose not to defraud her with a half-truth. "I don't see how he could have," she said instead. That, at least, was honest.

They were saved from wandering too far down that darkling road by a knock on the door.

"I'll get it," Anna said as Joan yelled, "Come in." Both, it seemed, welcomed the distraction.

Ron, the bear-team guy who'd given them a lift to the bottom of Flattop Trail four nights before, let himself in the front door. Those four nights had stretched into years in Anna's mind and she didn't remember Ron's name till Joan called out a greeting.

Big and bearish himself, Ron was well-suited to his profession. Descended from some sturdy sun-drenched people, he was of middling height with thick black hair, a glossy close-cut black beard and rambunctious black chest hair that sprang out of the vee of his uniform shirt.

"Joan has all the fun," he said seriously as he flopped his two hundred pounds into an aging Barcalounger with childlike disregard for the load limits of its infrastructure. "Then I was off when the search team was called out so I didn't even get in on that.

"Let's see. What did you guys miss down here at Adventure Central? Tom up at Polebridge ranger station"—Ron named the station on the northwest boundary of the park—"got to tow a gutted horse trailer from where it'd been illegally parked. Lord knows what they were hauling. The drug dogs didn't like it much but didn't hit on anything.

"On the east side Alicia had a lady she thought had symptoms of a heart attack—shortness of breath, bad color—and had her taken out by helicopter. Turns out the lady wasn't having a coronary. She was eighty-three years old and tired. Poor old gal will keel over when she gets the bill.

"And while you guys were out finding bodies, right here in the megalopolis of West Glacier, crime capital of the world, yours truly was called on to risk life and honor shooing a chipmunk out of some lady from Virginia's tent."

More laughter from Joan; too much for the nominally amusing chipmunk incident. Joan laughed a lot. It was how she let the pressures that built up inside her skull escape since her innate kindness and empathy forbade darker, more violent expressions. Anna was coming to know the nuances of her laughter. This was sharp with the relief a change of subject provided.

The change was short-lived.

"Tell me everything," Ron said. "I'm on till midnight so take your time."

Trading the conversation back and forth effortlessly Anna and Joan wove a picture of their four days in the high country. Joan's instincts were excellent and neither she nor Anna shared anything about the water bottles, the precise location of the body, the contents of the pack that had been found or any other detail Ruick might wish kept secret for investigative purposes.

"Wow," Ron said when they'd finished. "Could be anybody. But why would anybody do it?"

"That's it in a nutshell," Anna said.

Dead ends summarily reached, the conversation limped on for a while, Ron dragging his visit out as long as he could. The four-to-midnight shift could be deadly dull. Anna and Joan managed to yawn him out the door a little past ten. Shortly after that they both headed for the unparalleled luxury of a mattress covered with clean sheets and dry blankets, and under a roof.

At eight a.m. both women were in a conference room down the hall from Harry Ruick's office. Anna was filling out a statement encapsulating what she had experienced and observed regarding Carolyn Van Slyke's murder. Joan was filling out reports on the bear attack on their camp and her involvement with the search for Rory. Joan could easily—probably more easily—have done her work in the relative comfort of her own office. The resource management building was an older structure with fewer conveniences but had loads more personality than the bricks of headquarters.

She'd come with Anna to keep her company, she said. Anna suspected she also wanted to pick up any new information there might be about Rory's involvement, or lack thereof, in his stepmother's death. Ruick had no news on that score but, good as her intentions, Joan stayed with Anna till they'd finished and Anna left to meet with Ruick.

The chief ranger's office was several doors down on the right. His window opened onto an uninspiring view of the back parking lot.

As in Joan's house, Anna felt at home. The walls held cheaply framed posters of parks Harry'd worked and photographs of him, younger and thinner, grinning from the tops of mountains with like-minded men wearing fleece and wool and wind-chilled smiles. The tops of the ubiquitous metal filing cabinets held marksmanship trophies and strange pieces of rock and bone.

Ruick was behind a gray metal desk working through the pile of papers that had accumulated in his In box during his excursion to the field. His door was open. Anna tapped on the doorframe.

"Come in," he said as he glanced up to see who it was. When he noted it was her he stopped what he was doing and gave her his undivided attention. Since getting the full bore of his administrative persona was rare, Anna was flattered and mildly alarmed. She took her place in the armless metal visitor's chair and waited to be enlightened.

"I've got a little problem I'm hoping you can help me out with. I'm short-handed at the moment. As you know, two of my district rangers and four other law enforcement rangers are out in California on the Miranda fire."

Anna'd been out of the loop for a while and hadn't heard of this particular conflagration but was unsurprised. Great swaths of California burned most Augusts. High desert and dry, forest fires burned fast and hot and too often near heavily populated areas.

Ruick was looking at her. Dutifully she said yes to whatever it was he was expecting her to agree with.

"Thing is the fire was contained, burning itself out. The crew the Glacier rangers were on was to be demobed. I expected them today or tomorrow at the latest. Yesterday, while I was on Flattop with the Van Slyke thing, Miranda blew up, jumped the lines and took in another eighty-five hundred acres." There was just a hint of self-condemnation in his tone that led Anna to suspect Ruick felt Miranda wouldn't have dared misbehave so grossly had his attention not been taken up elsewhere.

"Looks like they'll be out another week or ten days. The FBI hasn't got any interest in this murder-in-the-outback kind of thing when it's got no drugs or gun overtones. We'll keep it single jurisdiction. The long and short of it is, I'd like you to work with me on this. Sort of Girl Friday."

Girl Friday was a significant promotion from step-'n'-fetchit, but this time Anna was offended not by the word "girl," but the concept as a whole. She said nothing, giving him a slow count of ten in Spanish to save himself. She'd reached *seis* when he did.

Horror dawned as her silence brought home the inexcusably sexist remark he'd just made. A political and personal *faux pas* that not only brought the blood burning to his face and neck but must have scared the bejesus out of him as well. In such opportunistic and paranoid times, a statement like that could get him dragged into court were it to fall into the wrong ears.

Anna waited for him to dig himself out. The hole was pretty deep. She rather looked forward to a circuitous round of creative half-excuses that, like air freshener, would alter but not eradicate the stink. She underestimated Harry.

He rubbed his face with both hands and for the first time she noticed how tired he looked. With his people gone to fight fire there was a good chance he'd been up late on a call-out chasing poachers or settling visitor disputes.

"Let me start with an apology. That comment surfaced from when I was a dinosaur and didn't know any better. That doesn't excuse it but—"

"Not a problem," Anna interrupted, sensing he'd merely been careless in his approach and was genuine in his remorse. Beside, there were those questions she wanted answered and it sounded like she was about to get carte blanche to ask them.

"I'm your girl," she said.

Ruick laughed. "Why do I doubt that?"

9

The remainder of the morning was dedicated to working out the details. It had never seriously crossed the chief ranger's mind that Anna might say no. "No" was not a real option for district rangers. He'd called Anna's boss, John Brown, and made sure he was clear to borrow her. Should the murder investigation interfere with the DNA project, Anna's stay would be lengthened and she would enter into the next phase of paper-pushing instead of fieldwork and learn what she could.

Matters settled to his satisfaction, Harry filled Anna in on the plans of the relevant parties. After the autopsy was completed and Lester could attend to the business of disposing of his wife's body, he was hiking back into Fifty Mountain. Harry had argued against it. Les was frail, inexperienced and, one might assume, emotionally distraught. An ideal recipe for disaster. But legally he could not be stopped. Suicide was a crime, stupidity was not.

Rory would be allowed to continue working on the bear DNA project with Joan Rand. Anna was not pleased with this turn of events. Weak as the case might be, Rory was a murder suspect. Because she felt she'd be betraying a confidence, Anna didn't tell Harry of the Rory–Luke connection in Joan's mind, but she was afraid it would color the researcher's view of the boy. She would not be careful enough of Rory and would respond to him more as a surrogate son than a potentially dangerous man. Ruick listened respectfully to Anna's concerns but, as she couldn't come up with any concrete ideas to better run the show, he stuck to the status quo.

Nominally Anna would still be working with Joan. She would accompany her and Rory into the backcountry, but her first priority would be the murder of Carolyn Van Slyke.

"Today I want you to interview Rory. I'll take his dad," Harry said. "Something's not kosher with those two but damned if I can figure out what."

Both Van Slykes arrived shortly before three o'clock. Anna met them in the foyer, a plain, barely decorated area just inside the glass doors where the receptionist's desk sat. A much older looking Lester occupied the only chair. His son, hands thrust deeply in his pockets, stood before a black and white photo of the old headquarters building studying it as if its architecture was going to be on a test they were about to take.

Anna sent Les down the hall to the chief ranger's office. She took Rory to the conference room. Joan was gone and Anna missed her. She'd not consciously admitted that she wanted Joan there for the interview but she found she did.

"Mind if I tape this?" Anna asked and put a recorder on the table.

"Whatever."

Anna pushed the Record button.

"You want anything?" she asked as he slumped into Joan's vacated chair and began mindlessly spinning it in slow circles on its axis. "Coke or coffee or anything?"

"Nothing. I don't want anything."

Anna was relieved. She'd made the offer out of habit. She had no idea where these amenities were to be found in Glacier's headquarters. "Me neither," she said and sat down. For as long as a minute, an exceedingly long time for silence between two people not long acquainted, she watched him, waiting to see what he'd do, which way he'd break under pressure.

He stopped his spinning and occupied himself by staring out the window watching the maintenance vehicles going by the parking lot to the maintenance yard beyond. There was a stiffness to his neck and shoulders that suggested he could play this game till the metaphorical cows came home. Evidently, in his young life, he'd become accustomed to protecting his inner world from outside storms.

Anna let another thirty seconds crawl by to make sure. Looking at Rory, the deceptively fragile frame, the thick sandy hair, coarse and falling like hay across his unlined brow, the deep-set blue eyes, she didn't think he looked like a boy who'd kill his mom. But then what did a matricide look like? In the imagination they were sly, sinister, horned and hairy. In reality they were just people. Kids. Whatever was broken was deep inside, out of the public view. Children murdering their own parents was uncommon but by no means unheard of. Often it was the "good" boys who did it. With the possible exception of Lizzy Borden it was always boys, Anna noted. She could call to mind three incidents in the past two years. Sons murdering Mom and Dad. But never mutilating them.

"I'm real sorry about your stepmother," she said.

Reluctantly, Rory brought his gaze back into the room. It settled not on Anna, but on the table between them.

"Yeah . . . well . . . it happens."

Anna breathed out slowly. *It happens? Jesus.* "How does it happen?" she asked neutrally.

"People die."

Anna could tell by his tone he was shooting for a matter-of-fact delivery. An underlying bitterness ruined the effect and she remembered his biological mother had died as well. This was a double trauma for Rory. The new coupled with the inevitable reliving of the old. Mentally, she readjusted. This upwelling of the severest of childhood wounds could account for any number of incongruent behaviors.

"Can't argue with that," she said and Rory's eyes met hers. In the blue depths she saw that spark kids get when adults surprise them by not being unutterably obtuse.

"Who'd want to kill your stepmother?" Anna made no attempt to soften the question.

If it jarred him, he didn't show it. His eyes strayed again to the parking lot, unseeing as he searched inside his skull for an answer. Anna thought she saw one briefly illuminate his eyes then fade. It appeared not to be so much rejected as hidden. Finally Rory said, "There's a few, but none of 'em here. I mean, who'd be here? Why not just run her over in a crosswalk at home in Seattle?"

Rory was nothing if not pragmatic about homicide.

"A few?" Anna pressed.

"Carolyn was a divorce lawyer," Rory said.

"Oh. Right. Anybody specific?"

"Maybe her ex-sister-in-law. Barbara something. She hated Mom."

"Mom" and "Carolyn" were running neck and neck. Some unresolved conflicts there. Anna dearly wished Molly were at hand. Rory's world was definitely psychiatrist country.

"I guess somebody could have followed her here." Rory sounded hopeful, and why not? He wasn't stupid. He'd know they'd be looking hard at both himself and his dad. Television had done a thorough job of destroying naiveté and replacing it, often as not, with misinformation.

"Could be," Anna said, but didn't believe it. Too intricate. Too much trouble. Rory was right, a crosswalk in a city would be a lot more likely.

Anna changed direction. "Tell me what she was like."

Rory flashed her a look of alarm that Anna didn't understand, then settled into a careful recitation of facts: height, weight, color of hair, occupation, educational background. Not the usual stuff a kid would choose to describe what a deceased parent was like. Anna didn't think he'd misunderstood the question. He was avoiding it.

"How'd she get on with your dad?"

Rory's face hardened slightly. "You'd have to ask him."

Anna let that lie between them for a while. Then she said, "So. You going to tell me where you got that water bottle?"

A blank look from Rory did more to convince her he'd not snatched it from the dying hands of his stepmother than a mountain of protestations would have done. The look cleared as memory returned. The transition was too natural and held too many shades of awakening to be feigned. "The one I had when you guys found me after the bear tore up our camp?"

"That very one. Where'd you get it?"

"I don't know," Rory said.

As improbable as that was, Anna found herself inclined to believe him. "Where'd you get it?" she repeated anyway.

"I can't tell you." He was beginning to sound desperate.

"Try."

"I didn't have it I don't think—no, I know I didn't because I got thirsty—real thirsty—by the time the rain started."

Anna thought back. That would have been just after sunup when she and Joan were gathering their wits and what was left of their bear-ravaged camp.

"So you were thirsty," she prompted.

"I was hot. I'd been running," he admitted. "I'd taken off my shirt. I lay down for a minute. The rain woke me up and the sweatshirt was gone and the water bottle was just there. After a while I guess I got to thinking I must have brought it from camp, but I didn't. Not really."

Anna could understand that. The brain's job was to make sense of the world. When the world refused to fall into line, the brain was perfectly capable of rearranging memories until at least the appearance of order was restored.

"Let me get this straight," Anna said. "While you were napping in the woods at dawn, lost to friends and family, someone or something stole your dirty sweatshirt and left you a bottle of much-needed water in its place. And all this without waking you up, asking if you were alive or dead."

"That's it," Rory said, the stiff neck returning. "My sweatshirt wasn't all that dirty."

"A kind of good fairy or guardian angel?" Anna asked, just to see if anger would shake anything more loose from the boy.

Rory stared at the table, his lips pressed shut, undoubtedly to keep language unsuited for adults in authority shut behind his teeth. Danger past, he unlocked his jaws. "Maybe it was exactly that. A guardian angel. I needed water pretty bad, and all that day and the next I never came across any. Maybe I'd've died without that happening."

Anna'd learned not to argue with magic. In her years of law enforcement, whenever a wizard had been pointed out she'd always been able to find the little man behind the curtain pulling levers. She suspected there'd be a mortal with feet of clay behind Rory's miracles as well. Maybe Rory's own size tens.

"I must have had two water bottles with me," Rory said suddenly, clearly pleased with the idea. "And I brought one out of the tent with me. I just don't remember doing it."

Anna's eyes narrowed. "You just said an angel gave it to you."

"Yeah. Well. That's stupid. I must've had it with me before." Rory's voice turned sullen and mulish. "I took it with me when I left camp. I'd just forgot. There was the bear and all and I didn't feel so hot."

Anna decided to let the matter go. For now.

She turned off the tape recorder, dragged out a map and for the next twenty minutes nudged, badgered and cajoled Rory into approximating as closely as he could his journey during his thirty-six-hour hiatus. Every attempt ended the same. Rory knew where he'd started and he knew where he'd ended up. The hours and miles in between were a kaleidoscope turning timelessly through forest and scrub and burn. When it became evident he could not or would not be more specific, Anna backed off. If he wouldn't tell her, there was no way to force him. If he really couldn't tell her and she kept pushing, eventually he'd make something up to get her off his back.

Convinced she'd gotten all she was going to at this juncture, she declared the interview at an end. Back in Harry's office she and Rory rejoined the chief ranger and Lester Van Slyke. A brief consultation convinced Anna and Ruick that an interview with Van Slyke, father and son, would not be a productive use of time. There'd been ample opportunity to watch the two of them interact when emotions were raw. By now defenses would be in place. They were excused with proper words of thanks and Anna was alone with Harry.

Civilization diminished him. In the backcountry with a life and death situation to put his back into, he'd appeared younger and stronger than he did behind his desk, awards and diplomas arrayed around him.

Anna caught a glimpse of herself reflected in his window. She was no great shakes either. Her short hair had more gray in it than she remembered noticing in the mirror and her age was beginning to tell its ever lengthening story in the marks under her eyes and in the softening at her jawline.

"For the family of the dearly departed these boys are behaving in a decidedly strange manner," Ruick said. "Les is still determined to go on with his damned camping trip and he said Rory's still dead-set on finishing up the DNA project."

"Rory talked to him?"

"Called him last night at the hotel."

Not having spent much time with Rory, Harry wouldn't

know how peculiar that was. Maybe the death of Mrs. Van Slyke was bringing father and son together.

"No sense letting a little thing like murder spoil your vacation plans," Ruick said cynically.

The Van Slykes' decision to remain in Glacier had its upside from a law enforcement point of view. Though they might have their suspicions, there was no evidence on which to hold Les or his son. In park crimes, there was always the added difficulty of perpetrators and witnesses dispersing to faraway places before the investigation could be completed.

"What do they mean us to do with the body?" Anna asked. "Leave it at the morgue in Flathead County till it's time to go home?"

"Sort of. Les has that all worked out. Soon as the autopsy's done he wants it cremated locally. He'll pick up the ashes after his camping trip."

"No funeral, memorial service, nothing?"

"Apparently not. He seemed to be genuinely grieving for his wife. He teared up a few times, if that means anything. More than that, though, he seemed angry at her."

"That's natural enough," Anna said, remembering her sister's lectures when she'd turned angry at her husband, Zach, after he'd died. Abandonment was as universal a fear as fear of falling. Fear had a way of turning inward. In women it usually manifested itself as depression, in men, anger.

"Nah. Not like that," Harry said dismissively. "I'm no shrink but this felt different. There was an element of spite in it. Like old Lester might kick his wife's corpse a good one if he thought nobody was looking."

"Rory intimated his folks were not experiencing unremitting wedded bliss, but he declined to elaborate," Anna said.

"Les didn't say anything outright against the missus and, like I said, he managed a few tears. What set me off was the way he was ordering up the cremation of the corpse. Sort of slam-bang and take that."

"Do you think he killed her?"

"He's got no alibi, of course. Things happen in the wee hours, and unless you sleep with somebody, you're not going to have anybody to vouch for your whereabouts. He's got some real mixed feelings about her being dead, that's for sure. But no, I don't think he killed her. If he did he'd be playing the grief card a little harder. And he'd probably want to get the hell out of here, post haste."

"Unless there was something here that needed doing," Anna said slowly. "Maybe something Carolyn stood in the way of."

They mulled that over for a time but came up with nothing. What could an old man and a boy want in the Glacier wilderness? There was no gold, no silver, no oil or natural gas, no buried Aztec treasure that anybody knew of. Glacier lilies had been dug up and spirited away but they were worthless, financially speaking.

Thinking of the lilies, Anna told Harry of Geoffrey Mickleson-Nicholson. Harry wrote down the name.

"No way to trace him without numbers," he said. "Social security, driver's license, date of birth—but I'll see if anybody with those names filed a backcountry permit."

"I don't know if he's even old enough to have a driver's license," Anna said. "But while you're at it, check for a Bill or William McCaskil. He was camped at Fifty Mountain when the Van Slykes were. He lied about how well he knew Carolyn."

Ruick wrote "McCaskil, William" on his legal pad. "What else?" he asked.

Anna couldn't think of anything.

Ruick stared out the window, tapping his pen absentmindedly, top then tip, like a tiny baton.

The clock on his desk said it was quarter till five. The day had slipped away. Indoors, cooped up with people, Anna had missed it. Afternoon light, strong and colorless, the sun high with summer, striped the parking lot with the shadows of the surrounding pines. A fantasy of a hammock and a good book teased up in Anna's brain. Unthinkingly, she yawned, her jaw cracking at maximum distention.

Harry looked at her and laughed. "Tomorrow is soon enough. I expect we've all earned an early night."

10

The sound of claws came in the night. At first Anna thought she was camped in the high country and fought the claustrophobic blindness of an enclosed tent. Slowly it came to her that she was fighting the covers on the bed in Joan's guest room. The window to the left of the bed was open, only a thin screen between her and the out-of-doors.

Panic opened Anna's eyes and, by the faint light of the few street lamps that polluted the night in the housing area, she saw a great shaggy hulk. As she watched, it blanked the light, took it like a black hole, then perforated it with the shine of ragged teeth.

Open-mouthed, she couldn't scream. Not a sound came out. Her arms and legs lay heavy as deadwood on the mattress. The teeth slipped through the screen, a faint tearing noise, then a paw, clattering claws so long they struck the sill, came through the wire. Still Anna was paralyzed, a poison, a weight in her limbs.

With a tremendous effort she fought to move. The resulting jerk woke her, freed her from the nightmare. For half a minute she lay in the bed reassuring herself that now, really, this time, she was awake, not merely dreaming she was, safe from the black quicksand of her subconscious.

Then the sound of claws was repeated and the nightmare began again. This time Anna could move. Quick as a cat she was out of the bed, mother-naked, back against the wall beside the window. Her heart pounded and she felt half crazy but she knew she'd heard it: scratching.

Joan had inherited the house with curtains. She must have.

Anna could not believe a member of the female gender would purposely choose those that hung to either side of the window.

Snaking her hand between the oversized geometric-patterned drapes and the wall, Anna eased the curtain out far enough to afford her an oblique view of the screen. Time passed, measured by the beat of her heart: a minute, two, maybe three. Nightmare cleared from her eyes and she noted the faint silver sheen of distant light reflecting off the fine mesh, the darker shadow from the overhanging eve. Across the street at an angle, she could see the garage of one house and the front entrance of another. All was still. No monsters.

Adrenaline subsided. Cold sank into her bare skin, worse where buttocks and shoulder blades touched the plaster of the wall, but she did not return to bed. Waiting was an art form. Seldom had she gone wrong with waiting, watching another minute. Another five minutes.

Scratch. Scratch. A claw, a single claw, the sere black forefinger of a crone, crept up from beneath the sill and raked at the screen.

Soundlessly, Anna backed away from the curtain. Crossing the bedroom in three strides, she snatched up shorts and shirt. In the hall she pulled them on. Her boots were by the front door near her day pack. She stepped into them and jerked the laces tight.

Joan lived like a pacifist. The only weapon that presented itself in the shadow-filled living room was a three-legged footstool beside the Barcalounger where Anna'd left her day pack. She tipped it clear of the remote control and a *Reader's Digest* and hefted it in her right hand. Heavy hardwood, well made; it would suffice.

Moving quickly, she let herself out the kitchen door at the back of the house and ran quietly around the garage, her boots nearly soundless on the lush summer grass. Bobbing like a duck for a June bug, she peeked around the corner then ducked back.

A shape was crouched beneath her bedroom window. Given the real and imagined beasts that had haunted her nights, she forgot for a moment who took honors for the most dangerous species, and was comforted by its human contours.

Whoever scratched at her screen had his back to her. Carrying the stool up against her shoulder, ready for defensive or offensive use, Anna stepped from behind the corner of the garage and moved slowly across the concrete driveway.

Scratch. The crone's finger was a stick the croucher pushed up to scrape the wires. The croucher wore a dark coat but his pale hair caught the light. Anna moved up close behind him. Fear at bay, she was rather enjoying the game.

Leaning down, mouth near the intruder's ear, she whispered, "Rory, what are you doing?" The result was most satisfying. Rory Van Slyke clamped both hands over his mouth. His twig went flying and he collapsed in a heap, his back against the wall of the house, his eyes huge above his hands.

The only thing missing was noise. Rory had not made a sound. Not a squeak or a grunt. Somewhere along the line he'd learned not to cry out. Anna wondered why.

She swung down the stool she'd been brandishing and sat on it. "What are you doing?" she repeated, this time in a normal voice.

"Shh," Rory hushed her. "I was trying to get your attention," he whispered.

"Why didn't you knock on the door?" Anna whispered back. Library rules: it's hard to speak normally when one's conversational partner is whispering.

"I didn't want to wake Joan," Rory replied. He sat up. "Can we go someplace? For a walk maybe?"

Sleep had been pretty much ruined for an hour or so, at least till the adrenaline had time to be reabsorbed. "Sure," Anna said. "Let me get a jacket."

"No. Take mine," Rory said, slipping out of a dark fleece coat. "I don't want to wake Joan," he said again.

Anna took the coat. It was soft and oversized and already nicely warmed up. "Lead on, Macduff," she said. Rory looked blank. "Where do we go?"

"Oh. Just anywhere." Beneath the fleece he wore blue jeans and a sweatshirt with "Mariners" stenciled across the chest. Shoving his hands into his jeans pockets, he walked across the grass to the street. Anna fell in step beside him. Briefly, she wondered just how big a fool she was being, lured out alone at night by a young man who was on a short list of murder suspects. For reasons she was not quite sure of, her alarms weren't going off. Maybe Joan's goodness was wearing off on her. Maybe she was getting old and sloppy, losing her edge.

Whatever it was, Anna felt no fear for her physical self, and a burning curiosity to find out what was on the boy's mind. For the length of a city block, till they came to a fork in the road, Rory said nothing. The houses they passed were dark and sleeping. Anna liked being out at night. It had been awhile since she'd moved like a ghost among the living, thinking her thoughts while they dreamed theirs. In the Mississippi woods the nights were too dark for wandering.

At the fork, Rory stopped for a second as if the decision of which way to go momentarily overcame him, then went on again, straight, toward headquarters and the main road. Tall trees lined either side of the lane, drawing curtains of impenetrable black alongside. Overhead the night was clear. Stars and a quarter moon gave enough light to see by. Anna was pleased to walk without flashlights. In true darkness they were invaluable. In anything less they only served to narrow vision down to where it was a distraction instead of a guide.

"So what happens now?" Rory said after a while.

"How so?" There'd been a lot of blood under the bridge in the past few days. He could be asking about any number of things. A natural reticence made her not want to spout forth unnecessary information.

"About the . . . you know . . . the death," Rory said.

Anna looked at him in the weak light from the moon. If he'd shed any tears for this stepmother he'd done it in private. His eyes were dry but she noticed he did not say Carolyn's name or call her "my stepmom." Regardless of where his emotions lay, it was natural that he would want to distance himself from the incident.

"There will be an investigation," she said carefully. "Chief Ranger Ruick will be heading that up. He'll try and find out who did it and bring them to justice." She realized she sounded prim and simplistic, but at the moment, she wasn't sure what else to say, wasn't sure what it was Rory wanted.

"You got suspects already?" Rory asked. They'd reached the road that led past the headquarters parking lot toward the maintenance yard. Rory turned down it. Anna hesitated. This way took them toward the machine sheds, garages, storage barns and, if they went far enough, the resource management building. They were moving away from the housing area where a shout would be heard and, because this was a national park, responded to.

In the end, she followed him. Time enough to turn around. She wanted to know where he was heading metaphorically if not geographically. "Nobody special, if that's what you mean," Anna hedged. "This wasn't exactly your smoking-gun sort of situation."

"On television they always suspect the husband," he said. "Do you guys suspect Les?"

Rory seemed oblivious to the fact that he, too, might be a suspect. Maybe he thought being incommunicado for a day and a half in his bedroom slippers was an ironclad alibi. Or maybe he was more cunning than Anna gave him credit for. Maybe he wanted them to suspect Les and that's what this little nocturne was playing up to.

"He's a suspect," Anna said because Rory already knew it was true. "Why? Do you think your dad killed your stepmom, that Les killed Carolyn?" She purposely used titles and names, wanting to bring it home, make it personal, to see what Rory would do.

A twitch? Too dark to tell. "Maybe I did it. Ever think of that?" he asked.

"Those were my very thoughts not more than a minute ago. Did you?"

"Dad didn't."

They'd reached the maintenance yard. Rory stopped by the gasoline pumps and turned toward her. "I don't think you ought to go poking around. Dad's not healthy. Can't you see that? He's old and his heart's not good. He's got high blood pressure. He can't handle this kind of stuff. Leave him alone."

This, then, was the crux of the matter. Anna looked around at the deserted maintenance yard, the rows of blank garage doors facing in on a paved rectangle, the hulks of machinery dead with the night, and rather wished she'd insisted they turn back earlier. Rory, several feet away, was studying her as intently as she studied her surroundings. His sandy hair gleamed in the soft light but the rough cascade of bangs, in need of trimming, threw his eyes into deep shadow.

"It's cold," Anna said. "Let's keep walking." And talking. Though emotionally taxing and often spiritually dangerous, talking was not a physically damaging sport. Anna wanted to keep him right on doing it until they got back into a more populated locale.

"Let's not," he said. She started off anyway as if she hadn't heard him, setting a casual pace that would take them around a sharp corner past derelict-looking buildings toward the resource management office and another residential area.

After a brief hesitation, he walked with her. Anna allowed herself a small inward sigh of relief. Determined though he might be, Rory was not yet ready to lay hands on her to get what he wanted.

"Why don't you want your dad investigated?" she asked mildly.

"I told you," Rory snapped. "His health isn't good."

His wife's health was considerably worse, Anna thought, but didn't say so. She just walked and waited to see if whatever was under the surface of Rory's filial concern would boil out into words. It didn't, and that concerned her. Kids, normal kids with fair-to-middling parents, might bluster in their adolescent years about not trusting anyone over thirty, but beneath that bluster dwelt the child whose long habit had been to turn to adults when in need. Rory'd had that habit broken for him.

Anna kept on at the same easy pace. They reached the corner where the maintenance yard bent into an L-shape. This was the farthest they'd get from windows and ears, a walled canyon of buildings, machinery and trees between them and the scattered houses. Realizing she'd tensed, Anna relaxed her neck to keep herself alert and ready. Consciously, she monitored the speed of her steps.

"I don't have any say in this investigation," she said easily. "I'm just visiting from another park. I've done a few chores for Harry but that's it. If you want your dad left out of things, the person you need to talk to is the chief ranger. I'd suggest you do it during regular business hours. Creeping around in people's shrubbery could get a fellow shot."

"It's you I want to leave Dad alone," Rory said and this time he did lay hands on her. Strong brown fingers curled around her upper arm forcing her to stop.

The touch triggered fear in Anna. If she were going to fight or run, now was the time. For small people without the skills or scriptwriters of Jackie Chan, exploding like a cherry bomb then running like hell was the best bet.

The spurt of fear was not enough. They were still talking.

"Like I said—" Anna began.

"No," Rory cut her off. "You. You leave him alone." The fingers tightened on her arm. "You're different. You pry and pry and wriggle into people's heads. You don't just ask what they've done. You watch and you wait like some fast little snake that looks asleep. Then there's that little tongue flicking out because you smell something. You pry into stuff that's none of your affair. That has nothing to do with anything. Nothing to do with *this*."

Rory was being his own pep squad, letting his own oratory whip him up like a speaker inflaming a mob of one.

Anna decided to break into it before he worked himself into trouble. "That's enough," she said quietly. With another boy she might have yelled, a verbal slap to get his attention, but she'd seen Rory with Harry Ruick. The boy definitely had a problem with authority. "Let go of my arm," she said just as softly. "I bruise easily and it is swimsuit season."

Either the tone or the absurdity got through and he let go. She began walking, glad to be leaving the spectral machines of the maintenance yard.

"Time we headed back," she said. "I don't know about you, but it's way past my bedtime." No longer curious as to what Rory wanted from her, Anna firmly dropped the subject.

After fifty feet of consideration, Rory picked it up again. The heat his speech had lent his words was gone. The icy edge that replaced it was far more alarming. "If you don't lay off Les and just do the bear thing or whatever, you'll be sorry. Real sorry."

The clichéd threat should have sounded childish, empty, but it didn't. No hollow undertone spoke of desperation or grasping at straws. Rory had something concrete in mind. Anna felt it with every chilled ounce of marrow in her bones.

Rory had missed his opportunity to thrash her. They walked now between two rows of neat houses, petunias, a riot of color in the light of day, spilling black as tar from window boxes. What could a high school boy do to her? Slash her tires? Leave burning dog droppings on her doorstep? Spray-paint "fuck you" on her garage door? If Rory planned a physical threat all she need do was report him to Harry and he would be shipped out of the park immediately with a ranger escort to the airport. Any threat he made would end the same way. Anna was grown up, connected. He was a child. He must know that.

"What will you do if I don't stop investigating Les?" she asked, genuinely curious.

"I'll tell everybody you sexually harassed me," he said evenly. Anna laughed.

"Pressured me," he went on. "That you used your position to coerce me into having sex. That you seduced me and made me do things I'm ashamed of."

Anna quit laughing. She quit walking. So did Rory. Together, face to face, they stood in the middle of the empty street. A horrible, gnawing anxiety began eating Anna from the inside. Rory had found the right threat. An accusation like that would get her, not him, shipped from the park. It wouldn't matter if it was true or not. It wouldn't matter if Harry Ruick believed it or not. The mere accusation would be enough. If Rory pressed charges, life as she knew and enjoyed it would dissolve into smirks, sneers, depositions, lawyers. Before it was over she'd be beggared emotionally and financially. The park service might back her, but they'd be running scared. Anxious to cut her loose and save themselves.

Even if they knew it wasn't true.

Rory's face changed and she realized she'd been fool enough to let her fear show on her face, writ so large a callow boy could read it by the meager light of a quarter moon.

"You're joking," she said, and, "It won't work." Both statements were untrue.

"When I was in junior high school this teacher got sent to prison for it," he said.

Anna remembered the case. It had created a feeding frenzy in the media. In the blink of her mind's eye, she saw herself with a hundred microphones shoved in her face. Bile rose in her throat. She gulped it back. Anger and fear mixed such a powerful potion in her blood she could feel the shaking from the inside out. Run, cry, smash the boy's face, rant, beg; the need to do these things simultaneously and at the top of her lungs held her as paralyzed as she'd been in the dream of the bear. This time her brain was paralyzed as well. She couldn't think.

Helpless. This was what it felt like, a squirming, raging flylike frustration caught in the fingers of an evil, wing-pulling boy.

"You wouldn't actually do that," Anna said hopefully.

"I'm sorry," Rory said and the shred of hope vanished. Had he been mean or vindictive she might have had a chance. Rory believed what he did to be the regrettable but necessary means to some greater end.

"Shit," Anna murmured and hated herself for her transparency. She turned and walked because she could think of nothing more to say or do. Repetitive movement fed her mind just enough; it could race, and thoughts began clamoring, scratching, fighting to find a way out of this predicament.

The moment she reached the house she could call Harry Ruick, drag him out of bed and tell him of Rory's threat. Preemptive strike. Perhaps it would do a little to predispose the chief ranger to believe her, but not much. It would be too easy to believe Rory did threaten her but not with a lie, threatened her with exposure. And why was she out walking alone with an eighteen-year-old boy after midnight anyway?

Harry didn't know her well. They'd been acquainted only a few days and only in a professional capacity. What did he know of her personal quirks or kinks? Only that she was a widow and had been without a man for many years. Rory was a nice enough looking boy. It wasn't out of the realm of possibility. "Jesus," Anna heard herself whisper and closed her teeth against any further involuntary outbursts.

Ruick would call her boss, John Brown Brown. But Brown didn't know her either. He'd call her field rangers in the Port Gibson district on the Natchez Trace. At least one of them, Anna knew, would like nothing better than to insinuate the worst. The case she'd recently finished on the Trace had been fraught with adolescent boys, several of whom she'd leaned on pretty hard. What might they be tempted to say to even up old scores? Regardless of the final scene, the play would be long, exhausting and she would not emerge unscathed. Right off, she would be slapped on the first plane back to Mississippi. Even if Ruick could believe Anna was blameless, he wouldn't dare keep her around; not on the case, not on the DNA project. Unlike Rory, she was not a minor, not a civilian. There would be no need to treat her with kid gloves. "Jesus," Anna whispered again, unable to help herself. "You're a fucking genius, Rory. You know that?"

"Sorry," he repeated sadly, and Anna wanted to strangle him.

He had seen her fear, heard it in muttered blasphemies. He knew he had won; she was on the defensive if not actually beaten outright.

Anna would go with that.

They had returned by a circuitous loop to the original fork in the road that led to Joan's house. As they turned down it, Anna let her steps falter and dragged her hand down over her face. "I don't feel so good," she said. It was no great stretch to make it sound believable.

"We're almost there."

Anna considered trying to squeeze out a few tears, but she was so long out of practice she didn't think she could pull it off. She comforted herself with the thought that it was too dark to get the full theatrical effect from them anyway.

Given Rory's staunch admiration for those who took no flack, Anna wasn't trying to win his pity or compassion. He was more likely to scorn her as weak, pathetic. That was just fine. All she needed to do was to keep him emotionally engaged a bit longer.

When they reached Joan's driveway, Anna allowed herself a weary sigh. "God, I'm thirsty," she whispered. "I've got to get a drink of water."

"You go," Rory said, hanging back. "I got to get to bed."

"No." Anna felt panic rise. "Please," she said. "I won't wake up Joan. We've got to talk. Just let me get a drink."

"You'll wake her," Rory said. "It won't do you any good."

"No, I won't," Anna promised. The last thing she wanted was to wake Joan Rand and force Rory to play his hand. "My day pack. It's just inside the door. I've got water in it. Just let me grab it. I won't be a second. I won't even go inside." Indecision worked across Rory's face. Revulsion was there too, though whether for her or for himself, Anna couldn't be sure. "Please," she pleaded. "Please. We need to talk."

"I won't change my mind," Rory said.

Anna took that as permission and dashed lightly up the concrete steps. Careful not to vanish from Rory's line of sight, she opened the door and leaned in. Her pack was behind the Barcalounger where she'd dumped it. Having rummaged briefly through its innards she emerged again into the night, pack in one hand, water bottle in the other.

"Here," Anna said and led him to the garage door. "We can talk here. Joan's room is at the other end of the house. She won't hear us."

"What if somebody sees us?" Rory asked.

He was getting skittish. Anna had to work fast. "Wouldn't that suit your purposes to a T?" she asked acidly. The sudden change in the emotional weather put him off balance.

"I guess," he faltered.

"Sit down," Anna commanded, the pleases and the pleadings gone from her voice. "If you're to blackmail me you better damn well get the terms straight."

Rory didn't sit but he hunkered down on his heels. Close enough.

"I don't see the point—" he began.

"The point is you don't want me, personally, asking questions about Les, that right, Rory?"

"Yeah. That's right."

"And let me get this straight, you kind of caught me off guard back there. If I don't stop investigating your dad, you're going to accuse me of sexually harassing you? Even though I never laid a hand on you or spoke to you in a sexual way ever?"

"I'm sorry," Rory said for the third time.

"That's what you've threatened to do, isn't it?" Anna pressed. He was fidgeting, looking over his shoulder. Any second he would spring to his feet and she would have lost what might be her only chance.

"That's it," Rory said. "And I'll do it, too."

Anna almost breathed a sigh of relief but stopped herself in time. "Even though I never behaved toward you improperly in any way," she pushed for good measure.

"Even so. I'll do it," Rory declared firmly.

Anna had what she needed. She relaxed back against the garage door, the day pack tucked protectively under one arm and at long last took a drink of the water she'd made such a fuss about needing.

"What's your dad got to hide that you'd sell your immortal soul to the devil to keep me from finding?" she asked seriously.

Rory sensed that something had changed but he didn't know what. Pushing himself to his feet, he glanced around as if expecting the neatly trimmed shrubs to be suddenly bristling with policemen. Nothing stirred.

"You're not afraid I'll find out Les killed his wife are you?" Anna asked sharply. "Or not just that. What is it?"

"I've got to go," Rory said. "I'll do what I said I'd do. Leave it alone." With that he loped off into the street toward the dorm he shared with a couple of other boys.

Anna stayed where she was and watched until he ran around a corner and a house swallowed him from sight. After that, she listened. For half a minute she could hear footfalls as he ran, then that was gone and the eerie stillness of the Glacier summer night reclaimed the neighborhood. Opening the pack, she located her pocket-sized tape recorder by its red running light. Without taking it out of the protective canvas pack, she pressed Rewind for several seconds, then Play.

"*Even so. I'll do it,*" Rory's voice came out of the small machine. The batteries were okay.

11

The night had been "early," as the chief ranger suggested, but way too short, the middle bitten out of it by Rory Van Slyke's blackmail plans. Anna'd slept the remainder of it with the cassette beneath her pillow, stowed in a plastic box taped shut. It was all she had to protect herself against untold mental cruelty. She would have no peace until she'd made several copies and cached them in safe places.

Between the fragmented naps that passed for sleep and, more productively, during the long hot shower she took before Joan woke up, Anna pondered what to do with her blackmailer. It hurt her to admit it, but on a very basic level she did not trust the National Park Service. This was nothing personal; she didn't trust any operation that was run by committee and few that were not.

Despite the fact that she had a tape with what amounted to a confession on it, she didn't want to go to Ruick with her story of Rory's threatened accusation. The tenor of the country was that of growing paranoia. Americans were happily forfeiting their freedom of choice for imagined increases in security. Mandatory sentencing hobbled judges, taking the intelligence and humanity from their jobs. Zero-tolerance policies for weapons in schools was forcing teachers to suspend children of seven, eight and nine for bringing butter knives to spread their lunchtime peanut butter. Taking away parole and time off for good behavior undermined the incentive system in prisons.

People as individuals were giving up their decision-making power because they did not want the responsibility. Society as a whole chose to believe one-size-fit all so they would not be troubled by the inexact science of justice.

The park service was no exception. The merest hint of litigation sent the brass scurrying. The threat of a sexual harassment suit rendered them virtually impotent. Even the discovery of a plot to make an unfounded accusation would land Anna in a prison of red tape and hushed conversations.

Before she subjected herself to that particular form of slow torture, she had two options: to find out whatever Rory wanted to keep hidden before he knew what she was up to and made good on his threat, or to use the tape for counter-blackmail.

She intended to do both.

Once Rory's secret—or more precisely, Lester's secret—was brought to light and broadcast, there would be little reason for Rory to carry out his plan. Revenge was the only one Anna could think of, and he didn't strike her as a vengeful person. Presenting him with the truth in one hand and the tape in the other would, she hoped, end the matter.

Setting out for the resource management office she crossed her fingers as she'd done when she was a girl and hoped Rory Van Slyke, like most adolescents, would sleep past noon.

Anna had been loaned a vacant desk and computer in the main room of the resource management office. Like most buildings of similar vintage it was painted green inside and out. Within the draping, needle-laden branches of the gracious old pines that surrounded it, Anna had a pleasant sensation of being hidden away in a forest bower.

Settling down in front of the computer, she studied the bulletin board above. It was full of eight-by-ten glossy color photographs of *Ursus horribilis* looking not in the least horribilis. A hidden camera on a motion sensor had caught the great bears in the act of frolicking. In photo after photo their magnificent play was frozen: bears rolling in the blood lure, tossing the scent-soaked wood high in the air, lying on their backs hugging their treasures like sea otters hugging abalone.

She forced herself away from this delightful display to the dreary gray and black of the monitor and took a deep breath. The ineffable odor of government saturated the air: an indefinable smell containing years of burnt coffee, spilled copy fluid and antique cigarette smoke, with a unique overlay of dusty file folders.

If the park service ever got rich and replaced these old offices with wall-to-wall carpeted off-white cubicles, Anna would have to resign.

Time mattered. She put aside the urge to dive into Lester Van Slyke immediately. Whatever secret his son was so dedicated to keeping she was sure it related back, however tangentially, to the death of his wife. Before she began rooting around in Lester's life she needed to build a frame of reference. Failing to do so might mean that when the secret appeared, should she be so lucky as to stumble across it, it would slide past her unrecognized.

Putting Rory, the threat, the tape and the previous night from her mind, she concentrated on the task at hand.

As a matter of course, she had collected the vital information on the people she'd interviewed. She had names, addresses, and numbers on Bill McCaskil, the Van Slykes and Mr. and Mrs. Roger Heidleman of Detroit, Michigan. They were the couple who'd told her McCaskil spent a considerable amount of time in the company of the murder victim.

Despite these easier paths, Anna chose to start with Geoffrey Mickleson-Nicholson. Ruick showed little interest in him and Joan felt positively benevolent toward this mysterious lone boy. Anna wanted to know who he was. Feminine intuition, or years in law enforcement, made her think he was somehow connected with the strange goings-on. Using a variety of spellings for each name, she ran him under both Mickleson and Nicholson.

Unsurprisingly there was no one by that name on the back-country permits list. No one by that name had received a ticket for a moving violation in the State of Montana in the last three years, though lacking any numerical data, the search was not as complete as it could be. She found no felony arrest warrants or convictions for either Geoffrey Mickleson or Geoffrey Nicholson.

Moving on, she was reassured to find the midwest as solid as ever. Mr. and Mrs. Roger Heidleman had done everything right. Their backcountry permit was in order. From that she got the plate number of their car and ran it to get Roger's driver's license number and date of birth—the keys to the kingdom as far as data was concerned. Other than a speeding ticket in 1998, fifty-three in a forty-mile-per-hour zone, Heidleman was clean. The missus didn't even have a traffic citation against her record.

Bill McCaskil had also filled out a backcountry permit. He'd filed for the full two weeks allowed at Fifty Mountain Camp. That struck an off chord with Anna. Two weeks is a hell of a long time to camp, especially in one place. The burden of necessary food would be enough to stagger a seasoned hiker. McCaskil looked to be a greenhorn, unhappy and uncomfortable in the natural world.

Using the license plate number on his backcountry permit, she followed the same route along the information highway that she had with the Heidlemans. The results were considerably more interesting. McCaskil was not a pillar of the community. He'd been indicted for fraud three times, convicted and served eighteen months in a Florida state prison. The first indictment was for credit card fraud. The one he'd served time for was a real estate scam. The third was for selling bogus fishing permits for protected marine areas. His prison record took some time but Anna was able to access it. McCaskil had spent five weeks in the prison psychiatric unit for "stress-related antisocial behavior." Given he was in jail, the phrase could mean anything. Other than the psych ward, he was an unexceptional convict, serving his time quietly.

McCaskil was not a good citizen, but other than the vague "antisocial" label, he was apparently nonviolent. Crooks dedicated to paper crimes—check kiting, insider trading, fraud—were usually no more likely to turn to murder than an average citizen, unless put under undue pressure. However, their chosen profession was more likely to bring them to that point by way of blackmail or fear of exposure than that of a welder or the checker at the neighborhood Albertson's. McCaskil's antisocial behavior was linked to stress. Crime was a stressful business.

Anna sat back. The computer screen had drawn her in till she'd been sitting hunched over with her head at an uncomfortable angle and her eyes too close to the screen. Twisting in her chair, she cracked her back in a satisfying rattle of bones. While she'd been lost in cyberspace, the office had come alive. There was the smell of fresh coffee and the hum of humanity at work.

Consciously, she relaxed the muscles of her neck and balanced her head properly atop her spine. Then she brought Carolyn Van Slyke into the mental picture she'd been building of Bill McCaskil to see if the two connected anywhere except around the cold fire pit of Fifty Mountain.

Could Carolyn have been blackmailing McCaskil? Had he

followed her to Glacier for the purpose of murder? Anna pulled out his backcountry permit and that of the Van Slykes. McCaskil had arrived three days earlier than they had. It was possible he'd discovered their vacation plans and come to the park to lay in wait. Possible but not probable. Why expose himself so unnecessarily? Fill out a permit, be seen in company of the victim, remain after the deed was done?

McCaskil was from Florida, Van Slyke from Seattle. They'd have to travel a long way to cross paths. Still, Anna made a note to check prior addresses and possible business connections, the obvious being a divorce where Carolyn represented husband or wife.

Unconsciously sacrificing good posture, she returned to the computer screen to digitally pursue the Van Slykes. Their vehicle, a grating combination of the Bavarian Motor Works and sport utility vehicle, was registered in Carolyn's name. Anna discovered the Van Slykes' home address, which she'd already obtained from Rory, and the fact that Carolyn was an inveterate speeder, seven tickets in three years. From that one could surmise that Mrs. Van Slyke fancied herself above the law or simply had a lead foot.

Anna went to the photocopy of Ruick's notes and observations during his interview with Les that his secretary had kindly made for her. In the upper righthand corner neatly printed was Rory's name, social security number, driver's license number and date of birth. It was what Anna'd been looking for but seeing it was an unpleasant reminder of her own deficiency. Knowing Rory—or thinking she did—and the fact that he was a minor had worked against her and she'd neglected to get his vital information. She could get the information from Joan's records but that wasn't the point. She'd gotten mentally lazy. It wouldn't happen again.

Yes it will, she corrected herself, but hopefully not for a while.

Even a minor could rack up wants and warrants. Murder was no respecter of age. Teen killings in schools were big news. Mass murder was relatively new, but kids killing kids was a horror floating mostly unseen and unacknowledged beneath the presumed innocence of childhood.

Molly had participated in a psychiatric study done in 1995 through the joint auspices of three east-coast medical teaching facilities. The findings were unsettling. On too many occasions to ignore, children as young as four years old had caused the "accidental" death of a friend or sibling: the child that died in a fall, the child that wandered into the bull's paddock, the one who drowned.

With these grim thoughts clouding any natural sunniness of spirit she might lay claim to, Anna ran Rory through the paces on the computer. No wants. No warrants. No moving violations. His only brush with the law had been when he was in his early teens. Twice he'd run away from home. Anna made a note to find out why.

Lester was next. No hits; Les hadn't so much as been caught running a red light in the previous seven years. There were those who could squeeze a whole lot more of Lester's life out of the computer, but Anna was not one of them. She would have to do it the old-fashioned way, lowering herself to the archaic practice of actually talking to people.

She went back to Harry's notes. Lester Van Slyke worked as a quality assurance engineer for Boeing in Seattle. His wife had been with the law firm of Crumley and Pittman, also in Seattle.

Two calls got Anna the number of Boeing's personnel department. She was shuffled around to three different people but finally got what she was asking for—a list of the company's quality assurance engineers. Lester was one of nine in the electronics department.

She called the eight. Three were available. Without out-and-out lying, she gave each the impression that she was making routine calls gathering general background information on Lester Van Slyke to the end that he would be granted a higher security clearance on a government project where he was acting as a consultant.

Ms. Tremane was suspicious and told Anna nothing. Mr. Burman was uninterested in helping Lester and came across as jealous of the fictitious government consulting job. He told Anna that Lester took a lot of sick leave, implied that he was accident-prone and hinted that the government could get a more dependable consultant, namely himself. Mr. Richmond was positively loquacious. He seemed to genuinely wish to help Lester get the apocryphal security clearance. He described Les as quiet, self-effacing, humble, intelligent, caring, hard-working and a slew of other adjectives that fit with what Anna already knew. When pressed, Richmond admitted that Lester had been down on his luck for a few years and taken a good deal of sick leave. It wasn't bogus, the well-meaning Richmond went on to say. Twice Lester had been hospitalized.

Richmond was one of those people who so love to talk that the pure joy of rattling their tongues between their teeth overcomes reticence and discretion. He told Anna Les was concerned about his son. Though the boy seemed to love his stepmom, he'd never really recovered from his biological mother's death and Les's remarriage. Riding the tide of gossip, he told her Les always spoke highly of his second wife but not with the love and humor with which he'd spoken of Rory's real mom. Carolyn, he said, seemed attached to Les. She'd call him at work three or four times every day and Les would get anxious when he missed her call and downright upset when he had to work late for any reason. Anna kept him on the line several more minutes in which "tired, harried and worried" were added to the list of descriptors, and she obtained the name of the hospital where Richmond claimed to have visited Lester.

When she'd gotten everything of value she was going to get out of Mr. Richmond, it took another five minutes to get off the phone with him. Ear and brain were overheated from so much talk; talk without faces, or body language, no setting, merely voices piercing a tangled web of impersonal wires. Anna took a few minutes to breathe, to feel her butt on the chair, her feet on the floor, to hear the pleasant bustle of the office and see the shapes and colors that made up her surroundings. Anchored again in the real world, she allowed the fragments of information regarding Lester Van Slyke to coalesce in her mind.

Harried. Worried. Scared of missing Carolyn's calls, of getting home late. Rory attached to stepmother, yet not forgiving Les the marriage. Rory's contempt for his father. Humble. Self-effacing. Sick leave. Hospitalization. This fit with what Anna had observed in Lester Van Slyke, though at the time what she'd seen had no meaning for her.

The information operator provided her with the phone number of the hospital where Lester had been treated. Unsurprisingly, Anna got nothing from them. Medical establishments were well aware of what information they could divulge and what they could not.

Even without verification, Anna was sure of what she had seen: the bruises on Lester's legs, some new, some already fading, the cuts on his forearms.

Folding her notes, she left the resource management building and walked the quarter of a mile past pine-shrouded employee housing to where Rory shared a dorm with three city boys in the park to learn appreciation for the flora and fauna.

An African-American youth in sweatpants and a New York Rangers T-shirt answered Anna's knock. Rory was upstairs in his room. Two lung-deep bellows brought him shambling down. He also was clad in sweatpants and a T-shirt and looked as though he'd been dragged from sleep.

Rather than invite Anna into the mess, he stepped out on the porch and shut the door.

Anna chose not to give him time to organize his thoughts or get his defenses up but squared off in front of him and asked him point-blank: "Rory, how long had Carolyn been using your father as a punching bag?"

12

Anna'd been hoping for a reaction to her jackbooted approach. She wasn't disappointed. As the words struck him, Rory stiffened, the muscles of his face paralyzed with shock. There followed a brief struggle where he forgot to maintain that paralysis, to keep control, or at least appear to. Emotion won out. The hardened cheeks, the wide-open eyes, the rictus of his lips began to melt. Then, in sudden collapse, they flowed together in a twisted malformation and Rory began to cry. Not as a boy cries but as a man who has denied tears for decades will cry with squeezed little whimpers, convulsive jerks and dry eyes.

Moments after this phenomenon began, rage roared up inside him, so strong it spun Rory around and brought his unprotected fists hard against the wood of the house, a fire out of control.

The porch was wide enough; Anna moved discreetly out of the way until the violence burned itself out. So vehement was his outburst, she knew it couldn't be sustained for long.

The pounding stopped. His knuckles weren't raw or bleeding. Even in extremity he'd chosen not to harm himself. A good sign. The constricted sobs subsided, leaving his face red and dry with unspent tears. At length he turned from the side of the house and looked at her, eyes empty after the storm.

"So," Anna said. "Am I to take it she'd been beating on him for a while?"

Rory collapsed. Back against the wood he slid down till his butt was on the porch and his knees poked up as high as his shoulders. The rough siding rucked his T-shirt up under his armpits but he seemed not to notice.

Anna sat down opposite him, her shoulders against the railing, her feet folded under her. After the weeping and wailing, the soft sounds of the park settled around them like a blessing. Needles in a great old lodgepole pine stirred and whispered overhead. From somewhere nearby came the purposeful skritching sounds of a squirrel squirreling away winter supplies. Into this Rory heaved a great sigh, blowing out unnamed mental toxins.

"Why don't you tell me about it?" Anna asked kindly.

Rory shot her a look as if her kindness was out of character. Anna was stung. She was *always* kind to animals and had been known to be kind to humans on those rare occasions when they deserved it.

"What's there to tell?" He looked past Anna, over the rail to the whispering pine boughs. By his tone she guessed he was shooting for blasé. He only managed deep weariness.

His question was one Anna couldn't answer so she sat quietly enjoying the sun on her face and arms. Ephemeral warmth with an underlying hint of cruelty, the northern sun touched with cleansing power. In Mississippi, in summer, the sun struck like a blow. Only idiots and Yankees stood anywhere but in the patches of shade provided by the gracious old oaks and pines. Anna'd missed the scalpel touch of sunlight at higher elevations.

Rory sighed again then began to give up the shame he'd been carrying in secret for his father for so many years. "I don't know why it started. Mom—my real mom—died when I was little and it was just me and Dad for a while. That was okay, I guess. I don't remember much, really. Just a lot of quiet and a lot of TV. A *lot* of TV. I remember I thought it was pretty cool that I could stay up late watching television with Dad when my friends had to go to bed at eight."

Dad. He'd used the word twice. Now that Carolyn was dead, Les had been given back his title. Anna took that as a good omen for the future.

"Carolyn came along maybe two years later. Dad met her at a party at Boeing. Or maybe it was somewhere else. I really don't know. I don't care. God." Rory stopped a minute, breathing out whatever memories had derailed his narrative.

Anna sat quietly, hoping none of the boys in the dorm would

come rocketing out and wreck the chemistry of the moment. She had a hunch if Rory stopped talking now, he might never start again.

"Mostly I remember how much fun she was. It was like we'd been living in black and white and all of a sudden our world got colorized. I guess Dad and I hadn't got out much since Mom died. I sort of remember I used to do things after school—you know, kid things like Little League or whatever. But sometime after Mom, I'd sort of stopped, I think. Dad worked late a lot. I guess there was nobody to take me places and pick me up or something.

"Then Carolyn shows up and we're doing things again. Lots of stuff: water parks and fairs and circuses and hockey games. She was always laughing, teasing Dad. She did everything for us. She'd cook and she cleaned the house. I remember that, though I couldn't have been much more than seven or eight. I came home from school one day and the house was bigger, lighter. The curtains were open. Dad's piles of newspapers and magazines were gone. My clothes were hung up and my bed was made. Like when Mom was alive.

"She was at our house all the time. Dad didn't work late much anymore.

"They got married pretty soon after that. They hadn't known each other six months. I know that for sure. Later Carolyn was always saying things like, 'I must've been out of my head marrying you when I'd only known you five months. Five fucking months. God. By month six I knew I'd made one hell of a mistake, that's for sure.'"

Rory probably related the words verbatim. As he said them his face curled into a sneering mask and his voice was charged with such contempt Anna winced. That particular scene had evidently been burned into his brain.

"That was later though. I guess I remember her teasing got mean and she got really jealous—had to know where Dad was all the time and went into a fit if he was like two minutes late home from work. She'd driven it and timed herself so she knew exactly how long it took. She got real picky about the house. It had to be just so. And dinner was at six-fifteen every night and don't be late or else. If Dad didn't say the right compliments about the food she'd go off on him.

"They started having huge fights. Not the big ones in front of me. Always after I went to bed. My room was upstairs and way at the back of the house but I could still hear them. Not words, just shouting. Crashes. Crying. In the morning sometimes things would be broken. I was older by this time, I must've been twelve because I remember Mrs. Dent, my sixth-grade teacher, sending me to a counselor because I kept falling asleep in class. The counselor was okay but sort of fixated on drugs, like I was a junkie. I didn't tell him anything."

Rory looked at Anna. It was the first time he'd dragged his eyes from visions of the past. "I thought it was Dad," he said clearly. "I thought Dad was beating Carolyn. They tell us about that stuff in school and you see movies about it on TV all the time. I didn't even know it could be the other way around. I mean, Dad was stronger than she was. Why didn't he stop her?"

The question was pushed out with such intensity Anna could tell he'd been living with it for a long time. Now, with childlike insistence, he was waiting for her to answer it, and she couldn't.

"Did you ever ask him?" she said instead.

Rory was disappointed. He slumped back against the wall and his gaze slipped away again to other times. "Once," he replied. "He said she didn't mean it. He said she was high-strung. He said it was hard for her to be married to an older man. He said he could be pretty aggravating sometimes." Rory was silent for a minute and Anna thought he'd finished. But he wasn't. In a voice constricted with rage and shame he said, "Then he told me *he didn't mind*. He was in the hospital when he said it. Carolyn had hit him in the face with this metal stool she kept in the kitchen to reach high shelves. The underside of the seat was real sharp. She nearly cut half his face off. You can still see the scar." Anna had seen it—the thin white line that marked off a semicircle of Lester's face. They'd been looking for a motive for the slicing off of Carolyn's brow, cheek and half her nose. This certainly fit the bill. For both father and son.

"Did she ever hit you?" Anna asked.

"Not really. She started to get after me once when I was thirteen or fourteen. I was in the backyard hitting a ball into the fence and something set her off. She came out and headed for me. It scared me so bad I raised the bat. I think I'd have used it too. By then I'd pretty much figured out why Dad was always bruised or limping—she'd already put him in the hospital twice, once for a broken collarbone and the other time for a ruptured eardrum, I think—anyway, her coming at me like that was scary. When she saw I meant to fight she just stopped. Then she laughed and said, 'That's right, Rory, don't take any shit. Not from anybody.'"

"She never knocked you around when you were little? Slapped you, shook you, anything like that?"

"Just Dad," Rory said.

In a sick sort of way it made sense. Carolyn wasn't into child abuse, just the abuse of men. At fourteen Rory had been becoming a man.

Maybe in Carolyn's world there were only two kinds of men: those whom you beat and those who beat you.

"You seemed to get along with her well enough," Anna said mildly.

"Yeah. Well. At least she didn't let anybody beat on her."

That pretty much summed it up. Rory'd gotten lost between a stepmother he feared and a father he'd been ashamed of. A child's natural survival instincts kicked in and he aligned himself with the stronger caregiver, learned from her to scorn his father. Anna had to wonder how far it had gone.

"Ever get so frustrated with Les you wanted to smack him upside the head yourself?" she asked sympathetically.

"Sometimes," Rory admitted. Anger animated his voice as he elaborated. "How could anyone not? He'd get like those little yippy dogs that squeal and tuck their tails between their legs before you've even kicked them. Then you *want* to kick them."

Anna understood the phenomenon. "Ever do it? Ever kick them?"

"Hit Dad?" He thought about what, on the surface, was a simple question for a long time. Too long to be fabricating a lie. Anna guessed that on so many occasions over so many years Rory had wanted to strike out against the humiliation he felt in the person of his father, that he was either making sure he'd never actually done it or he was counting the number of strikes. Anna dearly hoped it was the former. To be beaten by one's own child must be a torment only Shakespeare and God could comprehend.

At length Rory spoke. "I wanted to," he admitted. "But I never did. Mom—my real mom—wouldn't have liked it. I wanted Dad to fight back. At least I did at first. Sometimes I was glad when

Carolyn hurt him. He was so . . . so *pathetic*. It made me sick."

Rory looked sick. Anna felt sick. They sat in sick, wretched silence for a while, the ghosts of Rory's childhood twining about them.

Anna fought off the hopeless lethargy they exuded and asked, "Did you ever fight back for him?"

Rory'd been sitting, head back against the wood siding, eyes closed. The sun touched the down on his cheeks, lighting the fine golden hairs, giving him an ethereal, unfinished look. He opened his eyes at Anna's question and the lines of his face firmed up. "You mean did I kill Carolyn?" he asked without seeming much to care whether Anna thought him a murderer or not.

"More or less," Anna admitted.

"I didn't," he said simply. "I was just plain lost."

Anna couldn't tell if he was telling the truth or not. He'd closed his eyes again, gone away to someplace inside his head and she could read nothing but distance and weariness on his face.

"I believe you," she said. If he was telling the truth, her lie couldn't hurt. If he wasn't, it might put him off his guard. "Is this why you were blackmailing me?" she asked. "So I wouldn't find out your dad was beaten?"

Rory nodded wordlessly.

"Is that bullshit over?"

"It's over," he said.

"It sucked, Rory. Really sucked."

"I know."

"I've got to go." She levered herself up from the porch floor.

"You gonna talk to Dad?" Rory asked without opening his eyes.

"I thought I would."

"If Dad killed her I hope you never can prove it."

Anna didn't say anything. Had it not been for the butchery, she might have shared the sentiment. The act of cutting away Carolyn's face was anger gone so insane its perpetrator had best be caught and removed from society.

Sudden light-headedness reminded Anna she'd not eaten since the night before, and she set off on foot to walk the half-mile to Joan's house. Expecting to spend the day in the resource management office, she'd not thought to ask Harry for the use of a vehicle. After food, transportation was next on her list.

Rarely did Anna find it a burden to walk instead of ride. This afternoon was no exception. The mere act of putting one foot in front of the other, moving forward completely on one's own will and strength, gave life a sense of purpose and control. And there was that adage about regular movement of the legs that stimulated orderly progression in the brain.

Houses, trees, cars, gopher holes and thimbleberry bushes flowed by externally. Internally Anna pondered borrowed shame—Rory's for his dad—abandonment, fear, self-worth, violence, childhood trauma, family roles: scapegoat, victim, hero, mascot. The bits and pieces of codependency theory that she'd picked up from listening to her sister, Molly, had a place in the shattered family dynamics that Rory had grown up in the midst of.

His natural mother had abandoned him via death when he was five. According to Rory's account, Les had abandoned him over the next two years via depression. Then Carolyn came on the scene and the neuroses and psychoses really started to roll.

That sort of thing didn't make people into murderers. But it was bound to help. The circumstances of Rory's thirty-six hours missing had, at first, seemed to make his murdering Carolyn remote to the point of ludicrousness. Taken with this new information, Anna was seeing it in a new light. Rory is traumatized by the attack of the bear slashing at a person—Joan—for whom he cares, and threatening, indirectly since the bear did not see or approach him, his own safety. Rory runs, panicked. Then, quite by accident, he meets another frightening figure, Carolyn, who for much of his life played the same role as the grizzly. Under the influence of fear, opportunism and post-traumatic-stress disorder, Rory strikes out, kills her.

That was as far as Anna could spin her tale of Rory Van Slyke's mental gyrations. Hiding the body—sure, anybody who didn't want to get caught would do that. The same went for stashing the cameras and taking the exposed film if pictures had been snapped by the victim. Slicing off face-steaks and carting them away were something else again.

Joan wasn't home and Anna was disappointed. Not only did she want to lighten her load of slime by sharing it with her friend, but after the exposing of a wound Rory'd kept resolutely bandaged for so long, Anna figured he'd need a shoulder to cry on.

Since her own were too bony and prickly for wailing-wall duty, she'd hoped Joan would volunteer to check on the boy.

Joan's office number got Anna through to voice mail. The tale was too convoluted to deal with electronically and she hung up without leaving a message.

The refrigerator grudgingly offered up a piece of cheese the mold could easily be cut off of and a handful of miniature peeled carrots in a sandwich bag. Having rid the cheese of alien life forms, Anna shoved the lot into a piece of pita bread and ate as she walked back toward park headquarters.

Harry was out. His secretary, Maryanne, was out. It was lunchtime and everyone but the receptionist had gone elsewhere. Effectively stopped for the moment, Anna dumped herself in Maryanne's swivel chair outside the chief ranger's office to wait on her betters.

Snoopy was not how Anna chose to characterize herself. She much preferred the term "inquisitive" or, at worst, "impatient." Working on other people's timetables, waiting docilely until they were ready to feed her items of information, seemed a waste of time and good spirits. This theory went a long way toward happily blinding her to such crimes as trespass and invasion of privacy.

While she waited she sifted through the papers on Maryanne's desk, careful not to disarrange anything overmuch. Considering herself absolutely justified, still Anna chose not to get caught. Copies of the 10-343s and 10-344s—case incident reports and criminal incident reports—were stacked to one side of the computer. Harry Ruick was a hands-on sort of guy and had the park's reports come across his desk, even at the rarified level of management to which he had risen.

Leafing through them Anna got a dim sum of the crimes du jour in Glacier National Park. Taking her time, she read of littering, campfires out of bounds, a horse trailer towed up by Polebridge Ranger Station, two fire rings recently rehabilitated in the northwestern quadrant of Flattop Mountain, petty thievery in the campground, food improperly stored. She'd been in law enforcement too many years not to sweat the small stuff. Felons were consistently caught because they were speeding, loitering, littering and parking in front of fire hydrants. Except in the movies, criminals could usually be counted on to be careless. There was a

logic to it. Who, if willing to commit robbery or murder or mayhem, would have any qualms about driving with a taillight out?

From the incidents, she moved on to the crimes. Nothing
leapt off the pages at her. It was pretty standard stuff: driving under the influence, smoking dope in the campgrounds. One stolen
car, one statutory rape—both allegedly committed by concessions
workers in West Glacier.

The only report of any interest—and that only because she'd
heard it mentioned on the radio a couple of times—was the abandoned horse trailer found on the northside. She flipped back till
she found it and read through it again. Parked off the road, its location obscured imperfectly by brush dragged over the tracks,
was a 1974 Ford pickup truck, blue, with Florida plates. No insurance or registration papers inside. Attached to it was an old
horse trailer, no plates, gutted and used to haul something other
than a horse. Drug dogs were brought in. No hits. The truck was
registered to a Carl G. Micou of Tampa, Florida. The plates were
run: no wants, no warrants. An address was found for Mr. Micou
but the phone number given had been disconnected, no new
number listed. The old number had been traced to a business,
Fetterman's Adventure Trails on Highway 41 outside Tampa. Fetterman's had closed its doors about the time the phone was disconnected.

Odd but not pertinent. Anna put the report back where she'd
found it and looked around for something else with which to pass
the time. Maryanne's computer was only mildly tempting. Anna
was convinced that computers, like horses, could smell fear and
turn on the operator when mishandled.

A manila folder marked "C. Van Slyke" offered itself up from
the "Out" basket. Within were Harry's notes from the Les Van
Slyke interview, of which Anna had already been given a copy.
The transcription from the tape of her interview with Rory was
there, she noted, and was struck by Maryanne's efficiency. The remaining papers were new to Anna. The secretary had stuck a
Post-It note on the paper-clipped pages that read "cc to A. Pigeon." Anna felt a sense of failure. In her home park, the Natchez
Trace Parkway, she'd not been able to command the cooperation
from her field rangers that was being accorded her in Glacier as a
matter of course.

The lab report had come back on the water bottle found in

Rory's possession after his unplanned hike. The crime lab used by Glacier National Park was the Montana State Lab in Missoula.

It had been less than twenty-four hours since Harry had turned the thing over. Anna was impressed at the turnaround time. Harry Ruick obviously had clout.

The majority of the fingerprints on the bottle were Rory's, but four clear prints of thumb, index and middle finger had been lifted from the plastic. They belonged to Carolyn Van Slyke. To Anna's mind it was proof positive Rory had, if not killed his stepmother, at least been in close enough proximity to her the night he'd gone missing to obtain her water bottle. Though this was obvious enough to real people, Anna'd been around long enough to know it would mean little to a jury were Rory brought to trial. Any defense attorney would be able to argue that of course Mrs. Van Slyke's prints were on the bottle; she was Rory's mother. They could have been put there at any time before the boy'd taken the bottle camping with him. And could Anna swear, under oath, that he'd not had two bottles with him on the trip? No.

Had she not marked it when she took it into evidence, Anna would have had a tough time swearing that water bottle was *the* water bottle he'd had when he'd been found and not the one he'd used prior to the bear attack. The bottles were identical.

Two other partial prints, belonging neither to Rory nor Carolyn Van Slyke, were also on the bottle. At a guess they belonged to Lester, but they could be from anyone to whom Carolyn had given a drink. The hikers that found Rory could have held it for him. Still they'd be run through the AFIS, the automatic fingerprint identification system, as a matter of course.

The next page ended Anna's waffling. Traces of blood had been found on the bottom of the water bottle. As of the date of this report, the lab was unsure whether there was enough for DNA testing.

The remainder of the pages were just inventory lists: contents of the pack they'd found wedged under the log and the belongings of the deceased. Anna started to put the borrowed pages away and noticed the inventory of Carolyn's belongings wasn't duplicated. There were two lists: items belonging to the deceased and items found on the body of the deceased. At first they appeared identical. Then Anna'd noted the "belongings" list was short one item.

"I see you've made yourself at home," Harry said acidly.

"Yeah." Anna was too absorbed to notice the intended reprimand. "So the army jacket Carolyn was wearing wasn't hers?"

Ruick shook his head disgustedly. Since Anna'd not been aware of his implied rebuke, she also missed its annoyed follow-up at her obtuseness and took the headshake as a negative about the jacket.

"Lester's?" she asked.

"Les doesn't know where she got it. Come on into my office. I'll let you in on any details you haven't already found on Maryanne's desk."

"Thanks," Anna said sincerely.

Ruick muttered something that sounded like "skin of a rhinoceros," but, accustomed to the idiosyncrasies of the brass, she politely pretended not to notice.

As it happened, there was no more to tell than she'd discovered through her snooping. No leads on to whom the jacket belonged or why Carolyn was wearing it. Les told Harry that his wife had a habit of appropriating anything belonging to nearby males for her own use and thinking nothing of it. Had she been cold when she'd left that night, she might have snagged some camper's coat off a tree or rock.

"Les was careful to point out that his wife would never steal," Harry said. "That she just 'borrowed without permission.'"

"If the jacket's owner hiked on, we'll never know whose it was. Shoot, he might not even be a hundred percent sure where he lost it," Anna said.

"Follow it up," Ruick ordered.

"Sure." Mentally Anna added another forty miles hard hiking to her list just to chase down this wild goose for the chief ranger.

Army jacket dispensed with, she settled into the task of telling Ruick of her interview with Rory concerning the spousal abuse. She'd not taped it because she'd been afraid of inhibiting the boy's narrative on such a sensitive issue. She taped her recounting of it now while it was fresh in her mind.

When she'd finished, Ruick didn't say anything. Rocking himself absently in his chair he stared into the parking lot. Lunch was over. Cars were coming in. Even in a national park on a beautiful summer's day most folks drove the half-mile to work. No wonder America was the fattest nation on earth.

"The marks on his arms and legs. Bruises, cuts in various stages of healing. I'd have spotted it on a kid in a second," he said finally.

Anna made no comment. She would have too. On a child it would have set off all the alarm bells. One didn't expect it on a grown man.

"I've heard of course of wives beating their husbands," Ruick said. "I've just never come across it before."

Neither had Anna. She must remember to ask Molly just how rare the phenomenon was.

"It doesn't make sense," Ruick said. "Les is no Tarzan. I mean he is—was—what? Eighteen years older than his wife?"

"Eighteen," Anna confirmed from the birth dates on the notes she had with her.

"And in bad shape. Still he outweighed her by a good thirty pounds and is six or eight inches taller. What did he have to be afraid of if he fought back?"

"Being abandoned," Anna said with certainty. She remembered how it felt when Zach had died. What would she put up with not to feel that again? *It was like we'd been living in black and white and all of a sudden our world got colorized,* " Rory had said. Lester was scared to death to go back to that black-and-white world. Even black and blue must have seemed an improvement.

"Give me abandonment any day of the week," Harry said.

Anna guessed none of his wives had ever up and died on him. If he'd ever been married. She looked around his office past the ubiquitous NPS certificates and awards. No pictures of wives or kids.

"Are you married?" she asked apropos of nothing but her thoughts.

"Twenty-seven years. I played it safe. Eilene is a little bit of a thing who wouldn't hurt a fly. What do you say you and me go have another chat with Lester?"

13

Lester was doing what depressed and grieving people traditionally do: everything wrong. The curtains of his second-floor motel room were drawn. The room was overwarm and stuffy. He'd not showered or shaved or dressed. In a plaid flannel bathrobe he'd probably had since before his son was born, he'd been sitting in an unmade bed watching television.

When he opened the door to Harry Ruick's knock Anna was taken aback at how much he'd deteriorated since she'd seen him last. The thinning gray hair stood out in bed-wrinkled strands and colorless stubble highlighted the crease and sag of his cheeks. Puffy eyes rimmed with red attested to the fact he'd spent much of the intervening time weeping. That or he suffered from allergies.

Eyes watering at the sudden exposure to light—or reality—he said absurdly, "May I help you?"

"We'd like to talk with you for a minute," Harry said. He pulled off his straw summer Stetson and held it in front of him like a steering wheel. Anna didn't know if he did it from respect or good manners. Either way she liked him for the gesture. Her Stetson was at home on a peg in the closet in Rocky Springs, along with her service weapon and other needful things. Today she wore the goofy-looking green NPS billed field cap. It crossed her mind to snatch it off in deference to age or grief but the rules regarding women, manners and the wearing of hats had become blurred. One never knew, anymore, what was proper.

She left it on. Beneath its polyester squeeze her hair probably looked as bad as Lester's.

Mr. Van Slyke was baffled for a moment. Then his face cleared somewhat and he said, "Of course. Won't you please come in? Please excuse the mess. I . . ."

The brittle safety of polite platitudes fell away and his words dried up. Sidling by ahead of Harry, Anna looked closely at him. His skin hung loose over muscles devoid of elasticity; his was the face of a man who'd had a small stroke or was in shock. Taking his hand she shook it as if they'd just been introduced. "Good to see you again," she murmured. His skin was dry and warm. Not shock. Probably just old-fashioned depression. She shied away from a sudden memory of the weeks and months after Zach died when she'd moved in slow motion, pushing through a life grown thick and suffocating as Delta mud. But then Zach never beat her. Zach was the kind of guy who put mice out, then left the door ajar in case it got cold and they wanted back in.

Even without Carolyn's ghost, the room would have been enough to depress Anna. As Les had warned, it was a mess. The contents of a backpack and a suitcase were disgorged over the available surfaces, along with the remains of an uneaten fast-food supper. There was a single chair of that sterile motel hybrid between kitchen straight-back and easy chair beside a round table piled with the soiled and disorganized guts of Lester's day pack, and the bed.

Out of deference to rank, Anna left the chair for Harry. Sliding loose change and motel brochures to one side, she perched on the low dresser beside the television. Lester hadn't turned it off when he'd answered the door. Garish colors and rude noises emanating from the set proved the only life the room had: distorted, invasive, inconsequential.

Anna composed herself to let Harry take the lead and watched the men settle, Harry, hat in hand, at the small cluttered table and Les Van Slyke on the edge of the unmade bed, his bruised and bony knees sticking out from under the battered flannel robe. She was put in mind of Rory's image of Les as a whimpering dog. It was not a pretty picture, particularly of a boy to have of his father.

"Mr. Van Slyke—" Harry began.

"Lester, Les," the old man begged, and the humility on his face made Anna want to deliver a swift kick to his nether regions.

"Les," Harry amended. "We—or rather Anna here—has been

talking with Rory. He suggested your relationship with your wife, Carolyn, was not as smooth as you painted it."

Lester tweaked at his bathrobe, arranging it demurely over his knees. As soon as he let go it fell away again. He left it alone. After enough time had passed that Anna had to actively clamp a lid on herself to keep from jumping in with questions of her own, he said, "All couples have their little troubles now and again. Carolyn was quite a few years younger than I am. I suppose she got restless sometimes."

"Did you argue?" Harry persisted.

"Most married people argue," Lester said, making eye contact with the rug between the toes of his mangy brown carpet slippers.

"Did she ever get violent?" Harry asked.

"Carolyn did have a temper," Lester said and, to Anna's surprise, he smiled as if at a pleasing memory. "She was a feisty one."

"Did she ever get violent with you?" Harry pressed patiently.

At that Lester looked mildly alarmed. His fleshless white hands skittered about over his knees like frightened cave spiders. "How do you mean?" he asked.

"Hit you, clawed you, threw things at you," Harry explained. Ruick, like Anna, had to know Lester was playing for time, but for reasons of his own the chief ranger had chosen to give it to him.

"She'd get frustrated," Lester admitted. "She threw things once or twice. Carolyn was a complicated woman and I've always been a simple man. Sometimes it was too much for her. Especially with her having that high-stress job. She needed to let off a little steam once in a while."

Anna should have admired his loyalty but she didn't. Domestic abuse cases occurred wherever people cohabited, whether it be in houses or tents or camper trailers. Over the years her sympathies with the abused person's attachment to the abuser had hardened into an impatience that verged on anger. Molly had explained the psychological dynamics of the victim/victimizer relationship and, though Anna had come to accept it intellectually, viscerally it still pissed her off.

Other than the fleeting smile at his deceased wife's "feistiness" Lester showed no emotion. Now Harry shot Anna a look, eyebrows raised, lips crimped, that suggested, at least to Anna's mind, that Rory had been exaggerating or maybe out-and-out lying. Given Mr. Van Slyke's equanimity she could see how Harry might think that. But he hadn't been there, hadn't see Rory or heard his voice as the tale unfolded. Rory might not have his facts right, but Anna would have bet the farm that he believed the things he'd said.

She believed them too. Most people, when hit with the questions Harry had put to Les, would have said, "Why do you ask?" Les showed no interest. He'd been too busy evading, minimizing, rationalizing—major tools in the building and shoring up of denial.

Harry's eyebrows seemed to signal defeat. Anna took that as a call for backup and entered the fray.

"Mr. Van Slyke," she began and continued, bulldozing over his protestations that she must call him "Les." "When Harry asks about your wife hurting you, he means like the times she inflicted injuries that put you in the hospital. Your son said she broke your collarbone, burst your eardrum and once nearly cut your face in half with a kitchen stool."

The blunt assault of words didn't have the effect she'd been hoping for. Beneath the pasty sagging skin there was a rippling disturbance, but it could have as easily been brought on by Rory's bizarre lies as an unmasking of the truth.

"Why would Rory say that?" he asked, bewildered. Not quite bewildered enough. His left hand scampered up his right arm and his forefinger stretched out, gently stroking the scar that bisected his face.

Seeing the gesture, Anna willfully misunderstood his question. "Rory said it because the boy loves his father, loves you and seeing you hurt broke his heart."

That got the desired reaction. Not only are more flies caught with honey, more can be killed. Anna felt a pang of guilt for manipulating Les's emotions. It didn't last long.

He rubbed his eyes with both fists like a very small child. There were tears left like snail trails on his knuckles. The rounded shoulders shuddered with a convulsive sigh.

Harry had a look of annoyance on his face directed not at the weepy old man but at Anna. She huffed, a teensy puff of air from her nostrils. If he was thinking she should leap to the bed and put the feminine arms of comfort around Lester, he had another think coming. She leaned back against the mirror, made herself comfortable for the duration of the waterworks.

The chief ranger had, indeed, been expecting something of the sort. Seeing her settle in he put his hat on the top of the clutter on the table and stood. Stooping awkwardly, he patted Les's shoulder. Words failed him. Again Anna got the flash of annoyance. She considered suggesting the classic comfort "there, there" but thought better of it.

Lester calmed down. Ruick retreated with unflattering speed back to the safety of his lonely chair.

Painfully, Les pulled himself together, or as much together as he would ever get. A handkerchief was found, eyes dried, nose blown. Water was sipped, housecoat readjusted. Then he settled himself to answer honestly.

They didn't get anything in the way of revelations. Honesty is an individual perception. If Les had ever been able to view his situation objectively—or, more to the point, as others would view it—the ability had been lost. The need to feel okay about himself and still to stay with Carolyn had to be balanced. The only way to do that was to create a new truth, one where being a victim was acceptable, even admirable. Telling them now of his wife's transgressions, Lester could not go outside the reality he had made for himself. "She had a temper" and "sometimes she got carried away" were the best he could do. The broken collarbone, the ruptured eardrum were accidents. She didn't mean it. Lester had zigged when he should have zagged, etc., etc., ad nauseam. The blow from the metal kitchen stool that had scarred his face he simply slid over as if it wasn't worth mentioning. As if it had never happened.

Of Rory, for whom the sudden tears had presumably been shed since they clearly were not for his own miserable situation, he said, "The boy shouldn't have taken it so much to heart. *I never minded.*"

The words came to Anna's ear not in Lester's confused, sad voice but the desperate wail of his son when he'd said the same thing earlier in the day.

Harry gave Lester a few minutes more than Anna would have to collect himself then said, "We're just about done here Mr. . . . Les. We understand this has got to be a rough time for you. Real rough. We're sorry—"

For an instant Anna was afraid he would parrot the empty phrase in vogue in TV cop shows, "We're sorry for your loss," but he didn't.

"—to have to put you through more questions, but in cases like this we can't wait on good manners."

"I understand," Les said. He pulled the handkerchief from the pocket of his robe where he'd stuffed it and blew his nose loudly and thoroughly. "Go ahead."

"You said earlier that the army surplus jacket your wife was wearing when we found her was not hers. Do you have any idea who it belonged to?"

Les kept his face down and blew his nose again though it didn't need it. "I guess it could have been Carolyn's," he said. "She was always getting new clothes. I never paid much attention." He was lying. A husband might not notice if his wife bought a different shade of lipstick or a new blouse but if she suddenly started sporting oversized U.S. Army fatigues he'd probably sit up and take note.

Ruick nodded slowly. "I see," he said and Anna wondered if he was seeing the same thing she was: a skittering of weasel tail vanishing down a secret hole.

"We thank you for your time." Harry rose and reclaimed his Stetson. "We'll talk again before you make any decisions about what to do next."

Back in Ruick's pickup, painted white with the standard green reflective NPS stripe down the side, as she and Ruick buckled their seat belts, Anna said: "Our suspects stink."

"Kind of hard to picture that particular worm turning, isn't it?"

"Rory doesn't fit the bill much better."

"There's always the homicidal stranger just passing through."

"Fortuitous accident?"

"Could be. If it is and our murderous Mr. X has moved on, we're pretty much guaranteed a segment on *Unsolved Mysteries*," he said sourly.

"He was lying about that army jacket," Anna said.

"You think? I don't notice what my wife wears, much to her annoyance."

Anna explained her rationale.

"Good point," he conceded. "Supposing he does know where

she got the coat. To give him the benefit of the doubt, let's say he didn't remember yesterday and he's figured it out since. Why not just tell us? Who's he protecting? If the jacket was his—and Les doesn't strike me as an army surplus kind of guy—it wouldn't prove anything. Wives take their husband's coat all the time. First time around he said she had a habit of 'borrowing' things."

"Maybe it belongs to Rory. Maybe he thinks the two of them did get together and Rory killed her, made the coat swap at the same time he got that second water bottle," Anna suggested. She didn't remember ever seeing Rory in an army jacket, and given the new polypropylene microfleece nature of his backpacking wardrobe, a bulky heavy coat seemed out of character, but she couldn't remember for sure. "I'll ask Joan," she said.

Not because the coat question concerned her overmuch—Anna would have noticed if Rory had lugged a heavy army jacket into the woods—but to have something to do, she sought out Joan at the resource management office.

Joan was in a tizzy. The DNA lab at the University of Idaho had screwed up on the hair samples sent in from the bear trap they'd harvested before unpleasant adventures interrupted their research. There'd been a mix-up, Joan told her distractedly. The lab had sent back DNA results from Alaskan grizzlies, not those of the lower forty-eight. Though the same species, grizzlies in Alaska were considerably larger—thirty to fifty percent—and had enough other evolutionary and environmentally based differences that the tests could tell one from the other. Till she sorted out her bits of hair and scat, Joan was useless for any other topic of conversation.

Anna left, her departure unnoticed, and walked back to the employee housing area. Though she'd wanted to share the day's findings and frustrations with Joan, it was reassuring that not everybody spent every waking hour thinking about who killed whom and why.

The rest of the afternoon she dedicated to the familiar chore of packing for the backcountry. It was something she had done so many times in her life she found the Zenlike sameness of laundry and sorting and putting things into small plastic bags as freeing as a walking meditation.

Around five o'clock, as she was contemplating a nap in reward for her labors, Harry rapped on the screen door. The autopsy results had come. Northern Montana was not rife with murders and the medical examiner had worked up Carolyn Van Slyke's corpse first thing.

Much of it they already knew from observation: no defensive wounds, no sexual assault, no skin beneath the fingernails, no bullets in the body, no knife wounds but the filleting of the front upper quadrant of the skull where the M.E. approximated two to three ounces of flesh had been excised.

The cause of death was severing of the spinal cord between the first and second cervical vertebrae. That surprised Anna. Given the cutting on the face, she thought head injury would be the cause, that the removal of the flesh might have been done in part to hide the nature of the blow.

"Did he just twist her head till her neck snapped?" she asked. She'd seen it done in a dozen movies but never come across it in real life. For some reason the image made her queasier than the slicing and dicing.

"Nope," Harry said. "Weirder yet." He handed her the report he'd been reading from and she scanned the last half of a page.

Carolyn Van Slyke had been struck on the side of the head with such force her neck had snapped, not just crushing the cord but knocking the skull so fast and hard that it was propelled over the opposite shoulder and down toward the clavicle, pulverizing the outer edges of three vertebrae and hyperextending the muscles and tendons of the neck.

"She must have been hit with a tree trunk to get that kind of torque," Anna said.

"No tree trunk," Ruick said. "What's missing?"

Anna didn't like to be quizzed. Then again, she loved a challenge. For half a minute she skimmed what had been read to her and read again the final paragraphs. "Ah!" she said as the light finally dawned. "No injury to the skull. No point of impact, cracking, etcetera."

"She was hit by something soft," Ruick said.

"Like a man's forearm?"

"I've never met a man who could hit that hard."

"Kicked, hit with a booted calf, Jean Claude Van Damme style?"

"It would have to be one heck of a kick."

"What if she was already unconscious and the killer forced her head back and down?"

"That was the best I could come up with," Ruick admitted. "But Dr. Janis, the M.E., said doing it slowly like that would have squashed the spinal cord. The severing suggests a single, sudden, hard blow."

"That's helpful," Anna said dryly. "Did Dr. Janis have any suggestions?"

"One. She said a boy she'd seen in Helena had been killed that way. The kid was seven years old. His nineteen-year-old brother and his buddies got drunk and were swinging around a heavy padded boxer's punching bag on the end of a chain. The kid stepped out, caught the full force of it above his left eye, his head snapped back and down, producing injuries like those of our pet corpse."

"At least we know what to look for now," Anna said. "A guy in the backcountry with an oversized bolster. Shouldn't be too hard to track down."

"Wish I had something more tangible but this is as good as it gets."

They talked of Anna and Joan's return to the backcountry. Anna was against Rory going. They hadn't enough to arrest him for the murder of his stepmother. With him now claiming he may have had the two water bottles all along, he was barely a suspect, no proof to take to a grand jury. Ruick had reservations as well but wanted to keep the Van Slykes in the park; allowing Rory to continue with the DNA project would keep not only him in the area but Les as well. Rory's father was determined to return to Fifty Mountain Camp and finish his stay so he and his son could return to Seattle together.

"It's as if neither will leave till the other one does and both of them are hot to get back up on Flattop Mountain," Anna said. "Why?"

"That's what we've got to find out, I guess."

They struck a compromise. If Joan Rand said no, the deal was off. If she said yes, Buck, the stalwart backcountry ranger, would be detailed to go along as insurance.

Joan said yes.

14

As it turned out, hiking into the wilderness with a potential murderer was not what grated on Anna's nerves. It was hiking with a teenager seesawing unpleasantly between sulkiness and petulance. Gripping tightly to her hard-won adulthood, Anna managed not to engage. Armored with genuine compassion, Joan seemed impervious to the sporadic adolescent barbs. Anna was not. The best she could do was appear to be. Rory, like most teenagers she had met, could be the best of company. And the worst. Like heat-seeking missiles, people between the ages of fourteen and eighteen had an uncanny ability to sense weak spots and hit them with unnerving accuracy.

Has to be hormonal, Anna thought as she meticulously refrained from wincing when he wrote off a generation of the finest rock-and-roll musicians ever to overdose as "overrated bubblegum salesmen." There was a spark of hope to be gleaned: perhaps at menopause, when she underwent reverse adolescence, she, too, would become uniquely dangerous, even if for only a brief period of time.

Till then, she relied on the grainy endurance of middle age to out-walk the strength and suppleness of youth. As the ascent to Flattop grew steeper and hotter and dustier, she picked up the pace and soon walked alone. Almost alone. Drooping along at her heels, nearly as sullen as Rory Van Slyke, was Ponce, the ten-year-old gelding the park used as a packhorse. Doing double duty as DNA flunky and Harry Ruick's flunky, Anna had too much ground to cover on foot. Out of kindness of heart or weakness of mind she'd volunteered to walk the first twelve miles, four of them nigh onto vertical, so Ponce could carry Rory and Joan's packs.

Buck was to meet them at Fifty Mountain. They would overnight there. In the morning he'd go with Rory and Joan to work hair traps. Anna and Ponce would be on their own for the most part but, when feasible, would camp with the DNA research team. Harry had insisted on this not only for Rory and Joan's security but for hers. Anna'd not put up a fight. Much as she liked camping alone, she was not one-hundred-percent sure their lady-killer had left the park.

Despite the best Zen intentions, her mind did not remain un-cluttered during the hours of the hike to Fifty Mountain. In the burn her thoughts turned to the peculiar Mr. Mickleson-Nicholson and his digging of glacier lilies. As they neared the place in the trail where Rory had met up with the hikers, visions of extraneous water bottles danced in her head. No revelations were forthcoming, and by afternoon's end, she plodded on as dull as Ponce and was nearly as glad as he when they reached camp.

Buck was there to greet them and lend a beefy hand and a strong back to unloading and feeding the horse. Grazing was much frowned upon, and along with their gear, Ponce carried pellets for himself.

William McCaskil was still at Fifty Mountain—or at least his tent and pack were in the far campsite where they'd been two days before.

Tent pitched, Anna allowed herself the luxury of a cup of hot tea before getting on with business: finding and again chatting with the felon, McCaskil.

The sun slid behind the mountain, dragging the day's warmth down with it. In this clashing together of day and night, nature chose to unleash one of her showier moments. As Anna drank her tea, fog white as drugstore cotton began pouring down, feather-light liquid in stasis, from over the jagged mountain face to the east. Slow and silent in sinister majesty it cloaked the crags, slipped between them and flowed toward the meadows. In an instant so perfect as to seem eternal, the drift turned from white to wild flamingo. In its feeble human way, Anna's brain sought to categorize the sight: lava, chiffon, whipped cream, frozen fire. Her puny metaphors exhausted themselves and, for a blissful while, she sat in mindless appreciation.

Pink faded to gray. Tea grew cold. Wind breathed up from some damp mountain lung and she stirred herself. Dusk was long. She had at least an hour of half-light left in which to find and annoy at least one of her fellow campers.

McCaskil had returned from a day hike. When Anna trickled into his campsite he was shrugging out of his pack. His thick wavy hair was tangled and particles of high-country flora were caught in the nest. He'd been hiking cross-country in boots so new they blistered his feet. Anna could tell by the ginger-wincing way he pulled the footwear off. A confidence man, a city slicker, a greenhorn pushing his urban body through the thickets in search of what? Spiritual renewal? By the sour look on his face, it didn't look as though he'd found it.

"Howdy, howdy," she said, just to be irritating.

"Oh. It's you," he said repressively.

Anna took this as an invitation and settled herself comfortably at the base of a struggling pine tree. Fog flooded the camp. The evening had gone from chilly to cold. Pulling the hood up on her fleece jacket, she watched McCaskil, in shirtsleeves and shivering, glare at her from under well-shaped eyebrows.

"You're cold," she said pointedly. "Why don't you put your coat on?"

"I like being cold. And I like being alone. Nothing personal." He smiled then as if belatedly remembering some age-old warning about women scorned. "Except when there's a good-looking woman around." The first statement had come from the heart. The second blew out like a smoke screen.

Whatever he hoped to hide with it remained hidden. Anna was no match for him. She'd had a number of years to learn the art of ferreting out information. McCaskil had probably had twice that to practice fraud, deception and misdirection.

Flirting was the tool he chose this evening. Every query of Anna's was met with compliments, her remarks turned aside with double entendres. Fifteen minutes into the fruitless exercise, she realized she'd been lucky the first time and caught him off guard. For whatever reasons, his guard was up now. She would get nothing useful from him till she had a bigger pry bar. It crossed her mind to try and crack open the playboy façade with her knowledge of his conviction for fraud but she didn't know to what end. And she strongly suspected he knew she knew, was ready for it.

Several times she managed to shove Carolyn Van Slyke into the conversation. With the passage of time McCaskil's association with the deceased became ever more fleeting. When she'd first talked with him three days before, he'd referred to her as "the blond" and used her first name. Now she had been relegated to "that woman the bear ate." Since Carolyn had been murdered by a human hand, Anna wondered at McCaskil's seeming conviction that she'd died of natural, if fearsome, causes. When questioned he waved it away. "Whatever," he said callously. "I guess I wasn't paying all that much attention."

Cutting off the chitchat, Anna excused herself. Having walked well out of earshot she radioed Ruick. He'd been off duty for several hours but he was the kind of guy she figured would leave his radio on twenty-four hours of the day. She was right.

"I've got a hunch," she told him. "Run the prints on the second topographical map found on Van Slyke's body. The one in the pocket of the army surplus jacket."

The chief ranger said he would and didn't ask why. Being cagey and mysterious was an occupational hazard in law enforcement. Either Harry accepted that or was convinced Anna's hunch was as uninteresting as it was unimportant.

Grateful not to have to expose her fledgling theory to the harsh reality of nouns and verbs, Anna didn't care which.

The fog was not, as Anna had feared, a precursor to another day's cold rain. By sunrise it had moved on, moved up or simply vanished. The day was exquisite as only a high mountain summer can be: cool and warm at the same time, with breeze on one cheek and unfettered sunshine on the other. There was nothing in the air but air. Not the cloying touch of the moisture of the south, not the putrid undercurrent of a city's stink, not the bracing tang of salt from the seashore. Air so clear Anna felt if she stopped breathing she could soak it in through the pores of her skin.

Joan was gone with Rory and Buck, trudging back down West Flattop Trail to set up camp once more in the small meadow with the great flat boulder. On the surface it seemed unwise. Bears, like lightning, frequently struck twice in the same place. Joan had chosen to camp there again for a couple of reasons. One, Anna was sure, was a bad case of selective memory brought on by a prejudice in favor of *Ursus horribilis*. She couldn't help but notice that in Joan's conversations the bear had no longer ravaged, savaged or destroyed their camp but merely upset it. The rest of the researcher's logic was sound. There was no better campsite near where they were to dismantle and move the hair trap they'd been aiming for when life intervened with other plans and, too, the bear had found nothing in the way of a food reward. In the bearish sciences this meant it probably would not return.

Not being burdened with a scientific mind, it occurred to Anna that the bear, this bear, their own personal bear, had not been looking for food reward. What else a wild animal, not yet tainted by contact with the human race, might be seeking she wasn't ready to say, but the story of "The Ghost and the Darkness" came to mind. A true story of two lions—solitary hunters, according to scientists, naturally chary of human settlements—who had teamed up apparently for the sheer, unadulterated pleasure of creating terror and taking human life.

If people could go insane, who was Anna to say an animal, if only rarely, couldn't do likewise? Probably an animal smarter than the rest. Too smart for its own good.

"Get thee behind me, Dean Koontz," she said aloud, realizing she'd slipped into nightmare in the midst of the most stunningly beautiful of days. Joan was right. The meadow was a fine campground. Tonight, barring unforeseen circumstances, Anna would be joining her and the boys there. Till then she would enjoy the day, the solitude and pursuing to the best of her abilities the job she'd been given.

William McCaskil's camp looked uninhabited she noted as she lugged her tent and gear down toward the food preparation area and Ponce's makeshift paddock, a tying rail between the food area and the outhouse. A powerful temptation to search his tent coursed through her. The previous night she'd struck out with the slippery fellow. Or missed the basket or fumbled the ball—it was hard to know just what game McCaskil was playing. Had she been a private citizen, she might have given in to the urge. As a federal law enforcement officer she could not. Even in a tent in the wilderness, an American citizen had a reasonable expectation of privacy. If she found anything during an unauthorized search the evidence would be tainted and she would have done the investigation more harm than good.

After a night's sleep and a feed, Ponce was of a cheerier disposition than the day before and Anna's weight was somewhat less than he was accustomed to carrying. In easy companionship they started west, Ponce looking for anything tasty he might snag in passing and Anna looking for nothing in particular. Since there were no clues in the form of tracks or paper trails, and her meager list of suspects had already been interviewed within an inch of their tawdry little lives, she decided to return to the scene of the crime. *Third time's the charm,* she told herself, wondering who'd coined the idiotic aphorism. The true charm was being on horseback under a fathomless sky with nobody to answer to for the entirety of a splendid day.

Riding on flat improved trails was a luxury and a joy. But as she dismounted and tied Ponce to the log where Joan and the excitable ranger had waited while she and Ruick bushwhacked to the body, Anna was reminded that it had been a long time since she'd been in the saddle. What little padding she once had on her posterior had since lost its stuffing. Her sit-bones complained of miles of insult.

A strip of orange surveyor's tape indicated where the body had been taken from the brush. Anna entered the scrub and began the steep alder-choked journey down the side of the ravine. Alone, rested, the sun shining, she was able to give the now-battered path her undivided attention. She discovered nothing but a discarded Good & Plenty box. It had not been there prior to the murder. The cardboard paper had not been rained on. Anna knew she hadn't dropped it and she was sure Harry hadn't. No ranger had. Park rangers were subject to the ailments of the general populace: prejudice, stupidity, small-mindedness, malice; but she had never known a single one she suspected of littering. In the days since the body had been recovered the crime scene had been visited by an ill-mannered civilian.

With the exception of arsonists, who liked to see the fruits of their labors, most criminals did not return to the scene of the crime. Could be a curious visitor who had learned of the location by some means. Could be a hiker coincidentally chose that spot to take a leak and clean his pockets. Still, Anna bagged the candy box, marked the day, time and place she'd found it, and tucked it away. One never knew.

The Good & Plenty was the sum total of excitement. In the

irregular opening in the alders where Gary had found Mrs. Van Slyke, Anna sifted through leaf litter, crawled into the neighboring tangle of bushes, examined weedy trunks and found nothing.

At length, enjoying a childish morbidity, she lay down in the place where Carolyn had been dumped and, folding her hands behind her head, contemplated being among the quick, and the sure knowledge that one day she would join the dead. Molly said thoughts of mortality came with one's fiftieth birthday. Anna still had a few years to go. But then she'd always been precocious.

Free from what she expected to see, Anna finally saw what was actually there.

In law enforcement classes, teachers were always admonishing students not to forget to look up. In real life, officers, rangers, forgot. Unless it was obvious, evidence in treetops went largely unnoticed. Both times that Anna'd crawled into this ravine, she'd seen little above eye-level.

High in the scrub, hard to assess from a supine position but probably six or seven feet up, a handful of the dusty-looking leaves were striated. Had the marked leaves not been so far from the ground Anna would have thought they'd been brushed with mud, painted by a passing boot after the rains and, so, after the body recovery. High as they were, above where tracks could be found, they held less interest.

Plants, like other life forms, were subject to disease and death, molds and rusts and parasites. Anna wasn't well enough versed in the pathologies of Montana's flora to speculate what this augured and her mind drifted. Drifted far enough to notice no other leaves, no other bushes were affected.

The world of the shrubbery pressed around her, began to feel claustrophobic. Sticks poked in her side. Leaves stuck in her hair. Skinny bark-clad fingers scratched at her arms. Light was deceitful, playing tricks with leaf shadows stirred by a wind that scarcely ever penetrated down to ground level. Heat, held close and dusty, itched on her skin.

Time to abandon her macabre resting spot. She rose and pushed into the branches to pluck one of the marred specimens. The rust-colored markings were smeared from the rain, but protected by the leaves above, enough remained for study. Dried blood—in her chosen profession Anna had had the opportunity to see plenty of the stuff—was slathered on various surfaces. A spit test reconstituted the brown to red. She took a small paper bag from her pack and collected several of the leaves. Blood in trees was not as rare as it might seem. Predators roamed the skies. These twiggy boughs were insufficient to support a dining hawk or eagle but occasionally they dropped wounded prey. If this was the case the tiny critter's corpse had been whisked away by a lucky groundling.

Her gory find stowed in an inside pocket, Anna stood in the alder and waited. Flies found her. Deerflies with jaws like airborne Chihuahuas flew kamikaze missions at the backs of her knees. Absently, she slapped them into the next world.

At length the information she waited for came into view: another patch of the rusty leaves a couple yards deeper in the brush. Shifting her attention down she moved toward it carefully, seeking any further sign underfoot or lower on the bushes. Runoff from the rain had erased any trail that might have been left and the sturdy alders retained no sign of anyone's passing.

Having reached the second cluster of streaked foliage she repeated the process. It took a sweaty, fly-bitten two hours to travel the rest of the trail but before noon she reached its end. Had she been a crow she could have flown from the place Carolyn's body was dumped to the pine tree where the blood trail ended in a matter of seconds. The two places were no more than seventy feet apart.

A pine, a lodgepole, rose gracefully out of the thicket. Its shade and the acidity of the fallen needles had opened a small needle-lined space beneath the boughs into which Anna moved gratefully. Her assumption that this was the blood trail's terminus was based not on what she found but on what she'd ceased to find. Three quarters of an hour's careful search around the tree led her to no new manifestations of rust-streaked leaves. Since the trail had been laid overhead, Anna crouched on her heels and studied the interlocking green of the pine above her.

This time the search was short. Twelve or fifteen feet up, partially secured to a branch with string of some sort was a navy-blue stuff bag vomiting pieces of clear—or once clear—plastic. All had been ripped to ribbons, by talons probably, though a bobcat or cougar or even a very talented fox was a possibility. Other than that, Anna could think of no pawed and clawed carnivores who frequented the avian stomping grounds.

The bark ringing the tree's trunk was unscarred. Whoever had put the package there had not done so by climbing. Having shed her day pack, Anna shinnied up for a closer look. Straddling a comfortable branch she tried to put together the pieces.

It didn't take long. With understanding came fear's cold touch, sickening in the warmth of noon. The torn plastic was blood-smeared as the leaves had been and comprised several different sources, two sandwich bags cut open, and part of what would undoubtedly turn out to be the tail end of a cheap poncho, the kind one can buy at the check-out counter in gas stations and carry in purse or trunk for soggy emergencies. The navy cloth was from a simple stuff sack, the sort hikers used to stow extraneous things. This one was eight or ten inches wide and twice that long. Bag and baggies had been drawn into the tree on a rope pull. A line of torn threads fuzzed the bark where the makeshift rope had been thrown over the limb and dragged. The line was secured with a slipknot. The dangling remainder had been cut, the frayed end tossed up into the lower branches. The rope was as cobbled together as the packaging: strips of torn fabric, white with narrow blue striping, tied end to end.

Carolyn Van Slyke's face had been cut off. The bloody slabs of meat had been carried high like a trophy or a team pennant over the butcher's head, leaving traces of blood on the cloaking leaves as he passed through. Away from the body, the murderer had packaged up the steaks in what he had at hand—sandwich bags and a raincoat—stuffed them in a sack that had been used maybe to carry his lunch, and cached this new treat up high where bears and other animals couldn't make away with it.

He'd been saving Carolyn Van Slyke's face for later.

15

A nna seriously wanted to get the hell out of there. Each and every idyllic day in this most beautiful of places had shown an underside that suggested God's Country was under siege from His traditional nemesis. To Anna's mind the most hellish of weapons had been unloosed: fear. Fear was the root of all evil. The others could be tracked to it. Greed was fear of want in pathological form. Lies, fear of being discovered for who one was, punished for what one had done.

The unnatural actions of the bear, Rory's bizarre disappearance, needless murder, now this abomination; fear poured into Anna's mind. In the midst of the very things that brought her comfort, she was being drowned in it. For a moment she clung to the branch fighting a desperate need to run from the wilderness, from sunlight, from solitude and hide in a closed, dark room full of familiar faces.

"Goddamn it," she muttered. Over her forty-odd years the fates had robbed her of her husband and taken a good shot at her only sister. She would not be robbed of that which made all else endurable, the peace and perfection of the natural world.

Anger helped but did not heal. Her rage was manufactured from two parts self-pity and one part need. It lacked the self-propelling white-hot burn of righteously earned ire. She kept it alive long enough to scorch away at least the core of her panic. She could trust herself to function, not to topple from the tree or dash madly down the trails shrieking.

When her breathing evened out, she knew she could stay and

do her work, but peace of mind, joy, freedom, those gifts of the wild country had been stolen away. "Fuck," she whispered, then she prayed a jolly little prayer: "Dear Lord, please let me find a gun in my pack when I climb down. Love, Anna."

Backup was hours away, but she radioed Ruick to tell him of her find. Mostly, she admitted to herself, to report her location. Should she go missing, Ponce would alert them to where she'd gone off trail but who would think to seek as far as the bush-locked pine?

Harry was in a meeting. Maryanne wrote down the message and Anna was left with no choice but to break contact.

Flinching at every sound, freezing at every change in the shadow pattern, she made several trips up and down the dese-crated pine taking photographs of and collecting the shredded bags. The meat they'd held was long gone. Whatever bird or beast had worried it out of its packaging had carried it away and undoubtedly eaten it. *Too bad*, Anna thought. Unless the killer was of the Hannibal Lecter School of Fine Cuisine, he may have removed the flesh not to eat it but to take away a clue to his iden-tity.

But why string the stuff up if he'd merely been covering his tracks? Surely one would want the telltale flesh eaten or buried or at least exposed so that it might decay more quickly. If something is cached it's because someone means to return for it.

No birds stirred the leaves, no shadows moved with the wind, still Anna stopped breathing, listened, cursed the gods for ignor-ing her prayer for firearms. Moving as quickly as she could, she labeled each item as she packed it in a paper evidence bag to bet-ter preserve the blood samples. The navy stuff sack was old, sev-eral years at least, made by REI and common as cotton underpants. The same went for the baggies and the torn scrap of poncho: generic, easily obtained, ubiquitous in the backcountry. The strips that had been tied together to form the line used to swing the cache into the branches were what appeared to be shirt-ing. The cloth was equally unremarkable, probably J. C. Penney or Sears, cotton-polyester sold in bulk. However, if the shirt they had been torn from had once covered the back of the killer, they could prove important.

Regardless of value or lack thereof Anna spent no time study-ing the evidence. With ingrained care she packaged and stowed.

Mind, ears and eyes were occupied patrolling the perimeter around the tree for cannibals, bears, axe murderers and other manifestations of impending violence.

At last the job was completed, everything tucked in her pack. With the possibility of flight nearer, Anna found her unease growing. "Get a grip," she ordered herself unsympathetically. Before she could make her escape, she needed to canvass the clearing one more time in case she had missed anything.

Out from the tree at a north-northwesterly heading, five-feet-four-and-a-half-inches as measured by the carpenter's tape she carried for just such a purpose, she found a pile of what could only be bear scat. Whether grizzly or black, she couldn't tell. This time of year, both had about the same diet. The sheer size of the sample would suggest a male grizzly but black bears grew nearly as large at the upper end of their scale. For unscientific reasons, Anna felt certain it was not only grizzly scat but that of her own personal grizzly.

Given its half-melted then dried consistency, the scat had been left before the rain but not too long before. If it had been deposited much before the storm, it would have dried more completely. The downpour would have reduced it to its component parts, not merely smoothed it over

An educated guess put the age of this sample at five or six days, seven at the outside. Around the time of Mrs. Van Slyke's death not twenty yards away, around the time the flesh cut from her face had been cached in the tree.

The killer had been here. *The* bear—or a bear—had been here. It was conceivable the smell of the meat in the plastic bags overhead had attracted a passing animal. Their noses were exceptionally keen. But Anna could find no indication this bear made any effort to retrieve his prize: no claw marks on the trunk or lower branches, no disturbed leaf litter or soil around the tree as might be expected from a frustrated three-hundred-pound scavenger.

It appeared as if the bear had simply come to this minuscule clearing, quietly relieved himself and went on. No law against that. Anna thought of the old joke "Where does a bear shit in the woods?" and smiled in spite of herself.

Too much coincidence, though. Bears, grizzly and otherwise, were high-profile inhabitants of Glacier National Park, but given the park's forty-one hundred square kilometers, there weren't all that many of them. According to Resource Management statistics, less than three hundred. One of the things the DNA study would do was give a more accurate count. Wishing she'd thought to pack one of Joan's handy scat sample bottles, Anna made do with another evidence bag—plastic this time—and procured a spoonful for the bear researcher. Anna noted a few of the standard bear leavings: berry seeds, twigs, grasses, most in mint condition. The bulk of this scat sample was made up of a dull brown-gray grainy matter that looked to be closer to digested dirt than plant matter. Another mystery for Joan. As long as there weren't buttons or buckles or human fingerbones, Anna couldn't get too excited.

She was glad to leave the pine clearing, scared to reenter the thick of the brush. It was an act of will to move up the side of the mountain through the obscuring undergrowth at a sensible pace. The urge to claw her way frantically out of the shrubbery didn't abate till she was not only in the open sunny world of West Flattop Trail but upon Ponce's broad back. Cowboys were braver on horseback. It was a little known codicil to the code of the west.

For no reason more logical than a bad case of the willies, Anna put a couple of miles between her and the flesh-eating pine tree. At a bend in the trail, a hillside of broken stones created a thousand unique, earth-bearing planters displaying such a breathtaking show of yellows, blues and reds that Anna wondered how human gardeners could bear to enter the competition. She tethered Ponce to a downed tree deep in tasty grasses and emptied her pack: water, lunch, map, evidence packets. Lunch first, she decided. Scrambling up and down the tree had given her the insistent appetite of an active child.

A peanut butter and honey sandwich under her belt, she was better able to concentrate on her find. Donning a new pair of latex gloves, she examined the torn bags, all that was left of the macabre food cache. The blood, she had little doubt, would turn out to be that of Carolyn Van Slyke. As she'd discerned in the tree, other than these sinister smears, the plastic baggies had nothing to tell her. With its sophisticated equipment, the lab might do better.

The blue sack was slightly more forthcoming. Gray-green dust and a pale yellow residue of a delicate almost glittering nature, like pollen but more reflective, streaked the fabric. Whatever the substance was, it had been scuffed onto the sack recently. Perhaps the lab could use it to tell where in the park the bag had been before it was shanghaied into service as a ditty bag for the deceased. In a civilized environment, that information might lead to the killer. Here, time was a deciding factor. The days it would take to get the bag down to West Glacier, then to the lab and back, would be too long. The killer would no longer be "living" in the same place.

Having returned the evidence to storage and divested herself of the surgical gloves, she unwrapped her second sandwich. Her fingers smelled of the talc used in the gloves and tainted her enjoyment of the peanut butter. Ignoring that and the busy ticklings of flies, she leaned against the log where Ponce was tied and listened to the reassuring tearing sounds as he went on with his picnic.

The killer was still in the park. Either that or Anna's intuition had finally slipped over into paranoia. That was a distinct possibility. Sitting in the sun, in a world where she had felt comfortable and whole much of her adult life, she was unpleasantly aware that she gasped and started at every noise. Her eyes never ceased scanning the horizon, alert for danger.

Though the most obvious, the wilderness wasn't the only thing she was at odds with. With the possible exception of Joan Rand, Anna had not had anything even resembling a genuine connection with another human being since she'd come to Glacier.

She thought of Sheriff Paul Davidson, her—her what? Her boyfriend? Her sweetheart? Or merely her lover? Paul was a good man and once, a long, long time ago in mind, two weeks ago by the calendar, she'd fancied herself falling in love with him. Since her adventures began in Glacier he'd scarcely crossed her mind. She'd not even called Molly though she'd told herself she would. There was something about this case that was causing her to isolate.

Anna snorted. Sensing an equine conversation in the offing, Ponce snorted back. "Isolate myself more than usual," Anna said to him. Ponce lost interest once she reverted to the human tongue. He returned to his grazing.

Humans were tribal creatures. Isolation was a form of pun-
ishment so extreme even in prisons it was only used for serious
breaches of conduct. Those who isolated themselves usually suffered as a consequence. Anna'd long been aware of the tiny
cracks in what passed for normalcy when she'd purposely been
too long alone, locked inside the ivory tower of bone that served
as skull.

Shifting position, her back to the trail so her ever-vigilant eyes
could keep watch on the woods, she considered her slow with-
drawal. The unseen scratchings of a small woodland beast sent
her pulse rate up and she realized what it was. She had been dis-
possessed, made homeless. Not removed from her house and cat
and dog in Mississippi—the park housing she enjoyed on the
Natchez Trace Parkway was simply one in a chain of way stations. Her home, where she felt safe and centered, had always
been the wild country. Towns, streets, houses, dumpsters, PTA
meetings—that was where evil lurked. In the backcountry was
only the often pitiless but never malicious work of the gods.

In Glacier that amoral purity was gone. A wrongness stalked.
Had it been only the warped and hostile actions of people, Anna
would not have felt the same. But it wasn't. Nature herself was
being unnatural. The bear that had torn up their camp was behaving in a creepy, unbearlike way. When human beings were evil
they were merely, if the Christian teaching was to be believed, ex-
ercising their God-given right to free will. When nature got personal, then whatever passed for Satan was surely afoot.

No wonder she'd bonded so completely with Joan Rand,
Anna thought. The researcher was the only person she could talk
to about their bear. Joan had been there. Joan felt it. To others,
even Molly or Paul, she would seem just another scared tourist
anthropomorphizing and exaggerating, the sort who submit reports in lilac ink of grizzlies juggling hedgehogs.

The next hour was spent riding back to Fifty Mountain in hopes Bill
McCaskil would have returned. But for a brief interlude with two
visitors from Washington State, an incredibly chirpy middle-aged
man hiking with a serene and homely woman Anna presumed was
his wife, she spoke with no one. The Washingtonian had been afire
with the news that there was a "Boone and Crockett elk" a mile

down the trail that Anna must see. The animal had moved on by the time she and Ponce came to where it was sighted and she was mildly disappointed. She'd never heard a creature referred to as a "Boone and Crockett" but given Daniel Boone and Davy Crockett's legendary stature, it must have been a grand old bull.

Bill McCaskil had gone the way of the elk. His campsite was empty, pack gone from the tree in front of his tent. What Anna had intended to ask him she wasn't sure but she needed to do something with her time. And though it was so uncharacteristic she didn't recognize the motivation, she wanted to do something around other people.

Against the wishes of both his son and Chief Ranger Ruick, Lester Van Slyke had hiked back to Flattop. He was taking up residence in his abandoned camp when Anna walked down from McCaskil's site.

Les was gray with the effort the twelve-mile walk had cost him—a coronary wandering around in shiny new boots. He carried an NPS radio, probably at the insistence of Harry Ruick. Other than that he seemed as ill-prepared for the rigors of camping as ever. He didn't want to talk to her, didn't want to explain his persistence in remaining in the backcountry, didn't want to discuss his former wife's violent behavior. After a quarter of an hour she was glad to leave him in peace and start back the way she'd come, returning to the tiny meadow where she, Joan and Rory had first set up camp.

It was as it had been before the bear attack. New tents were pitched, not where the old had been, but on the far side of the flat rock as if Joan, or more likely Rory, had suffered an attack of superstition and decided the old pattern had to be broken. Food and other bear attractants were cached high in a tree. A different one from where Rory's stepmother's corpse had hung.

The researchers were not in evidence. Anna watered Ponce at the little stream that cut through the clearing, found on her topo the place Joan had marked the next hair trap to be disassembled, then remounted and set out to find them. Ponce, erroneously thinking his day's work had been done, carried her with ill grace.

He was further discomfited when she found the others and it fell to him to carry the heavy rolls of barbed wire and the researchers' packs to the site of the next hair trap. Anna, leading Ponce, walked beside Joan. Rory chose to trail behind for reasons of his own. Buck walked with him but the two didn't speak. Anna was not offended at their choice. It wasn't that she disliked Rory; it was more that he carried about him an oppressive darkness, as if neurosis or deep injury had created in him a small black hole into which good cheer and rationality were sucked away.

A day's hard work in rough country had put Joan in a good mood. The cobwebs left by generating reports and packaging samples for the lab were burned away.

"This trap was pretty paltry pickin's," she said. The heat from her face made her brow glisten and the top quarter of her glasses fog up. That and the alder leaves poking through her hair gave her a look of the clichéd mad scientist. "No scat. A few wisps of hair. But at least the love scent hadn't been torn down. This one must have been hung high enough." Joan babbled on happily about barbed wire, lab reports and other resource-manager-type details. Anna half listened, enjoying companionship not content. After a quarter of an hour the going became rugged, the ground broken and the scrub dense. Conversation was replaced by heavy breathing and aggravated grunts. Ponce punished Anna for the arduous duty by pushing her in the middle of the back with his long bony face just infrequently enough she never expected it.

The new hair trap was to be strung up less than half a mile from the old. Wire taut, love scent high and inviting, rotten wood piled and doused with the irresistibly vile blood lure, they finished near six that evening. The work cleansed Anna's psyche as it had Joan's and she managed the trip back to camp restfully free of dark forebodings and acid contemplations. Off the beaten paths, they encountered no park visitors and Anna was glad. At peace, for the moment, in her own reality, she had no desire to be dragged into anyone else's.

In an unusual burst of intraspecies appreciation, she remembered the chipper fellow from Washington who had delighted her with his odd turn of phrase.

Anna decided to share. "I heard something funny today. A guy'd seen a big bull elk and called him a 'Boone and Crockett' elk." Joan and Buck looked blank. "Like in Daniel Boone, Davy Crockett," Anna explained. "You know, bigger than life." Still nothing. Gifts rebuffed, she was annoyed.

"Shall we tell her?" Buck asked.

"I think not," Joan said. "You don't know her like I do. She is exhibiting an uncharacteristic enjoyment in bipeds. It's a train of thought that would be a shame to derail so close to the station."

"Tell me what?" Anna demanded.

"She insists," Joan said.

"'Boone and Crockett' are the ultimate word on trophy animals," Buck told her. "They have a whole rating system depending on the size of the animals. Well . . . the size of their heads. That's where the numbers come in."

"My little guy was talking about the elk *dead?*" Anna was aghast.

"As he pictured him on the wall of his den," Buck confirmed.

The creepiness that had been temporarily held at bay by the advent of real work returned. Even apparent innocents from the great state of Washington harbored deadly intentions.

It wasn't until they'd been back in camp for an hour or more and been revived by an internal application of hot drinks that she spoke again and then it was of the dark subjects that had been consuming her mind.

Summarily banishing Buck and Rory simply because she did not wish to feel the impact of a stranger in the first instance and an adolescent in the second, Anna fired up the hissing glare of a Coleman lantern, set it on the wide flat table of stone and spread out her gruesome evidence collection for Joan's scientific perusal.

"I don't know diddly about human forensic pathology," Joan warned her as they knelt like aging White Rock fairies on the edge of the stone.

"All evil is not human," Anna said apropos of nothing but the growing unease Glacier's backcountry had instilled in her.

"If not, it stems from humans," Joan said, either exposing a cynical streak Anna hadn't suspected or infected with Anna's pervasive sense of dislocation.

Anna didn't argue with her. "Look at the pieces left of the blue bag," she said. "See here where it's streaked with dust and this yellow pollenlike stuff? I can't remember seeing anything hereabouts that would leave residue like this. Not that I've been looking," she admitted.

Joan shoved her glasses up on her head the better to see close up and, fabric pinched delicately between gloved fingers and thumbs, she examined it in the cold and noisy light from the Coleman. After a minute of two of this she stopped, retrieved a large Sherlock-Holmes-style magnifying glass from her day pack, said, "I wish I had my microscope," and studied the torn fabric for several minutes more.

"In my book, dust is dust is dust," she said at last and returned the navy stuff bag to Anna. "This is fine, grayish green, could be from argillite—alpine talus. Up high. Way high. Like tops of mountains. Or it could have come from under the bookcase in my bedroom. Lab tests would tell you what it's made of and maybe what kind of rocks it came from but, contrary to public opinion, rocks are not stationary. They slide and tumble, fall, wash down creeks.

"The yellow dust is different. I can't be a hundred percent sure but I don't think it is pollen. It looks more like scales, the weensy feathery scales you'd find on the wings of moths or butterflies."

Anna wasn't completely flummoxed. On Isle Royale, just outside the screen doors of most of the lean-tos, she'd seen butterflies crowd together en masse. They came to get the salts left behind by sleepy campers who, rather than stumble through the dark to the pit toilet, merely stood on the shelter step to urinate.

"Something in the bag attracted butterflies? A lot of butterflies?" As she said it, Anna knew it made little sense. Even if they'd been drawn to the bag in great numbers, when they beat their tiny wings, the scales didn't fall off.

"Not exactly. Above treeline we have incredible blooms of army cutworm moths June through September. The moths lay their eggs on the Great Plains and the caterpillars mature there. Then they migrate to the Rockies to feed. In the fall they go back. Lay eggs and die. There're not so many as there once were. They spray crops in Iowa, we lose moths in Montana. An argument for global environmental policies local politicians won't hear. Putting that together with the white dust, I'm guessing your bag was set down or dragged around somewhere above treeline on Mount Stimpson or Mount Cleveland or, oh, shoot, I don't know, one of them. We get aggregations of the cutworm moths from about twenty-one hundred meters in elevation up to about twenty-eight hundred meters. They like south and southwest faces." Joan took in the dark jagged ring of mountains cutting into the night sky around Flattop.

Sick of man-made light and racket, Anna turned off the lantern. In the sudden and blessed balm of night's silence, the two of them sat without speaking, watching the mountain peaks from where the blue sack had purportedly traveled.

The moon was waning, but in the thin clear air over the Rockies, its light was strong. Trees inked black on the shoulders of the mountains. Above their reach slivers of glaciers and the pale, much shattered talus that spent a majority of its life beneath the snow, caught the moonlight. The longer Anna stared the brighter the peaks became until, in their glory, they kindled a healing awe within her. "I wouldn't think there'd be much in that part of the world to attract people."

Joan laughed. "You sound so wistful. There's not much. Hardly anybody goes up there. Mountain goats."

"Trails?" Anna asked.

"Not that high."

"Just goats? I thought the bears denned at the higher elevations."

"Higher. Not that high. They do go up there in summer, though. The moths are a major source of protein for the grizzlies. They tear up whole hillsides of alpine talus, turning over the rocks and licking up the moths. See? Global. Spray wheat in Minnesota, starve a grizzly in the Rockies. Who'd know?"

"They know now," Anna pointed out. Neither bothered to add, "Who'd care?" Just a small circle of friends, as the old song went.

"Our butcher went up there for some reason," Anna said after a while. "Since he apparently isn't in the park to enjoy nature—at least not as we like to think of it—he must have had a pressing reason to travel so far off the beaten path. Ponce will not be pleased when I tell him tomorrow's itinerary."

Anna's radio ended further speculation.

"Your hunch paid off," Ruick said after they'd exchanged the requisite call numbers. "The prints on the second topo found in the army coat match those Bill McCaskil put on file when he was arrested for fraud. Looks like the victim was wearing his coat when she was killed."

16

Anna did not ride to Fifty Mountain at first light. She was under strict orders from Harry to delay until the cavalry arrived in the person of four law enforcement rangers from down in the valley.

Camp in the ill-fated meadow with its altar rock was broken. Joan and Rory, alone by necessity and Joan's choice now that Buck and Anna were needed elsewhere, left to service the next hair trap on Joan's list. This one was on the far eastern edge of Flattop Mountain near the confluence of Mineral and Cattle King creeks. After they'd gone, Anna packed her gear on Ponce not knowing when she would be rejoining the bear DNA research project as a productive member.

Far from chafing at the delay, she was glad to saunter over with Buck around noon. Several broken bones and knife wounds ago she'd lost her taste for facing unsavory types on equal terms. No right-thinking law enforcement officer wanted a fair fight.

When they arrived, the chief ranger and four others whom Anna didn't recognize were sitting in the food preparation area with Lester Van Slyke, talking in low voices. Ruick came over to where Anna tethered Ponce to the hitching rail.

"Our bird has flown the coop," he said, leaning on the rail, a water bottle held easily in one hand. Ruick seemed at home, in control everywhere Anna had an opportunity to observe him. "Les said he was here last night, saw him go to the outhouse once. He didn't use the food prep area or speak to anybody as far as Les noticed. Then Les sees him all packed up and heading out in the dark."

"What time?" Anna asked.

"Around eight, eight-thirty." Their eyes met. Anna hadn't out-thought him. "He knew we were coming to have a word."

"Les has a radio," Anna said.

"That's crossed my mind. You think Les told him? Some kind of conspiracy? Hired assassin?" Ruick laughed and Anna found herself laughing with him. Outside the confines of a movie theater the phrases sounded absurd. Lester Van Slyke from Seattle, Washington, hiring a con man with no history of doing hits for pay to murder his abusive wife in the Montana wilderness.

"People have their own twisted logic," Anna said, responding as much to her thoughts as Ruick's words. "There's too many ties for there not to be some kind of a connection." She leaned on the rail, elbow close to Ponce's nose. Occasionally she felt the flick of his tail on her backside and was content to let him keep the flies off the both of them. "Maybe we've been going at the connection from the wrong side," she said, the theory forming as she spoke. "Because it was Mrs. Van Slyke who was killed I've been trying to connect her with McCaskil as an enemy. McCaskil in the role of killer: come on purpose to kill her for his own reasons, a chance psychotic episode in which he kills her, or hired by the abused husband to do the deed. What if Mrs. Van Slyke and McCaskil were pals, in league for something more natural to a divorce lawyer and a fraud? She was wearing his coat when she was killed. Or at least a coat with his topographical map in the pocket. What if they were hatching some scheme that went sour? Mrs. Van Slyke dies. McCaskil stays in the park to finish his business? He sure doesn't fit the profile of a nature-lover and backwoodsman."

"Where does that leave our murderer?"

"I don't know. Maybe a falling out among thieves?"

"Or we're back to Les. If he weren't so . . ." Ruick glanced over his shoulder at the group on the hill behind them. ". . . so damned ineffectual, I'd have found some reason to arrest him by now."

Ruick squirted water into his mouth and swooshed it around more to entertain himself than to quench any real thirst. "What kind of fraud could a city-bred con man pull up here? Glacier's got nothing in the way of gold, silver, precious stones, gas, oil. One of the reasons it's been left alone is nobody ever figured out how to make any money out of it."

"Timber?"

Ruick looked at her. Not only was the terrain too rugged to log, cutting and stealing timber wasn't exactly a subtle crime. In a park where helicopter tours flew over on a daily basis, even a small-scale operation would be shut down less than twenty-four hours after it started.

"Right," Anna said. "Rare plants?"

Harry shook his head.

"Poaching?"

"Sure, some. But why bother? There are ranches just over the hill in British Columbia where you can legally shoot elk, bear, you name it. And since they're hand-raised, you can get 'em trophy-sized. They don't count that way, not with the big-league hunters. They insist the prey be 'wild.' But there's probably ways around that."

Ruick had pretty much shot down any ideas Anna had, so she said nothing. She couldn't figure out if this particular murder had too many clues and too many suspects, or too few. Why carve the face but not enough to confuse identification? What was easily obtained or carried into the backcountry that could deliver a blow powerful enough to sever the spinal cord yet soft enough not to crush or crack the skull? Why was the victim wearing a stranger's coat? Why didn't everybody leave right away? McCaskil, Lester, Rory—they had to know they were or could be suspects. If they'd done it, why stay? If they *hadn't* done it, why stay?

"We'll ask the s.o.b. when we find him," Ruick said philosophically.

Anna'd told him in greater detail about the macabre tree ornament she'd found near where Carolyn's body had been dumped. As she filled the chief ranger in on the details, she wished she'd never mentioned it over the radio. Too many listeners.

Ruick took possession of the ripped and bloody bags, forming the next link in the chain of evidence. He and his rangers had come to Flattop on horseback. One man would be sent back down to take Anna's find to the lab. The remaining three and Harry would track down McCaskil if they could.

Decisions to disturb the wilderness aspect of a national park were not made lightly. Helicopters, bulldozers, chainsaws, even tracking dogs were not brought in at the first whimpering of human discomfort. In Anna's years of watching park politics, some of the most courageous choices she'd seen upper management make were those made *not* to pour technology on a problem, not to bring in guns and dogs and forklifts and borate bombers, but to fight nature on nature's terms. Or, more courageous still, not to fight at all, to let the fire burn, the river change course, the historic crumble without replacement.

Often enough to make it an act of bravery, these administrators lost their careers. The public hated nature when she wasn't in their control. Ruick had chosen to hunt William McCaskil on foot and horseback. The body recovery of Carolyn Van Slyke had already invaded the sanctity of the park experience enough. If Ruick was wrong, if he didn't catch McCaskil and McCaskil turned out to be Van Slyke's killer and killed another visitor, Ruick would pay the price. He'd probably end his days as a chief ranger at some Civil War battlefield two acres across.

Anna respected him for it. Someday she'd have to tell him so. For today she had ground to cover. She was not to take part in the manhunt but to head above treeline to where the moths came to breed and die, where the stones were bleached, where the navy-blue stuff sack had traveled.

The night before, Joan had given Anna a crash course on the grizzly and the army cutworm moth. There were nine identified moth aggregation sites in Glacier that were known to be used by the bears. All were above twenty-one hundred meters in elevation, all on south- or west-facing slopes. The moths aggregated in glacial cirques on talus right below steeper headwalls.

Joan had ended the lesson with strongly voiced disapproval of Anna's venturing into any of the aggregation sites. As a researcher she did not like the impact on the bears that was inevitable when human beings—even one so small and light-footed as Anna—penetrated areas where the animals traditionally roamed undisturbed. As a good-hearted woman she was opposed to Anna's venturing into feeding grounds used predominantly by females with cubs and sub-adult bears during the peak of their use season.

"You're just making yourself an attractive nuisance," Joan summed up. "A recipe for disaster."

"No pun intended," Buck added, stone-faced.

"Ranger-on-a-stick," Rory said.

Warnings and disclaimers given, Joan had begrudgingly gone over the map, pointing out the sites closest to Flattop Mountain.

Anna took out the topo Joan had marked and showed it to Harry. Logic, a commodity to all appearances singularly lacking in the individual they pursued, suggested the aggregation site Joan had circled on the southern slope of Cathedral Peak. Cathedral, over seventy-six hundred feet high, was the only army cutworm moth site within easy—using the term loosely—commuting distance from Flattop, where the moth-dusted bag had been found. Given the amounts of both moth-wing powder and the grayish-green Joan guessed were traces of argillite remaining on the fabric, the bag had not traveled too far or too long between its dust collecting days and its incarnation as a receptacle for human flesh.

The country Anna was headed into was rugged and steep and dry. Too much for the shamble-footed Ponce. He would have the night off and Anna would walk. Much of the time she would be scrambling. There were no trails, no lakes, no creeks. Only seep springs, and that only if they still had water. Though the cirque she sought was not far in miles, it was a long way in time and energy. Probably she would need to spend the night on the mountain. There would be no trees in which to cache food and, if this aggregation site was being used, grizzlies, mostly females with cubs, would be in attendance. Toothpaste, insect repellent lip balm, and soap remained at Fifty Mountain. Anna ate as much food as she could and packed just enough for one more meal. There would be no breakfast the following morning. Because of the steepness of the terrain she traveled light: no tent, no stove, just camera, tarp, down vest, sleeping bag, water and filter. Even a seep spring could produce enough to refill canteens if one was patient. Or thirsty.

By one-thirty she was headed east away from Fifty Mountain. For the first mile or so, she walked Highline, an improved trail that followed the ridge east of Flattop Mountain, winding back to the Going to the Sun Road where the trailhead was. At about seventy-two hundred feet in elevation, where Highline dog-legged south, Anna turned north, traveling cross-country toward the glacial cirque below Cathedral Peak's south-southwestern slope.

High as she was, even small changes in altitude marked the

landscape dramatically. Soil grew rocky and rust-colored. In the distance, on the stern face of the mountain, she noticed small white specks: mountain goats feeding and rambling in their impossible places. Vegetation thinned till only the hardiest of pines still grew. A life of fighting showed in stunted and twisted limbs. Anna felt honored to be moving amid this stalwart troop of rebels battered by the elements but still alive. Much of the time, she traveled baboonlike on feet and hands, the slopes slippery with broken stone and a meager covering of shortened needles the pines let go. Periodically she stopped to rest and, braced against a gnarly trunk, looked westward across the emerald green meadows north of Fifty Mountain Camp to the blue-forested shanks of the mountains beyond. In this land of abundance, of water and game, other deserts thrust up: mountaintops like the one she hoped to gain where nothing grew and the life of rocks was visible to the naked eye.

Just after four p.m. she scaled the last stone massif, a forty-foot gray wall of crumbling argillite that showed its treachery in tens of millions of cracks and crevices, in the deep pile of shattered stone heaped at its base. Glacier was not a park favored by climbers. The rock formations that created its mountains were of soft stuff that would not hold pitons, ledges that could fall away at the merest hint of weight.

A half-mile's scrambling through dwarf pines brought her to just beneath the dramatic upthrust of Cathedral Peak. There lay a classic cirque, a chunk of the mountain gouged out by glacial movement leaving a steep amphitheater two or three hundred yards across and half again that long. Its uppermost end was marked by another massif. From there up was the ever-more-vertical run to the mountain's peak. A quarter of the cirque was still covered in snow. In midsummer, Anna knew it would be of the dry crusty variety of no use for melting and drinking. The rest of the cirque was floored in grayish-green alpine talus, flat loose stones ranging in size from teacups to tabletops.

At present the landscape was free of bears. Joan had told her the pattern of both grizzlies and black bears was to feed on the moths in the morning, rest nearby through the middle of the day, then feed again in the evening.

The long climb had tired Anna but it behooved her to make her explorations during the bears' off time. Just because she couldn't see them didn't mean they weren't around. Wild animals seldom flopped down to nap in plain view. Even in a place they'd always known as safe they tended to hide themselves away. An area as apparently free of secrets as the cirque could easily have hollows beneath stones. Surrounding rocks might harbor caves or even dens, though the bears tended to den up slightly lower, below treeline.

At this altitude there was nearly always wind, often greater than sixty kilometers an hour. In summer it came mostly from the southwest, but with no protection, it blew cold, and as the sweat from the climb dried, Anna grew chilled. Zipping herself into her down vest she rallied her shaking legs and trudged up the incline to the bottom of the cirque. The aggregations of the cutworm moths, and so the feeding grounds of the bears, were usually at the head of the cirques below the massifs. As she picked her way upward over the talus, fatigue was replaced with the not completely unpleasant hyperawareness Daniel might have felt in the lions' den.

Not every aggregation was fed on every day. Like everyone else, bears had their trends and preferences. This site had not been monitored since 1995. Glacier researchers prided themselves not only on the quality of their studies but on completing them in the least obtrusive manner. Joan had lectured Anna on the evils of disturbing the site with her presence, then made her promise to observe carefully and take accurate notes. Since she must defile this bit of habitat with her essence, she might as well come away with data.

The observation Anna was most interested in at the moment was that of beds. Habitually the bears fed from six a.m. till one p.m. then rested till around six in the evening. For their siestas they dug beds in the scree or the snow. From the air the sleeping beasts might be easily seen. At ground level it would be way too easy to stumble into the middle of somebody's nap.

Having reached the headwall of the cirque unharmed, Anna found a perch atop a square chunk of argillite tumbled down from on high, and took out her binoculars. Her eyes would cause less disturbance than her feet. Not to mention they were not as tired. Mentally gridding the long crescent-shaped area, she searched the ground. There were many piles of scat; most looked old and dried-up, but a closer view would be needed to be sure.

She spotted five of the oval-shaped excavations she'd been told to look for and was astounded once more at the sheer physical power of the grizzlies. In places, the digging went down a foot or more, and the volume of rock moved was in the tons.

Content she was alone and would not be providing anyone an afternoon snack, she put aside the glasses and slid off her rock. Fascinating as bears' lives were, she had not spent the day scratching up a mountain in search of that, but of traces of a person carrying a navy-blue stuff sack. Tracking over a stone surface, even soft argillite, was not a promising prospect. She would have to hope for luck and, if the gods were smiling, litter.

Working slowly, her attention divided between the ground and a horizon that could suddenly bloom with bears, she moved along the base of the massif. There were abundant samples of bear scat but she found nothing that looked to be fresher than two or three days. The scats were thick with the tiny fragmented exoskeletons of the moths, the only part of the insect that provided no nutrients. Joan would be disappointed, but Anna chose not to take the time to collect any samples.

The excavated ovals had been licked clean but Anna did see a number of itinerant moths. The cutworms were unprepossessing little yellow creatures with powdery wings. Where the bug hunting had been particularly good the yellow scales left streaks on the pale talus. In a place like this, then, the blue sack must have been laid down or dragged. To what purpose, Anna could not imagine. The cirques were dry, windswept, dangerous and hard to get to. Who would wander here?

A thought surfaced, so ugly it stopped her in her tracks. Bear researchers would come here. Men or women with an overweening interest in *Ursus horribilis*. They would be able to move through the park unremarked. They would be the ones who would wish to remain in Glacier regardless of who they'd killed because the bears were here, their work was here.

Anna sat down abruptly, scarcely noticing the bite the angular stones tried to take out of her behind. Carolyn Van Slyke was the mother of a bear researcher—a temporary baby bear researcher, true, but it was a link. Carolyn was a photographer with no film, murdered, sliced up, bits of her put in a stuff sack smeared with dust and scales from an extremely out-of-the-way bear eatery.

Had she accidentally or otherwise been photographing a Glacier bear researcher doing something for, against or to a grizzly that they oughtn't, and then was killed because of it and the telltale film stolen?

The train of thought, rattling along the track at breakneck speed, derailed suddenly, upset by the same old questions: Killed her with what? Carved her face why? And what could a researcher be doing that was so vile that an observer must die lest she tell? People could harass the bears but it was the harassers that came out the worse for wear. For a chilling moment Anna was jerked back into the tent in the dark, the bear destroying the camp. The shallow, almost healed scratch on her shoulder began to itch.

Murder by bear? Could someone who knew what he was about creep into a camp at night and salt it with love scent or blood lure in hopes of enticing disaster?

Sure.

Could Rory have done it?

Easily.

Joan Rand, huddled in the night, matching Anna scream for scream, was blessedly free of suspicion. She had the only genuinely ironclad alibi: she'd been with the investigating officer at the time of the incident.

A bear could be attracted in that manner. It wasn't guaranteed but definitely possible. That the bear would kill anybody was a long shot, and that it would kill a specific target so long as to be preposterous. It followed, then, that if the bear had been intentionally attracted to their camp and if the individual responsible for it was sane, the bear had been meant only to frighten or, with luck, injure one of them. If universal malice was ruled out as a motive, the only things left were revenge on Anna, Joan or, maybe, Rory—if he wasn't the perpetrator—or a desire to frighten them off from what they were doing.

Because in doing what they were doing they would discover what *he* was doing.

Anna laughed out loud, startling herself with the sudden noise. "What the hell were we doing?" she asked the rocks and bugs. "Collecting information on bears," she answered herself.

Like Carolyn Van Slyke was with her camera?

Like Anna appeared to be doing right now?

The wind grew a little colder, the cirque a little more isolated. Anna waited for a cloud to pass over the sun to complete the picture, but the clear summer sky wouldn't cooperate. Breathing deeply of air so cool and thin and pure it seemed to negate the possibility of deceit in any who breathed it, she stared down the talus-raddled cirque and across the green and black summit of Flattop. What on earth could a bear researcher need so desperately to hide?

The puzzle she'd been so assiduously working on began to deconstruct. How, if at all, did Bill McCaskil with his borrowed coat and his history of financial fraud fit into the picture? There was money in research. Where there was money there could be con men trying to get it. Those sorts of evils transpired in offices over phone lines. The perpetrators didn't actually go into the woods where the work was being done. There was no money at that end of the stick.

Thinking was getting her nowhere, and sitting motionless in the wind, she was getting cold. Anna returned to her task. The rocks were soft enough that in many places marks had been left on their surfaces by the claws of the grizzlies. Of the bear family, the grizzly was one of the most perfectly adapted to digging. The four-inch claws were virtually unbreakable and the characteristic hump on the shoulders, a silhouette that struck fear into the human observer rather like that of a shark's fin cutting through the water, was a lump of muscles that provided the bears with tremendous power in their forelegs. The better for digging up moths.

Anna saw residue of that power in the claw-scored argillite and the upheaval of tons of rock in the width of the cirque. Of the habits of the bears, she learned a great deal over the next couple of hours. Of the person who had visited an aggregation in the last few days she found nothing, not so much as a gum wrapper.

The magic hour was approaching. Bears siesta'd from thirteen hundred to eighteen hundred hours, Joan had said. Anna knew the numbers were approximate, varying, one would assume, from bear to bear. Still, as the minute hand on her watch closed the gap between five-thirty and six o'clock, she grew increasingly nervous.

Earlier, from her elevated perch, she had spotted five oval excavation areas. She'd inspected three. Alert for signs of returning diners, she hurried toward the fourth. She never got there. Halfway between the third and fourth was a bear dig of a very different aspect. It was linear, the rocks turned over in neat rows and not as deep, six to eight inches at most.

Things natural tended to eschew straight lines. Lines were a mathematical construct taught to the disordered minds of children until, in adulthood, people favored them, writing, digging, planting and, when possible, walking in them.

On hands and knees, Anna crawled along the linear upset of talus. Rocks had not been dug per se, but pried loose and over-turned. On closer inspection she could see marks in the stone; not the evenly spaced scrape of claws but sharp, angular scratches that had to have been made with a shovel or Pulaski. A person, most probably the person Anna sought, had been to the cirque for the same reason as the bears: to dig up army cutworm moths.

Sitting on her heels, eyes roaming the edges of the depression for interlopers of any species, she thought about the strange young man, Geoffrey Mickleson-Nicholson. The day they'd seen him, before the grizzly had come to their camp, they had passed a field of glacier lilies, another preferred food of the Glacier bear population. Someone with a spade had been digging them up. Most likely the obvious choice: Geoffrey Whoever. At the time it seemed of little importance. Illegal certainly, but one man with a shovel and a backpack was not going to dig the lilies to extinction.

There was nothing to indicate the digger of moths was the same person as the digger of lilies except that people pilfering the natural food of bears was an oddity. Rare to catch one doing it; statistically improbable to find two. The young man with the lovely smile and the suspicious habits was not a bear researcher; Joan would have known him. At least he wasn't a bear researcher in Glacier.

Could an adolescent rogue researcher be murderously mess-ing about with Glacier's grizzlies? The concept was absurd but Anna didn't throw it out entirely. She merely consigned it to the heap in her brain where other absurdities connected with this case lay.

Because it was cold and she was tired and the sun was going to be down in a couple of hours, she thought of werewolves. As a rational westerner, Anna didn't believe in the existence of the mythical monsters. As the sister of an eminent psychiatrist, she knew there were nutcases wandering the moonlit streets who sincerely believed they were werewolves. People suffering from lycanthropy. On rare but recorded occasions these individuals lived out their psychosis to the point of killing, ripping out throats and drinking blood as they believed they must in their wolflike state. Was it possible a person could believe himself a grizzly? Why not? People believed they were Napoleon, the Virgin Mary, the reincarnation of Michelangelo. In Mississippi, Anna'd dealt with a woman who believed herself to be the mother of eight children, all penguins.

Why not a bear?

Like those suffering from lycanthropy, could the psychosis go so far as to drive the sufferer to seek to live as a bear would live, eat as a bear would eat and kill as a bear would kill?

Anna thought back on the night she and Joan had been visited. Neither of them had seen an animal, merely heard what they believed to be an animal. They had only Rory's word for it that there'd been a bear and Rory was not exactly the poster boy for mental stability.

A deep and rotten core of fear opened in Anna, making her nauseated. She and Buck had been siphoned off to assist Ruick. Joan was alone in an isolated camp with Rory Van Slyke, an excellent candidate for the Bear Boy.

"Wait, wait, wait," Anna said, calming herself. Rory could have done many things but he couldn't have come to the cirque with a navy stuff bag, and it had not been he who had been digging lilies. The altitude, the solitude, a long day's work were scrambling her thoughts.

Creating a trancelike state induced by self-hypnosis that allows the fears and wish-images of the subconscious mind to be accessed by the conscious mind. Anna'd heard Molly say that in a lecture at Yale once ten years before. Then, she'd thought it a wonderfully phrased crock of shit. Now she wasn't so sure.

"Werebears," she said out loud to mock herself out of the heebie-jeebies.

It didn't work. The missing flesh so carefully cut from the face of Mrs. Van Slyke—a person using a knife rather than teeth and claws to pull the edible flesh from the prey? An absorbing if macabre theory. Much that was known didn't fit with the were-bear tale: the specificity and tidiness of the flesh removal, caching the flesh, stealing film, moving and hiding the body.

Anna put it from her mind and concentrated on trying to track the individual with the shovel. Shovel: that was a reassuring indicator of sanity. A person so far gone with mental illness as to imagine himself a bear by night would surely dig with his hands.

Six o'clock; time was up but Anna was not finished.

Clearing her mind of everything that was not visible on the ground, she slid easily into the tracker's zone, a quiet place where one could wait for as long as need be for the minutest sign to come clear. The shovel dig was fresh, not more than twenty-four hours old.

The fine layer of silt on the bottoms of the overturned stones was dry on the surface but, when scratched, still retained vestiges of moisture beneath. Overturning the stones carefully, she saw that the moths licked up by real bears had here been scraped off by human hands. The trail the fingers left during the harvest was clear. The navy bag had told Anna the gatherer of moths had visited this site. Had he used the bag to store his moths to eat later? Did he eat the moths, as the bears did, al fresco, one rockful at a time?

There was no way to tell which end of the linear dig was the beginning and which was the end. Anna stood a moment choosing the most logical direction from which the digger might have come. The same way she had, south from Highline Trail. She began with the opposite end of the line of disturbed talus, the end from which he had most likely departed. Squatting on her heels, she focused loosely on the ground and waited.

The low angle of the sun was perfect for tracking. And besides herself and bears, the digger was probably the only human who'd walked here for maybe years. Had conditions been otherwise she would not have been able to track over such an inhospitable surface.

A tread mark in the dust half obliterated by what must be the print from an enormous padded paw. A scuff, straight and smooth that could be made only by the side of a shoe—leather or rubber. Four yards farther on a veritable signpost: a single slab of talus overturned by the edged tool. Why that one, Anna couldn't guess. It must have looked particularly mothy to the guy.

A puffing, like a small steam engine straining uphill, broke her concentration. Before she looked she knew what it was. She'd heard it the night of the bear visitation. Fear, sudden, new, remembered, washed down from throat to belly to bowels.

The bears had come to feed.

17

Breathing in slowly, Anna calmed herself. The breath didn't come easily. Her chest had tightened into a straitjacket of muscle. The second attempt provided better results. Fortified with oxygen, she slid her eyes in the direction from whence the sound had come. On the far eastern side of the cirque, about halfway up, a sow with two cubs, new this year, watched her. The sow was swaying back and forth, weight shifting from paw to paw, head moving in slow arcs. The cubs, less focused, divided their attention between Mom and Anna ready to do as they were told.

Anna was down on one knee, close to the ground. *Be big,* she remembered. *Stand, wave your arms above your head, make loud noises so the bear will run away,* she'd been told. *Don't make eye contact; stand in profile, be as nonthreatening as possible,* she'd been told. *Sit down, stand up, fight, fight, fight,* the old high school cheer rattled through her mind and brought with it an almost overpowering need to giggle. Almost. *Don't run.* That was one consistent rule.

She breathed again and felt, to her surprise, the fear that gripped her loosening its hold. These were real, honest-to-God bears, bears in broad daylight doing the things bears were supposed to do. Far less terrifying than the half-mad half-man, half-beast imaginings she'd allowed herself earlier. Less terrifying than the bestial slashings that came in the night.

She looked away from the trio to her escape route, the trail she'd been following toward the western side of the cirque. She was nearly there, maybe a hundred feet, then an easy scramble up a rocky escarpment eight or ten feet high. Beyond that was fifty yards of scree and then the beginning of the scruffy pine belt that marked treeline. Not that trees would save her. None were substantial enough to climb should she be so lucky as to reach them.

Anna's life now existed at the whim and pleasure of the sow. Realizing that produced an odd calm. When there was nothing to be done, one was free of the responsibility to think of how to do it. Risking a moment of eye contact, she gave the sow an almost imperceptible nod, conceding the field of battle, and returned to her tracking. Minutes passed before her concentration reasserted and she could see again. Her eyes, the ones in the back of her head, saw the sow charging, but her ears heard nothing. Anna forced herself not to look, to move slowly, close to the ground as before, seeking out signs left by the human digger who had been here before her.

When she reached the low escarpment and was as yet undevoured, she chanced another peek. The two cubs were cavorting in the talus. In the strong evening light she could see the startling pink of their tongues as they licked moths from the bottoms of rocks their mother had turned over for them. Momma Bear wasn't digging but paced back and forth between her cubs and Anna. At either end of her path, when she stopped to turn, she looked in her direction.

A bargain seemed to have been struck. If Anna went quietly away, she would be allowed to live. It was a good deal and she took it, crawling as unobtrusively up the escarpment as possible, to disappear momentarily from the bear's sight behind a natural ridge no more than two feet high.

Once safe out of sight, reaction set in and Anna realized she'd not given over to the she-bear with quite the Zenlike equanimity she'd thought. Relief rushed through her until she felt mildly hysterical, wanting to laugh and cry with equal intensity. In the end she did neither, just lay in the weakening rays of the alpine sun, letting small wordless prayers of gratitude drift from her mind to whichever god looked after bears and lady rangers.

Niceties observed, she turned her mind back to more earthly pursuits. Time had abandoned its petty pace somewhere between her first notice of man-tracks and the last farewell to the family of grizzlies. Two hours had slipped by like the shadows of westward flying birds. In thirty minutes the sun would be down. Already the light had faded to the point where tracking was becoming more difficult.

It was time to stop, to find a camp for the night, but Anna kept on. Following trail had an addictive aspect not unlike that of eating Doritos. *One more, then I'll stop,* Anna found herself promising each time she found a partial print, a scuff, a wrinkle in the scree that told of a shod footfall.

Below Cathedral Peak the mountain flared, enough earth collected to sustain plant life and provide a walking surface for animals and people. The individual Anna followed had taken the path of least resistance, traveling downhill on the tree-studded skirt at an oblique angle to the peak.

On this surface, despite the failing light, tracking grew suddenly easy. Everywhere the person stepped on the sharply angled ground a mark had been left. Anna moved forward at a footpace, stopping only twice when a clear bootprint presented itself and she paused to photograph it. At last there was some genuine information: waffle tread cross-training shoes, a man's size ten to ten and a half, not new, with a distinct wear pattern on the inside of the heels as if the shoe's owner was slightly knock-kneed.

Keeping to the curve of the mountain, she followed the prints into the stunted forest of pine. Shadows merged and light diffused but the trail remained clear. Anna forgot the coming darkness.

At a small stone abutment, rust-faced with lichen and darkened with a brow of trees so dwarfed and twisted by the weight of winter snows that they more resembled mutant shrubs than stately pines, the trail ended abruptly.

For a moment Anna was still, her eyes searching, her senses on full alert. At the base of the rocks was a cleft, three feet wide and perhaps that high; the entrance to a small cave. The twisted arms of a squat pine tree partially obscured it. A place where grizzlies might den or lunatics hide. Awakened from the narrow dream of footprints and broken needles, she became aware of how little sunlight was left, how cold the air had become, how lonely the place where the trail brought her. Her intention was to follow and find, not to confront. For that she would want backup in the form of many burly rangers. Discreet departure was the wisest course of action.

An alien noise penetrated these thoughts. It was the merest

whisper of sounds, needles sliding over one another or the shush of fabric against bark, but it shrieked against Anna's heightened senses with the force of a gale through high wires. "Shhh," she breathed to herself, though all that moved or sounded within her was the rapid beat of her heart. Noiselessly she crabbed away from the den's mouth to put her back against the rock. The sound had not come from inside but from down the hill, opposite from the direction she'd come.

The sun was long gone. The light that remained was of the clear gray quality that reminds one that the sky is not a blanket of blue benevolently spread over the earth but only the beginning of cold and impossible distances. Acutely feeling her isolation and vulnerability, Anna thought to free her radio from her pack, call in her position. She should have done it hours ago. In the all-absorbing grip of tracking, she had forgotten. Now she found herself afraid to move, to make the unavoidable noise of finding and calling. If she was invisible, unnoticed, she could not be hurt

Dread of being trapped in an external frame pack heavy with drinking water and a sleeping bag galvanized Anna and she unsnapped the harness at chest and hips and, letting the rock take the pack's weight, slid out of it. Five seconds scraping and a muffled thump and she was free. Breathing heavily as if she'd performed a terrific feat of strength and endurance, she listened again, desperate to hear over the machinations of her own heart and lungs.

A skittering watery sound of pebbles moving brought her head up an instant before a fine rain of rocks fell from the top of the incline she'd taken refuge against. With it came a huffing grunt and the heavy grind of moving stone.

Cautiously, she stepped out from the massif and looked up. Twenty yards above, something dark and lumpish, not yet a bear but, in the dull gray evening light, not entirely human either, was curled down, shoulder against a boulder three or four feet high and that much across.

The rain of pebbles stopped, and in the sudden silence Anna saw the boulder give up its tenuous hold on the unstable mountainside and begin to roll, dislodging smaller rocks as it passed. The abutment she stood near was too low, not vertical enough to provide shelter from a landslide, even a small one.

Perhaps she could not run from bears but running from people was almost always a good idea. No time to think or to re-trieve pack, water or radio, she fled headlong down the moun-tainside, angling away from the vertical, hoping the rock would roll straight. Crashing sounds of her own progress mixed with the crashing of the rock and she could not tell if the entire mountain was coming down upon her, or if her half-man half-beast had fol-lowed the rock and was upon her heels. One sound did cut through the rest. The unmistakable report of a gunshot. Just one, just once, but it lent her a burst of speed that the onset of ava-lanches and grizzlies could not.

Anna never looked back, never fell and never stopped until she was deep in the dwarf forest and had reached the ledge atop the cliff dividing the high country from the more hospitable climes significantly below treeline.

There she collapsed. A furtive look back showed no pursuer. The gnarled trees were steeped now in a night that seemed to gen-erate beneath their branches and move upward to darken the sky. Crawling into a crack in the rocks that topped the crumbly cliff face, she covered her mouth and nose with both hands to muffle her breathing. Stilling herself, she listened.

With the abdication of the sun, the wind had picked up, whistling from the valleys, complaining as it crossed the ragged rocks where she'd gone to ground. Between the breathing of the mountains and that of her own belabored lungs she was deaf-ened. Frustration and fear tried to get her to poke her head out.

She hadn't the strength to run any farther. It was too dark to climb safely down the treacherous wall of argillite. She had noth-ing to defend herself with but sticks and rocks. Taking a lesson from bunnies, ducklings and others of nature's most helpless creatures, Anna stayed hidden. Her breathing returned to nor-mal. Knees and shoulders wedged against the sides of the crevice, head cocked, she listened through the crying of the wind.

Nothing. Nothing proved nothing. She settled herself in as best she could. Haste, not comfort, had dictated her choice of hiding places. The crack into which she wedged herself was hardly large enough to hold all her parts. Definitely not large enough to hold them in any configuration that wasn't torturous. Still, she was grateful to have it and in no great hurry to venture back into the woods in search of better.

Darkness wove its imperfect cover. South-facing, the cliff collected heat from the day and, though Anna was cold, she would not die of exposure. Pointed chunks jabbed at her left buttock and pried under her right shoulder blade, but she could move a little and that kept her legs and feet from going to sleep.

She listened. She dozed. She felt sorry for herself and angry by turns. She dozed again. A crack, a snap, two pieces of wood banged together or the dream memory of a gunshot woke her. Listening only made her ears ache. She drifted. In a dream, she heard the soft padding of a huge bear outside her temporary tomb, dreamed it so close she could hear the questing whuff-whuff and smell its breath. *Dog breath*, she dreamed, foul and familiar.

Thirst became an overriding factor around three a.m. She'd fled without water. The run had cost her. Here and there throughout her career, Anna'd suffered the usual discomforts of dwelling outside civilization: heat, cold, hunger, high altitude, sore feet, insect bites and stinging plants. The most insistent of these was thirst. The body knew it would survive the stings and itches, pain and even, for a while, hunger. Water it had to have.

Determined to stay in hiding till first light, she passed the hours wiggling fingers and toes and resolutely not thinking about liquids in any form. Near five o'clock the quality of darkness at the mouth of her hidey-hole began to change. Despite the dire misgivings she'd had, the sun was going to rise again and she was going to be around to see it.

Fumblingly, she found her feet and pushed to a standing position, head and shoulders above the lip of the ledge. From this rabbit's-eye viewpoint she took stock of the black and gray predawn world. No gunmen lounged nearby waiting to blow her head off. For once the wind wasn't blowing. The silence of the morning was so absolute that, had it not been for the cracking of her joints as she unfolded, she would have suspected she'd gone deaf overnight.

Nowhere was the sound of birds waking, water running, squirrels doing whatever it was squirrels did at this hour of the morning. Slowly she became aware of a slight smacking sound intruding on the perfect peace. It was her tongue as it tried to drum up enough saliva to wet her throat.

As she realized again her thirst, a water bottle materialized. It had been there all along but in the grainy morning light she'd not noticed it. Like a mirage in the desert it stood alone and upright not ten feet from where her head stuck up out of the cliff's top. By itself, sitting on a slab of rock the wind had swept free of needles, it looked like bait in a clumsily laid trap.

She'd carried no water on her helter-skelter run down the mountain. She'd neither dropped it nor, in her haste, forgotten. While she'd slept, someone had crept close to where she was hiding and put it there. Something had visited her. Who would try and crush her with a boulder, take a shot at her, then track her to her lair to leave water? Before fear could take over, it was gone. Anyone, anything, who brought water must be a benevolent spirit. Unless the water was poisoned. Absurd. Surely it would be infinitely easier to smash her skull with a chunk of argillite while she slept than to poison water and leave it for her to find.

Having visually searched the still-empty area along the cliff top she looked again at the bottle. It was hers, taken from the pack she'd abandoned. Near the top, written in red nail polish, the most indelible of all marking substances, PIGEON was printed in block letters.

A sense of unreality swept over her. It was so strong her vision blurred and she reeled in her cramped space, her pelvic bones rapping painfully against the stone. Like a bad comic, she did a double take then rubbed her eyes with her fists. But when she looked again the apparition was still there, bizarre in its homely mundane form.

Thinking of the Lost Boys and the poisoned cake, Hansel and Gretel and gingerbread, Anna eased from the crack in the rock one stiff, chilled inch at a time, emerging like a lizard too long out of the sun. The crevice she'd squished herself into was no more than a shallow vertical chink in the rocky drop where a rectangular piece of argillite had fallen away. She crawled on hands and knees to the water. Resisting the temptation to snatch it up and pour it down her throat, she studied the plastic bottle. White with blue lettering, she'd gotten it free when she'd joined the health club in Clinton, Mississippi, the previous spring. The bottle was as she remembered it but for two puncture marks about a quarter of the way down from the mouth. One dented the plastic. The other pierced it through. Had it not been set carefully upright, the water would have leaked away.

Teethmarks. Anna remembered her dream of padding paws

and dog breath. A bear then, not a dream. A bear had brought her water to drink. Savoring the fairy-tale image while the unreality of it made her head swim, Anna watched her hand reach for the water, her fingers curl around the cold plastic. She popped open the nipple and drank.

If it was poisoned, so be it. She wouldn't have missed the spurious magic of the moment for the promise of ten lifetimes.

18

Because she was truly thirsty, Anna could follow the water down her throat, feel it spread out in her stomach, soak through the walls, thin her blood and plump up her skin. Not a trace of poison anywhere. No one, nothing, sprang from the woods to strike her down as she drank. The water was a gift, not a trap, and she was as grateful as she was mystified.

The body satisfied, the mind was able to expand its focus past where the next drink was coming from. Carrying the bottle, empty now but far too interesting with its puncture marks to be left behind, she moved partly to get the blood flowing and because, gift or no gift, she did not want to linger in a place she'd been found out.

Walking slowly into the trees, where morning's light had not yet cleared away the shadows, she put together a rudimentary plan. Had the water not made its miraculous appearance, she would have headed down toward camps and creeks immediately. Given a short reprieve, she needed to go back to where she'd left her pack. Not to find, capture or confront evil-doers, she promised herself, but to look without being seen and to get her stuff back, including the 35-mm camera with film containing pictures of her attacker's bootprints. Or Gunga Din's bootprints. Could the roller of the rock and the bringer of water be one and the same? It made even less sense than Anna's image of a beneficent bruin carrying her water bottle in its kindly jaws.

Taking her time, moving with an ear to her own footfalls and an eye to keeping trees or rocks between her and the ridge where the pack had been left, she walked in a long ellipse so she would come upon the place from the north and above. This time she would be the stalker.

Movement and the return of the sun restored her equilibrium. Hunger, burning lightly in her middle, was a pleasant companion, reminding her she was alive and had much to look forward to. Within thirty minutes she had wended her surreptitious way back to where her reckless sprint had begun the evening before. Above and to the right of the den's—if it was in fact a den—entrance she made herself comfortable, her back to a green and gold boulder rapidly warming in the sun. The branches of two pines, tangled like ancient lovers fighting, created a pierced screen between her and the world.

A woman in purdah, Anna watched in security. She even began to enjoy herself as befitted a person given a front-row seat in a crown jewel park. Her pack was not where she'd dumped it, but ten or fifteen feet away. The sleeping bag had been pulled off, unrolled and thrown aside. The pack itself was open and the contents spilled out. From this distance she couldn't tell what was missing. It occurred to her that the camera—or at least the exposed film—would be taken or destroyed. Probably her radio would have suffered a like fate. She hoped her notes had been overlooked.

The boulder that had been pushed down toward her had come to rest below the pack, maybe six yards. Beneath its bulk poked the crushed arms of a small tree. From her elevated vantage point it wasn't hard to see the tree branches as the scaly withered arms and legs of a flattened witch. Anna let the Wizard of Oz take over and, in her imagination, saw the witch's legs shrivel and vanish beneath the fallen house.

The mind game shifted and she saw herself beneath the rock. Her own life crushed, her own legs and arms made sere and dry. That, after all, was what had been intended. She thought about that for a while. It hurt her feelings and offended her delicate sensibilities but, sequestered in the warmth of the sun, safe from prying eyes, she wasn't afraid. The rock and the tree milked for all the drama they had to offer, her thoughts moved on.

The brush that had been banked against the bottom of the rocky outcrop, partially obscuring the slot in the stones, had been dragged away. The opening was considerably larger than she'd imagined, several feet high and eight or ten feet wide, tapering down at either end. A nice place to pass the winter or hide out from the law.

Since it was not near denning time Anna had given little thought to disturbing a bear inside. Now she thought of the mother and cubs she'd seen the day before and wished she knew more about the habits of the grizzly. Did they use their dens in summer? Take naps there? Water the plants? Dust? She seemed to remember that, given the choice, a bear would return to the same place to den winter after winter but adapted fairly easily if the den were made uninhabitable by some natural disaster: flood, avalanche, ski resort.

Snug on her hillside, the thought of bears in residence did little more than delay her slide and scramble down a few minutes more. Her long watch was for two-legged animals. An hour passed. Anna neither heard, saw, smelled nor sensed anything to suggest that she was not alone.

One of the items tumbled from her abandoned pack was a one-liter wide-mouth plastic water bottle. With the mountainside warming, Anna took a greater and greater interest in it.

She was too old or too crusty to pass for Snow White or Rose Red. She could not expect a bear to bring her a beverage a second time.

Shortly after nine-thirty, convinced there was no one near and grown significantly thirsty again, she left her secluded niche and worked her way as quietly as she could on the sliding scree to the gash beneath the rocky overhang. There she waited once more. No sounds from within. No cool exhalation that she'd come to expect out of the mouths of big caves. This, then, was what it looked like; a shallow grotto beneath the rock. Still, she skirted it respectfully, careful her shadow did not fall across the mouth, and went to her pack.

The camera was there, though the film, both exposed and unused, was gone. The NPS radio Ruick had issued her was gone. Her flashlight had been smashed. The greatest disappointment was the water bottle she'd packed in. It was undamaged but the contents had been poured out. Her portable water filter was missing. All the evidence envelopes were gone. Her notebook had been left but the pages with writing on them had been ripped out

and taken. Near as she could tell, everything else had been ignored: map, underwear, socks, pens remained.

Whoever had messed with it had cared only that she go away
and go away with no record of the things she'd seen. The items
taken or destroyed decreed she must hike out and soon.

Why empty this water bottle, steal the filter, then go to the
trouble of tracking her down to leave a gift of water outside her
hiding place? Why try to kill her with rock and gun, then let her
sleep unharmed through the night? Dr. Jekyll and Mr. Hyde? Or,
like the werewolf, kind and humane by day, ravening beast by
night?

Moving quickly, not allowing herself to mourn the loss of the
water, she stuffed the goods, including the sleeping bag, willy-
nilly into the main compartment of the pack.

Having finished, she turned her attention to the den. During
her musings and stuffings she'd never once turned her back on it.
Without the flashlight, she was even less anxious to go poking
into its shadows than she had been before. But there was nothing
for it. Either she looked as best she could or the inspection was
put off a minimum of twenty-four hours while she hiked out and
made her report.

Approaching the gash from the side, she went down on one
knee in the runner's starting position in case a tactical retreat became suddenly necessary. In her right hand she held the can of
bear spray she wore at her belt. The stuff was made mostly of
pepper. She knew for a fact it worked on people. She had only the
manufacturer's word that it worked on bears.

The sun was not yet overhead. Far from shining helpfully into
the cave's mouth, it cast a black shadow there. Anna scooched
down slightly and thrust her face in under the overhang, listening,
sniffing, letting her eyes adjust to the gloom. Her nose processed
the most information. The smells were many, mixed and strange.
Underlying them was the familiar smell of rock and damp in otherwise dry country. Probably one or more seep springs had gone
into the making of the cave, though Anna knew better than to
hope for any open water. The lesser smells, the newer smells, were
what intrigued her. A trace of gas was in the air. Butane maybe.
Kerosene, wax, maybe. Perhaps she smelled not the gas itself but
the odors left from heated metal, extinguished wicks. Someone

had been staying here for a night or more. Someone who'd been willing to smash her to defend his territory.

Though the morning proved quiet, memory of the boulder reminded her not to dawdle. Her guess was the roller of rocks and filleter of faces had moved on after using the time she'd cowered in her crevice to clean all trace of himself out of the cave. Still, he might return. To kill her, if for no better reason.

She sniffed again. Traces of human food, certainly, but something more. The odor was exceedingly familiar but she couldn't place it; sweetish. Hay? Dustier, flatter. Anna gave up. Her eyes had adjusted. The cave was much as she'd expected it would be, shallow and uncomplicated, a shell-shaped cut in the mountain with no passages or rooms. At its maximum it was four feet from floor to ceiling. Using the half-light from outside she did a quick search. On one narrow ledge she found candle wax. That was all. The cave had not only been cleared, it had been swept. Looking back toward the crescent of pale light filtering in, she could see the marks of her own passage crossing a field swept into tiny ridges by a pine-needle broom.

Combing the tidy dirt on the floor she came up with half a peanut, a dime and a piece of what looked like dog biscuit. She sniffed it and found the source of the mysterious sweetish, hay-like, dusty, flat odor. Anna was shocked and then laughed aloud and scared herself with her own noise. Why would she be appalled that a person who would commit murder would have the unmitigated gall to bring a dog into a National Park Service–designated Wilderness Area? If they ever caught him, in addition to "murder in the first degree," she'd make sure Harry wrote him up for "dog off leash."

Evidence bags had been stolen along with film, radio, water and notes. Anna carefully buttoned the peanut, the dime and the dog biscuit into her shirt pocket. She was determined not to return from Cathedral Peak with nothing to show for herself.

It took over three hours to get back to Highline Trail. Knowing she had no water made Anna far thirstier than she would have been otherwise. Knowledge she was in no danger of actually dying before she got to Fifty Mountain Camp, where she would undoubtedly find at least one camper willing to lend her a filter pump, did nothing to alleviate her discomfort. So much for mind over matter.

On Highline she had the good luck to meet up with two women who'd hiked in from Going to the Sun Road. For the first time in her life, Anna wished she'd had children so she could trade her firstborn for a drink. The hikers didn't drive quite so hard a bargain and were glad to have the privilege of rescuing a ranger.

"Drink as much as you like," a hippy blond with wonderful eyes and badly sunburned cheeks said. "We'll top off at the next creek."

Anna took her up on the invitation and, thirst slaked, fell in with them as they hiked downhill toward Flattop. The women were good company. Both were from Oberlin, Ohio. Every year for seven years they backpacked together in a different national park. They collected stories, they told her, stories and pictures. On winter solstice they held a remembrance party and relived their adventures of past years.

"Now we've got you," the blond said, and Anna had to submit with apparent good grace—they had given her water after all—to having her picture taken, the better to illustrate what would probably be entitled "The Idiot Lady Ranger" story.

"Two good stories today," the other woman said. Emma or Ella—Anna had been too busy swallowing when introductions were made to hear properly. She was the older of the two, in her thirties, with inky black hair cut short like a man's. One nostril was pierced and she wore a tiny diamond there that flashed in the sun when she talked. "A while ago we stopped for lunch. We like to get off trail. You know, not just a few feet but half a mile or so, so we can really *be* here," she told Anna, the diamond winking conspiratorially. "We were pushing down through some brush to what looked like kind of a nice little clearing with a terrific view. We get there and there's this boy. Just this boy all by himself out on this rocky ledge and he's just sitting there crying his eyes out. Bawling. How weird."

"There's a story right there," the blond said happily. "I mean, I'm sorry he was crying. He seemed like a sweet guy, but you've got to admit it's got 'story' written all over it."

"No picture though," the possibly-Emma woman said.

"Maybe he was ashamed." Anna was still feeling mildly humiliated at her own story potential.

"Oh, we didn't shove the camera in his weepy little face like some demented newswomen," the blond said. "We believe in leaving no trace, not even footprints."

"Especially on people's faces," the other woman threw in and laughed, a boisterous, barroom laugh that tickled Anna. "He was really an unhappy citizen. We tried to talk with him but he wasn't much for that. He dried up the minute we showed. Real sweet fella."

"Till the camera came out. Then he became Mr. Freaky."

The story was beginning to interest Anna. "What did he look like?" she asked.

"Around five-ten. Young, exceedingly young. Too young to be out without his momma. He couldn't have been more than fifteen or sixteen, tops. What do the you think, Emma? Fifteen?"

"Thereabouts," Emma concurred.

"Soft, soft brown hair. Some wave. Big old hazel eyes with lashes out to here." The blond held a stubby forefinger adorned with chipped burgundy polish a couple of inches beyond her nose.

"Boxy jaw," Emma said. "Square guy. Not fat, square. Looked strong."

It was about the best description of a person Anna had ever gotten in her years as a law enforcement officer. These women were of that rare breed that saw what they were looking at.

She compared the description with her memory and decided they had seen the elusive Geoffrey Mickelson-Nicholson.

"Did he wear a length of chain wrapped around his waist and have a smile like St. Francis of Assisi?" Anna asked.

"I was getting to that," Emma said, in the injured tone of a raconteur whose flow is interrupted.

"Do you know him?" the blond asked.

"I've met him," Anna said.

"Do you know why he was crying? He wouldn't tell us."

Anna didn't. It crossed her mind that his heart was broken because the boulder he'd rolled down the mountainside had failed to squash her, but she didn't say so. The stories she collected weren't the kind that made for good memories on a deep winter's night.

"How long ago?" Anna asked.

"Maybe an hour," Emma said.

Too much time had passed to follow him on foot. Anna needed film, a weapon, a horse, water and a much better plan. She continued on to Fifty Mountain Camp with the ladies from Ohio.

19

Fifty Mountain was at peace, new campers not yet come, old
campers either out exploring or lounging in the church-
quiet of backcountry camp at midafternoon.

Anna went first to Ponce. He'd been fed by one of Ruick's
crew the night before, as they'd arranged if Anna spent the night
out. The bay was utterly content to be doing nothing and gave
her a big-hearted welcome that left horse snot down her right arm
from shoulder to elbow. Given the sad shape of her uniform shirt,
a smear of equine mucus was a mere drop in the bucket.

Beyond the hitching rail, the National Park Service had provided a tall pole firmly planted in the ground with metal hooks
near the top. Propped against a nearby tree was another pole.
This one was long and slender and tipped with a hook of its own.
Taking up the slender pole, Anna used it to lift off the pack she'd
left behind, cached high and safe. The NPS put these primitive in-
struments at the heavily used camps. Caching food in trees, done
repeatedly and inexpertly, not only damaged the trees over time
but, too frequently, resulted in the bears getting the goods anyway. Bears learned quickly, remembered and, rare among wild
creatures, passed that knowledge on to their young. Bears were as
good as rangers at spotting a cache that, with a little effort, could
be had.

Food, a sponge bath, cleaner clothes, resting in a tent; Anna
enjoyed the things that allowed people to maintain the thin veneer of civilization. Without a radio there was little else she could
do but while away the time till she got word from Ruick. As was

customary when one ranger went off alone in questionable pursuits, she'd been instructed to report in each evening. Since she'd failed to do so, Ruick would be looking for her. It behooved her to stay put so she could be found.

Renewed and rested, she ventured forth a little after five. She wandered by McCaskil's campsite. A young couple were pitching their tent there, arguing companionably about which direction the slope went. McCaskil wouldn't be back, not unless he was an idiot. He'd run. He had a radio, Anna was sure of it. Either that or he'd fortuitously overheard their conversation regarding him over Lester Van Slyke's radio. Not impossible in a town built of cloth.

If he had any sense, he was long gone from the park by now. Unless he had unfinished business here, and Anna couldn't imagine what it would be. Rolling rocks down on her? That made little sense. Anna couldn't tie McCaskil in with the excavating for moths or digging glacier lilies and she knew it wasn't he who'd dwelt in the den she'd found. He'd spent every night but one at Fifty Mountain.

She could connect McCaskil with Carolyn by way of the map and the coat. She could connect Carolyn and the blue stuff bag by way of blood and proximity. The mysterious Geoffrey Mickleson-Nicholson she connected to the blue stuff bag by way of the moths and the glacier lilies. So far she couldn't connect Geoffrey with Carolyn except through the blue stuff sack. Who the hell was the boy with the chain around his waist who wept and dug and, Anna believed, denned up in the high country like an out-of-season bear?

Full of questions and needing to pester somebody, she climbed the gentle hill through the blackened campsites and dead trees till she reached the uppermost one, the one where the fire had simply stopped of its own volition, often in the middle of a tree leaving half charred and dying, the other half determinedly thrusting green needles out to catch the sun.

Lester was there. He sat on a rock, elbows on his knees, hands hanging down, doing nothing. So seldom do people actually do nothing that to see it creates an impression of deadness. That's what Anna felt as she approached him. "Hey," she said feeling a need to announce herself though scarcely six feet separated them.

Like a man in a trance, he swung his face slowly toward her. His eyes were vacant, as if he took up no space on the planet. "It's Anna Pigeon," she added and some small reassuring life returned to his face.

"Yes. I was waiting for you."

For reasons she could not put her finger on, his words gave her a creepy feeling, much as the Grim Reaper's might when he called her name. Les stirred himself and the feeling was gone. "Chief Ranger Ruick told me to wait here, and if you came back, tell you to call him." He reached down and retrieved a radio propped against the stone at his feet.

Anna took it and radioed Ruick. Her first question was, "Is Buck back with Joan?" Ruick answered in the affirmative and her relief let her know how worried she'd been.

"Why didn't you call last night?" he demanded.

"Lost my radio." Silence fussed over the air as he waited for her to explain. She didn't. Radios were not safe. "I need to talk with you in person," she said instead.

Either Ruick understood her reluctance to chat or gave into it. He didn't press her. "We're no longer in the backcountry. Hiked out. Come down," he ordered. "Call me on the phone when you get here."

There were a couple of hours of daylight left. With Ponce for conveyance, Anna could have made it down the mountain by shortly after dark. Given her state of fatigue and the vagaries of recent nights, she didn't want to be alone on horseback that late. "First thing in the morning," she promised, uncomfortable committing even that much of her itinerary to whoever might be listening. She longed to quiz Ruick on what, if anything, they'd found in their search for William McCaskil, but didn't. If they'd found him, Harry would have said so. She could only assume they'd given up the search or it had led them out of the high country.

Radio chore completed, she sat on the ground near Lester Van Slyke. She kept the radio. If he cared about it one way or another, he didn't let on. She guessed he didn't. By the look of him, he didn't care much about anything. If he'd appeared old and sick and gray when they'd met, he looked three days dead now. The sparse hair was greasy and stuck to his pate in dark strands. His skin hung loose, the sagging jowls rough with two days' growth of beard. His pale blue eyes were rimmed in red and he blinked a lot as if he had trouble focusing.

"Why do you stay here?" Anna asked on impulse.

"I have to," he said vaguely. "Maybe there's something . . ." His voice trailed off. She waited. "Something I can do," he finished finally.

"About what?"

A minute passed. The drop of life that had animated him when he gave her Harry's message drained away.

"I can't do anything," he said so softly she barely heard him. He wasn't talking to her but to himself, undoubtedly repeating the mantra of ineffectualness the second Mrs. Van Slyke had spent so many years literally and figuratively beating into him.

For a while Anna watched him grow grayer and smaller. Lester was very nearly catatonic. The man was deeply disturbed and had withdrawn to a potentially pathological extent. Molly would know what to do. Fervently Anna wished her sister were there, would take over, make things right as she'd so often done when Anna was little. But Molly would have wanted to take the tack that was best for the patient, for Mr. Van Slyke. Anna just wanted answers.

It was not that she was without compassion, at least she liked to think she wasn't, but there was that about Les that brought out her anger. She could understand why his son hated him instead of the woman who tormented him. She could see how he would attract and incite abusers of every stripe. Les Van Slyke was the flesh and blood equivalent of the tar baby. He seemed to invite violence by his self-negation, acceptance of violence only enraging his attacker. Anna put the thoughts inside. They made her uncomfortable. Sweetness, comfort, safety, would that allow him to open up? Or was he so accustomed to responding to abuse from women that Anna would have to don the guise of his dearly departed wife to rouse him?

Maybe because she feared her own tendency to want to kick the cringing dog, she opted for sweetness and light. To make it ring true she closed her eyes, pictured him not as a self-involved, self-pitying shell of a man but as an old tomcat, battered and beaten till it could barely move, a cat who'd been so misused, when approached by a human hand, it could no longer even hiss but only close its eyes, wait for the blow and hope, this time, it would kill him.

For animals, compassion came easy. Keeping the vision of the tomcat firmly in mind, she began to speak and was pleasantly surprised to hear her words sounding genuinely kind.

"I can see that you're tired, Les," she began. "Tired almost to death. And you're alone like you've been alone for a long time, but now it's somehow worse. Everything's worse. Before, you were alone and you were hurting but she was there. She kept things going, moving, like she'd got things moving after your wife died. She was hard and she was angry but she was alive. You were alive. At least a little. And now she's gone and you're tired. Too tired almost to breathe." Les had not moved since she'd begun speaking but tears filled his eyes. They spilled down over his cheeks, divided and divided again as they dripped into the creases time and worry had cut into his face. Bleak as it was, it was a sign of life, and Anna pressed on not knowing whether the experiment would prove cathartic or would break the last weight-bearing wall in his poor old brain. *Practicing without a license,* Anna thought. She kept her voice low, monotonous, as hypnotic as she dared make it without sounding theatrical. She didn't want him to think for a while, just hear and follow.

"Without her, things have gotten in such a mess. You don't know how to make things right. You've never known how to make things right, not since your first wife died. At least Carolyn made things real. She made things happen, didn't she?" Anna hazarded a gentle question.

Les nodded. Satisfied, she went on, spinning an inner landscape for him, wondering as she went how she was going to get where she was headed.

"Now you're tired and you're scared. You're afraid of what you've done—"

Les's hands, till then hanging like dead leaves between his knees, twitched. Anna'd got it wrong and the jar threatened to wake him.

"—you're afraid of what you've done to Rory," she amended. The twitch stopped. Rory then. Anna followed that. "All those years, Rory loving his stepmom and not you. How could you know he knew? The beatings you took were for him, weren't they?" Anna asked, suddenly knowing that in Les's mind this was true. "You took them to keep the marriage together, because Rory needed a mom, because you couldn't bear to see him lose her a second time."

The tears fell harder. Les nodded again and weak mewling

noises made their way out from a deep well of emotion Anna suspected was liberally salted with neurosis in the form of martyrdom, joy of victimhood, self-aggrandizement, and other smarmy and seductive feelings.

Desperately she rifled through her brain. For whatever sick reasons, Les let Carolyn beat on him. To live with himself he convinced himself he did it for his son. Now he'd convinced himself he was staying in Glacier because he was scared, not for himself, but for his son. Did that mean Les thought Rory killed Carolyn, and by remaining, Les might be able to "do something" along the lines of impeding the investigation or tampering with evidence? Or that he killed her himself and, by lousing up the investigation, could salvage himself—a dad—for Rory?

Anna couldn't guess which and she dared not remain silent. If the tears were any indication, Les was believing her, hearing her speak as if she knew the innermost secrets of his mind, as if she were in some way his own voice. A wrong guess now and she'd break the spell.

She came from another direction, feeling her way carefully. "You knew Carolyn was gone that night," Anna said. "You knew she'd left the tent."

"I knew," Les mumbled, "but I didn't think anything of it. She used to leave at night. She . . ."

"She'd go out," Anna affirmed.

"She'd meet men," Les said.

The light dawned. "She met men," Anna said. "She took things from them didn't she? She *borrowed* bits of their clothes, things you'd find so you'd know. Like she borrowed the army coat she was wearing."

"She did it to hurt me," Les said. "I never let on, but it hurt. It hurt a lot." More tears.

"That's why you pretended you didn't know where the coat came from? You thought she'd been with Bill McCaskil? Had she known him before? Met him anywhere? An internet chatroom? A courtroom? A conference? Anything?"

"No. I don't think so."

"She just meets him around the campfire and hops in the sack with him?" Anna said skeptically.

"You didn't know her. It didn't take long. It didn't matter who. She'd go off with bellboys when we stayed at hotels. Or the bartender. When I was in the hospital she got to my orderly. A boy no older than Rory is now. I didn't want Rory to know. The coat and all. I didn't want Rory to know."

One mystery solved: why Carolyn had McCaskil's coat on and why Les was so peculiar on the subject. None of that factored into why Les stayed on, unless he wanted vengeance on McCaskil and, after the bellboys and bartenders and orderlies, why bother?

"You think Rory saw McCaskil and his stepmother together and killed her for it," Anna said, her voice sudden and harsh.

Les jerked as if she'd slapped him then covered his face with both hands. "Yes," he managed.

"Well, that's a crock," Anna said sympathetically.

"It is?" A thread of hope cut through the molasses of tears in Les's throat.

Maybe it wasn't. Scared by the bear, maybe Rory had run home to stepmomma, found her in the arms of the latest blunt instrument she'd chosen to beat her husband with, followed, chased or lured her a few miles from camp and killed her. It was the best scenario she'd come up with yet. It even explained why McCaskil would run. Even if he was innocent, who'd believe him when he'd been having sex with the deceased under her husband's nose? It happened every day, and in the usual run of things all three parties survived. But juries liked moral payback. A man with as many brushes with the law as Bill McCaskil would know that.

Anna kept these thoughts to herself. Lester Van Slyke had convinced her of one thing, he didn't kill his wife. If he could be made to believe Rory wasn't suspected either, maybe he'd go home or to a motel. Anywhere would be better than plopped down confusing what was already a sufficiently mind-numbing investigation.

"Rory's going to be okay," Anna said because that's what one says. "You don't have to stay here anymore. Tomorrow you'll go down with me."

"Okay," Les said, docile, empty.

Anna sighed. Of course the old guy would ride Ponce unless she wanted to be all day on the trail. She'd have to walk. Even pretending to be compassionate had consequences.

Tired as she was, Anna did not sleep well. Her nerves were sufficiently raw that the chance scraping of her wedding ring against the plastic zipper of her sleeping bag was enough to bring her to a sitting position, heart pounding. She was continuing to suffer an alien and disquieting need to flee from nature and hide out behind four strong walls, concrete sidewalks and tended lawns.

The previous night's tears and sleep had revived Les Van Slyke. He was, if not quite his old self, at least mobile. They were on the trail before sunrise and, thanks to Lester's radio, there was a truck and horse trailer waiting for them at Packer's Roost when they hiked out around noon.

Harry Ruick was in meetings till three-thirty. Anna celebrated this reprieve in Joan's house bathing, anointing herself with perfume, putting on clothing unsuited to rugged terrain and otherwise armoring herself against the wild things with the mundane soothing pastimes once called indulgence but, in the nineties, renamed "self-care."

If Ruick noticed that she looked or smelled better than when last they'd met, he was too much a professional to comment. Seated in a relatively comfortable chair in his office, the afternoon sun painting a warm square across her knees, Anna reported. She told him of the army cutworm moth excavation made not by claws but by a spade, of the den, the rock, the gunshot. She told him of the cave swept clean but for the wax on the ledge and the peanut half, the dime and dog biscuit fragment overlooked in the dust. She kept till last the part about the water bottle punctured by pointed teeth that had been left for her. Law enforcement officers do not like fairy stories, head investigators do not like underlings with overactive imaginations or a penchant for the romantic.

It crossed Anna's mind to withhold the incident entirely as irrelevant and damaging to her credibility. The decision to include it came only when she remembered a similar incident had happened before. Maybe had happened before.

"Remember Rory and the water bottle nonsense?" she asked. "He's since changed his story, but originally he said he lay down to sleep without one and woke with one beside him."

"Right. One covered with his murdered stepmother's fingerprints," Harry said warningly.

Looked at in the harsh light of reason, the benevolent bear spirit that brought drinking water to lost souls was pretty irrational.

"Just a thought," Anna said and let it go at that.

"This guy who brought the water shot at you?" Ruick asked skeptically.

"Yes." Anna'd done elaborating. Harry was as frustrated as she.

"You're sure? You saw the gun?"

"Heard the shot."

The chief ranger drummed his fingers on his desk pad and gazed out his window. "Before the rock was rolled, or after?"

"After," Anna said. "During."

"So the shot came at the same time the rock was crashing down?"

"That's right." Anna could see where the rock Harry was rolling was going to come crashing down too, but there was nothing she could do to stop it. She couldn't even find it in her heart to blame him. The murder was nine days old. Trails were cold. Witnesses, what they had of them, had scattered. There were no leads but Bill McCaskil, and the case against him was paper-thin. Harry would not want a reason showing up that would demand he pull his already depleted ranger force from their primary duties for the chasing of wild geese on Cathedral Peak.

"So you could have heard something else," he said, as Anna knew he would. "The boulder could have busted some smaller rocks or snapped a tree limb. That can sound like a gunshot."

"I could have heard something else," Anna agreed. Harry looked at her with what might have been a hint of apology in his eyes.

What he said was, "Could you have been mistaken about a person rolling the rock? Could it have been dislodged by accident? Someone hiding behind it, knocked it loose, that sort of thing?"

Anna thought about it for a moment. "No," she said at last. "It was pushed."

"Okay." Harry accepted her statement at face value and Anna was relieved.

She watched the sun creep up her thighs. Harry watched the maintenance vehicles come and go from the cluster of buildings down the road beyond the parking lot.

"We're pretty much up against it," he said finally. Anna realized then she'd been waiting for the subtle blame-placing, when lesser men begin the slippery process of easing fault off their own shoulders onto the shoulders of others. Ruick was not a lesser man.

"We don't have much to go on," he said. "I agree with you that Les probably is in the clear. His motive, even if the missus was flaunting McCaskil in his face, is too old. Les has been there too many times. If we had a straw-and-camel's-back situation with Mrs. Van Slyke's latest adultery, Les would have snatched up a rock or whatever. It would have been a crime of passion occurring at the scene, and more likely than not Les would have remained with the body and confessed to the first person who showed up. He wouldn't steal film, move the body, defile the corpse and cache the flesh."

"He'll be staying in a motel till Rory's done," Anna said, just to contribute something.

"Thank God for that. When he keels over from a heart attack they can damn well dial nine-one-one and let the police take care of it."

Harry sounded so callous toward human life Anna laughed.

"If I'd ever thought Rory was worth much as a suspect, I'd never have sent him back up with Joan," Harry said. "Even though we don't have enough for an arrest, there are ways."

Anna took the opening and outlined the story that had been haunting Lester Van Slyke, that Rory had run to Fifty Mountain after the bear attack on their camp, caught Carolyn *in flagrante* and killed her. On the hike out, Anna had given the theory a good deal of thought. In the end she'd found it flawed. She repeated it now because which information was valid and which was not was Harry's call, not hers.

He considered it much as she had, and in the end rejected it for the same reasons. Rory'd had no knife, no blood on him. Did he run to Fifty Mountain in his slippers, bumble into the wrong tent, catch Carolyn with McCaskil, then Carolyn dresses, hikes three miles, he follows and kills her? Or did he accidentally meet Carolyn on the trail in the dead of night in the arms of her lover and strike her down? With what? He was strong but slight. The story didn't hold together.

"William McCaskil's still in the running," Anna said without much enthusiasm.

Ruick just grunted. McCaskil might have had sex with the

victim, might even have lent her his coat, but neither of those things were illegal. What made him interesting was the fact that he had run, but there were lots of reasons for that. McCaskil was a convicted felon. It made sense that he wouldn't want to be mixed up in a murder investigation, especially if he was involved in something shady that he didn't particularly want to talk about. Unless they could connect him to the victim in some substantial way or prove he'd committed like incidents in the past, all they could do was talk to him and let him go.

"We'll get McCaskil," Ruick said. "His car is still here and we've got an APB out on him. He'll turn up. If you run across him, don't mess with him. He's got a history of minor violence. More than that, he's been convicted twice on felony charges. If he's the one who took a shot at you, he's facing his third strike. That'll be a hell of a lot of years. McCaskil's probably long gone and good riddance. Until my rangers get back from the fires, I don't have the manpower to keep this up. I'm not blowing off the attack on you, Anna. I'm not. I'll get a couple of my backcountry rangers over there tomorrow. But you and I both know what they'll find."

"What I found," Anna agreed, "less half a peanut."

"We're not giving up," Harry said, mostly to save face. "The investigation is ongoing. We've just got to figure whoever killed Mrs. Van Slyke has left the park. Until we find something more to go on, I can't see any point in committing my people to this at the height of the season. They're needed elsewhere."

Anna didn't like it. Intuition told her there were connections, somehow, somewhere, between the seemingly unconnected events, that if she could find the right vantage point she would be able to see how a Florida con man, a promiscuous Seattle divorce lawyer and a mysterious young man with a chain-link belt and a beautiful smile, were related to punctured water bottles, army cutworm moths, glacier lilies and murder.

Because she could not find her way to that vantage point, she said, "What do you want me to do?"

Ruick brought his gaze in from the parking lot and let it rest on her. Harry Ruick was as uncomfortable as she was with backing off the investigation. Unlike her, he was responsible for the safety of the entire park. National Park Service law enforcement was designed to keep tourists from damaging the resource and

each other. It was not set up to conduct long-term in-depth investigations. Parks were federal lands. The Federal Bureau of Investigation was the department used to that end. But, on occasion,
the FBI had bigger fish to fry—or fishes closer to home—and the
investigation was left to the park where the incident had occurred.

This was one of those times.

Carolyn Van Slyke's murder was very probably going to slip
through the cracks, along with a staggering number of other
homicides that would never be solved.

"What I'd like you to do," Harry said, "is keep at it for a
while. Joan will be up there for another five days. I can't see any
point in you turning around and going right back unless you just
want to for the DNA study. She's got Buck with her to fetch and
carry, and that's more than she's used to. Why don't you make
use of Joan's office and her computer? See if you can't dig up
something, *anything* that might tie some of this together. If you
don't come up with anything, you can consider yourself off my
duty roster and go back to work for Joan."

"Sure," Anna said. She'd start in the morning. In the bookcase under Joan's television she'd seen a video collection including such classics as *Die Hard, End of Days,* and *Aliens.* Tonight
she was going to enjoy a little vicarious kicking of ass.

20

The following morning Anna took possession of Joan's office.
On her way in she'd been greeted with a few friendly hellos
and had the coffee machine pointed out to her, but there'd
been no questions about the murder or anything related to it. Researchers were wonderful in their dedication. If it wasn't about
bears, virtually no one in the great rambling building gave two
hoots about it.

With Ruick's blessing, she had taken copies of every report
generated, every piece of evidence gathered and any and all lab
reports returned. Joan's office was devoid of clean flat surfaces.
Every inch of space was covered in folders, papers, pamphlets,
books and pieces of bears gathered over the years. Knowing this
well-feathered nest was as Joan wished it to be, the sprawling
form dictated by her professional needs, Anna chose to disturb
nothing. The relics of her investigation she placed carefully on
top of Joan's piles. She sat in the midst of them and opened her
mind to let plans and patterns form if they might.

Carolyn Van Slyke's autopsy report was to the right of the
computer on a half-consumed bag of gummi bears. Anna reread
it, looking for any connection to McCaskil. Other than the coat,
there was nothing. As a matter of course the body had been
checked for sexual assault. None. If Carolyn had been involved
with McCaskil, the sex had been consensual and a condom had
been used.

Anna had only Lester Van Slyke's word that Carolyn had
been adulterous. Though she believed him, there was a remote

possibility he'd been inspired by the army jacket, seen the accusation as a way of casting suspicion on McCaskil, not realizing in doing so he was giving himself yet another motive for killing his own wife. Since Anna had no positive leads, she took the negative.

Having found Carolyn Van Slyke's work number and address in Seattle, Anna called her place of business. Francine Cuckor, Carolyn's assistant, was happy to answer questions. Whether divorce attorneys were more open than most about adultery or whether Francine just liked to talk, Anna would never know, but according to Ms. Cuckor's bawdy tales, a few of which sounded apocryphal and bordered on admiration, Carolyn not only had sex with a large number of men but was open about it. Francine did say that Carolyn was an ethical practitioner of the law. Her exact words were: "She'd never fuck a client or a client's husband until the case was settled." From the way Ms. Cuckor said it, Anna guessed she pretty much thought Carolyn a candidate for the Lawyer's Hall of Fame on grounds of self-control.

Francine went so far as to offer Anna the names and phone numbers of others who could confirm her stories. Anna declined. She was merely fact-checking, not gathering material for letters to *Penthouse*.

She hung up and filched a gummi bear to cleanse her palate. She was not a prude. She'd enjoyed her share of fornication. Still, she was old-fashioned enough to feel adultery should be done on the sly, in great secrecy, and that it behooved the adulterers to feel ashamed and guilty. The libertine sentiments of Ms. Cuckor and the late Mrs. Van Slyke left her with a sense of sleaze that was unsettling. Anna had never cheated on Zach. A cynic had once told her it was because he died before their marriage reached the philandering years. Anna chose to believe otherwise. If she married again she would bring to the new union that same Pollyanna belief in fidelity.

If she married again. Thinking that startled her. Several years earlier she'd finally extinguished the torch she carried for her first husband. It had never crossed her mind that she might marry again.

She ate another gummi bear and picked up the reports generated by a computer search on one William Adkins McCaskil, a.k.a. Bill McLellan, Bill Fetterman, and Will Skillman. It was a point in the man's favor that he had registered for a backcountry permit under his own name. That he'd registered for a permit at all suggested that either his pursuits were innocent or, given he was well versed in the ways of crime and law enforcement, he knew in obeying the minor rules one was far more apt to get away with the major infractions. A significant number of felons were rotting in the federal penitentiaries because they got pulled over for failing to signal on a right turn and then one thing led to another.

McCaskil had been born in Sarasota, Florida, on December 27, 1949, to Gerald and Suzanne McCaskil. At sixteen, he'd gotten his driver's license suspended in Tampa, Florida. At twenty-nine, he'd been convicted of mail fraud, selling low-cost life insurance policies through the mail to elderly people. He'd served six months. At forty-eight, he'd been convicted of real estate fraud, selling one-acre lots over the internet that belonged to the Florida fish and wildlife service. For that, he'd served eighteen months and gotten five years' probation. Because of the light sentences, Anna guessed large sums of money had not been involved. That or McCaskil had connections.

Connections. Anna stared at the report without really seeing it. There was something there that was jiggling a lever in her mind trying to turn a light on. Again she read the first paragraph: a.k.a. Bill McLellan, a.k.a. Bill Fetterman, a.k.a. Will Skillman. McLellan and Skillman were of a piece. People often chose the initials of, or a play on, their given names when choosing an alias. Fetterman seemed out of place. Fetterman rang some distant bell.

Anna started with NCIC, the National Crime Information Center. Two Fettermans had wants or warrants, one was a twenty-two-year-old black male out of Philadelphia wanted on a burglary charge, the other was a thirty-one-year-old white male from Los Banos, California, wanted for grand theft auto. No tie-in that Anna could see with her a.k.a.

The obvious route petering out, she began a people search starting with the Fettermans of Sarasota, Florida. Fortunately, Fetterman was not a common name. Only three turned up: Dr. Peter Fetterman, A. Fetterman, and Fetterman Marine supplies.

A. Fetterman was Amanda Fetterman, the spinster daughter of the owner of Fetterman Marine. Anna told her she was from the Florida State Alumni Association trying to track down a

William or Bill Fetterman for the class of '74's upcoming reunion.

Amanda knew no Bill or William. Anna tried McCaskil and McClellan out on her and struck out both times. Finally, too many questions made Amanda suspicious and she began asking questions of her own. Making a hasty retreat fueled with "thank yous," Anna disconnected. She called the marine supply store next and spoke with Papa Fetterman. Same story told in less time: he knew no Bill Fetterman, McCaskil or McClellan, no Skillman either and what the hell was this all about anyway?

Peter Fetterman was a doctor of marine biology. The number Anna'd gotten off the internet was apparently his home. Being an efficient man, his answering machine informed callers of a work number where he could be reached. Just because he sounded so sensible, when Anna reached him, she told him that she was doing background checks for three men who'd applied for law enforcement positions. The doctor knew no men by those names. The only Fetterman he knew of was a man in Tampa. Their paths had crossed over an incident regarding a shark poached illegally from a study area. He wouldn't tell Anna where, other than to say "off the coast." He seemed to suffer from the delusion that few people could resist the lure of frequenting shark-infested waters.

Tampa was where young Bill McCaskil had his first recorded brush with the law. Anna moved on. To have phoned three people and gotten hold of them on, if not the first, then the second try was a phenomenal bit of luck. It seemed the more electronic paraphernalia people purchased to remain in touch with an ever-scattering herd served only to separate them further. In the course of various investigations Anna had spent days of her life on pointless rounds from answering machines to pagers to voice mail, never once speaking to a real live human being.

Consequently it was no surprise that Lady Luck dumped her in Tampa. No Fetterman was listed, either as an individual or as a business. Anna taxed the phone company's much-touted, new-and-improved information system that promised to find numbers to places with forgotten names. Nowhere in or around Tampa was a place of business with the name Fetterman in the title. The telephone operator Anna had hooked up with was probably as close to a saint as the phone company had on its rosters. She was willing to keep on trying when Anna decided to throw in the towel.

"We could try recently disconnected numbers," the operator suggested.

"You can do that?" Anna was amazed not at the technology but at the operator's access to those files, and her willingness to take the time.

"It'll take a second."

Anna couldn't think what good a disconnected number could do, but she felt an obligation to wait. After all, the woman had worked so hard it seemed ungrateful somehow. The strange quiet of telephone lines, not pushed full of Muzak, trickled into Anna's ear; faint hushing as of a distant sea, barely audible clicks and hums; the intercourse of the world kept at bay by a thin wall of rubber.

"Well," the operator came back on the line. "We've got something."

"Let's have it," Anna said. To prove she was paying attention, she sat up straight and held a pen at the ready over a sheet of scrap paper she'd nearly obliterated with doodles.

"Fetterman's Adventure Trails on Highway Forty-One."

Anna repeated it back to her. A name had been found, the operator seemed to feel at last her job was done and she could leave Anna in good conscience.

Rubbing the ear she'd compressed into the phone receiver for so long, Anna looked at the words angled in amongst the rococo permutations of bear tracks inked on the page. The name Fetterman had rung a bell. Fetterman's Adventure Trails set half a dozen clanging. Leaving the office in its state of productive disarray, she jogged the half-mile back to the headquarters building.

Harry was out to lunch. Maryanne was eating at her desk, delicately holding a sandwich in one hand away from the keyboard while she hunt-and-pecked corrections with the other. Anna hoped Harry knew how lucky he was.

The sandwich and the typing were set aside while Anna was settled in Harry's chair and copies of the past three weeks' 10-343s and 10-344s case and criminal incident reports were lifted from the files and placed before her.

On a case incident report submitted ten days earlier by the district ranger on the northwest side of the park, Anna found what she was looking for. No crime had been committed; it was the report of the truck and trailer abandoned off-road within park boundaries. The truck was registered to a Carl G. Micou out of Tampa, Florida. Anna rechecked the report on the abandoned truck. The only phone number on the vehicle registration turned out to belong to a business phone that had been disconnected, the phone number of Fetterman's Adventure Trails on Highway 41.

Anna had what she wanted but she didn't know what she had. For the next hour she read reports from the time the truck and trailer were found to the present but there was nothing else pertinent. A call to the Polebridge ranger station and another to dispatch let her know that no one had come forward to claim the vehicles. Anna photocopied the 10-343, thanked Maryanne and walked back to the resource management office.

The secretary's sandwich reminded Anna it was lunchtime but she was too preoccupied to take time hunting and gathering. Back in Joan's office she made do with candy. She was going to owe the researcher a bag of gummi bears before the day was through.

To impose order where none naturally suggested itself, Anna rearranged her papers atop those left by Joan Rand: Carolyn Van Slyke's autopsy report; the list of items found on the body, including the coat with McCaskil's topographical map in the pocket; then what information they had on Bill McCaskil a.k.a. Bill Fetterman; Anna's much-doodled-on notes tracing Fetterman to Fetterman's Adventure Trails; and, last in this papered line of thought, the 10-343 connecting a truck and horse trailer abandoned near the northwest corner of Glacier to the defunct business on Highway 41 outside Tampa, Florida.

Too much for coincidence, not enough for sense. Could the truck and horse trailer belong to McCaskil or have been borrowed or stolen by McCaskil? Sure. But then why was his own legally registered vehicle parked in a frontcountry parking lot? Who was Carl Micou? Did McCaskil have a confederate and, if so, a confederate in what?

None of this brought Anna any closer to a connection between McCaskil and the murder victim; still, she was pleased with herself. The morning had not been wasted.

Back on the phone, she reconnected with Francine Cuckor. Ms. Cuckor had her own brand of professional ethics. She'd been only too happy to share in gory detail the fact that her boss had

had sex with all creatures great and small. When asked to say yea or nay to names of clients, she got cagey. Eventually Anna was bumped upstairs to Claude Winger, a junior partner in the firm.

It was not advisable to spin tales for a past master at the art of professional dissimulation, so Anna told him, as her father would have said, "the whole truth, nothing but the truth and damn little of that."

"I'm Officer Anna Pigeon investigating the death of Carolyn Van Slyke. Could you answer a few questions for me?"

A pause, then a careful voice as devoid of regional inflections as that of a radio announcer said, "Ask your questions." Anna noted the lack of commitment to answering them.

"We have a couple leads, both weak at this point. We're trying to establish any prior connection between Mrs. Van Slyke and our possible suspects," Anna said, using frankness like bread upon the waters.

It was not returned tenfold. "And you want me to . . . ," the voice came back.

"Answer a few questions, if you would."

"Ask your questions."

There would be no softening up or slithering around Claude. Anna cut to it. "Has or was Carolyn Van Slyke working on any case involving a Bill McCaskil, Will Skillman, Bill McClellan or Bill Fetterman?"

"We can't divulge any client information."

"The fact that a person has engaged the services of an attorney does not fall under attorney-client privilege," Anna said. So often the attorney, doctor, priest and whoever-else client privilege was claimed for wasn't for the protection of clients. It was claimed, legally or not, because people were either too lazy to bother giving information to help out the police, or harbored vague worries that to cooperate would open up their own activities to scrutiny. Anna suspected Claude claimed it as a matter of course to avoid involvement and work. She thought of threatening to subpoena his files but knew it was an empty threat. The rank-and-file investigated and reported. It wasn't for the likes of her to go throwing around legal ultimatums. Claude Winger would know that.

She waited through a clearly audible sigh breathed out in an office in Seattle. "I'll put you through to the secretary. Give her

the names. She will tell you if any of them have engaged the professional services of Carolyn Van Slyke in the past year. She won't
go back further than that and she will not tell you anything else."

"Thank you," Anna said but he'd already put her on hold.
Minutes later, when she was beginning to think she'd been put on
hold to grow old and die, Francine came on the line. Winger had
evidently spoken to her firmly. She was businesslike to the point
of rudeness. Anna read off her list of names, adding Carl Micou
as an afterthought. She was answered by the huffy snicking sound
of fingernails on a keyboard.

"No persons by those names have contacted Ms. Van Slyke in
her professional capacity," Francine said mimicking an automaton.

Had the sentence with its convoluted precision come from
someone else, Anna might have suspected them of hiding something. From Francine it just sounded petty and pompous.

"Thank you," Anna said again and pulled her soul back from
the black and voice-filled void of the telephone to Joan's homey
office.

No cheese down that hole, Anna remembered one of her field
rangers, Barth Dinkins, saying. "No cheese," she said aloud.

Carl G. Micou, registered owner of the abandoned truck and
trailer, the man who'd given the Florida motor vehicles department the number of Fetterman's Adventure Trails as his home
number, remained a mystery. Anna turned back to her electronics.

Mentally apologizing to Joan for a phone bill she would
probably have a devil of a time getting her department reimbursed for, Anna called Information and, throwing caution to
the winds, charged the extra fifty cents and let them dial the
Tampa Better Business Bureau for her. A pleasant young man, at
least he sounded young and handsome and virile but may well
have been a nasty old poop with a nice voice, told her Fetterman's Adventure Trails was a licensed business owned and operated by Woody Fetterman. Fetterman's Adventure Trails had
operated at the same location for twenty-six years. The only address for Woody was that of Adventure Trails. There had been
no complaints against Fetterman's from either the buying public
or other businesses. Fetterman's Adventure Trails had recently
closed its doors but he did not know why. He suggested she call
the Tampa tourism department, as he thought Adventure Trails

was a theme park with rides and so forth. They might be able to help her.

The department of tourism could tell her little more. The woman who answered the phone offered to send Anna a brochure, then couldn't find one. They'd gone out of business, Anna said, possibly the brochures had been thrown out. That was probably it, the woman agreed. She wrote down Anna's address at Glacier anyway, promising to send it along if she found it. Anna would have been touched by the desire to please if so long on the phone finding out so little hadn't made her crabby.

An hour's work had provided her with one first name, if "Woody" was legit and not a nickname. Maybe Woodrow. Since Woody had been in business in the same place for twenty-six years he was no fly-by-night. It had been in the back of Anna's mind that Fetterman of Fetterman's Adventure Trails and Bill McCaskil might be one and the same. Twenty-six years, changed that. She couldn't see McCaskil quietly running a business while being indicted and arrested repeatedly for fraud under a handful of other names.

McCaskil was from the Tampa area—or had been there as a teenager. He could've seen the name Fetterman on his way to work or school every day and remembered it when he needed an alias. If it wasn't for the name cropping up again by way of the owner of the abandoned truck, Anna would have chosen to believe that.

"Woody Fetterman." Anna wended her way through the phone lines to the Tampa courthouse, records department. Yes, there was a certificate of death for a Woodrow Fetterman. He had died at age eighty-one of natural causes six weeks before.

Another possibility exhausted. Bill McCaskil a.k.a. Fetterman was not the Fetterman of Adventure Trails. He was not connected with Carolyn Van Slyke by way of divorce. According to Lester, McCaskil hadn't known her before they met at Fifty Mountain Camp.

"Damn," Anna whispered. The truck and the trailer. The name Fetterman. McCaskil and his aliases. Another possibility entered her mind and she went back to the 10-343 report. Carl G. Micou was born August 4, 1938, considerably older than McCaskil. Still, "Micou" could be one of McCaskil's aliases. Perhaps it wasn't listed because it was unknown or not yet used at the time William McCaskil was indicted for real estate fraud.

She spent forty more minutes on the phone and eventually ended up back at the records department in Tampa. The search took longer this time but Mr. Micou's death certificate was found. He had died of congestive heart failure in April of 1995, nearly six years ago.

"His truck is still alive," Anna said wearily.

"I beg your pardon?"

"Never mind. Thanks." Dead men, dead ends.

Sprinkled around the edges of Joan's office was all the information that, by any wild stretch of the imagination, could pertain to the death of Carolyn Van Slyke. Anna had already run to ground what little Fetterman, Fetterman and Micou had to offer. She'd verified that Lester's wife was indeed the queen of sluts. Swiveling Joan's chair slowly she let the other bits and pieces slide by: the army jacket with the topo and the file card. Anna rolled over and, without touching it, reread a copy of the card found in the pocket of what would undoubtedly be Bill McCaskil's coat. "B & C" was written in a loose hand across the top. Below those initials were numbers, measurements by the look of them: 12 11/16, 17 13/16, 30 12/16. The last, 30 8/19, was underlined in heavy ink.

When they caught McCaskil, if she were around, Anna'd ask him what the numbers meant. Probably nothing. His waist size. Who knew? She examined the photocopy of the topo. It had been reduced in size till it fit on two fourteen-and-a-half-inch sheets of paper taped together. Most of the type was too tiny for eyes that had seen more than forty years. There was nothing new since she'd looked at the original, no nifty clues pencilled in the margins, no big red X where the body had been found.

Anna rotated the chair another quarter turn and glanced briefly at her notes on Rory Van Slyke. Rory's dad was an abuse victim. Rory'd gone missing for thirty-six hours. Rory'd turned up having lost a sweatshirt and gained a water bottle, probably his dead stepmother's. Anna's mind drifted and she let it. No lunch, half a bag of gummi bears, her blood sugar was sufficiently screwed up her mind might actually go someplace interesting. It didn't. It merely cast back to the night on Flattop when Joan had divvied up the scattered remnants of the bear-ravaged camp, the ones she and Anna had stuffed unceremoniously in a sack before jaunting off with Harry in search of the lost boy. It was then Anna'd noted the extraneous water bottle in the bag beside the strange stick she'd picked up just outside the camp.

Rory had denied any knowledge of that stick, Anna remembered, just as he'd denied knowing how the water bottles had proliferated. A foot long, worn smooth, of hardwood, not pine or aspen, unweathered, Anna and Joan had known it was carried in recently so when they'd found it they'd saved it. Rory said he'd never seen it. Anna hadn't thought much about it at the time. It was a stick of wood not a stick of dynamite. Now she worried it around because it fit neatly into her collection of bizarre things that didn't fit.

Anna had kept the stick. Force of habit caused her to pack it out as she would any piece of litter. Unless the house had been burglarized by beavers it was probably on the floor of Joan's spare room, where it had been dumped when she unpacked before the last foray into the wilderness.

Thinking about it, she picked up a ruler, close in length to the mystery stick, though a good deal skinnier, and began to fiddle with it. If Rory had not been lying about the stick then it had been dropped in the little meadow by someone else on or about the time they'd been camped out there. Not more than a day or two prior to their arrival. Wood, even hardwood, weathers quickly out-of-doors.

Experimentally Anna waved the ruler about, trying to ascertain the possible uses for a finished length of hardwood, several times the thickness of a ruler, packed into the backcountry. Perhaps a woodcarver, seeking his muse in the mountains, might carry in a prize piece of wood. If she remembered right, the piece she and Joan found had been battered and worn smooth with much handling. Perhaps a woodcarver who went for long periods of time between artistic inspirations.

To the detriment of the ruler's edge, she drummed it lightly against the chair arm as she thought. The minor cracking sound as she played startled her. Before and, she thought but wasn't sure, during the attack on their camp by the bear, she'd heard the crack of wood on wood. That same sound had awakened her from her troubled sleep in the rocks on the flank of Cathedral Peak. Both times she'd written it off to twigs snapping under the weight of real or imagined marauders. Whacking the chair's arm again she noted the distinct quality of the sound.

So what? So somebody was banging pieces of wood together while a bear ransacked the camp or, even less likely, while a bear thoughtfully returned Anna's water bottle to her. Did Rory hear in his dreams the crack of wood before his mother's water bottle was left beside him the night he'd been lost? Why? A signal? Nervous habit? Voodoo ritual?

"Damn," Anna repeated to herself. All roads led to blasphemy. She put the ruler back where she'd found it.

The rest of the reports had little more information to be wrung out of them. The lab report on the blue stuff sack had yet to be returned but she expected no surprises. From her intimate and prolonged traverse across the alpine talus with its moth-bearing rocks, she had no doubt the traces on the bag were just as Joan had said: rock and moth-wing dust. The bloody traces within might be other than that of Carolyn Van Slyke, but Anna doubted it. The lab report on the peanut and biscuit fragment would probably be equally unenlightening. Most often things were precisely what they appeared to be.

Because she was there and could think of nothing better to do, she filled out a BIMS, a bear incident management systems report on the sow and two cubs she'd seen feeding in the cirque below Cathedral Peak. After she'd finished, she thumbed through BIMS submitted since she'd come to Glacier. She didn't know what she hoped for.

"Validation," she said aloud. Since she had no hard evidence to base it on, she'd not bothered to put it into words for Harry Ruick, or even more damning, into writing on any reports, but she had an overweening sense of bear, a bear padding through the incidents in Glacier. The obvious was the tearing apart of the camp. Less so was the flesh of the victim cached out of reach of a bear. A man digging the food of and dwelling in the den of a bear. The water bottle with teethmarks of a bear.

Nothing striking presented itself. The BIMS that were totally bogus, the lavender ink describing the bear juggling the hedgehog and the report of the dancing bear, Anna set aside. The rest, including the report of the attack on their camp, painted an active but not extraordinarily so, picture of bears being bears.

Shuffling the crazies back into the pile, Anna felt a sudden sympathy with the lavender ink. Things were not necessarily untrue simply because they were unbelievable.

She had done what she could. Her ear was hot from being pressed to a phone all day. Her stomach was full of complaining gummi bears and the light was going from Joan's window.

Anna went "home." Home for so many years had been wherever she fed the cat. Walking through a rapidly cooling twilight enlivened by mosquitoes bent on fueling reproduction with her blood, Anna found herself terribly lonely for her critters, Piedmont's comforting purr and even Taco's three-legged bounding, leaping, licking, declaration of welcome that she'd come to expect whenever she opened the front door. Sheriff Davidson, Paul, the new man in her life, she missed as well but not with the same childish want. Davidson hadn't seen her cry like Piedmont had, hadn't saved her life like Taco had.

The next morning Anna slept in, then typed up the scraps and snippets of information she'd gleaned in a day's calling and turned them in to Harry. He read them through carefully and, in the end, could find nothing more enlightening than she had.

"We'll follow up on this Fetterman thing," he said. "I'll call Tampa and see if we can't get the local police to make a few inquiries for us."

He didn't sound overly enthused. Anna didn't blame him. If they could connect the name of Fetterman to Van Slyke, which they'd failed to do, it might be of some interest but probably wouldn't go far toward solving their murder.

"We got the lab reports back," Ruick said. "Rush job because I hinted it was part of the murder investigation but I think what you stumbled across on Cathedral Peak was an amateur entomologist with a dog off leash." He pushed the folder across the desk and Anna read it without picking it up. The peanut was, near as they could tell, a peanut. The crust of biscuit she'd found was broken down: twenty-three percent protein, four percent fat, ten percent fiber, seven percent ash, a little calcium and a dash of phosphorus. The rest was dry matter and moisture.

"Dog food." Being a responsible pet owner she'd read the backs of dog food bags to make sure Taco got a balanced diet.

They sat for a bit. Maryanne stuck her head in the office and reminded Harry that the fire management officer from Waterton was due in a few minutes.

"Well," Harry said, "I hate to keep you tied up when there's no point in it. Not to mention when I borrowed you, Glacier started paying your salary." He smiled to let Anna know it was a joke. Anna smiled back politely, pretending she believed him. Budgets were counted out by nickels and dimes. Money was always tight. "You can either pack it in and go back to the Trace or go on up. Joan's got another four days before this round of traps is completed. You can probably pick up enough about DNA testing to convince John Brown we didn't waste your time completely."

"I'll give him a call," Anna said. "See what he wants me to do." The interview was over. She pushed up out of the chair.

"I'll see an official letter of thanks gets into your personnel file," Ruick said. He stood and shook hands with her. He was warm and friendly, but she could tell she was already sinking out of his sight. Chances were he'd barely remember her name when next they met. The chief ranger was moving on to the next crisis to threaten his park. Or his career.

"You can leave your gear with the receptionist any time today," Maryanne told her as she left. A nice way of reminding her the radio needed to be checked in ASAP. Ponce had already gone back to the comfort of his paddock.

"Will do," Anna said, feeling mildly miffed. In her mind she heard her tiny, mean, long-dead grandmother cackling: *Think you're so important? Put your finger in a bucket of water, pull it out and see how big a hole it leaves.*

21

John Brown, Anna's chief ranger on the Natchez Trace Parkway, was markedly grumpy about the disruption of her learning project, somewhat mollified by having had her off the payroll for over a week, and amenable to allowing her to remain four more days to finish up, or attempt to, her training on the use of DNA research in the management of park wildlife.

Dispatch notified Joan of Anna's return. Rather than try to give detailed directions that draggled off trail through rugged country, she kindly agreed to meet Anna at Fifty Mountain so she could walk with them to the next trap site. Buck had been cut loose from the project and was hiking out as Anna hiked in, though by a different trail. He had a girlfriend in Waterton, Canada.

Civilization, much as she'd looked forward to it, had proved a disappointment. The sense of order, safety and rationality she had fantasized about had not been forthcoming. In place of safety she'd found dullness and isolation. Order and rationality had consisted of scribbling the crazy parts down on report forms and filing them, imposing not order, but an appearance of order. People so desperately needed an illusion of control to give them courage to get up in the morning.

Anna's illusion of control had been smashed years before with the sudden, meaningless death of her husband. In the years since, she'd made an effort not to give in to the need to put the pieces back together, but to see and know and accept with some degree of grace that life is meaningless. There is no Grand Plan. Everything doesn't happen for the best. One can knock till one's knuckles are bloody and the door may not be opened. Those who didn't know her well construed this to mean she was cynical or even bitter. Anna felt it allowed her to see past expectations to what *was* and freed her from the need to figure out what it *meant*.

Unfortunately, this cultivated mind-set was only half useful. It was good to see what was. But it was her job to figure out what it meant. She had failed at her job. That others had failed too was of little comfort.

Heading into the wilderness with thoughts such as these muting her senses, she found she was disappointed in the out-of-doors as well. The realization was so alarming she stopped walking and stood in the heat of the sun. She'd grown disenchanted with the natural world because it had been behaving in what seemed an unnatural manner, and disappointed with the world of people because it behaved precisely as she'd come to expect it would.

This way madness lies, she thought and took some time to realign her brain. For twenty minutes she stood sweating in the heat of the switchback noting only the breezes, the color of thimbleberry, the feather-light scratch of needles against the sky. Finally, having found her way back into her own skin, she walked on with a lighter load. Expectations abandoned, now whatever occurred, however strange, would be as nature intended. Everything would make sense. That she could not see the pattern was a fault within herself, not an aberration within the natural world.

Joan and Rory were waiting for her at Fifty Mountain Camp. They looked and smelled as if they'd been in the bush for three days and Anna was delighted. Joan's nose and forehead were sunburned and she had a scratch on one cheek from battling the shrubbery. Rory had grown brown and, to Anna's eye, taller, stronger and clearer since the death of his stepmother. Not being a Christian soul, Anna believed there were those who belonged on the Better Off Dead list. She didn't doubt that the toxic Carolyn Van Slyke was such a person. Next time she saw Lester, Anna would be disappointed if he, too, had not begun to flourish now that the influence of his violent wife was removed. Disappointed, not surprised. There was that about Lester that Anna suspected craved the violence, that he might seek out another wife who, if not actually prone to physical violence, would at least verbally and psychologically abuse him.

"Are you going to college, Rory?" she asked abruptly in the midst of their reunion.

"What? Yes, next year," he replied as the questions soaked in.

"University of Washington in Seattle?" she demanded.

"No. I'm going to school in Spokane. I got the grades to get in."

Anna was satisfied. He wouldn't be living at home. Lester Van Slyke would never be convicted of anything in a court of law. Lester was a victim and, as such, Anna supposed deserving of pity and understanding. That was fine on the surface but now and then victims, people who chose to be or to remain victims, did as much damage to the offspring of the union as the abusers did. Politically incorrect as the theory was, Anna'd kicked around long enough to know it was true

"If Rory's future is settled to your satisfaction, perhaps we might go?" Joan said and smiled with her lovely crooked teeth. Her exceedingly round cheeks pushed her glasses up.

Anna laughed. "Lead on."

"I'm glad you're back," Joan said as Rory helped her on with her pack. "We've been needing a treat."

Anna was considered a treat. Things were looking up.

The previous day Joan and Rory had dismantled a hair trap beyond the burn area to the south at a confluence of two avalanche chutes. The barbed wire was rolled and the samples secured. Rory took the hard-sided case with the blood lure and the love potion. Joan had the samples from the last two traps. Flattered to be welcomed and glad, after so long spinning her proverbial wheels, to be of service, Anna lashed the heavy rolls of wire to the frame of her pack and rotated herself into it.

Enough daylight remained that they could hike to within striking distance of where the new hair trap was to be and set up camp. Joan in the lead, they set off northward across an expanse of glorious green meadow littered with immense squared boulders. Wildflowers, late blooming because winter had held on overlong, spangled the grasses and occasionally a rare pond, tiny, midnight blue and seemingly as deep as an ocean, gleamed darkly in the undulations left by a retreating glacier.

Rory, healed by the good mountain air or exposure to Joan

Rand's idiosyncratic brand of sanity, followed Joan, chattering away like a healthy teenager.

Anna was happy to let the sound flow by with the staggering beauty of the scenery. Her own cure was at work, and normalcy was flowing back into the void murder and mayhem had carved out. Before long she added her own cheery sound pollution and whistled a tune her father had taught her, one that meandered and had no words.

Beyond the meadow the trail dropped off steeply, leading down into the valley that would eventually widen out to hold the splendor of Waterton Lake. The first mile was of switchbacks carved through rock. As it descended, the foliage thickened. Trees grew taller and mountainsides of ripe huckleberries slid away in old avalanche chutes above and below the trail.

"Great bear country this time of year," Joan hollered back. "They come for the huckleberries. So make a joyful noise. We don't want to startle anybody." Joan acted on her own direction by belting out the first line of "The Battle Hymn of the Republic" in a scratchy alto.

The light, gold with late afternoon, drenched hillsides shoulder-deep in wildflowers of every hue, pushing out from cracks in the rocks. They hiked and they sang and Anna realized balance had been restored. She was having a good time. More than that, she was having a good time with people. If that wasn't well balanced, sanity was highly overrated.

As they crossed a wide, flat shank of hill, the trail a narrow ribbon carved from the slope with pick and shovel, Joan pointed out where they would go in the morning to set up the next trap. There was no break in the ragged alder skirting. When they left the trail they would fight their way up an avalanche chute to where it converged with another, smaller chute on what Joan promised was a flattish spot.

To find a place suitable to camp, they hiked another couple of miles descending into the forest proper. So far north, with so much moisture to draw on, it came close to a forest primeval in Anna's eyes. The trees were huge, great piney boughs obscured the sky. Beneath, ferns grew tall, well overhead. There was a deep hush of needles and leaves underfoot. A crashing and a glimpse of brown through the green-cast shadows announced that they'd invaded the domain of a moose cow. Probably there was water nearby.

Anna laughed and pointed as if the others could have missed
the cow's noisy departure. Anna liked moose. She'd fallen in love
with them when she worked on Isle Royale in Michigan. The
Bullwinkle Syndrome: though moose were immense, potentially
dangerous, wild animals, their bulbous noses and shambling dis-
jointed stride always made her want to play with them. Good
sense and respect for their dignity had kept her in check.

"Moose," she said idiotically.

"There're a lot in this part of the park," Joan said.

"Cool," Rory put in.

Cool indeed.

Camp was deliciously sylvan. Doused with DEET, the mosquitoes were tolerable. The quiet was so deep it was tangible, a
force that cradled the brain in soft folds. Civilized quiet of the
same intensity made the ears ring. Here it made the soul expand.
Anna breathed it in. The gentle chitchat of camp did nothing to
injure the silence but dropped onto its surface like petals on a
pond. Anna listened to Joan joking with her young protégé, hearing the voices in pleasant counterpoint to the forest's peace.

"Story time," Joan said when supper had been eaten and the
dishes—plastic sacks into which hot water was poured to recon-
stitute various carbohydrate substances—were cleared away and
cached in a tree for the night. "What's been happening all these
three days while we've been working for a living?"

In the hours since she'd realigned her brain and enjoyed the
rejuvenating effects of Joan Rand and the wilderness, the murder
investigation had retreated so far as to seem ancient history. Anna
brought it to the fore without rancor, a puzzle only, valuable as
entertainment around a single candle Joan always burned, her
own private "campfire."

A look at Rory let Anna know the tale, though of his stepmother, held no real horrors for him. Early on, Anna knew he'd
suspected his dad. It had been that, more than Carolyn's demise,
that had tortured him. Anna guessed between pouring fish guts
and blood and nailing barbed wire to trees, he'd had a significant
amount of therapeutic conversation with Joan.

Leaning on her sleeping bag and pack, Anna told them about
her phone calls, the name of Fetterman, the unclear connection
between the truck and trailer abandoned on the northeast corner
of the park and McCaskil's aliases. The only phone conversation

she omitted was the one she'd had with Francine out of Carolyn's office. Maybe Rory'd not been as close to his stepmother as had first appeared but he didn't need to have her memory trashed.

No competition in the way of TV, radio, the Internet or floor shows, Anna had a good audience and found herself rambling on more than she intended. She told them about the night she spent hiding in the rocks on the shoulder of Cathedral Peak, how she'd dreamt of a bear padding around and woke to find her water bottle punctured by what could have been teeth, how she'd searched the den, finding it swept clean but for the peanut, the dime and the part of a biscuit.

"We're nothing if not thorough," Anna finished. "Harry even had the biscuit analyzed."

"Flour and water?" Rory ventured.

"Protein, fat, fiber, ash and a few other things," Anna told him. "Dog food was our guess."

Joan sat up, the look of passive interest sparked by something deeper. "How big was it?" she asked. "About the size of a charcoal briquet?"

"It was broken," Anna said. "But about that. Why?"

"Do you remember exactly what it was made of?"

Anna squeezed her eyes shut, trying to picture the sheet of paper. "No percentages. What I said maybe, plus calcium. The bulk, I remember, was dry matter. Sounded sinister to me."

"Omnivore food," Joan said.

Anna opened her eyes. "Omnivore food?"

"It's what we feed bears in captivity. A normal-sized bear will eat about six pounds of omnivore food and about that much in fruits and vegetables every day."

"Somebody's feeding the bears?" Rory said. "I mean, feeding them bear food?"

Anna laughed. Feeding bears intentionally or otherwise in the national parks was an ongoing problem, but Rory was right. Nobody fed them bear food. "Why would anybody do that?" she asked. "To lure the bears?"

"Bears eat it," Joan said. "Bears aren't finicky. But it's no great lure. We spent years developing lures. Omnivore chow isn't even in the top one hundred. The stuff hasn't got much of an odor. The scent not only doesn't broadcast, it's not all that alluring. You might feed bears with it but I doubt you could use it to attract them."

"You could habituate them," Rory said unexpectedly. "You know, always have food for them at the same time and the same place so they come there over and over."

Anna and Joan thought about that for a while. "You could," Anna said slowly. "But why?"

Between them they listed the obvious reasons: to shoot them, observe them, capture them, photograph them. All were possible, none practical. Glacier National Park was a place where bears were protected, monitored. Their numbers, habits and activities were scrutinized by rangers, researchers and an increasingly informed public. If a person wished to manipulate the bears in any of the suggested ways, there were thousands upon thousands of acres just to the north in British Columbia where, on private lands, it could be done either legally or with a much greater chance of remaining undetected.

"Boone and Crockett," Anna said, remembering the Washington man evilly ogling the elk. "A trophy-sized bear, one that could tempt a poacher?"

"Not in the lower forty-eight," Joan said. "Because of food, genetics, etcetera, our bears are on the small side. A big old male could weigh maybe five hundred pounds. Maybe. Four or four-fifty would be more like it. The trophy hunters do Canada up north, or Alaska."

"An idiot?" Anna suggested. "Wandering around like some demented Johnny Appleseed feeding bears?"

"There's always room for another idiot," Joan admitted.

Anna had her own tent this time out and she found she missed Joan's company. Through the cloth walls she could hear the other woman snoring in an unladylike fashion and found the noise soothing. Sleep was eluding Anna and it was good to know someone was resting.

The nerves and hyperawareness that had poisoned her last night in the backcountry had passed. She was not lying awake waiting for the clack of sticks and the onslaught of toothy beasts. The man who had rolled a stone down at her and fired off a round didn't concern her much, either. He had not stalked her. It was she who'd sought him out. If he'd not already finished whatever he'd been up to and left the park, he was probably staying as far away from anybody in green and gray as he could.

Telling her story to Joan and Rory had loosed the scraps and facts she'd managed to tuck away. Now they blew about till the inside of her skull looked like Fifth Avenue after a ticker-tape parade. Joan and Rory; the conversation had triggered something. Anna lay comfortable in her bag, fingers locked behind her head, eyes on the perfect darkness beyond the screen of her front door, waiting for the scrap that would fit to sort itself out from the others. Feeding the bears, trophy bears floated by, Boone and Crockett. That was it. Boone and Crockett, the last word on what was and was not a trophy animal and where it fit in the hierarchy of biggest and best based on skull measurements—taken after death, naturally.

In the pocket of the surplus army jacket Carolyn Van Slyke was caught dead in, the jacket they were pretty sure belonged to William McCaskil, was a piece of note paper. "B & C" was written at the top. Below was a list of numbers. Boone and Crockett and the measurements of a trophy animal, Anna was willing to bet. In the morning she would radio Ruick and get him to check it out.

What, if anything, it had to do with Van Slyke's murder, she couldn't fathom. Had Carolyn seen and photographed this animal and so been killed and mutilated, her film stolen? Glacier didn't have trophy-sized bears, but there were other creatures: moose, elk, mountain lion. That didn't account for the omnivore food. And who would kill and mutilate a photographer for taking a picture of the animal? How would one be caught in a compromising position with a trophy-sized animal? It was feasible the poacher could pack the kill out. They needn't take the whole animal. Just the head.

Now there was a grisly picture.

Anna shook her head in the dark. By dint of great mental strain, she'd solved one more small mystery: what the list in the army jacket meant. And nothing but nothing was cleared up.

"You asleep, Joan?" she whispered on impulse.

No answer from the neighboring tent.

"Goodnight then," she said and resolutely shut her brain off for the night.

Work was good: hard, hot, deerflies biting. Wretched scrambles through cutting brush with a heavy pack on was what Anna was good at. Like fighting wildland fire, it was deliciously mindless in that just staying on one's feet and doing one's job took total concentration. Joan Rand was an added blessing. When Anna had a boss she trusted, she found enormous relief and contentment in just following orders.

Shortly after two p.m. they had the DNA hair trap assembled. Rory predicted the pickings from this site would be slim. He expressed the opinion that the North American grizzly was too intelligent to work as hard as they had just to roll in essence of rotted fish and eat a few huckleberries.

Rory was showing signs of being a kid and not the scared, suspicious shadow of an adult that Anna'd seen when they'd first met. She was beginning to enjoy his company. Joan always had, but then when it came to adolescent boys she saw through the eyes of a mother. Anna's were more akin to those of a parole officer.

The eighty feet of barbed wire stapled in a rough circle around a place that was only flat in Joan's imagination, they began the butt-and-heels slide down to the trail.

The next site to be disassembled was back the direction they'd camped. A luxury—since they'd be several nights there, they didn't have to carry all their gear on their backs during the day.

With a minimum of cursing and scratches, they regained the trail. As they caught their breath, the radio crackled out Joan's call number. It was the chief ranger asking for Anna.

"You got a fax," Ruick said. "From some gal at the Tampa tourism office. Looks like a brochure for Fetterman's Adventure Trails. Nothing on it clicked with me. I'm guessing the alias was a fluke."

"Describe it for me." Anna waited while Harry marshaled his thoughts.

"Nothing out of the ordinary. It's a fax. The resolution isn't all that great. Fetterman's looks like a lot of those tourist trap places. Fun for the whole family sort of thing. There's a picture of what's probably an alligator. Let's see. Animal shows. Souvenirs.

Looks like a kind of swamp tour thing with nutria being fed to gators. Kind of a mom and pop operation. There's a group picture on the back. Faces are a blur. Underneath. Let's see . . . 'Looking forward to new friends, George and Suzanne Fetterman, Carl Micou, Geoffrey Micou, Arthur Gray and Tunis Chick.'

"The gal who sent it has written in the margin, 'Adventure Trails was closed down after George Fetterman's death earlier this summer.'"

"How old is the brochure?" Anna asked. "Can you tell?"

"Hmm. Lemme see, lemme see. Here. Nineteen ninety-six. Old. I expect nothing much changed in Adventure Trails from year to year."

Anna gave the radio back to Joan. Harry had just called as a courtesy. The brochure held little interest and less information. Neither she nor he had any desire to waste airtime playing twenty questions to figure out what if anything a derelict roadside attraction in Florida had to do with a dead and mutilated Seattle divorce lawyer in Montana.

In fact, Anna's mental gears had been sufficiently shifted over to the DNA project that they had hiked two miles down the trail before she figured it out.

"Joan! Stop!"

Joan and Rory turned to look back at her. Anna had stalled in the middle of the trail.

"Tell me about that boy you've been e-mailing. The one making the map," she demanded of the researcher.

22

Normally it would have been a hike of four hours or more from where they were to the tiny meadow where they had camped nearly a week before. They covered the ground in just over three, arriving an hour before sunset.

Having left tents, stoves, sleeping bags and the rest of their camping gear behind, they traveled light and moved quickly. Without the amenities the night would be uncomfortable but Anna had not wanted to lose the time it would have taken to return and strike camp then climb back up to the plateau on Flattop carrying the added burdens.

In truth she'd not wanted the added burden in the persons of Joan and Rory but, after she'd traded her theory for Joan's information, they refused to be left behind. It increased her sense of responsibility, yet she was glad not to be alone. Because she suspected the park radios were being listened to by people other than rangers, she'd made the decision not to call Ruick to send backup.

The decision was not as foolhardy as it appeared on the surface. No one could start for the high country till morning anyway. Anna had all night to change her mind.

Leaving the trail before it neared Trapper Peak, Anna, Joan and Rory followed the slope in a southerly direction along the side of Flattop. This flank of the mountain was west-facing and caught the brunt of the afternoon sun. Several tiny lakes, carved an eternity before by glaciers and fed by small streams carrying snowmelt, provided water. It was prime huckleberry country and the berries were at the height of their season.

A half-mile or so beyond their old campsite, on an upthrust of rock, Anna stopped. Partly she was motivated by the sounds of heavy breathing behind her. She'd set a punishing pace. That she, too, was breathing hard was of no consequence. If she was right, time was of the essence, not only to save a valuable life but to see a sight that she would never forgive herself for missing.

A grunt and sucking sound told her Rory had dumped his pack at the base of the rock and gotten out his water bottle. Joan crept up beside Anna, aping her pose, elbows on the higher stones, body crouched behind. The researcher's round face was alarmingly red. The hair that curled from beneath her ball cap was glued to her cheeks with sweat, and the upper regions of her oversized glasses were beaded with moisture. Despite the physical costs, Joan's first words were, "Do you see anything?"

"Not yet. Tell me again about the e-mails," Anna said.

"Okay. Right. Let me think." *Breathe* would have been as apt a word. Anna waited while Joan recovered and lined her thoughts up for a round of scientific reasoning.

"First e-mail about six weeks ago. Maybe more. The screen name is Balthazar. He says he's a high school student doing a research project on grizzly bears. He wants to know their ranges, denning habits, eating habits, if they're protected at Glacier, or if we allow hunting. Sensing an acolyte, naturally I fell all over myself to answer."

"Naturally." Anna unboxed her binoculars. Above the little lake, the land was sloped and thick with undergrowth. Nearer the water the bushes thinned out, creating a small natural meadow. The pine forest straggled down unimpressively, the trees thirty and forty feet apart.

"And you figure this Balthazar really was a high school student, not just some guy?"

"Maybe not high school but young. He never made any attempt to show me what he knew. The more education you get, the more irresistible that becomes."

"Six or eight weeks ago," Anna said as much to herself as Joan. "About the time George Fetterman was kicking the bucket."

"Several more e-mails like that," Joan went on. "Late July around then. Then no more for a week or so. Then the map idea comes up. The questions become very specific. Where the bears eat, when."

"About this time we're packing to head out for the first round of DNA traps. Same time as the truck and horse trailer are found abandoned," Anna said.

"Yes. Near as I can figure."

"And you told him . . ."

"Flattop burn, glacier lilies."

"Then we go down with the dead woman and you've got mail."

"I tell him Cathedral Peak for army cutworm moths. And, in a week or so, Flattop, west side, huckleberries."

Rory pushed up beside them. "You think some guy is trying to trap a bear or something? Like to put in a side show?"

"Not exactly," Anna said.

Rory came and went. Napped in the last of the sun. Anna and Joan stayed where they were, raking the hillside with binoculars.

Once Joan nudged Anna and pointed. A black bear, nearly the size of a grizzly, ambled out from the scrub below the clearing. Through the glasses Anna could see its nostrils open and close as it checked for danger. By good fortune and foresight they were downwind. Dressed in muted colors, lying low on the rock, they watched it unseen.

A quarter of an hour later a small grizzly sow, probably not quite three hundred pounds, came from higher up. She was a rich brown, almost the same shade as the black bear who, like many of his compatriots, was black only in name, not in hue. With her was a single cub, one born this season. The cub ran after her, nipping and tugging at her ankles. Anna smiled as she and Joan simultaneously said "awww" under their breath.

Half an hour more and Anna was getting wiggly. Joan had spent so many hours in uncomfortable positions watching empty tracts of land that she'd slid easily into research time and moved not at all. But for the slow arcing of the glasses as she scanned the area, Anna would have suspected her of having fallen asleep.

Ten minutes before sunset, when down-canyon winds, the night breath of the mountains, was chilling the back of Anna's neck, Joan whispered a prayer.

"Oh, my heavens," she said. "He's a god. I must apologize to the lab at the University of Idaho."

"Where?" Anna demanded. "Where?"

"Shh. There. Twenty degrees west of the last tree. Closer in. There. Rory!" she hissed. "Wake up. Come up. Bring your glasses."

Anna was scanning the huckleberry-choked hillside, seeing nothing but a blur. Then he was there, standing on his hind legs easily eleven feet tall, easily twelve hundred pounds and an incredible golden color. The rays of the setting sun struck him full on the side, the light flaring like fire on his pelt, running in sharp liquid flame over the pale guard hairs of his hump and the tops of his ears. "Jiminy," Anna breathed. "Boone and Crockett, eat your heart out."

"See him?" Joan whispered to Rory, who had belly-crawled up between them. "An Alaskan grizzly."

The magnificent creature was no more than twenty yards from where they lay. He had been feeding on the huckleberries that grew thick through a low cut in the hillside, little more than a ditch, but sufficient to hide him from sight until he stood up on his hind legs.

"I see him!" Rory hollered, sudden and loud in his excitement.

"Shh," Joan hissed, but it was too late. The great golden head turned in their direction. The nostrils flared and the huge paws twitched. Even at a distance of sixty feet, Anna could see the claws, four-inch nails, dull white against the slightly darker fur of the animal's belly.

Brown eyes looked at the three of them, locked with Anna's then the bear looked away, growled as if uncertain. His great forelegs swung, the incredible power in them rippling smoothly beneath the backlit hide.

The black bear, the sow, even the little cub stopped feeding. The black bear huffed and snorted, the sound an unhappy pig would make. For an instant it looked as if he would stand, meet the challenge. Then he chose the better part of valor, turned and loped away, quickly hidden by the ensnaring tangle of brush.

The cub squeaked and hopped in excitement and earned a stern cuff from its mother. Silence settled back, unbroken by the noises of foraging animals. Unbroken by the sound of breathing. Consciously, Anna stopped holding her breath.

Crack. Crack.

Not nearby but carrying clearly in the still air; the sound of twigs breaking, or of wood on wood. The sound Anna had heard the night the bear tore up their camp, the night she'd dreamed a bear stalked her hiding place in the rocks on Cathedral Peak.

Crack.

The great golden bear looked back at Anna's rock and roared, a huge and awful sound that shook the hair on its chest and bared teeth red as blood in the failing light.

"You go," Anna said quietly.

"Anna—" Joan whispered.

"You fucking *go!* Take Rory." Anna didn't—couldn't—take her eyes off the bear. Behind her she heard hurried scraping as Joan and Rory slid down the back of the rock out of the bear's line of sight. Anna doubted her vehemence had convinced Joan to leave. Rand would be intent on saving the boy. A fear of bears, faced with a bear of this magnitude, was bound to melt Rory's mind.

"Don't let him run," Anna whispered. It didn't matter that Joan didn't hear her. Joan knew more about bears than Anna ever would. Except maybe what it felt like to be eaten by one.

Crack.

Again the bear roared and dropped to all fours, never once looking away from Anna.

Fleetingly she wondered if she'd been wise sending Rory and Joan away. Bears were less likely to attack groups. There were records of grizzlies attacking groups of three and four but it was less common than attacks on a single person.

But this wasn't a regular bear. Joan knew it too—or sensed it. That's why she'd gone.

For a moment the bear waited, huge golden paws flattening the grass, his great head swaying from side to side as tiny bear thoughts in his small bear brain shook into alignment. Anna had not moved. She could not decide whether to make herself small and nonthreatening or as large and imposing as possible. She had a hunch with this bear it wouldn't matter a damn what she did. The need to run made her legs trembly. She ignored it. Not from bravery but because the image of the bear lunging at her back was too terrifying.

She slipped the can of bear spray from her belt. Coming from behind her was rustling, then a thump. Either Rory or Joan, like a Japanese maiden in a horror movie, had tripped and fallen while fleeing the monster.

The great bear heard it too. His head ceased to sway. A roar built in the massive chest as his eyes focused to the left of Anna's rock. Springing to her feet she began waving her arms over her head. Large and imposing it was to be then, though at five-foot-four and one-hundred-twenty pounds, Anna felt woefully inadequate.

"Hey bear, hey bear," she shouted.

Crack. Crack. Crack. A low whistle.

The grizzly charged. Never would Anna have believed an animal that size could move that fast. The sun dyed his coat red and the fur rippled as he came, beautiful and shining like that of a well-groomed golden retriever. Anna was so transfixed by the uncanny beauty she forgot to be afraid for a second, forgot to turn profile, forgot she was not supposed to look the animal in the eye, forgot she held bear spray in her right hand.

The bear came on, his powerful legs moving over the broken ground with liquid grace. Roaring was done. He was intent only on Anna. She could hear the labored whuff of breath. He was enormous. Rising from the low swell of ground her rock lookout topped, he towered over her.

"Not running, not running, not running," chanted through her mind as she raised the can of bear spray, a fly swatter against an avalanche.

A scream cut through to her. Not her own. A sharp cry that made the bear flinch.

"Drop the pepper spray. God. Please."

Anna had heard the voice before. Faith, not trust, opened Anna's fingers and the pepper spray fell away. Curling down after it, she rolled up like a pill bug, her arms covering her ears, hands clasped over the back of her neck, knees pulled up to protect her more vulnerable parts. The fetal position. This was how she'd first been introduced to the world. Was this how she was going to leave it?

A blow that nearly uncurled her pounded into her shoulder and she felt herself knocked down the backside of the rock like a hockey puck off broken ice. Her kneecap struck stone. Anna felt nothing but the impact. Pain would come later.

Pressure. The bear was on her. She could feel the weight of his chest against her side. Fur, amazingly soft, pressed down on her bare legs. She felt the squash of the great arms as the bear tried to crush her or roll her over. Her face was buried in its pelt. Heat and smell and fur surrounded, suffocated. The bear was absorbing her, smashing her into its very being. Heavy hot breath smelling of huckleberries and things less pleasant washed over her face. Like a child, Anna squeezed her eyes shut whispering, "Go away, please go away."

Crack.

The weight lifted. The animal growled, low and questioning, then roared and another blow fell. This one did unwrap Anna from around herself. She felt her legs fly out, her head snap back and she was rolling down the stony hillside. Her skull smacked against rock and she cried out. Her eyes flew open. She saw the bear and the darkness descending on her together.

Anna had not expected to wake up; or if she did, to wake in the tradition of Jonah, in the innards of Monstro. First came thought, a sense of mind creeping forth from a place far more distant than sleep. She knew she was thirsty and she knew she was cold. Opening her eyes, she knew she was blind or had gone to a place where sight did not matter. It was as black outside of her skull as it had been within.

It wasn't that Anna did not care, it was that she could not think, so fear didn't follow. As she lay in the black she noted she was breathing. With that fragment of earthy information she began to assume she had not left the world she'd grown accustomed to. Surely in heaven, hell, purgatory, Valhalla or wherever, the incessant labor of lungs would no longer be mandatory.

Form came next, form in the darkness, shades of night. She lay on her side in a patch of stone exposed by an old avalanche twenty feet or more from the rock where she, Rory and Joan had sat watch. Night had come. If the moon had risen it was weak and distant. Only the faint light of stars separated the earth from the sky.

Confusion engendered by a bash on the head and waking in the dark was as brief as it was intense. Time, place and circumstances reinstated themselves. The bear had left her for dead. Possibly the fact she'd banged her head on a rock and gone unconscious had saved her life. A black bear, a bear who attacked not to intimidate and frighten off, but to procure dinner, would have taken a few pounds of flesh. Satisfied she was no longer a threat the grizzly had left her in one piece.

One battered piece. Without moving much, lest the bear had not gone away, Anna assessed the damage as best she could. No claw or bite marks. None. That was a surprise. Cuffed about as she had been, she thought surely she'd been cut. The only blood she found was below her left ear where she'd collided with a rock. Her head ached fiercely but the truly significant pain was in her knee. When she rolled to all fours and tried to push herself up she nearly cried out loud. Standing was actually an improvement, and though it hurt to do so, she was relieved to find she could put her weight on it. The joint was not damaged but the kneecap itself was either cracked or badly bruised.

Why hadn't the bear clawed or bitten her? It was in the nature of beasts to use claws and teeth, to worry and strike and bite. The last she remembered before the bear had bowled her down the hill like a hedgehog had been the furry overpowering sensation that the creature was trying to embrace her.

Hedgehog . . . what had the report written in lavender ink said? *Bear activity: juggling a hedgehog. Observer activity: standing amazed.*

Anna had been juggled, bowled and left, but for a chance accident, entirely unscathed.

Alive and well and standing amazed, Anna thought and hobbled to a stone where she could sit down, the damaged knee unbent. The clearing was empty, no sign of the eaters of huckleberries. No sign of Rory and Joan. Anna looked at her watch. She'd been unconscious a long time, maybe twenty minutes or more. Another ten had been used up while she metaphorically put herself back together again. Where the hell was Joan? Why hadn't she come back to see if Anna lived or died?

Because her head hurt and she'd been left in the dirt by a giant bear, Anna attempted to entertain the idea that Joan had abandoned her, run all the way back to West Flattop Trail intent on saving her own skin.

The story wouldn't wash. Not only would it be out of character for Joan as a good woman to leave another to die, it would be out of character for Joan as a good researcher to leave a fantastically out-of-place golden Alaskan grizzly without photos, scat samples and much in the way of scientific contemplation.

Joan was around. If she hadn't come back it was because she couldn't come back. Anna felt the sickening boil of fear as she wondered if Joan had come back too soon. If the bear had left Anna to pursue more lively prey.

She opened her mouth to call out, thought better of it and closed it again. No time to go off half-cocked. A few minutes limping and fumbling located her day pack. She took inventory. A little food. Plenty of water. Pliers, hammer, staples, small hard-sided case with the last skunk love-scent canister inside and a well-used topographical map. Since she'd fully intended to be back in camp before sundown, she'd not brought a flashlight. Joan had the radio and, search as she might, the can of bear spray she'd dropped was not to be found.

Feeling unarmed and fragile, she sat again on her rock. The cold was deepening. She didn't have a jacket with her for the same reason she was without a flashlight. The Boy Scout motto came to mind. A lesson to be learned. Again. The hard way.

Without light she couldn't search for Joan. Without a radio, she couldn't call for help. The one thing she could do was move from this exposed place. Pushing to her feet, she limped slowly toward the thickening screen of alder that heralded the pine forest proper. Chances of encountering a bear or *the* bear were greater in the coverts, but like any hurt and frightened animal, Anna felt the need to hide.

Moving slowly, favoring her bad knee, she picked her way over the rock-embedded land past the miniature lake. Till the moon rose, her eyes were of questionable use and she stopped every few steps to listen. Partly she listened for Joan and Rory; mostly she listened for any sign that the bear was still in the neighborhood. The only sounds she heard were those of her own making.

Beneath the alders darkness was absolute. Anna lost all sense of direction and, knowing what she did was illogical and dangerous, she pushed on. Nowhere seemed safe. Nowhere seemed a good place to stop. The small clearing was too exposed, too near the water source where bears would come to drink. The thicket was too closed in, too dark. Her knee was swelling, her head had left its dull ache to throb, but still she could not bring herself to stop.

Because the patron saint of lost souls—or fools—guided her footsteps she came not to the edge of a cliff or ravine but out of the thicket and into the more open land beneath the pines.

The moon had yet to rise, but there was a hint of ambient light from the sky. After feeling her way blindly through the brush, Anna felt relief as her eyes came alive once more. The need to keep moving abated somewhat. That and the pain in her knee finally convinced her it was wiser to stop.

Back against a pine, she straightened her leg, drank water and listened. From a ways away—a mile, a yard, she couldn't tell— came the shush of a body passing through brush. The water froze in Anna's throat. Forcing herself to swallow it, she flinched at the audible gulping sound she made.

More listening. Faint, very faint, a hissing roar like that of distant water rushing down a narrow gorge. No rivers this high, no streams of that magnitude; Anna wondered if she was suffering an auditory hallucination brought on by a bang on the head. Far away, disturbingly hard to get a sense of, the hissing continued. Then, just as faint, just as clear in the still, crystal air, a clink. Metal, the key to the aural conundrum.

The hiss was the familiar obnoxious noise of a Coleman stove, the clink a pan or lid. Someone was making dinner. Anna pushed herself up, started toward the sound in too much of a hurry. The knee gave out and she fell. When the pain ebbed, she sent a tiny prayer of gratitude into a heaven she believed to be deaf and dumb.

Joan would not leave her knocked out in a rocky field while she calmly prepared dinner less than a mile away. Joan didn't have a stove or camp gear. Anna, in her rush to be right, had dragged her and Rory into this mess as unprepared as she herself was.

For a time she remained sprawled on the soft carpet of needles, unsure whether it was better to go see who was camping in her woods or to run away.

The rumble from the Coleman stopped. An angry voice, just one, the words unclear but the savage tone unmistakable, made the decision for her. Setting her mind beyond the pain in her leg, Anna moved toward the source of the noise with infinite care, one step, one tree at a time. Twice she was stopped. Twice she thought she heard the stealthy padding of oversized paws on the pine needles in the darkness behind her.

The steps stopped when she stopped. Maybe it was only the crush of her own booted feet placed with such care. Maybe she imagined it. Whatever the source, Anna no longer wanted to run away. The terror behind her was as insistent as that which lay ahead.

The ranting voice, though more unsettling, was easier to track through the dark than the amorphous hiss of the stove had been. A person venting with such energy also made enough of a racket to cover the unavoidable sounds of her progress; she covered ground quickly.

Speed acted against her in a peculiar way. The faster she moved, the more she believed she was being pursued, the better she could imagine the glowing eyes and bared teeth inches from the nape of her neck. It took effort and a damaged knee to keep her from giving in to childlike panic and running toward the sound of a human voice.

A misstep. The knee twisted and Anna was forced to a halt. Her breathing was ragged. She'd broken a sweat that would soon turn to chill. *Out of control,* she warned herself, and *Breathe.*

Not making noise in body by movement or in mind by fear of the dark and the monsters that dwelt therein, Anna began to hear distinct words: "Out. Not a fucking game. By Christ I will."

Sobered, she moved again. Closing out the vision of the bear, she returned to the calming slowness that had marked her progress in the beginning, careful to make no sound, barge into no solid objects in the dark.

Another minute and she stopped abruptly. Perhaps fifteen feet in front of her was a dark form. A man, she guessed. He held a flashlight that he was pointing into the woods in the opposite direction from where she stood. By its backwash she could see he was tall and under his right arm he held a long-barreled rifle. In the pale spill of the flash she saw Joan and Rory.

Joan's face was colorless but for black around one corner of her mouth that could be blood or dirt. Her wrists and ankles were tied together so she had to sit hunched over, elbows around her knees. Rory was beside her. His ankles had been lashed together but his hands were free. He held them palm up in front of his face as if he felt for raindrops. At his feet the Coleman stove lay on its side, a pan tipped over nearby.

Rory'd been put to cooking, Anna guessed. In a rage the man with the flashlight had kicked over the stove, burning Rory's hands in the process.

"Goddamn it," the man bellowed. The light swung like a sword, piercing the darkness several feet to Anna's left. Staring right at her, Bill McCaskil screamed, "Come out now or I'll blow their fucking heads off!"

23

The McCaskil who held the rifle and the flashlight was a different man than the shifty Lothario Anna remembered. Days alone in the wilderness had had an adverse effect on the city boy. His beard was rough, his hair matted and spiky by turns, his clothes dirty. The biggest change was the eyes. McCaskil was scared, scared to the point of unreason. Even in the dim backwash of the flashlight Anna could see his irises were entirely ringed in white as his facial muscles pulled the lids away. Whatever edge he'd been running toward when he came to Glacier, McCaskil had been pushed over it.

A crazy man, a scared crazy man, with a rifle and hostages. In law enforcement this was what was referred to as a worst-case scenario.

"Out," McCaskil cried in a voice ugly with fear. He swung the rifle toward Rory and Joan, and Anna raised her hands, stepped forward. She never made it into the light. McCaskil was wheeling, screaming, the flashlight raking the trees. He'd not seen her.

"I'm not going to hurt him." His voice became wheedling as he turned. Silence followed, deepened by the darkness and the trees. "Balthazar's mine!" he shrieked and Anna flinched. Whomever he shouted for, it wasn't her. Joan and Rory must have told him they were alone. Anna blessed them for their courage and began creeping around the circle. McCaskil was beyond negotiation even if she'd had anything to negotiate with. Running away was the best option. With the cover of night she could do it easily if she left Joan and Rory.

A gut-numbing roar froze the cowardly thoughts; bear—*the* bear—close by. McCaskil screamed high and shrill, and the rifle at his side fired, the glare of the muzzle harsh and bright and then gone, leaving a red wound seared across Anna's night vision.

"I'll kill them. You'll have killed them," he screamed into the night. "Like you killed that Van Slyke woman. Butcher. I'll do it."

A great gush of terror brought the contents of Anna's stomach into her throat and she had to fight to keep from retching. The slicer of faces was somewhere in the darkness with her. He, and a great bear that seemed to have an agenda of its own.

Run away, run away, she thought and moved to the next tree, closer to Joan and Rory.

The two of them sat shoulder to shoulder about fifteen feet from the mad McCaskil. Ranting, a second round fired, the thrashing of his booted feet as he made short, aborted dashes at sounds only he could hear, covered the noise Anna made as she moved.

The west-facing slope was dryer than the valleys, and there was little undergrowth, not much in the way of cover but shadow and luck. Behind Rory and Joan, several yards in the woods, Anna parked herself in the shelter of a tree that she hoped was wide enough to hide her should McCaskil's light come back around. Her shirt was gray, her shorts green—all to the good—but in the near-perfect darkness under the pines, should light touch on her bare arms, her legs or her face, they would shine like beacons.

Making herself small in mind if not in body, she wriggled out of her day pack and set it squarely in front of her where probing light would not fire its burgundy hue in a dun and green landscape. Working by feel, Anna groped through it. Her breath was coming in short shallow gasps, audible, panicked. Her scalp was tingling and she was losing sensation in her hands and feet. *Hyperventilating,* she warned herself. *Too scared.* Lifting the pack to her face in lieu of the traditional paper sack, she breathed into it, then out. The smells of her short history in Glacier were all there: peanut butter, skunk, sweat, fish guts, grease, dust. The skin on her head loosened, her heart ceased to pound in her ears, her fingers began to feel like fingers. Ten breaths more, counted out over a brief eternity, and she put the pack down again. In her hand were the wire cutters, quicker and more sure than a Swiss army knife dulled from years of promiscuous use.

The light flew erratically past. She waited a moment for the sound of a rifle shot and the sudden blasting away of an exposed elbow or knee, but she'd not been spotted. Further out into the trees, drowned in the impossible ink of a woodland night, she heard the stealthy sound of padded feet moving over duff.

Nothing she could do about that. She pushed it from her mind.

A quick peek let her know McCaskil had turned again and faced away from her. He stopped shouting. In a voice dead calm and more frightening because of it, he spoke to the darkness, "In one minute I will kill the boy. You can save him. Balthazar's life for the boy's. One minute." He began counting down in a loud voice.

Out of the frying pan, Anna said to herself and rolled from the cover of her tree. Ignoring the burst of pain in her injured knee, she moved as rapidly as possible toward the others. In seconds she knelt behind Rory. "Not a sound," she hissed in his ear. She showed him the wire cutters and he understood. Quickly and quietly, he swung his feet around.

Joan's head turned. Without light Anna could not read her expression. She trusted in Joan's good sense. What she could not know was how much of it fear had eaten away. As there was nothing to be done to reassure either the researcher or herself, Anna ignored her.

Closing her mind to the possibilities, Anna felt at Rory's ankles. Thin, hard plastic; McCaskil had bound his prisoners with the disposable cuffs policemen carry as spares. Clearly he'd come prepared. Though virtually impossible to break, he couldn't have picked anything more vulnerable to fence pliers, and Anna was grateful.

"Twenty-nine," McCaskil called. "Twenty-eight."

Snip, snip.

Anna clipped a bit of Rory's flesh along with the plastic and he hollered, "Ouch!" The wretched rotten boy actually said ouch. "Sorry," he whispered too late.

"He's turning," Joan hissed.

"Run," Anna said and pushed Rory to his feet, "run!" She shoved at unidentified bits of boy anatomy as she scrambled to her feet to follow.

A hailstorm of words, shrieked and screamed from what

sounded like the throats of a multitude of demons, rained down.
McCaskil's threats, Rory's squeaks, Joan's exhortations and
Anna's own sailorlike vocabulary of meaningless obscenities. Mc-
Caskil's flashlight shivered and snapped. In her mind Anna heard
Teddy Pinson, an old college friend, intone, *"'The vorpal blade
went snicker-snack!'"*

Rory disappeared in darkness followed by a gunshot close
and loud, a blow on Anna's eardrums. Cutting through trauma-
induced deafness came a scream. Anna's mind folded down in
confusion. The metallic swallowing sound of a bolt-action rifle
and another round was chambered. Anna'd fallen. Had she been
shot and screamed? Had the bullet found Rory in the dark? Before enough time had elapsed to draw a full breath, Anna knew
she'd not been hit. Her knee had given out as she'd lunged for the
cover of the woods.

"No!"

That was Joan. Anna rolled and the butt of McCaskil's rifle
pounded down, not the killing blow to the back of the head he'd
intended, but a glancing strike to the shoulder that made Anna
cry out.

McCaskil had thrown aside the flashlight. The beam ran
along the ground catching up the rust of the needles, illuminating
the man's booted feet. Anna bunched up her weight on her left
hip and kicked out. The sole of her boot connected with Mc-
Caskil's ankle. Fierce pain shot up from her bad knee but she
scarcely felt it. McCaskil went down on one knee.

Writhing across the slippery bed of needles, as single-minded
as a sidewinder, Anna struck out again, connecting this time with
his shin. The man bellowed in rage and fell back on butt and
heels. No time to rise and shine. Knowing she had more strength
in her legs than her upper body, Anna propelled herself after him.
Crablike, snakelike, scuttling like a scorpion, hoping like any low
and little thing to strike quickly enough and with enough venom
to survive one more day.

McCaskil retreated. He hit the fallen flashlight and the beam
spun, a drunken beacon, then stopped, spotlighting the two of
them. McCaskil had the thirty-ought-six, a Weatherby, Anna
noted from habit, raised to his shoulder, the barrel pointed between his knees past the toes of his boots at her face. Even a mad-
man would not miss at this range.

"Easy, Bill. You're okay, Bill. It won't work. Rory's gone; a witness. You can't do it, Bill. Give it up, Bill."

Joan was talking: smooth, calming as if to a wounded and wild beast. She was doing, saying all the right things, using the man's name, trying to bring him back to himself.

It was too late. Whatever indicates reason, an indefinable inner light in the eye, had gone out in Bill McCaskil. Shadows scraped up from the cockeyed light, making of his nose a mountain that eclipsed one side of his face from the piecemeal sun. His upper lip, long, well formed, the skin darkened with a week's growth of beard, curled up exposing teeth that shone white and feral. With that small movement McCaskil's face ceased to be human and Anna knew he was going to kill her. She did not want Bill McCaskil's to be the face that went with her into eternity. She turned her head, looked at Joan Rand.

A roar shattered the tableau, so close, so visceral, the wild rage of the world and of the mind gathered into a sound so dark and awful, the night itself seemed to have turned on them. Mingling with it were terrible screams and the hopeless sound of a David being torn to pieces by a Goliath of fur and fury.

"Rory!" Joan cried.

McCaskil jumped. The rifle barrel moved an inch off center. Anna grabbed the barrel and kicked at his knee. Bones loosened by the thunder of the bear, McCaskil let go. Anna yanked the rifle from his nerveless fingers. Dragging it, she crawled away in an undignified but necessary retreat. Close fighting was not for the small of frame.

The horrible roaring deepened, intensified, and Anna found herself crouched, gun across her knees like a frightened hillbilly. Breathing past the primal terror, she forced herself to her feet, braced her back against a tree to stop her shaking and to take the weight off her weak knee. McCaskil made no attempt to rise, to run, to finish killing Anna or to be killed by her.

The roaring went on and on pinning him to the ground, Anna to the tree and Joan to the tiny patch of earth her bonds had made her home for too long.

The flashlight rocked back and forth, making shadows wild. Finally it stopped. The roaring stopped. Time itself stopped, or so it seemed. Anna's arms were quivering, the rifle hard to hold.

Thin whimpering percolated through the new-made stillness: hers, McCaskil's, Rory's, Joan's—it was impossible to tell.

The darkness just beyond the reach of the flashlight shivered, changed. Anna leveled the Weatherby at the manifestation and waited somewhere beyond fear, just this side of insanity.

Ripples of gold unsettled the shadow, catching the imperfect light of the flash. Out of the woods padded the great grizzly, beside him the crying boy with the smile of a saint. On the bear's other side walked Rory, the same Rory whose screams had indicated he was snack food.

The spinning effervescence of a fairy tale snatched up Anna's brain. This bear was with them, of them, glittering gold protector of babes lost in the woods. A dozen stories of wild things become human, princes enchanted, curses fulfilled, were physically manifest and Anna was ensorcelled, charmed, turned to wood and bark like a recalcitrant wood nymph. Her limbs could not move. Her voice had locked itself away deep in her throat.

"Don't shoot him," the boy said, as if Anna could have destroyed that much beauty even to save her own worthless hide. "His name is Balthazar."

"How do you do?" Anna croaked idiotically. To her amazement the bear raised a single huge paw to shake and she laughed, sounding, at least in her ears, a little on the hysterical side.

Recovering from the bear theatrics—given that Rory's skin was still whole and he was in it, that's what the roaring must have been—McCaskil crawled toward the enclosing ring of darkness. The bear's enormous head swung toward him and an echo of the bone-melting roar rumbled in his chest.

"Keep that goddamn bear off me," McCaskil cried, his voice ragged from yelling.

"Balthazar doesn't like him," Geoffrey said. "When we were little he used to tease us something awful."

We. The boy and the great bear had grown up together. Staggered by the unreality of the scene, Anna found herself wondering if they were brothers.

Enough of her training survived this onslaught of otherworldliness that she continued to watch McCaskil with one eye and half of a reeling brain. He feared Balthazar more than he feared her or the Weatherby.

"You can't let that bear come after me," he said. "That's illegal."

Anna said nothing. Should the bear eat William McCaskil, her greatest concern would be for the animal's digestion.

Her head hurt, her knee was killing her, she was very tired. Overriding these fleeting discomforts was a bear of legend not ten feet from her. More than anything, she wanted to touch him, play with him, listen to the stories he might tell. It crossed her mind to let McCaskil go. His nerves shot, his rifle taken, he was of little threat to a party of five souls, particularly when one of them weighed over a thousand pounds and came from the factory equipped with an astonishing arsenal of edged weapons.

Ruick would pick McCaskil up in the frontcountry or the Montana state police would nail him eventually. Maniac turned craven, the man actually looked rather pathetic oozing toward the woods and temporary freedom. Being captured by a crippled-up lady ranger would only add to his humiliation.

That thought brought with it the tug of petty revenge that pulled Anna back to a sense of duty. "Stay," she ordered McCaskil.

"You can't shoot a man if he runs. Not unless he's a threat to life. I read that," McCaskil said, but he made no move to test the theory.

"You qualify," Anna said flatly. McCaskil had given up. Anna did not think she was fooled. She'd seen it enough times: the deflation as the tension of keeping up the fight, or the lie, or the act was given over. Still, she did not lower her guard. Cleverer people than she had been tricked, and died because of it.

Rory found the wire cutters and freed Joan. Joan held the flashlight and Anna the rifle while McCaskil bound his own hands and feet with more of the plastic disposable cuffs Geoffrey found in his pack. Balthazar, the great golden bear, sat on huge haunches, ancient eyes watching like a primitive god.

The sense of unreality was such Anna felt giddy and could not stop herself from being flippant and cracking jokes. Tension still on but terror fading, the others, with the exception of William McCaskil, caught her mood and the dark between the trees took on a mad-tea-party feel.

Checking McCaskil's bonds, Anna had to force her discipline, school her mind to pay attention to detail, to take seriously the business of catching and keeping a felon.

When their makeshift camp had been made as safe as plastic ties could make it, Joan righted McCaskil's stove and boiled water for hot drinks. Anna would have traded her boots for a good dollop of brandy to give her tea backbone but was grateful for the beverage even without it.

Given the homely activity of serving tea and cocoa, normalcy might have been expected to return but for the fact that a huge bear sat among them, his dark eyes following their puny movements, his pale golden belly round and Buddha-like under paws the size of serving platters.

"We'll talk," Anna said when the rushing of the stove was silenced and she'd once again checked on McCaskil, cuffed and chained to a tree with the links that usually served as Balthazar's lead.

"Your name is not Mickleson-Nicholson, but Geoffrey Micou, isn't that right?" she asked.

The boy sat with his arms around his knees looking weary and relieved and terribly sad. He wasn't as old as Rory, maybe fifteen. The silky brown hair was greasy, flattened against his skull by a ball cap that Balthazar had gotten hold of and was in the process of dismembering with delicate nips of his inch-long canines.

"I'm Geoffrey Micou. I just—just made up that other name."

"Carl G. Micou was your dad?" Anna asked and he looked surprised. The line about old age and treachery winning every time came to her mind. Geoffrey was at an age where he could still believe each and every one of his thoughts was new, unique to the world. He had yet to learn that all the stories have already been told. What remains is to choose the story one likes best and live that.

"We found your truck and trailer—your dad's truck—" Anna explained. "The tags were registered in the name of Carl Micou."

"Oh." Geoffrey sounded disappointed, magic losing its charm once the trick is explained. "That was what we used to move Balthazar. Dad had it made over."

"I know," Anna said. "The ranger found omnivore food in it." She didn't add that, until recently, they hadn't known it was omnivore food. It served her purposes to appear omniscient. Besides, it was fun.

"He fucking stole him." McCaskil dripped his acid into the circle. "That bear's mine."

Joan turned to him. In lieu of her traditional campfire candle, they had put McCaskil's flashlight butt-down in their midst, needing the security of watching their prisoner and, for Anna at least, the unending awe of watching the bear. In the dim fallout, Joan's face was hard, its customary softness hidden away from the man chained to the tree.

"Don't talk," she said. "We don't want to talk to you. We don't care what you think or feel." Her voice was so devoid of humanity Anna was made cold. McCaskil must have jumped way over onto Joan's bad side when he took a shot at Rory.

McCaskil subsided.

"I did steal him," Geoffrey said with a fond look at his monolithic companion. "Nobody should own a bear like Balthazar. He's not just a thing."

"You're my map boy, aren't you?" Joan asked.

Geoffrey blinked a few times, long dark lashes settling like feathers below wide-set hazel eyes. Then the sense of what she was asking came to him. "Yes, ma'am. I thought if I knew where the food was, I could take Balthazar there and teach him to eat it."

"Reintroduce him to the wild," Anna said, thinking of the looting of glacier lilies, the mining of cutworm moths. "Why the park? There're plenty of places in Canada and Alaska."

"You don't let anybody shoot them in the park," Geoffrey said simply.

"Ah." The logic was indisputable. One does not take a friend to live where murderers are waiting to take his life.

"Why didn't you ask for help?" Years of motherhood and carrying pain for children ached in Joan's voice.

"You'd've said no," Geoffrey answered. "Everybody would have said no."

Neither Anna nor Joan was naïve—or dishonest—enough to argue with him. The bear belonged to somebody else. Geoffrey was a kid. He would have been blown off on several accounts.

"That bear's my property," McCaskil felt bound to pipe up. Reassured by the company of others, safe from the bear and, in a strange way, safe within his bonds from the responsibility for decision or action, William McCaskil was recovering his equilibrium. Anna liked him better mute and cowering.

"Can't have pets where you'll be living for the next fifty years," she said.

Anna guessed the bear really did belong to William McCaskil if it was legally obtained as a cub. The brochure had listed the owners of Fetterman's Adventure Trails as George and Suzanne Fetterman. McCaskil had been born to a woman named Suzanne. Anna's bet was Fetterman was Suzanne's second husband, McCaskil's stepfather. Hence the use of Fetterman as an alias. He'd have been grown when Geoffrey was young but evidently visited Mom often enough to torment a little boy and a little bear. McCaskil must have inherited Adventure Trails when old man Fetterman died.

The thought process rippled quickly through Anna's mind. It could be verified easily enough. At present she chose not to speak of it. She didn't wish to give William McCaskil the right of anything.

"Mr. McCaskil was going to sell Balthazar," Geoffrey said.

"I found a home for him, a nice ranch in British Columbia where he would roam free," McCaskil said virtuously.

"Boone and Crockett," Anna snapped. "Balthazar would have been shot as a wild bear by some slob hunter for a trophy. What were they offering? A hundred thousand? Two? That must've seemed a fortune to a small-time fraud like you. Or could you get more because Balthazar would stand and roar on cue, add to the drama? Even charge and attack without any real risk to the hunter. You're a son-of-a-bitch, McCaskil. Be nice and shut up or you will be shot trying to escape." As a rule, Anna refrained from abusing prisoners in her custody. The venom she poured out on McCaskil was tied directly into the loss and outrage she felt looking across the flashlight at the quiet miracle eating a red ball cap and thinking of him destroyed for the sake of a little entertainment and bragging rights.

"Mr. McCaskil told me that's what he was going to do," Geoffrey said. "He said I could visit Balthazar's head after it was on somebody's wall. He said that to me. That's when I took Balthazar. I wrote you from the road," he told Joan. "I've got a laptop and a cell phone back where my stuff's at."

"Does the bear—Balthazar—do whatever you say?" Rory spoke for the first time. Anna covered her mouth to hide her smile. The envy was heavy in Rory's voice. What boy, what person of any age or gender, wouldn't want a twelve-hundred-pound omnivore as friend and backup?

"Pretty much," Geoffrey said. "My dad was Mr. Fetterman's animal curator. They got Balthazar when he was really tiny and I was about ten. We grew up together and I helped Dad train him and we'd do shows together. People liked seeing us, a bear and a little boy. After Dad died, Mr. Fetterman kept me on. I lived in his wife's old sewing room—Mrs. Fetterman had been dead a year or so before Dad went. I took over with Balthazar. He's a trained bear but he's not a pet," he warned and Anna noted he shot her as severe a glance as he did Rory. "He's a wild animal. They've got their own rules and you can't go around breaking them. Balthazar can't be scared or hurt or teased. He doesn't understand it. That's why he hates Mr. McCaskil so much. When he smells him he knows something bad is happening and he goes back to bear rules to save himself."

"Fucking menace," McCaskil growled.

Balthazar growled back and McCaskil shut up.

"How do you tell him what to do?" Rory asked.

"Lots of ways. He responds to a few verbal commands. He'll sit down and play dead to whistles. Some tricks he taught himself and just does them for fun when he's happy. He likes to juggle—kind of play catch really—with pinecones. Sometimes he just starts in to dance even when there's no music."

"I guess I'll pay closer attention to bizarre bear management reports in the future," Joan said, and Anna laughed.

Geoffrey went on, "For the show, Dad taught him to growl and stand tall and charge by different numbers of raps on pieces of wood. He picked the wood because the noise was natural and it would seem more real."

"We found one of your clacking sticks," Anna said. "After the night you and Balthazar tore up our camp."

Geoffrey looked away, fixing his eyes on the flashlight between them. "I'm sorry about that. I just wanted you to leave. Balthazar got into some kind of trap thing. A tree with wire around. It took me fifteen minutes to get him to leave. He'd got hold of a little thing that smelled like cherry candy up in the little tree and wouldn't stop playing with it. I figured it was one of those traps you'd told me about that day we met. I was afraid you'd find out somehow."

"Ah," Joan said. "And here I blamed the last team for hanging the love scent too low. Who could know?" She smiled.

Geoffrey continued with his story, "I was trying to teach Balthazar to dig lilies around there. We'd tried other places but there were other bears and they scared him. I thought if we did that—you know, to your camp—you'd be scared away."

Joan reached out. She must have thought better of touching Geoffrey because her hand stopped partway. "You can't scare away researchers by letting them know there's a subject in the neighborhood," she said.

"I didn't know that then."

Joan boiled more water. More hot drinks were made. Out of a sense of duty, Anna made a cup of cocoa for McCaskil. When they'd settled again, she said to Geoffrey Micou, "Why don't you tell us about Balthazar killing that woman?"

Rory gasped audibly. McCaskil laughed. "They're going to shoot that killer bear," he said. "He'd've been better off with me. Maybe he'd've run off and lived." Geoffrey covered his face with both hands, a gesture both theatrical and genuine.

"Anna!" Joan scolded her for insensitivity. To Rory she said, "Are you okay with this?"

Anna had forgotten the dead woman was Rory's stepmother. Guilt nudged her but curiosity was stronger and she didn't withdraw the request.

"I'm okay with it," Rory said. Joan looked at him hard trying to see past strange shadows and high school bravado. Apparently she was satisfied.

"The woman who died was Rory's stepmother," she explained to Geoffrey.

The hands over the boy's face crawled up into his hair to become fists, strands of brown spiking out between the fingers. Whatever Micou felt floated to the surface where it could be easily seen by anyone with eyes. Perhaps growing up brother to a bear had denied him humanity's greatest defensive weapon: the lie.

"I'm sorry. I'm so sorry." The words squeezed out through a throat full of tears.

"It's okay," the older boy said. "I've got my dad."

Fleetingly Anna wished Lester Van Slyke had been there to hear Rory say that. Not that Lester deserved it. Realistically it would probably not be long before he compromised his son's respect with another self-assassinating relationship.

"Go on," Anna said.

"Go ahead with your story," Joan repeated, with more gentleness and better results.

"Balthazar and me had done your camp to scare you away. I knew you'd gone off," he said to Rory. "When Balthazar smashed your tent it rolled like a tumbleweed and we knew you weren't in it. That's why I let him play with it. We wouldn't have hurt anybody. Anyway, afterward we were both wired and shaky and ran back to the trail. I thought we should get a ways away before we hid out. We couldn't be anywhere there were people when it got light. Hide out till you guys left and we could come back for the lilies.

"The lady was coming down the trail just as it was getting light and I dove for cover and started whistling for Balthazar but he was up tall and sniffing and growling like she was some big scary something. He's used to people. I've only see him do that when—"

"When Mr. McCaskil is around?" Anna asked.

"That's right. He's scared of him."

"This lady was wearing Bill McCaskil's coat," Anna said. "She took it from his tent before she started out that morning."

"Stupid slut," McCaskil said.

"Watch it," Anna retorted.

"That's it then." Geoffrey turned to Balthazar. "I was worried about you," he told the bear. To the people waiting he said, "This whole thing has been stressful for Balthazar. I mean, I'd never been out of Florida but Balthazar's never been anywhere. The other bears scare him. Deer scare him. He almost ran off that cliff up by the army moth place. He's never been in a world that had cliffs in its floor. I was afraid maybe it was too much for him He'd been off his feed and some of his hair fell out. I thought maybe when he saw that lady he had a nervous breakdown. You're okay, pal," he said to his friend. "She was just wearing Mr. McCaskil's coat."

Balthazar exonerated, he turned back to his human audience.

"She started taking flash pictures, pop, pop, pop. He's used to pictures but I think in the low light like that and him being already upset and all—I don't know, maybe it blinded him or something. He started roaring and walking toward her on his hind legs. I know by now Balth isn't himself and I'm out yelling and whistling like mad. This lady keeps popping and getting closer and I'm yelling for her to stop and Balth to stop and nobody's listening to me. Then Balth gets almost on top of her and she pulls out a little can like that stuff you had." Geoffrey nodded at Anna. "She squirted him and he just went nuts—he swung and her head snapped over. Way over. God."

His hands came down out of his hair where they'd been pulling at it during the telling and covered his face again.

The riddle "What was soft enough not to cut but could be swung with enough force to sever a woman's spinal cord" was answered.

"But her face was cut off—" Rory began.

Geoffrey started to cry, silently, the tears working their way through his fingers to paint pale tracks in the grime on the back of his hands.

Anna quieted Rory with a gesture. Joan patted him on the knee to let him know she didn't mean to be so abrupt.

"Balthazar's claws left marks on her face," Anna said.

Geoffrey nodded. "You'd've come looking for a killer bear. You'd've found us."

For a minute Anna sat sipping tea already grown cold. A fifteen-year-old boy dragging the body into hiding then cutting away the flesh, probably with his pocket knife, weeping as he wept now at the memory of it. She doubted Timmy would have gone half the distance for Lassie.

"You put the—ah—clawed pieces in a tree after."

"I didn't want anybody to see or you'd know but I was afraid if I buried it another bear might dig it up. You know, get a taste for it. Then get himself into trouble."

Geoffrey recovered from the tears. Anna suspected his life at Fetterman's Adventure Trails had had its share of life and death. He'd get over Carolyn's. He scrubbed his face until the tears had been smeared around.

"You took her water bottle and the film," Anna said. "I can understand the film, why the water?"

"I didn't mean to. It had fallen out of her pack on the trail. I found it after. I didn't want to—to go back. So I took it. Then when I saw him—you, Rory—and I knew you'd run off without anything. I left it by you to drink."

"You took my sweatshirt," Rory said, sounding more honored than offended.

"I'm sorry," Geoffrey said. "My shirt had stuff on it. Blood. And I'd tore it up to make a rope so I could hang the bag with the . . . you know. I thought if hikers caught sight of me with no shirt they'd remember me."

"You left me water, too," Anna said. "Up on Cathedral Peak after Mr. McCaskil here tried to kill me."

Geoffrey nodded. "I'd read a person can live a long time without food but not without water. I'm sorry about the bottle. Balthazar got to playing with it. We'll buy you a new one."

He looked across the upward beam of light at Anna, his clear hazel eyes as old as stone.

"What will happen to Balthazar now?" he asked.

"Nothing bad," Anna promised.

"Hah." McCaskil.

"Nothing bad," she repeated. "I swear that on the worthless life of our prisoner."

24

Anna came to look back on that night with the odd dreaming reality with which she remembered much of her childhood. A time when everything was new and hence nothing was strange. Miracles were commonplace and, so, unremarkable. The rules, not yet pounded into the fabric of the mind like great rusted nails, were easily suspended.

A circus of arrest and rescue came to them the following morning, masterfully planned and efficiently ringmastered by Chief Ranger Harry Ruick. Buck was with him and Gary, both armed with Weatherby Magnum bolt-action rifles—enough "stopping power" for a bear the size of Balthazar. They'd need it if anything went haywire, Anna thought, because they'd have to shoot through the person of Geoffrey Micou before they got to the shaggy body of his brother. Anna turned over the thirty-ought-six McCaskil had donated. It wouldn't stop a bear but would do a lot of damage.

The shortest route out was down McDonald Creek, the western half of a large loop trail that started and ended at Packers Roost. Though her knee was bothering her, she eschewed horseback and walked most of the way out. She wanted to be near Balthazar. She found unending delight in the play of sun and shadow over his fur, the lumbering grace of his walk, the sharp accents his long claws made on his tracks in the dust. Because of the potential for problems, Harry closed the trail to visitors, citing the uninteresting excuse of dead elk near it causing a potential bear hazard. Balthazar's trailer and the pickup to pull it had been taken out of impound and would be waiting at the end of the trail.

At Packers Roost the bear and the boy were separated. Balthazar was taken to a holding pen loaned by a West Glacier entrepreneur who ran a Bear Country attraction where tourists could see black bears.

Bill McCaskil was taken to the county jail to be held until formal charges and setting bail were arranged for. With his list of aliases and a charge of kidnapping researchers and attempting to murder a federal law enforcement officer, he would probably await trial behind bars.

Rory agreed he had had enough of the DNA project and would be going home to Seattle with his dad. Joan promised to clear everything up with Earthwatch.

Geoffrey Micou proved a bit of a problem. He was just turned sixteen, a minor and an orphan. Mr. Fetterman had taken care of him after his father's death but he hadn't bothered to make the boy go to school. Geoffrey dropped out in the seventh grade. He was extremely bright and had taught himself a great deal but was officially truant. Montana Child and Family Services were brought in. Though Joan fought to keep him with her at least until his future was settled, he had been spirited away.

Anna was left with the promise she had made that nothing bad would happen.

For three days she and Joan and Harry contacted zoos and research facilities. Grown Alaskan grizzlies with Balthazar's peculiar history were not in demand. No one wanted him. He could not survive on his own. Despite the goodwill surrounding the magnificent beast, Anna became afraid the only solution would be a Final Solution. Then the trust of a boy and a huge chunk of magic would be ripped out of a world already short on both.

Anna flew out of Kalispell headed for Dallas knowing she had failed. Solving a murder case, catching a felon—these things were necessary on some level but in essence mundane. The world was not bettered by the knowledge that Carolyn Van Slyke died by accident. Perhaps Florida's finances were marginally safer by the removal of one con man from the premises, but there would be others to take his place. At his core, William McCaskil was not a violent man, Anna believed. He was a greedy immoral man pushed to violence by his own fears. The thirty-ought-six he'd said he bought for self-defense. Anna figured he meant to use it to threaten Geoffrey: "Do as I say or the bear gets it." Until Geoffrey put Balthazar back into the transport trailer for him, McCaskil had nothing. Whether or not, no longer panicked, he would have killed Geoffrey, Anna would never know. She didn't think so. Geoffrey was no real threat to him without Balthazar.

Her failure had been in the most important element of the crime: saving the wonderful bear.

Back in Mississippi, she prayed to various gods known to have a soft spot for animals and felt a fool and a hypocrite for doing so. She was surly to her field rangers, avoided her boyfriend and was unmerciful to speeders.

On her fourth day back she received a Federal Express package from Joan. Anna had been praying to the wrong gods. Help had come in the form of Glacier's former superintendent, now serving in Yosemite. The park service is a small town. Glacier's old superintendent was friends with the superintendent of Canyonlands. Outside the park, near Moab, Utah, lived a man who trained most of the large and dangerous animals Hollywood used in its movies. He would take Balthazar. That was the good news. The great news was that he would take Geoffrey Micou as well, as an apprentice.

"Hallelujah!" Anna said.

The package had come to the ranger station in Port Gibson, where she was stationed. Unable to wait, she'd ripped it open in the outer office and read it standing in the middle of the floor. Randy Thigpen, one of her field rangers with whom having a lady Yankee boss did not sit well, was at his desk. "What'd you get?" he demanded.

"The bear's going to be okay." Randy knew the story and Anna didn't elaborate.

"Whoop-ti-doo," he said.

Anna's good cheer was undaunted. "And I got a present." A small package wrapped in gold foil and marked "A souvenir of your trip. Love, Joan" had been stuffed into the bottom of the cardboard envelope. With childish impatience Anna tore it open. Inside was a glass vial filled with brown liquid and mosslike matter. "Balthazar" and the date were penned on the sticker pasted to the side.

"What is it?" Thigpen asked.

"Shit," Anna said happily.

"I guess just everybody loves you," Thigpen growled.

Joan had sent her a scat sample. After all, what were friends for?

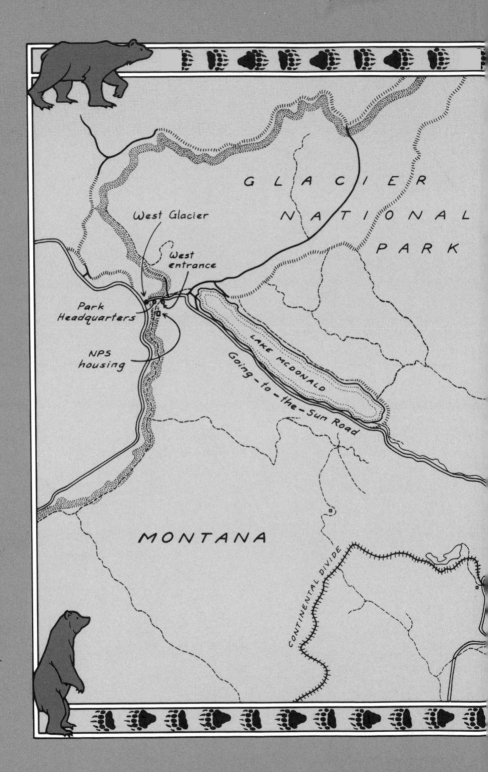

GLACIER NATIONAL PARK

West Glacier

West entrance

Park Headquarters

NPS housing

LAKE McDONALD

Going-to-the-Sun Road

MONTANA

CONTINENTAL DIVIDE